Wall of Fire

J.G. Holtrop

Published by: Brushbow Books

Editing: George August Koch
georgeaugustkoch@aol.com
www.GeorgeAugustKoch.com

Graphic Design: Aurora Gabrielle Slinkman
auroraslinkman@aol.com
www.AuroraSlinkman.com

Image Credit: neil/stock.adobe.com
Roman/stock.adobe.com

A CIP record for this book is available from the Library of Congress Cataloging-in-Publication Data

ISBN-13: 978-1-7334000-1-5

Printed in USA

Wall of Fire

J.G. Holtrop

ACKNOWLEDGMENTS

I give thanks to God my Savior, who gave me a love of His Word, His people and His land. I praise Him for this story and for giving me the ability to write it. I am grateful to Him for blessing me with friends and family who have supported and encouraged me during the writing of this book.

A special thanks to Sam and Jill Wat, who were the first to read a portion of the manuscript. Their encouragement, insights and suggestions added a depth of meaning I would not have achieved on my own. Jill has been by my side every step of the way supporting me with prayer and encouragement. Thank you, Jill and Sam.

I am also appreciative of all those who gave generously of their time, to not only read but also to critique the manuscript. In addition to Jill and Sam, I would especially like to thank Judy Davis, Murray Roujansky, Jessica Shluessler, Barb Walker and Marie Yunker, all of whom not only gave me valuable feedback on the overall story, but shared which parts impacted them the most. Thank you all for your honesty, prayers and encouragement.

My heartfelt thanks to George August Koch, who edited the manuscript. He was much more than just an editor. He not only corrected the grammatical and spelling errors but also made improvements to sentence structure and word choice. He made sure all the different plot / storyline threads were consistent throughout and also ensured the continuity of the formatting. His gift for detail and knowledge of language has made *Wall of Fire* eminently more readable, understandable and enjoyable. His editing was thoughtful, comprehensive, and essential. As an additional blessing, George has become a valued friend. Thank you, George, for all the long hours you spent making this book the best it could be.

I am also grateful to Aurora Gabrielle Slinkman for developing the cover design, and for formatting the interior. Even though I changed the book title several times, Aurora kept coming up with new designs, never complaining, always with a smile. Thank you, Aurora, for your patience and creativity.

Finally, I thank my husband Dale, whose positive attitude and sense of humor kept me somewhat sane during the many years of writing.

In memory of my beloved sister and friend,

Barb Brouwer

Who held my hand as we walked through life,

Supporting and encouraging me in every way.

May her memory be a blessing.

Contents

PART ONE

THE FINGER OF GOD

Do not fear them, for it is the
LORD your God who will battle for you.
Deuteronomy 3:22

Nate watched as the El Al airliner touched down on the runway at Ben Gurion International Airport. As he watched the plane taxi toward the terminal, he thought of all he had experienced in the last two months.

As a volunteer with ELISHA FUND he had traveled all over Israel, delivering food, clothing, medicine and other necessary items to needy Israeli communities from the Golan to Gaza. He had brought the same aid to the needy communities in the areas controlled by the Palestinian Authority. He had observed for himself the interactions between the Israelis and the Palestinians. He had seen for himself the impact of the BDS movement. He had seen for himself how the Palestinian Christians had two entirely different views of Israel and the Jewish people.

He also remembered the day, two months ago, when his plane had landed at this same airport; he remembered the excitement he had felt at arriving in Israel.

After finishing his first year at college, Nate had seized the opportunity to go to Israel and volunteer with ELISHA FUND. He had worked in the Tel Aviv distribution center, delivered supplies to the ELISHA warehouses, even helped rebuild a warehouse in Sderot. The old warehouse had been destroyed in one of the rocket attacks from Gaza, and even as they rebuilt, the rockets had kept coming. He remembered how terrifying those attacks had been—there had only been fifteen seconds to find shelter! He remembered the people he had met. Despite being surrounded by enemies and under constant threat of terror attacks, the Israelis were the happiest people he had ever been around.

Everyone was convinced that war was coming. Supplies were pouring into the ELISHA warehouse and needed to be inventoried and organized. Food, medicine and clothing needed to be distributed to those in need. The new warehouse in Sderot needed to be restocked.

Nate watched as a plane soared off the runway and disappeared into a crystal-blue sky. Soon he would be boarding a plane and heading back to the States. It was time to return home, but he wasn't sure he wanted to leave. He wanted to be in the fight that was coming—not shuffling supplies or working in the warehouse…but in the IDF or something…

He watched the passengers disembarking from the plane. They were smiling and talking as they looked for the signs indicating where they would meet their tour groups.

Should he stay and help Israel? he wondered. *Should he go home to Dad and Mom, JJ and Josie? Should he go home, get ready for college and start thinking about what he wanted to do with his life? Or should he stay…* He couldn't seem to shake the feeling that he was being turned around.

Nate studied his boarding pass. His plane would be ready soon.

Looking up, he was startled to see that the scene had shifted. Instead of happily and calmly walking from the plane, people were rushing **toward** the planes—running across the tarmac carrying only backpacks. Nate sensed a feeling of panic among them.

He shut his eyes tightly for a moment. *What was going on?*

When he looked up, he saw passengers calmly leaving the plane, just as before. He shook his head. *What was that about?*

2

Nate searched through his duffel bag and pulled out a worn Bible. He held it a minute before opening it. Then he read: "Verily I say unto you, inasmuch as ye have done it unto one of the least of these My brethren, ye have done it unto Me." Matthew 25:40 That was the mission of ELISHA FUND: to show the love of Y'shua to the Israeli people. *What should I do?* he prayed. *Stay or go?*

Nate picked up his old duffel bag, stuffed his boarding pass and Bible inside, and headed out of the terminal—away from Ben Gurion and a flight back to the States.

Nate headed back to Tel Aviv…

CHAPTER ONE

Tel Aviv
-1-
And I saw a beast rising out of the sea…
and the beast that I saw was like a leopard,
its feet were like a bear's,
and its mouth was like a lion's mouth.
Revelation 13:1-2

In an office deep inside a nondescript building in Tel Aviv, Gen. David Yash'el (Ret.) scrutinized the map behind his desk. The whole region was in chaos. Egypt was unraveling; Syria was imploding; Turkey was destabilizing; violence in Iraq was escalating; Hezbollah was stockpiling missiles; Gaza was firing rockets; Iran was continuing to pursue nuclear weapons—this was a map of a disaster in the making. When the internal fighting ended, Israel's enemies would unite and come against the Jewish State.

David recalled the hundreds of thousands of Muslims in Tahrir Square in Egypt, after the fall of Mubarak, responding to an impassioned speech by the leading imam of the Muslim Brotherhood: "We will march to Jerusalem! We will shed our blood in Jerusalem! We will die as martyrs in Jerusalem!"

David closed his eyes for a moment. No matter what was happening now, it was going to end up in Jerusalem. The Prophets had foretold it. It would come to pass. "I'll tell you something, the final battle will be at Jerusalem, just as you foretold Zechariah," he said, as if the prophet were standing next to him.

"Yeah," he heard a voice behind him say.

Startled, David turned away from the map to see a young man standing in front of his desk. He too was intently scrutinizing the map. "I think this is just the beginning," the young man said. He was of average height; dusty blonde hair; deep blue eyes. He looked like he was in his late teens or early 20s. He wore baggy jeans and a navy T-shirt. He carried an old army-green duffel bag.

"I'll ask you something. Who are you? What are you doing here?" David demanded, wondering how he had gotten past security. "Why are you here?"

The young man turned toward David. "I was looking for someone. I just—well, I came into this building and kept walking until I saw you."

"Who?" David said. "Looking for who?"

"I—I don't know."

David stared at him, waiting.

The young man ran a hand through his hair. "I wanted to talk to someone about helping out … maybe joining the IDF or … something."

David evaluated the man. His Hebrew was poor but understandable.

"You are from where?" he asked.

"United States," the young man replied.

"Name?"

"Nate—Nathaniel—Grange."

"You are Jewish."

"Ah … no. I'm American. A Christian."

"You're in Israel—why?"

"I'm working with ELISHA FUND. We—"

"I know of ELISHA FUND," David interrupted. "They send you here? ELISHA FUND?"

"No." Nate shook his head. "I was heading back to the States. I was turned around."

"Who?"

"What?"

5

"Who turned you around?"

"I don't know. I was headed for the ELISHA warehouse, and I ended up here."

David sat down and gestured for the young man to take a seat. David studied Nathaniel. He would find out who he was and how he happened to be here—in his office.

"I'll tell you something. If you're not Jewish, it is not possible to join the IDF," David informed him.

Nate thought about that.

Nate's eyes turned to the map. "What do you see?" David asked.

Nate studied the map. "It's complicated," he said.

"Say something," ordered David.

"It looks like a great beast, waiting to devour Israel." Nate walked to the map and traced the mouth of a beast, formed by the countries that surrounded Israel.

David nodded; it did look like the mouth of a beast.Nate turned to David. "They are still trying to rebuild the caliphate."

"I'll tell you something," David replied. "The caliphate is everywhere. It is not about territory, it is the Muslim Brotherhood, the radical ideology."

Nate said. "The prophet Daniel wrote about it. So did John."

"Daniel I know, but who is John?" David asked, leaning back in his chair.

"He wrote the last book of the Bible. It's called Revelation." He looked back at the map. "The three empires Daniel wrote about … John said they would all combine and become one great empire."

"The Ottomans did that long ago," David said. "Then the British came. 1917. It was the end of the Ottoman Caliphate."

Daniel 7; Revelation 13

"They were wounded with the sword of the British. John said that would happen."

"Daniel. He said something?"

"He did." Nate frowned. "I'm still studying this. ... Remember Nebuchadnezzar's dream? The one about the great tree?" Daniel 4

David nodded.

"Well, after it was cut down, it was bound with a band of bronze and iron. I'm thinking that the bronze is the British and the French and the iron is the dictators and monarchies. The British and French carved up the old Ottoman Empire ... made a bunch of countries. These countries were ruled by dictators and monarchies. That's what's kept people like the Muslim Brotherhood from taking control and forming the caliphate again."Nate looked at David. "Does that make sense?"

David considered what Nate had said. It was true, but was that what Daniel had written about?

"We'll wait and see," he said. "This Arab Spring. It began all these big changes."

"Yeah," said Nate. "Summer is near, then everything the prophets wrote about starts to happen."

David studied the young man sitting in front of him. Most Israelis didn't study the Tanakh. Most didn't know what the prophets wrote. This young man was Christian, studying the ancient prophets in the Tanakh and the Christian Bible.

David thought about the Iranian propaganda film *The Coming Is Near*. The Muslims were waiting for the return of the Mahdi along with their version of Jesus. The Christians were anticipating the return of their Jesus, and the Jewish people were looking for their Messiah. The movie claimed that Iran would soon help expedite the appearance of the Mahdi—the 12th Imam. The Iranian government viewed the rebellion and chaos in the

Middle East as a sign that the Mahdi was soon to appear. The movie stated that Ahmadinejad, President of Iran, would conquer Jerusalem prior to the coming of the Mahdi. Ahmadinejad was no longer President, but the Mahdi's imminent arrival was still being proclaimed. When the Mahdi arrived, he—the Mahdi—along with Jesus, who they called Isa—would lead the armies of Islam and conquer all non-Muslims. Isa would crush the cross, declaring Islam the true religion and Allah the only god.

"I'll tell you something. The Muslims believe they can bring the Mahdi by creating chaos and bathing the world in blood. You know of the Mahdi?" David asked.

"Yeah … he's coming too," Nate said. "There will be war. The Lion of Judah with his sword of fire will come and destroy him."

"Israel will look to our Deliverer when war comes. We will look to HASHEM, the Holy One of Israel. He will deliver us." David said. "Perhaps the Messiah will come. Perhaps it is the time."

"When Y'shua comes," Nate said, "He will come from God to deliver Israel. Everyone will know—for sure—that He is the one you've been waiting for. He is the Lion of Judah."

"How? How will everyone know?" David challenged. Nate spread his hands, looking intently into David's eyes. David returned Nate's gaze, wondering…

"Christians think they can hurry the return of their Messiah," he finally said.

"Y'shua will come at the appointed time. Nothing anyone can do will change that," Nate said.

✡✝✡✝✡✝✡

Gen. David Yash'el had commanded young men and women in battle for decades. He had seen many with courage and purpose. He had seen more than a few serve with selfless bravery. Some of them were Machal—volunteers from abroad. Israel owed a great deal of its success, especially in the1948 War of Independence, to the Machal's contributions. Nathaniel wanted to be a Machal— but he was not Jewish. Also, did he have the courage? There was something unusual about this young man. David felt connected to him in some strange way. His eyes narrowed slightly. Too many unanswered questions. David decided he was going to get all the information he could about Nathaniel Grange.

"To join the IDF as a foreign volunteer is respected by Israel, especially with war coming," David said.

"I'll tell you something, no exceptions are made. You must be Jewish."

David slid a pad of paper in front of him. "There is Sar-El," he said. "You can volunteer in Sar-El."

Seeing Nate's questioning look, David explained: "Sar-El means Service for Israel. Volunteers work at different army bases—do what is needed behind the lines to keep the IDF running smoothly."

Nate sat silently, staring at the map. "It would be a start," he said.

David finished writing the Sar-El information and handed the paper to Nate.

"Your visa? You have it?" he asked.

Nate placed his duffel bag on the desk. "Yeah, it's in here…"

The duffel bag was very old. WWII vintage, David observed. He noticed a serial number stenciled on the side of the bag and jotted it down.

Nate pulled a packet of papers out, sorted through them, and handed his passport and visa to David.

David opened the passport. One entry. Departed United States. Entered Israel. The picture was current. Nathaniel had entered Israel two months ago. David examined the visa, and rose to copy both items. "It will take three or four weeks to be approved for Sar-El," he said. "Apply soon."

"Yeah," said Nate, retrieving his passport and visa from David. "I'm on it."

Nate turned to leave.

At the door he spun around.

"Do you know a Captain Jacob Yash'el?" he asked. That took David off-guard. There was nothing in this office that had his name on it. "You ask … why?" he said carefully.

"During the Gaza War—Operation Cast Lead? —my grandma saw Captain Yash'el interviewed on TV. She wrote his name down and has been praying for him ever since. She's—well, we all are—praying that he will be protected in battle, that he has peace in his life…"

Nate looked at David expectantly. "She asked if I could find out how he is."

"I am Yaakov's grandfather. I am General David Yash'el."

"No way!" Nate exclaimed. **"That's** why I was supposed to come here! To meet you!"

"Yaakov is well. He is alive. He is happy. He is still in the IDF."

Nate had begun rummaging in the battered duffel bag. "Grandma wrote him a letter …it's in here … somewhere…" He extracted a wrinkled envelope and handed it to David. "It's not sealed. You can read it if you want."

David took the letter, turning it over in his hand. "To Yaakov I will give this. Thank you."

-2-

David sat at his desk and opened the letter.

10

Dear Capt. Jacob,

When I saw you interviewed on TV during the Gaza War, I adopted you in my heart. You are in my (our) prayers every day.

I pray that the Almighty will hide you in His shelter in the day of trouble; that He will conceal you under the cover of His tent; that He will lift you high upon a rock. Psalm 27:5 I pray that even though an army encamps against you, that your heart will not fear; though war arises against you, you will be confident. Psalm 27:3 I pray that the Holy One of Israel will be your refuge and your fortress; that you will trust in Him. I pray that He will command His angels concerning you to guard you in all your ways. I pray that they will bear you up, so you will not strike your foot against a stone. Psalm 91:2,11 I pray that the Most High will be your stronghold and your rock of refuge. Psalm 94:22 I pray that you will be delivered from evil men; that you will be preserved from violent men, who plan evil things in their heart and stir up wars continually. Psalm 140:1–2 I pray that Adonai will be your rock, Who trains your hands for war and your fingers for battle. That He will be your steadfast love and your fortress, your stronghold and deliverer, your shield and your refuge. Psalm 144:1–2

I pray that the Almighty will protect you, strengthen you, and give you peace.

In the name of Y'shua, the Lion of Judah.

If this letter reaches you, know that you are loved and brought before the LORD each day,

Janna Grange

David replaced the letter in the envelope. Closing his eyes, he remembered…

On December 27, 2008, the IAF had launched an air strike against Hamas terrorist cells in the Gaza Strip. Israel had finally responded to the thousands of rocket attacks on Israelis' southern cities.

Once the operation began, Hamas increased the number of attacks and was now firing an average of 80 rockets into Israel each day. Rockets were being fired into Ashdod and Ashkelon. Grad[1] rockets were hitting Beersheba. Hamas had been deliberately firing rockets into civilian centers, including multiple kindergartens. All the schools within range of the rockets had been closed.

The IAF struck Hamas terrorist cell headquarters throughout the Gaza Strip, including a Hamas training base and outposts, as well as Hamas government complexes. They attacked rocket launchers and Grad missile stockpiles. Houses of senior Hamas terrorists were targeted. Tunnels used to pass weaponry into Gaza were also struck.

Before each air strike, the Israeli government warned the people of Gaza. To avoid civilian casualties, calls were made to apartment complexes that were known to house Hamas forces. Ninety thousand Palestinian homes in Gaza received phone calls warning of an air strike. Only when the complex was believed to be empty of civilians did the IAF strike.

One week after the start of Operation Cast Lead, IDF ground forces prepared to move into Gaza. Watching the coverage, David had switched between Israeli, Arab and U.S. newscasts. The American station showed hundreds of soldiers moving forward. It was a line as far as the eye could see. They were to move on Gaza in 15 minutes. One of the soldiers was being interviewed. It was Yaakov!

Was this the newscast Nathaniel's grandmother had seen?

"This is Capt. Yaakov Yash'el," the reporter said to the camera. Then, turning to Yaakov, he asked, "Can you tell us what's going on? What are they saying to all the soldiers?"

A soldier on each side of the road was stopping each of the troops as they passed.

"They're asking if they have their dog-tags," Yaakov replied. "They're telling them to put their number on pieces of

---

1 Russian-made rocket. The name means "hail."

paper and to put one in each of their boots … so they can be identified if they're blown to bits."

"It's going to be that tough," the reporter said, sounding concerned.

"It's going to be like going into hell," Yaakov said, deadly serious. "They've been preparing for us. Everything has been booby-trapped. Hamas is dug in with stockpiles of ammo and rockets. They know where we'll be coming in. They're waiting for us."

The camera showed each soldier being handed a card.

"What's that? What are they giving them?" the reporter asked.

Yaakov glanced over to where the camera was pointed. "They're handing them cards with a prayer for going out to battle," he said as he turned and ran to rejoin his men.

The camera now focused on a huge huddle, hundreds of men, which had gathered around a rabbi. David could hear the rabbi's resounding voice:

"You are the army of Israel! You are going out to war! You will not be afraid! God is going out to war with you! God is going to fight your battle for you!" Deuteronomy 3:22

David had lost sight of Yaakov. His stomach was gripped with anxiety.

David had left the TV on when he went to the Israeli television studio. There he would give his "expert analysis" as Gen. D. Yash'el (Ret.), and not think about being a grandfather while Yaakov walked into the jaws of hell.

The sun was beginning to spread its warmth when David returned home. The picture on the TV showed armored vehicles returning from battle. Weary soldiers walked around and behind them.

"We have just been informed," the reporter said, "That there have been **no casualties**! I repeat—**no casualties**!" The reporter looked bewildered. "All these men, these soldiers, have returned

alive." Someone had come up and handed the reporter a piece of paper. "A slight correction—there has been one injury," he said, reading the paper. "One soldier was injured when a chunk of concrete flew out of a building and hit him on the arm. It tore his uniform. He is uninjured except for a scratch on his arm."

David bowed his head and thanked the Almighty for His protection, as tears filled his eyes.

David raised his head when he heard the reporter exclaim, "Look at that. LOOK AT THAT!" All the vehicles and men had come to a standstill. Above their heads was stretched a huge double rainbow. All the soldiers were looking at the sky. They started reaching up with their hands. They were cheering: "He's with us!" "We went into Gaza and God went into Gaza with us!"

Later Yaakov had told him how it was. "We walked into a world full of explosions and smoke. Rockets exploding, bullets flying all around us. We wouldn't have been surprised if there had been dozens of us dead."

"The whole time we were wondering: *How come the explosions aren't hitting us? How come bullets aren't hitting us? The trip wires—we see every one! How can we see everything?!* It didn't seem right; something was not right."

"After the battle, when we got back, we could see armored personal carriers with their hatches open. …We wondered … *How many guys bought it? How many dead?* We looked into the hatches, looking for blood. I asked an officer, 'How many of us got hurt? How many got killed?' He said, 'Nobody. Nobody got killed.' All those explosions and shooting and nobody got killed!"

Yaakov had sat silently for a long time before he said, "God went into Gaza with us."

"It was the finger of God," David said. [2]

---

2   The account of the battle in Gaza is from a video made by Ariel Siegelman. He joined the IDF and fought in Gaza. To hear this true story in his own words: www.youtube.com/watch?v=Fa9E1X6NybE

A truck nearly backed into Nate as he entered the ELISHA FUND DISTRIBUTION CENTER. "Hey Darryl!" he called.

Darryl leaned out of the window of one of the trucks. "Thought you were on a **plane** already."

"Decided to stay."

"**Great!** Look at all this **stuff!** We can **use** you, man!"

Nate looked around. Pallets of supplies were everywhere. The warehouse was packed.

"We have to get this stuff **organized** and **moved out**. More comin' every **day**." Darryl said, waving a clipboard.

"Show me where," Nate said, glancing at a forklift.

"Toss your stuff in the **bunkhouse**. How 'bout **nights** for you?"

"I'm on it," said Nate.

"Everything comes in during the day …nobody wants nights. I tell ya, I'm goin' day and night. Can't keep up."

The bunkhouse had been partitioned off the back of the warehouse. This was where the male volunteers stayed. The women had a much nicer facility. The bunkhouse area was comprised of a row of bunks, a shower room, a galley kitchen, a fellowship area, and a small room that used to be an office. Nate had taken over this room during his two-month stay. He dropped his duffel on the bunk, not knowing how long he'd be staying this time.

The sun was beginning to set when David sent Nathaniel's information out to be vetted. As an afterthought he sent the number that had been stenciled on the old duffel-bag.

Nate gazed at the Mediterranean Sea. His well-worn Bible was opened beside him.

The sea was peaceful. The sun was coming up.

Nate saw in his mind's eye people struggling through the surf on moonless nights. Refugees from Europe. Survivors of the Holocaust. Evading the British patrols. With nothing but their soaked clothing, they reached the beach. Waiting for them were members of the Haganah. The refugees were quickly and quietly loaded into waiting vehicles and taken to Tel Aviv. They were the fortunate ones. The majority were seized by the British and brought to detention camps on Cyprus.

There they waited ... it was 1947 ...

Suddenly what he saw changed. The people were going away from the beach, struggling to reach boats that would take them away from Israel. Nate shook his head. *What? Again? What was that about?*

A stiff breeze sprung up off the Mediterranean Sea.

The pages of the Bible rippled and, as the breeze quieted, the Bible lay open. Nate read:

And the woman fled into the wilderness,

where she hath a place prepared of God,

that they should feed her there

a thousand two-hundred and threescore days.

Revelation 12:6

Gen. David Yash'el leaned back in his chair. He reviewed the briefing he had just read. Israel was doing all that could be done to prepare. They had made ready sealed rooms to protect against chemical and biological weapons. They had stocked them with emergency supplies: food, water, medicine, radios, flashlights, batteries, toilet paper…

The IDF was working to complete the task of delivering a gas mask to each citizen. Drills were held so each person knew what to expect and how to react.

A few years ago, Israel had conducted the largest nationwide emergency drill in its history. It was held to prepare the Israeli people for war on multiple fronts: chemical warfare; an uprising of the local Arab population; terrorist attacks. Other disasters, such as earthquakes or an epidemic, were included in this worst-case scenario. The drill had improved Israel's readiness and ability to deal with any and all emergencies. The exercise had also revealed areas that needed improvement, and solutions had been found. But none of them had foreseen the rebellion that had cascaded throughout the region.

David pulled up one of the hundreds of Facebook pages that were calling for a Palestinian terrorist Intifada. He read:

"O Israel, burn, the Arab rebels are coming."

"We will finish what Hitler started."

"Dear Jews, don't be afraid, death will be swift. Expect an Arab deluge, we are coming. We will help the religion of Allah and Palestine to triumph. Death to the Jews, murderers of the prophets…the offspring of the sons of Zion are going to Hell.

"80 million people defend Egypt; 31 million defend Iraq; 21 million defend Syria; 10 million defend Tunisia; 7 million defend Libya, but 1.2 billion Muslims will rise up for you, Palestine.

O Palestine, millions of martyrs are marching toward you."

David took a long deep breath. 1.2 billion Muslims was more than 100 times the entire population of Israel. May 15, on the secular calendar, was the anniversary of Israel's being reborn as a nation. Once again, a tsunami of hate was threatening to sweep over the Jewish State.

David opened his inbox. He checked to see what had been learned of this Nathaniel. He opened one with a subject line that stated, *"RE: Serial number / Still vetting your guy…"* The email read:

Serial number 21102315
Sgt. Nathaniel Grange 1919–1947
WWII – 1944–1946
42nd "Rainbow" Infantry Division

David read the report with growing interest. *This must be a relative of young Nathaniel.*

Buried in Nachlat Yitzchak Cemetery, Tel Aviv.

David went to the Nachlat Yitzchak Cemetery website and printed out the grave-finder map.

✿✡✿✡✿✡✿

Nate woke up when the pillow hit his head.

"Get up!" Darryl yelled. "Somebody's here **lookin'** for you! You better get out here **pronto!**"

Nate followed Darryl into the warehouse. "This better not be **trouble,**" Darryl was saying. "What you been **doin'**? This guy is **lookin'** at **everything**…"

It was the General. "Come. I show you something," David said.

Nate tossed his duffel bag onto the backseat, and David pulled into the morning Tel Aviv traffic.

"I tell you something," David said. "Before and during the War, in 1947 to '49, there were volunteers that came to fight with Israel. They were called the *Machal*. Some of them volunteered aboard the ships of the *Aliyah Bet*. Some served in the early Israeli Army; seventeen *Machal* from the United States died in combat, fighting for Israel. One of them is buried in a cemetery near Tel Aviv. I take you there."

David could see Nate nod his head, absorbing this information.

"The soldier buried here helped Jewish refuges get out of Europe and into Israel. That was in 1947. When Israel was attacked later that year, he stayed in Israel and fought with the *Haganah*."

"I'm listening," said Nate.

"During WWII," David continued, "he served with the 42nd Division, 222nd Infantry Regiment.

He liberated Dachau."

David heard Nate breathe in sharply.

"Dachau—you know this place?" he asked, turning to look at Nate. Nate's face had hardened and his eyes were grey. He lowered his head.

"I had a teacher whose father had liberated Dachau. He told us about it and showed us pictures. He wrote it all down and gave it to us. It was so real. I could even smell it."

"Say what he told you," David said.

"He said the smell was overwhelming; it wrapped around him before he even entered the camp. He passed open freight cars filled with corpses. There were scraps of striped uniforms among the bodies. When he entered the camp, there were thousands of corpses. They were piled in heaps. Some lay scattered over the ground. Some were neatly stacked by the crematorium. He showed us pictures of everything."

"Buried in the corpses were people who were still living. He could tell—the eyes were blinking."

Nate's eyes were blinking as well, brushing tears out of his eyes.

"Some of the living were walking around. It looked like the dead were walking. They had no flesh, only skin stretched over bones. Some were squatting down. When the soldiers walked up, they would try to stand up. 'Amerikanish?' they would ask."

"When he entered the barracks there were more survivors, lying with the dead. They were piled up on the narrow shelves that were used as bunks. They were all sick. Stuff dripped from the top bunk down to the next, to the next, and finally to the ground. The smell hung in the air. He said it was like a thick fog, like a shroud of death."

David watched Nathaniel intently. He was talking as if he was seeing and smelling it all—almost as if he had been there.

Nate raised his head. His expression had become less harsh.

"A couple of days later he went into some barracks in another part of the camp. It was dark inside. Voices came out of the darkness asking, "Do you know my uncle?" "Do you know my father? … Sister? … Aunt?"

Nate paused. "Then there was a weak quavering voice that said, 'I had a brother. We lived together.' The voice told where he and his brother had lived; told how his brother had left and gone to the United States; told how his brother had become a rabbi."

A small smile had begun to light Nate's face. "The voice asked, 'Do you know my brother?'"

"There was a chaplain, a rabbi named Klaussner. When he heard the voice, he realized there was something familiar about it. 'Yes, I know your brother,' he answered the voice. 'I am going to bring your brother to you right now.' Rabbi Klaussner rushed out of the barracks. When he returned, he had a soldier with him—it was Chaplain Abraham Spiro. They had come over on the same ship, and what the voice in the darkness had said made Rabbi Klaussner sure that Chaplain Spiro was this man's brother. And he was! Spiro was his brother! What a reunion that was. It was a miracle from God."

Nate looked at David. "It was the finger of God! God was at Dachau that day."[3]

"Where was God before that day?" David asked with deep sadness in his voice.

Nate's eyes looked intently into the General's. "He was there. Suffering. Enduring pain, sorrow, tears, starvation, thirst, beatings. God was there..."

After a long silence David said: "And you? This story you tell. You feel you were there?"

"Yeah," said Nate softly. "It was like I was there."

Nate remembered how he had seen the pictures in his mind as he read his Bible. Before his teacher told him about Dachau. Before he saw the photos his teacher's father had taken.

✿✞✿✞✿✞✿

David and Nate walked in silence through Nachlat Yitzchak Cemetery. When they arrived at the gravesite, David stooped and brushed off the dust that had obscured the name carved into the headstone.

Nate crouched next to David. "That's *my* name!" he exclaimed. He looked at David questioningly. "Who is he?"

"A relative?" David asked.

---

3 Compiled from eyewitness accounts of the American soldiers who liberated Dachau, and the memoir of Rabbi Klausner.

"No." Nate was staring at the name—his name. "I, ah, did my whole family genealogy … needed the extra credit." He glanced at David. "There was no Nathaniel Grange … I would have remembered. No Nathaniel at all. … I went back hundreds of years."

Nate brushed the dust off the rest of the stone. A Star of David. A cross.

"Was he Jewish? Was he Christian?"

"I'll tell you something, there were maybe ten Christian Jews in Israel then," David replied.

"I have a question for you," said Nate. "What happened to Sgt. Grange? How did he die?"

"A battle, on the road to Jerusalem," David replied. "I'll tell you something. Where it happened, I will show you."

"Really?!" Nate said.

"Now I ask you something," David said. "Where did you get your duffel bag?"

Nate's eyes rested on the bag. "I didn't get it; I've always had it."

David raised his eyebrows, "Always?"

"Yeah. I had toys in it when I was a little kid. I carried my books in it when I went to school. I put my football gear in it in high school." Nate paused, a puzzled expression crossing his face. "That was when I found…"

Nate had stopped speaking. "Found?" David prompted.

Nate looked at David. He slowly nodded his head. "I'll email my mom. Maybe she knows."

After a long silence Nate asked, "Why did you want to know where I got my duffel bag?"

"On the side, a number. A U.S. military serial number. It belonged to Sgt. Nathaniel Grange. Your bag belonged to Sgt. Grange."

22

Nate closed his eyes and ran his hand through his hair. "Something's not right," he said. "Something is **not** right."

David remembered Yaakov saying those same words about Operation Cast Lead.

In silence they walked back to the car.

Suddenly Nate grinned. Looking at David he sang:

> **"When I hear that trumpet sound**
> **I'm gonna rise right outta the ground.**
> **Ain't no grave**
> **Can hold my body down!"**

"What is that?" David asked, startled.

"It's from a commercial; for *Deadliest Catch*, a program about the Alaska crab fishermen."

By the time they arrived back at the ELISHA warehouse David knew all about crab fishing out of Dutch Harbor, Alaska. "Maybe you should be in Alaska instead of Israel," he said to Nate.

"Are you serious?" Nate said, astonished. "That's the most dangerous job in the world!"

✡✝✡✝✡✝✡

"Where you **been? You** in **trouble? Talk** to me, man!" Darryl demanded as he walked out of the warehouse toward Nate.

"Cemetery," grinned Nate. "Saw where Nathaniel Grange is buried."

"**What?** You saw your **grave?** You plannin' on **dyin'**?"

Nate told Darryl about Sgt. Grange.

"You're **weirding** me out," Darryl said, shaking his head. "If I saw my name on a grave, I'd be outta here!"

✤✡✤✡✤✡✤

Nate watched the clock: 3p.m. in Tel Aviv. Soon it would
be the Sabbath and no one worked in the warehouse on the
Sabbath. Back home it was early Saturday, 7 a.m.—or was it
6? JJ and Josie would be up by now, watching cartoons. *Mom
should be getting up … making coffee…*

He clicked the Send button and waited.

Re: duffel bag
Mom – this is important – where did my duffel bag come from??

…turning on the computer…checking her email…

Nate watched his inbox.

A reply! Finally!

Re: duffel bag
I have no idea

Re: duffel bag
Really need to know – when did you give it to me?

Re: duffel bag
Don't remember giving it to you – why?

Re: duffel bag
Something's come up – ask Dad Grandpa Grandma anybody

Re: duffel bag
Will do – u ok?

Re: duffel bag
Yeah – just wondering – really need to know.
Bible you gave me? Where did it come from?

Re: duffel bag
Bookstore – it's on your shelf – can't believe you didn't take it

Re: duffel bag
Not that one – the one you put in the duffel bag

Re: duffel bag
There's a Bible in your duffel bag? Not from me

Nate reread the emails: Mom didn't know where the bag had come from? She hadn't given him the Bible? Had the Bible belonged to the other Nathaniel Grange? Had his special Bible had belonged to someone else?

Something's not right, he thought. *Something is not making sense.*

Re: duffel bag
What's going on? I'm your mother – I get to know

Re: duffel bag
U.S. military serial number on bag. Belonged to Sgt. Nathaniel Grange. He fought with Israel in 1947. He's buried here. I have his duffel bag.

Re: duffel bag
You have his duffel bag? Who is he? How did you get it? What's this about a Bible?

Re: duffel bag
I'm asking you
Bible – found it in the bag – right after I was baptized

Re: duffel bag
Really?! K see what I can find out

Nate had never told anyone what he saw as he read his Bible. Even Mom didn't get to know.

✡✝✡✝✡✝✡

Nate sat on his bunk, holding his Bible. It was really worn. It must be really old. The leather was beginning to crack.

Nate opened it and read what was written inside the cover.

There was his name:

Nathaniel Grange

A note:

When you read the words contained in this book
Your eyes will be opened and you will see
The glory of the Holy One of Israel

A verse:

I have spoken it; I will also bring it to pass.
I have purposed it, I will also do it. Isaiah 46:11b

Another verse:

Thus says the LORD of hosts: "I am exceedingly jealous for
Jerusalem and for Zion. And I am exceedingly angry with
the nations that are at ease, for while I was angry but a
little, they furthered the disaster."

Therefore, thus says the LORD, "I have returned to Jerusalem
with mercy; my house shall be built in it ... my cities shall
again overflow with prosperity, and the LORD will again
comfort Zion and again choose Jerusalem." Zechariah 1:14-17

✿✝✿✝✿✝✿

David picked up the phone. He would see if he could learn
what had been in Sgt. Grange's duffel bag when he died, and
where his belongings had been sent.

-4-

Gen. Yash'el leaned back in his chair, deep in thought.
Nathaniel's account of Dachau was disturbing. He had spoken
as if he had actually seen, actually experienced, actually
smelled Dachau. And then there was Nathaniel's statement that
God was at Dachau. Why would HASHEM, who was Holy and

26

Pure, allow Himself to be in the middle of the suffering, the degradation, of Dachau? And why would HASHEM allow so great an evil as Dachau and thousands of other camps to exist? HASHEM was just. Where was the justice?

Now there was another great evil, another Holocaust, rising like a great wall of water, pushing its way over the entire Middle East and flooding into Europe. David stood to look at the map hanging behind his desk. He had circled in red the tiny sliver of land that was the State of Israel. It had become an "exceedingly great army," a formidable military power, just as the prophet Ezekiel had written. Ezekiel 37:10 All options were on the table when it came to defending the Jewish State. How could Israel respond to an enemy determined to shed its blood on the streets of Jerusalem? To enemies who identify themselves as martyrs?

Ben-Gurion had said "salvation comes from the sky," referring to the need for an Israeli air force. The IAF was one of the best in the world. The Israeli Defense Forces were the best-trained, best-equipped in the world, except for the United States. But David knew "salvation" didn't come from military power. When Israel won the wars of 1948, 1956, 1967 and 1973, she hadn't had the military capability to win against the Arab nations that had attacked. Salvation had come from the sky, but it was HASHEM who had fought for Israel. David had seen that salvation for himself. He had fought in the battle for Jerusalem in 1948. He had fought in the Six-Day War in 1967. He had fought in the Yom Kippur War in 1973. He had been twenty-eight years old in 1967, maybe a decade older than Nathaniel was now.

He would bring Nathaniel to Jerusalem, he decided. He would tell him what it was like when God was there. It wasn't anything like Dachau.

CHAPTER TWO

Jerusalem

-1-

...the LORD will protect the inhabitants of Jerusalem,
So that the feeblest among them on that day shall be like David,
And the house of David shall be like God,
Like the Angel of the Lord, going before them.
Zechariah 12:8

"I'm not applying for Sar-El," Nate said as David pulled away from the warehouse. "I'll be staying at ELISHA FUND." David raised his eyebrows at this news. "I think I'm needed there," Nate said, though he didn't sound convinced.

David nodded. He thought for a moment and reached into the glove compartment. He took out a blue notebook with the IDF insignia on the cover. Handing it to Nate, he said, "I'll give you something."

Nate looked at him questioningly. "A manual," David explained, "to help you understand how the IDF operates. Maybe you'll change your mind. This will help you with your Hebrew—it's the language of the military."

Nate looked through the notebook. "The CD," David added, "will help with speaking."

"Thanks," Nate said, glancing up.

"In the back, another CD. Arabic. To know some Arabic is useful."

"Whoa," Nate said slowly. "I have to learn Arabic too?"

"No," David assured him, "just a few phrases."

"This is the old road to Jerusalem," David remarked as he turned onto Route 1 out of Tel Aviv. "I'll tell you something. In 1947 it was narrow, just a strip that led from the sea through the Judean hills to Jerusalem." Nate looked out the window at the rolling forested countryside that bordered the road while David continued to talk.

"Arab villages were on each side. The Arabs swarmed out of their villages, attacking lines of vehicles loaded with supplies for Jerusalem. I'll say something. They were like locusts. They were everywhere. They made roadblocks and mined the road. Mines would blow up one vehicle and the rest of the column would have to stop. The Arabs would be waiting in ambush. The drivers and guards of the convoy would be defenseless, out in the open. This was the most critical and terrifying road in all Israel."

Nate nodded, studying the road intently.

"It is here, on this road, that Sgt. Grange died," said David. "The convoy had been stopped. The Arabs were coming like a flood, attacking the men defending the supply trucks. One of the men—his gun jammed. He was trying to clear it when bullets started roaring toward them. Grange threw his body on

the man with the jammed gun, forcing him to the ground and covering him. Seconds later he was dead."

"He died a hero, then," said Nate.

"I'll tell you something, it is not a small thing to give your life for another man," David said.

"'Greater love has no one than this, that someone lay down his life for his friends,'" Nate quoted. "Y'shua said this." **John 15:13**

David said nothing.

"Do you know who the man was? The man he saved?" Nate queried.

"Yes, yes. I'll tell you something. He became the father of thousands in Israel," David answered.

"Thousands?!"

"Yes. He escaped the Nazis. After the *Kristallnacht*, he got out of Germany and joined the Resistance. He spent the war smuggling Jews, mostly children, out of Europe. They tried to bring them into Palestine or some other place of safety. Then, the war with the Germans ended. There were many children, without family, without fathers or mothers. He found a place for them in Israel—the Ya'thom Kibbutz. It is here that he became the father of the fatherless. Many thousands grew up in Ya'thom.

"When the war with the Arabs began, he fought with the Haganah. After this war he did not fight in wars again. Every war, every terror attack, brought children to Ya'thom. He said his life had been spared for a purpose—to provide a home for the children who had suffered so much. So, he is much-loved in Israel.

Thousands call him 'Abba.'"

Nate replied, "It was the finger of God." *...and I have Sgt. Grange's duffel bag and his Bible, he thought. Is that the finger of God too?*

"I think it was near this road…further ahead…that he died," Nate said.

"Sgt. Grange?"

"No…" Nate paused, focusing his thoughts. "There was a Jewish man. He came up from the grave and fought near here."

"Up from the grave?" David asked, mystified.

Nate turned to David. "A Jewish man was hidden in a grave during WWII. In Poland. In a cemetery. He stayed in the grave until dark. Then he came out and ate the food that had been left for him. He could walk around a little, and then had to go back into the grave. He stayed in that pit for years—until the end of the war."

"And he fought here?"

"He made it to Israel." Nate had directed his attention back to the road. "As he got off the boat, he was taken—somewhere—he didn't know where. He was given a gun—he had never held one before. He was told something in a language he didn't understand. When he died, he had only been in the country two weeks. He died in a field of gold. I don't know his name. I can only see his face." [4]

---

4 Adapted from the account of Lisa Cook, granddaughter of a Polish family who hid the Jewish man in the cemetery. See *Jews, Gentiles, and the Church* by David Larsen, pg. 107, for parallel account of Jews hidden in graves in Wilno, Poland.

David studied Nate. "This you know? How?" he asked. "You see his face? How?"

Nate dropped his head, looking at the old duffel bag lying at his feet, thinking about his Bible.

"I don't know how to explain," he said, "I just don't know."

"I'll tell you something," David said thoughtfully. "There were many battles along this road, but only a few in a field of gold."

Nate raised his head, listening intently.

"The field of gold. It was a field of wheat, which looked like gold in the spring of 1948. These were the wheat fields of Latrun, the fort that guarded the access to the Sha'arHaGai pass. This was where the Jerusalem Corridor became narrower with a stony ravine rising on each side. Without this pass the Jerusalem road could not be defended. Arabs had control of the Latrun fortress. Ben-Gurion insisted that Latrun must be taken. It was the only way to save Jerusalem."

David glanced at Nathaniel, who was giving the account his full attention.

"The Haganah was stretched very thin. Fierce battles were being fought throughout the country, and there were not many men to spare for an attack on Latrun. As Haganah officers rapidly laid out a battle plan, new immigrants were literally taken from the boats and brought to a staging area. They were trained for barely a week. The immigrants spoke a dozen different languages. No one understood Hebrew—the language of the military. It was chaos. There was a shortage of weapons, of water, of any kind of equipment."

David pulled into the Armored Corps Museum at Latrun. Armored vehicles, including tanks from the War of 1948, surrounded the Fort. Parking the car, David continued:"The first attack was planned as a surprise pre-dawn action, but it began late. The sun was already rising and exposed the Haganah troops charging through the wheat field. The attack fell apart as Arab bullets began slamming into the raw recruits. They panicked, broke ranks, and were mowed down like the wheat that surrounded them."

31

As they got out of the car, David added, "I'll tell you something. They had a lot of courage. They had no training, poor weapons and not much discipline, but courage—that they had."

Nate stared at the old fortress and nodded. "This is the place."

Nate was scrutinizing the assortment of tanks. "These we used in '48," David pointed to the virtually defenseless tanks that had been improvised for the assault on Latrun. David grinned. "And over here are Russian tanks we were given by the Arabs. During the Six-Day War, one of the Egyptian commanders abandoned all his tanks and artillery. He wasn't the only one. Scattered all over the Sinai were tons of Russian military equipment—tanks, small arms, ammunition—which fell into the hands of Israel."

Nate was grinning as well. "'Do not be afraid because of this vast army. For the battle is not yours, but God's,'" he paraphrased. [2 Chronicles 20:15]

"I'll tell you something," David said. "It was the finger of God."

"American?" Nate questioned, gesturing toward a more modern tank.

David nodded. "Yes, a large part of our arsenal."

He directed Nate's attention to an Israeli *Merkava*. "This one is considered one of the best tanks in the world."

Nate examined it. "Maybe I would be working on these if I joined *Sar-El*."

As they approached the museum, housed in the old fort, David pointed out the shell holes still visible in the thick walls. "I'll tell you something, the second attack nearly succeeded. It was commanded by Mickey Marcus, an American colonel—a *Machal*. Israeli armored cars penetrated the courtyard, but enemy artillery and a series of mistakes brought defeat. There were four attempts to take Latrun; none succeeded."

David and Nate stopped in front of a long wall outside the museum. Engraved on the wall were the names of the armored corps soldiers who died in action. There were no names of the immigrant soldiers, who in their first weeks in Israel had died in the attack on Latrun. Their names and faces remained unknown—except for the face Nate had seen, and even Nate didn't know his name.

-2-

"I'll show you something," David said as he and Nate walked toward the Harel Outlook. "Here you can see the road that passed by Latrun."

Looking at the steep, rough, rocky features of the land below, Nate saw a marked difference between this and the gently rolling hills on the opposite side.

"This mountain protected the Burma Road from the guns of Latrun," David said.

"Burma Road?" Nate questioned.

"Col. Marcus, the *Machal*, took charge of making this trail into a road like the one the British had made in Burma during WWII," David explained. "The Jerusalem Corridor was protected by the Haganah, the Palmach, but it was impossible to defend. Not enough men or weapons to keep it open. The fighting was fierce; there were many casualties. In the end the Arabs controlled the Corridor, and Jerusalem was under siege. There was no way to supply the Jews of Jerusalem. There was no way to bring food, water, fuel or ammunition into the City."

David paused, remembering how desperate Jewish Jerusalem was in those days. "I'll tell you something, 100,000 Jews were in Jerusalem. We were suffering. We were freezing. We were starving. Without the convoys bringing supplies, we would die. This road had to be made quickly. Not only were Jews starving in Jerusalem, but the ceasefire was soon to be declared. West Jerusalem had to be secured before the ceasefire or it would be lost."

Nate looked at the now neatly blacktopped road. "Why didn't they make this road earlier, before all the attacks on Latrun?"

"We didn't know it was here! A dirt track, it was discovered during the fighting. A Haganah soldier, Amos Horev, remembered it. He told Col. Marcus, and at night he and another soldier took a jeep to see how far they could go. The road was rough, and they were exhausted. They stopped and slept for a while. Then! I'll tell you something! They woke to see headlights coming from the direction of Jerusalem. They discovered it was a jeep. Someone from the city had the same thought—then they knew they could supply Jerusalem this way, if it could be made passable."

"Sweet!" exclaimed Nate. "Like Hezekiah's tunnel!"

"Yes, yes! It is the same. God opened eyes," agreed David. "Open eyes were not enough. Much work was ahead. A bulldozer—we had nothing else. This road was built by gangs of young Jews from Jerusalem. They hacked out this road by hand as rapidly as possible, under the cover of night. There were still casualties, but it was defensible. They started on May 18 and by the time of the truce—June 11—they had already broken the siege."

Nate was staring at large oversized silhouette figures directly across from the Outlook. "Who are they?"

"I'll tell you something," David replied. "Without these porters, the siege would not have been broken."

Seeing Nate's puzzled look, he explained: "At first there was a three-mile gap between the road from Tel Aviv and where it met the road from Jerusalem. No vehicles could come through. About 200 men from the *MishmarHa'am*—the Home Guard— were conscripted, right off the streets of Tel Aviv. They were in their 50s, didn't know where they were going or why. At the same time cars, trucks—any vehicle—was requisitioned off the streets. They were taken, with their drivers, loaded up with the supplies and the porters. Then they were driven as far as possible up the Burma Road. When the road became impassable, the men were given 45-pound packs. They carried these packs for three miles, over difficult terrain, in the darkness, until they met the jeeps from Jerusalem. By the

7th of June, twelve tons of supplies were getting through each night. The siege was broken."[5]

"Many roads have been built since Oslo to bypass hostile Arab villages all through Judea and Samaria," David said. "These are the most dangerous roads in all Israel. Those traveling can be shot or stoned. Now, with Hamas and the P.A. joining together, there are threats of kidnappings."

Nate looked down at the road. He imagined how it had been to build this road, how it would have been to carry all those supplies for three miles in the dark under Arab fire. He wondered what it was like to live in an Israeli settlement. He thought about the family that had been murdered on the road to one of the settlements just last week.

Before leaving the Harel Overlook, the two stopped inside the entrance. A simple plaque, positioned between the trees, honored the American volunteers who fought in the War of Independence. "Sgt. Grange was killed on the road to Jerusalem," David told Nate, pointing at his name. "I'll tell you something. We don't forget the sacrifice."

On the plaque was a Scripture verse:

All the men of valor among you shall pass over armed before your brothers and help them.
Joshua 1:14

-3-

"During the War," Nate turned to look at the General, "where were you fighting?"

"I'll tell you something," David replied. "I was too young to be a fighter, but we were all fighting for life in Jerusalem. Before the British left, few supplies came through. No guns or ammunition, only whatever food and fuel could survive the trip on the Jerusalem Road. Some guns, some bullets, we managed to smuggle in. Not many. It was freezing cold that winter. We were

---

5   Account of Amos Horev, who discovered the old road. From the documentary *Against All Odds.*

all cold, but the Haganah and Irgun fighters were the worst off. No warm clothes. No place to get out of the cold."

David paused, thinking of his father shaking in the freezing weather.

"As soon as the Mandate ended and the British left, the Arabs cut off the water supply to Jerusalem. The Arab sections could get water, not the Jews. We knew this would happen, so we were prepared."

David glanced at Nathaniel. Yes, he was listening.

"Under the rule of the Turks, each house had been given a cistern. When the British came, the houses got running water. We secretly collected and cleaned all the old cisterns and brought them to a certain place. We filled them with fresh water. Jerusalem had enough water to last four months. All the cisterns were sealed, and only an authorized person was allowed to open them. Water was distributed in special containers, loaded onto trucks and horse-drawn carts each day. Everyone lined up to receive their daily ration. The Arabs were sniping at any Jews they saw on the streets. My mother … she was killed in this way. I was one who took water to the fighters. And the food."

"How old were you?" Nate asked.

"Nine years. My mother—killed. My father—in the Haganah." David's face was somber. "He was killed too. Before the truce. It was while people were collecting their rations that they were killed by snipers. I was small and fast. I ran the rations to the fighters and to some of the people. By the first week of June there was almost no food. Then! I'll tell you something! Five jeeps with weapons and men made it to Jerusalem. They told us about the Burma Road. These five jeeps turned around and met the trucks loaded with food and fuel. Jerusalem was saved! A few days later there was the truce."

"General," Nate said, "I can't…I can't even imagine… nine … your mom and dad…"

David could still feel the grief. "Yes. Yes. They died for Israel, for Jerusalem. So I will fight for Jerusalem and Israel. Every war, I was in the fight. Now, my son and grandsons—they fight."

"My father," David continued, "was defending the Zion Gate, entrance to the old city. They had taken the Zion Gate on the same day the Burma Road was begun. There were 1700 Jews under siege in the old city. It was a desperate fight. The Palmach was surrounded by hundreds of Jordanians. They had only 25 bullets left. After the last bullet was fired"—he looked at Nate—"the Jordanians started shouting, 'Abraham! Abraham!' They dropped their weapons and ran!"

"Whoa! No way!" Nate exclaimed.

"Yes! I'll tell you something. Years later, one of the soldiers who was there with my father, met one of the Jordanians. This Arab said they ran away because they had seen a vision of a huge figure standing over the Jewish fighters. They saw him as Abraham, the father of the Jews. They ran away. They were terrified!"[6]

"Angel?" Nate asked.

"The Almighty sends His angels to fight for us," David answered. Yes. The finger of God."

"The Lion of Judah," said Nate. "The Angel of Adonai, over Jerusalem."

✿✞✿✞✿✞✿

Easing his way back onto Route 1, David glanced at the young man sitting next to him. Nathaniel was different. His intensity and seriousness were all in contrast to a joy that broke through in a broad smile, an expression of amazement or even a song. David had felt a bond forming between himself and Nathaniel. It was a bond that began when he learned of the prayers Nathaniel's family offered for Yaakov. A bond that was strengthened with Nathaniel's spontaneous stories—heartfelt and troubling—and with his recognition of HASHEM'S hand in the events of Israel.

6   Account of Ira Rappaport, one of the Palmach soldiers who witnessed the occurrence on Mt. Zion. He later met a Jordanian soldier who told him why they had run away - a vision of Abraham defending the Jews in the sky above the Israelis. From *Against All Odds*.

David smiled to himself. Or, maybe it was more about having a young friend, whose eyes were open, to share his stories with.

As they passed an old truck, rusting by the side of the road, Nate looked questioningly at the General.

"From the fight for the Jerusalem road," David explained. "They have been left as a memorial, so it is not forgotten how many gave their lives in this desperate fight."

Nate stared at the truck, then at the road. He felt his heart pounding. This was the place … the place Sgt. Grange had died.

"I'll tell you something!" David announced. "The day, the very day, the Burma Road was beginning to be carved out, the Syrians, with 200 armored vehicles—including 45 tanks—attacked Degania, the oldest kibbutz in Israel. The only heavy weapons in all of Israel were four ancient howitzers. They were like the ones used by the French against the Prussians in 1870. Two of them were dismantled and rushed to Degania. The commander there was Moshe Dayan. You know Dayan?"

"The guy with the eye patch, right?"

David nodded and smiled. "As soon as they arrived, Dayan had them reassembled. At that moment the first Syrian tanks rumbled through the kibbutz perimeter. The old field gun was fired and struck the lead tank. The Syrians, including all the tanks, rapidly turned and went back up the mountain road! They didn't realize that these two obsolete guns were half of Israel's entire arsenal!"[7]

David turned to Nathaniel. "Do you see?"

A broad grin spread over Nate's face. "Yeah. The finger of God!"

"This was not the end of the Syrians," David said. "Their army regrouped east of the Galilee. They were waiting to be re-supplied. At the same time a column of Israeli trucks and cars, with their homemade armor, were on their way to relieve another kibbutz that was under attack. They took the wrong

---

7 From "Israel, A Nation of Miracles" at BibleToday.com

road and crossed the border into Lebanon and ran head-on into a column bringing supplies to the Syrian Army.

There were dozens of truckloads of ammunition, a string of light artillery and 20 new armored cars. The Israelis fired point-blank at the first truck. It was a tanker filled with gasoline. When it exploded, it set on fire the next truck, which was loaded with hand grenades. The grenades going off were like a series of rapid explosions that could be heard for miles around. The terrified Syrians abandoned their cargo. The Israelis barely had enough men to drive the supply column back into the Galilee. When they reached the kibbutz, they learned that the Arabs had heard rumors that the Jewish army had invaded Lebanon and had fled from *Eretz* Israel!"[8]

"Finger of God!" Nate nodded, still grinning.

"I'll tell you something! There is more!" David said, "Are your eyes open still?"

"Wide open!" Nate said, anticipating the story.

"At Safed—this is near the Sea of Galilee—a small unit of Israeli soldiers were holding off at least a thousand Arabs. Suddenly a storm came up. The Israelis, in desperation, took what was left of their gasoline, poured it over 50 empty drums, set them on fire and rolled them down the hill. The storm, the flaming barrels tumbling down the hill, making a deep roaring sound as they hit the rocks, was too much for the Arabs. They thought this was some kind of secret weapon and fled for their lives."[9]

"That's it!" Nate exclaimed. That's what it was!"

"What? What is it?" David asked, surprised.

Nate leaned back in his seat and closed his eyes. Smiling, he said, "Just something I couldn't figure out."

"Tell me something," David pressed. But Nate didn't say anything.

---

8   Ibid.

9   Ibid.

As they continued to Jerusalem, Israel National Radio filled the silence:

> The truth of the Palestinian Authority's intent was just made public in an article in the UK's Guardian newspaper written by a prominent Palestinian intellectual and former PLO negotiator. Ahmad Samih Khalidi admits quite openly that the two-state paradigm is a thing of the past. He reveals that the new Arab strategy, and I quote, "bypasses the notion of an independent Palestinian state on part of Palestinian soil" and set its sights on "the entirety of Palestine before 1948." This admission—that it's all or nothing—is quite sobering, since up till now we have only heard it delivered as a warning coming from Jews and Israelis on the right who are usually dismissed... The Palestinian Authority president says that Jerusalem will be the Palestinian capital city...In the estimation of NBC foreign correspondent Richard Engel, "the Arab street is virulently anti-Israel" and "over time this thing ends in Jerusalem"...

-4-

Nate could hardly take in all the people in the Western Wall plaza. They seemed to have come from every corner of the earth—Ethiopia, India, China, Europe, Russia, America, as well as the Middle East. It was like being in downtown Chicago, except this was Israel and these were Jews from every country. There were tourists as well, with buses parked nearby. Men and women were separated, he noticed. Men were swaying as they recited prayers from a *siddur* [10] or read the Torah. Others stood quietly, reverently. Everywhere Nate looked there were Israeli soldiers, rifles slung over their shoulders. Their eyes were alert, their movements casual. They were a quiet but forceful presence. Nate looked up at the blue sky overhead, almost expecting to see the Lion of Judah keeping watch along with them.

---

10   A Jewish prayer book.

"Come," said David, gesturing at Nate to get a *kippa.* "I'll show you something." Putting the small cap on his head, Nate followed the General as he approached the wall. "It is here I said my first prayer at the Western Wall. There was no plaza then; it was narrow. When more people came, they had to wait in line to touch the stones."

"When was the plaza built?" Nate asked.

"I tell you something," David said. "In 1967, two days after capturing the wall, with no government order, the military demolished the entire Moroccan Quarter, making the plaza. The next Sabbath was *Shavuot.* Many would come to pray. It had to be finished by then."

Nate looked around, searching for something. "Is there a ditch around here?"

"Yes, yes. It is called the trench. Archeologists have dug it."

David pulled his prayer shawl over his head, reached out his hand and leaned against the ancient stones. Nate stood a moment. *There hadn't been a plaza—or a ditch—until 1967?*

He looked at all the men praying. Then he too rested a hand on the wall and bowed his head in prayer. He pressed his forehead against the ancient stones, feeling their warmth.

When he raised his head, he saw the General placing a folded piece of paper between the stones. At Nate's questioning look, David explained: "A prayer. Placed here before the eyes of the Almighty."

Nate searched his pockets for a scrap of paper. Nodding, David handed him a pen. "It is always before the eyes of HASHEM."

Nate wrote:

Father in heaven, in Y'shua's name, allow me to fight with You in Jerusalem.

He folded the note and placed it between the stones.

A moment later he pulled it back out and added: *In the IDF. Thanks, Nate Grange.*

He surveyed the wall, found a niche that didn't have any prayers in it, and carefully placed his prayer before the eyes of God.

Nate turned and looked around the plaza. The sky had become overcast. There were no people except the soldiers, and they weren't Israeli. Nate felt a chill come over him. Closing his eyes, he leaned his forehead against the wall. *Why is this happening?* he prayed. *What does this mean?*

"Come," David said. "I'll show you something."

They made their way through the crowded plaza. The sun was shining. The Israeli soldiers were standing in groups of two or three, talking as they kept watch.

-5-

Nate had devoured half his sandwich before he said: "I've always read that Israelis are secular."

"Yes. This is what they say. I'll tell you something," said David. "Ask an Israeli, 'Do you believe in the Almighty?'; they will say, 'I am not religious. I am secular.' They do not say 'I do not believe in God.' It is not possible to live in Israel and not believe the God of Israel is keeping watch. They close their eyes. They do not want to be religious. They do not want to keep the Law. Example: Sabbath laws—do not turn on a light, do not carry a match, do not drive a car, and do not spit. And more."

"'Don't spit'?! What's that about?" Nate asked.

"To spit in the dirt is to dig a hole. To dig is work."

Nate grinned. He thought of Y'shua spitting on the ground to heal the blind man. [John 9] Was that on a Sabbath? He couldn't remember.

42

"Rules for everything. No one can keep them all. I'll tell you something: Follow the writing of the Torah. It is enough."

"That's what Rabbi Y'shua taught," Nate agreed. "To keep the Torah, not the traditions of men."

David stared at Nathaniel for a moment but said nothing. Then he changed the subject and smiled.

"The IDF, they know the Almighty fights for Israel," he said. "Even your West Point knows. I remember something. A General from West Point said that 'the U.S. Military Academy does not study the Six-Day War. What concerns West Point is strategy and tactics, not the miraculous.'"

As David savored his meal, Nate looked for something more to eat.

"Yes. I forget—young man, big appetite," David said, signaling for another plate to be brought.

Nate looked around the square, enjoying eating outside under the blue Jerusalem sky. There were cafés, souvenir shops, snack bars, and on the west end was a synagogue. "The Hurva," David informed him. "You know the Hurva?"

"Weren't the Arabs upset when it opened?" Nate asked, vaguely remembering.

"Arabs," David said dismissively, "are always upset. … I tell you something. About the Hurva. This is the third time it has been built. First time: 1700. The Arabs burnt it down 21 years later. Second time: 1864. The Jordanians blew it up May 27, 1948. Third time: March 15, 2010. The Israeli police had to send in reinforcements to prevent the Arabs from rioting. The Arabs don't like the Hurva. They know the prophecy."

"What prophecy?" Nate asked.

"Rabbi Elijah ben Solomon Zalman—you know this Rabbi? The Rabbi Gaon from Vilna?" David asked. Nate shook his head. "I have no idea."

"He was a legendary rabbi. He prophesied the Hurva Synagogue in Jerusalem would be destroyed twice and built three times. He said this in the 1700s, when the Hurva was the most magnificent synagogue in the world. He said that when it was rebuilt the third time, then building of the third Temple would begin. That is what upset the Arabs. The building of the Temple."

"Are they building it soon?" Nate asked.

"I'll tell you something," said David, "the whole Middle East would be in flames."

"Another prophecy was made by the Vilna Gaon," said David. "He said that when you hear that the Russians have captured the city of Crimea, you should know that the times of the Messiah have started, that His steps are being heard."

Nate leaned forward and stared at the General. "That just happened," he said. "Seriously. It was just a few years ago!"

David nodded. "He also said that when we hear that the Russians have reached the city of Constantinople that we should put on our Shabbat clothes and don't take them off because it means that the Messiah is about to come."

Nate thought about that.

"You fought at the Western Wall?" Nate asked, eating a second sandwich.

"Ammunition Hill. We'll go there on the way back to Tel Aviv." Folding his napkin, David recalled: "In Jerusalem, maybe at the same time, in the night there was an IDF truck loaded with ammunition parked next to a building. It was to re-supply the outposts on the front lines. If this truck was hit by enemy fire, the explosion of ammunition would have brought down all the buildings in the area killing the people inside. Then! I tell you something! An incoming enemy shell made a direct hit on the truck."

David paused. "No explosion! That Arab shell rested on the top of all the ammunition and never exploded!"[11]

"Whoa! No way!"

"Yes. This is how it is when God fights for us." David paused again. "I remember something. You know Ariel Sharon?"

"Yeah, he was Prime Minister," Nate said.

"Before that he was a commander in the IDF. I'll tell you a story. Sharon's forces were following a wadi through the desert. Even after night fell they continued. In the darkness they ran into a minefield and lost one of their armored troop carriers. They could go no further at night. In the morning, at dawn, they continued. Suddenly! I'll tell you something! A whole brigade of Stalin tanks—you know the Stalin tank?"

Nate shook his head.

"The heaviest tank on the battlefield," David explained. "A whole brigade! Facing them in the desert. Behind the tanks were self-propelled guns. Sharon's tanks raced forward to attack, but the Egyptian tanks didn't move at all. Cautiously the Israelis approached. This is what they found: Every tank was intact but deserted!"

"What?!" Nate burst out.

"Yes! Later Sharon talked to the commander of this Egyptian tank brigade, who had been taken prisoner. He explained that he did not believe he could withstand the Israeli attack, so he decided to escape with all his men, but didn't want to blow up the tanks because the Jews would have heard him."

"Sweet!" Nate was grinning.

"I'll tell you more." David thought a moment. "Yom Kippur, 1973. A single IDF soldier in the Sinai led a captured Egyptian column to the Israeli lines."

"Only one?" Nate asked.

---

11 "Israel, A Nation of Miracles"

"When the Egyptian officer was asked why he surrendered the entire tank column to one Israeli soldier, the officer answered, 'One soldier? There were thousands of them!' The Israeli soldier didn't see the Army of the Almighty, but the Egyptians did!"[12]

Nate grinned as he quoted: "One man of you puts to flight a thousand, since it is the LORD your God who fights for you, just as He promised." Joshua 23:8

"The finger of God," said David.

-6-

"I'll tell you something. I was scared, but did not think about it," David told Nate as they approached Ammunition Hill. "We rode a bus to the battlefield. On the way we wrote farewell letters. Some are in this museum."

"This was not my first war, my first battle, but this was the worst," he continued seriously. "We fought face-to-face with the Jordanians. In the mountain were dozens of trenches. One trench would provide cover for other trenches. We were in some, the Jordanians in others. We just fired at each other and threw hand grenades. At the top was a huge reinforced concrete bunker. That made capturing Givat Hatachmoshet even more difficult. Finally the bunker was blown up. Our courage came from the Almighty Himself! There were three times as many Jordanians as we expected. It was a bloody battle. We lost 36 killed, 90 wounded. I was injured, not serious. The Arabs, 71 killed. Then! I'll tell you something! One of our scouts captured the hill by mistake!"

"By mistake?!" Nate exclaimed.

"Yes! The night was moonless. He fell into a Jordanian trench, started firing his rifle—from the hip, you say in the U.S.—and captured the Hill!

"Thirty hours later, we broke through the Lions' Gate, and re-united Jerusalem. This was the finger of God!" David

---

12 Ibid.

exclaimed. "The first paratroopers reached the Western Wall...there never were and never will be a moment like that. We were not prepared for this. Only God, who directed the whole thing, was prepared. Everyone was weeping—overcome by emotion. Commander Gur radioed: 'The Temple Mount is in our hands!' We were praying Kaddish for all our comrades who had died. Rabbi Shlomo Goren. He blew the shofar. Then there were shouts of joy and singing of Hatikvah."[13]

"We were not planning on going through the Lions' Gate. We planned to blow open the Eastern Gate and surprise the Arabs. There was a rabbi with us. 'You cannot enter the Eastern Gate,' he ordered. '*Ha-Mashiach* only can open the gate, when He comes.' He said the prophet Ezekiel had written this."[Ezekiel 44:2]

David looked at Nathaniel. "This is when I began to study the Tanakh to see what the Prophets say will happen to Israel."

Nate grinned. "I'll tell you something: I'm studying that too. Seriously, you have to read the end of the Book. You have to know the end from the beginning."

✿✞✿✞✿✞✿

Outside, as they walked through the original fortifications and trenches, David remembered what it had been like. "The Egyptians, Syrians, Iraqis, Saudis all came against us," he said. "In Jerusalem, it was the Jordanians. 182 Israeli soldiers gave their life-blood for Jerusalem. These trees"—he gestured at the 182 olive trees planted around the site—"each one is dedicated to one of the soldiers."

David and Nate wandered slowly through the museum. It was in the reconstructed bunker, underground.

Inside they read the farewell letters, examined the weapons, and scrutinized the maps and battle plans. As they watched a video presentation of the heroes of the Six-Day War, Nate saw that David was attempting to hold back his emotions.

---

13 Israel's national anthem. The title means "The Hope" in Hebrew

A few minutes later David said, "Some of the Jordanians said they saw a huge brilliant figure holding a sword of fire, with an army behind him, standing over Jerusalem."[14]

"A sword of fire over Jerusalem," Nate said. "I'd like to see that!" *Maybe I will...*

During the drive back to Tel Aviv, David and Nate were absorbed in their own thoughts. When they were nearly in Tel Aviv, David broke the silence. "Nathaniel," he said, "I'll tell you something. I have a reason for taking you to Jerusalem. I took you there to show you how the Almighty fights for Israel. In Dachau, the Jews were abandoned by HASHEM. He had turned His face from them. You see? God is here. He was not at Dachau."

Nate prayed: *How do I explain?*

"God's people are His servants," Nate said slowly. "Sometimes He allows His servants to suffer. He doesn't allow them to suffer for no reason. He suffers with them."

"What is His reason? How can He suffer?" David asked.

Nate answered: "'He was despised and rejected by men; a man of sorrows, and acquainted with grief... He has borne our grief and carried our sorrows ... He was wounded for our transgressions; He was crushed for our iniquities.' Isaiah 53 This is the prophet Isaiah writing about the Messiah."

David said nothing.

✿✟✿✟✿✟✿

"I'll ask you something, David said. "How can you see Dachau, a field of gold, a man's face?"

Nate took a deep breath, then reached down and took the Bible out of his duffel bag. He held it a moment before lifting it up for David to see. "Sometimes when I read this Bible I see things, like pictures or a video. I don't know what it is that I see, sometimes for years. Then someone will tell me something

---

14 "Israel, A Nation of Miracles."

or I'll be somewhere, and then I know what I saw." His voice trailed off. *This sounds crazy,* he thought.

After a moment David asked, "So…you are a prophet?"

"Me?! No! I don't know why this happens. I don't want it to happen—it just does."

David pulled over to drop Nate off at the warehouse. Then he said: "I remember something—come for Shabbat. Yaakov also will come."

"Yeah, that will be great," Nate said enthusiastically. "Did he get Grandma's letter?"

"Yes. Yes, he wishes to meet you. I come for you before sundown."

Nate lifted his duffel bag out of the car. It had been a long day. He was tired. He had a lot of thinking to do.

✿✝✿✝✿✝✿

"Where you **been?** It's **dark** already!" Darryl fired questions at Nate, waving his clipboard, as he entered the warehouse. "We got **three trucks** to load! They leave for the south first thing… grab **that pallet**…"

-7-

Nate collapsed on his bunk. After a day spent in Jerusalem, all night working in the warehouse, he was exhausted. *One more thing,* he thought, *before I can sleep…*

Nate turned on his laptop. It was 6a.m. in Tel Aviv. That would be…he counted on his fingers…10p.m. back home. Dad should be getting home soon—unless he'd arrested somebody and had paperwork to do.

Nate checked his inbox. There was no reply from Dad yet.

Mom had emailed: No one knew when he had gotten the duffel bag; no one knew anything about the Bible, nor about a Sgt. Nathaniel Grange.

When he had asked about money being transferred from his college account, and said he was staying in Israel for a few more months, Mom was not happy. "Talk to your father" was her final email.

Nate read what he had sent yesterday:

Re: college account
Dad –THIS IS IMPORTANT – Staying in Israel volunteered few more months. need $ transfer college account?

What he had saved for this trip was nearly gone. ELISHA FUND had the bunkhouse, but he still had expenses. He needed a phone, a vehicle, a way to get around. That would cost, and he was out of cash. The only money he had was in his college fund, but his parents had to sign for it.

There it was! Nate opened the email that had just appeared.

Re: college account
Your mother and I have discussed this. We feel that it's time for you to come home. Talk to Elisha Fund and opt out. You will need time to prepare for your fall classes. College account is for college only.

Nate replied:

Re: college account
Applying Hebrew University, staying Israel. I am of age. John 9:23
[John 9:23, "he is of age; ask him"]

Nate had applied for a student visa when he had gone for an extension of his volunteer visa. He hadn't mentioned to his folks that he was thinking of applying to Hebrew U. and he hadn't actually applied yet. That would be first thing tomorrow…

RE: COLLEGE ACCOUNT
You're already registered at Northwestern. You may be "of age" but you are not financially independent. We are also watching the situation in the Middle East. Looks like war may be coming. The enemies of Israel are saying, 'Let us wipe them out as a nation." Ps. 83:2,4. We want you home before the whole region explodes. [Psalm 83:2,4, "Your enemies make an uproar; those who hate you have raised their heads…they say, "Come, let us wipe them out as a nation; let the name of Israel be remembered no more!]

Which was why he **had** to stay…?!

Re: college account
I'm trusting in the LORD. The LORD is my refuge and my fortress. Proverbs 3:5–6, Psalm 91:1–2.
[Proverbs 3:5–6, "Trust in the LORD with all your heart, and do not lean on your own understanding. In all your ways acknowledge Him, and He will make straight your paths.]
[Psalm 91:1–2, "He who dwells in the shelter of the Most High will abide in the shadow of the Almighty. I will say to the LORD, 'My refuge and my fortress, my God, in whom I trust.'"]

Re: college account
Son listen to your father. Pay attention. Proverbs 4:1.
[Proverbs 4:1, "Hear, O sons, a father's instruction, and be attentive, that you may gain insight."]

… the things to come were coming!

Re: college account
The Spirit of truth will guide me. John 16:13. Even if you forsake me. Psalm 27:10.
[John 16:13, "When the Spirit of truth comes, he will guide you into all the truth, for he will not speak on his own authority, but whatever he hears he will speak, and he will declare to you the things that are to come."]
[Psalm 27:10, "For my father and mother have forsaken me, but the LORD will take me in."]

No reply. Nate waited …and waited…

Nate yawned. Still no reply from Dad…he waited…couldn't stay awake anymore…he fell asleep.

Nate woke up with a start when he heard the email alert. He stumbled over to his laptop, running his hand through his hair. *Need a haircut,* he thought.

Re: college account
Son, we're not sure what's going on with you, but we're going to trust your decision. We'll transfer 10k today. We would appreciate regular updates, something more than two sentences every couple of weeks. We're trusting the Lord for you.

"Thank You Lord!" Nate said with all his heart.

Re: college account
Thanks! Been really busy. Today went to Jerusalem with the general. You won't believe the stories…

That's two pages, Nate thought as he hit the *Send* button.

✿✟✿✟✿✟✿

Nate squinted at the clock and groaned. He had to get up. The General would be arriving soon.

Nate ran his hand through his hair again. *Really need a haircut...*

No time for that; he had to find something to wear. He pulled out the black jeans and white shirt that had been stuffed into his duffel bag. He tried to smooth out the wrinkles. The jeans would be all right, but the shirt...maybe if he steamed it...Nate hung the shirt near the shower and turned the hot water on. Steam was pouring out of the bathroom. *That should do it.* He couldn't go to Shabbat dinner with a wrinkled shirt, could he?

✿✟✿✟✿✟✿

David reviewed the file he had received earlier: Nate was from a regular middle-class, American-Christian family; football in high school; average grades; no police record. One item of interest. Nate had been involved in an automobile accident a year ago. His courage and clear thinking had saved the life of the injured party. He had completed one year of college before coming to Israel as a volunteer with ELISHA FUND. It also noted that he had no known connection to Sgt. Nathaniel Grange and no known Jewish heritage. David saved the file and opened an email that had just come in.

RE: serial number
Sgt. Grange duffel bag: no next of kin. 'Decoration of State Warriors' affixed
to War of Independence campaign ribbon placed in duffel
Stored in warehouse Tel Aviv. Warehouse torn down 29 April 2001.
No information on present location of duffel bag.

David leaned back in his chair. April 29, 2001 was the day Nathaniel had been born. David didn't believe in coincidence; it wasn't kosher.

CHAPTER THREE

Shabbat
-1-

Observe the Sabbath day, to keep it holy,
As the LORD your God commanded you.
Deuteronomy 5:12

"Nathaniel." The General's wife, Hannah, smiled. "Welcome to our home." Taking his arm, she led him into a room where there were three men standing to meet him. "This is our family, you see?"

"This is Abbas' young man, Nathaniel," she announced.

"Here is son Yaron," she said, introducing the older of the men to Nate. "Yaron makes the harps of David."

Yaron stepped forward and shook his hand. "Welcome," he said with a smile. "We make them in Jerusalem."

Introducing two other men, Yaron said, "These are my sons, Eyal and Yaakov. Eyal lives in a settlement in Samaria. Yaakov is stationed in the Negev."

The two stepped forward and looked appraisingly into Nate's eyes for a long moment. Then with broad smiles they greeted him.

"Welcome!" said Eyal.

"I finally meet you," said Yaakov. "It is good."

"I meet you too!" said a small voice. "This," said Yaakov, dropping his hand to the little boy's head, "is my son, Yosi."

"Hi there," Nate replied, as Yosi ducked behind his father.

"My family is not here," Eyal commented. "It's become too dangerous to leave the settlement."

Yaakov directed Nate's attention to one of the women on the couch. "My mother, Abigail. And my wife, Sara." Both women welcomed Nate with generous smiles.

"And this," said Yaakov, looking tenderly at a small child who was sleeping in Sara's arms, "is Gilana."

"It's great meeting all of you," Nate remarked, putting down his duffel bag. "Thanks for having me."

Eyal studied the pendant Nate was wearing. "You are wearing this?"

Nate nodded. "I don't know what it is exactly, but I wear it all the time."

David came and examined it.

"Usually it's under my shirt," Nate explained.

"You got this—when?" David queried.

Nate was becoming uncomfortable. "Is something wrong?"

"This is the metal given to the *Machal* who fought during the 1948 war," David replied.

"How did **you** get it?" asked Yaakov.

"It was in the duffel bag?" David guessed. Nate nodded.

"Later I will tell you something," David said. "Now there are other things to talk of." He turned and led the way into another room.

Nate looked around. Maps on the walls, shelves overflowing with books, a cluttered desk, some kind of radio, and a computer filled the room. As they faced a detailed map of Israel, Nate tried to follow the rapid Hebrew as they pointed to different areas.

"They are fighting each other," David said. "Sunni against Shia, Egyptian against Egyptian, Syrian against Syrian, brother against brother. It is the four winds of heaven, stirring them up."

"Then they'll turn against us…"

David jabbed his finger at the map. "Here, here, and here." He pointed to the cities most likely to come under chemical, biological or nuclear attack.

Yaakov traced the borders with Syria, Lebanon, Gaza and Egypt. "We're prepared for what will happen when we hit them…"

Yaron contemplated the possibilities. "How ready are we?"

Eyal pointed to Samaria. "We are under attack now! The Palestinians destroy our fields, steal our livestock and attack our vehicles. We have no defenders! We have almost no supplies!" He looked at Yaakov. "We're not allowed to defend ourselves!"

"We're working on a plan," Yaakov said cautiously, glancing first at Nate and then at David. Yaakov stepped out into the courtyard with Eyal. Nate could see Yaakov talking rapidly and Eyal nodding.

Yaron began giving David some details of what was going on at Eyal's settlement. The Palestinians were attacking primarily with rocks, causing accidents and injuries. A family had been murdered. A young girl had died from a lack of medical supplies she'd needed … kidnappings were attempted … a car with a baby inside was hijacked…

Nate looked down at his *Machal* pendant. *I can do something,* he thought. Then he said it aloud.

David and Yaron turned and looked at Nate.

"I can get medical supplies," Nate remarked.

"How? Where will you get them?" asked Yaron.

"I tell you something," said David, "the agreement with ELISHA FUND and the government is to give drugs only to hospitals and certain clinics."

"Yeah, I know," Nate answered.

David looked into Nathaniel's eyes. "Count the cost," he said.

"I'll need a list," Nate told Yaron.

Yaron stepped into the courtyard. Nate could see him telling Yaakov and Eyal what he had said. Eyal glanced over at Nate and nodded.

A woman's voice broke the silence. "Time to light the Shabbat candles." The men gave the map one last look before beginning to leave the room. Nate turned to see a young

55

woman with amused eyes and a friendly smile looking at him. *Sababa!* Nate thought. *I wasn't expecting this!*

"Welcome to the war room," she said.

"Hi," Nate replied. "Nice meeting you. You are…?"

"Yaakov's sister, Tahlia."

Nate nodded and smiled. He followed her into the dining room. Should've got that haircut, he thought.

The Shabbat table was set with a white tablecloth, pale-blue china and polished silver. Centered between two silver candlesticks were an elaborate Kiddush cup and two loaves of challah. Nate thought of how his mom set the table for special family times.

He looked over at Hannah with a smile of appreciation for her beautiful Shabbat table.

Hannah put a delicate lace shawl over her head and said:

"The Sabbath is a delight, the holy day of Adonai, a day to be honored. May You bestow on me and my family a full life. Be gracious to us. May You bless us with many blessings, and cause Your Presence to dwell among us.

Compassionate Father, extend Your loving-kindness to me and my loved ones so they walk before You in the ways of the upright, holding fast to Your Torah and to good deeds. Keep far from us any shame, grief and sorrow. Set peace, light and joy in our home, for with You is the source of life; in Your light, we see light. Amen."

Hannah reverently lit the Shabbat candles. Covering her eyes, she prayed:

"Blessed are You, Eternal our God, sovereign of time and space.

You hallow us with Your mitzvoth and command us to kindle the lights of Shabbat."

Laying his hand on Yosi's head, Yaakov blessed his son:

"May God make you like Ephraim and Manasseh. May you grow into a multitude in the midst of the earth."

Laying her hand on Gilana's head, Sara blessed her:

"May God make you like Rachel and Leah, who together built the house of Israel."

Holding the Kiddush cup, David said a blessing over the wine:

"Blessed are You, Eternal our God, Sovereign of the Universe, Creator of the fruit of the vine."
He then said a blessing over the bread:

"Blessed are You, Eternal our God, Sovereign of the universe, Who brings forth bread from the earth."

The table was loaded with food. It reminded Nate of Thanksgiving dinner. Various chicken dishes, a selection of salads, vegetables, fish—he hadn't seen this much good food since before leaving home. He filled his plate with chicken, fish, carrot stew, and much more that he wasn't familiar with.

Sitting across from Tahlia, he couldn't help but notice how her eyes softly reflected the candlelight.

Conversation flowed around him. "…know we didn't get all the shipments. Hezbollah has some of Syria's biological or chemical weapons…" "…only about 60 to 70% of the people have gas masks…" "…they lighten up on sanctions, Iran will just keep going until they have nuclear…" "…what's the United States doing?! This isn't the first time they've betrayed us…" "…Iran's just going to continue until they have nuclear…" "…what's the United States going to do if that happens?"

Nate realized that last question was directed at him. "I have no idea. This President says he won't put up with a nuclear Iran, but I don't know what he'll do. One thing I do know, you can count on us to back you up if the time comes. The last administration threw you under the bus, but this one won't."

Yosi chimed in: "I go under the bus too!" Sara shushed him.

"There's no more room under the bus," Nate quipped.

"I tell you something: War is coming," stated David. "This year, next year, we cannot know. We must be prepared."

"The IDF is ready. Our military has never been as prepared as they are now," asserted Yaakov. "Israel has its own Responsibility 2 Protect." Yaakov's gaze rested on Sara and Gilana as he lifted Yosi onto his lap.

"We must consider everything," David said. "I'll tell you something. Much has happened quickly. We have said, something is pushing these things to happen, like a schedule is to be followed."

Yaron, Yaakov, Eyal and Nate all nodded in agreement.

"Also, a third intifada is being threatened."

"There's already an intifada against the settlements!" Eyal commented.

"Israel has almost no room to maneuver," David continued. "What will America do?"

"I have no idea," Nate again replied.

"What of Iran?" Yaron wanted to know. "Will the United States stand with Israel if we need to go after their nuclear sites?"

Nate shook his head. "It could go either way. America's talking about lifting sanctions. Nobody wants another war."

"War is coming. Maybe this year. Iran is getting closer every day to a nuclear weapon," Yaakov stated. "Without the United States, Israel will be alone."

"Israel is never alone, and we have taken out nuclear sites before," Yaron responded. "Do you remember what happened in 1981?"

"I was, like, not born yet," said Nate. "I don't know anything about 1981."

"It was June 7," said Yaron, "when the Israeli Air Force bombed the Osirak nuclear reactor in Iraq. It was on the eve of Shavuot, the anniversary of the day Israel conquered the old city of

58

Jerusalem. It was a Sunday, a day when the French technicians who were helping Saddam build the reactor would be off work. This was the day chosen to stage the raid on Osirak. The reactor was near Baghdad, beyond the range of the F-16 Phantoms. To fix this problem they added extra fuel tanks, which they would jettison when they were empty. This was potentially very dangerous. There were 1000-kilogram bombs on the wings of the plane, right next to where they'd be jettisoned. If one of the tanks even touched a bomb, it would explode. There was nothing else to be done, so the risk was taken."

"That was just one problem," Yaron continued. "The Iraqis would have our pilots in their sights for fifteen minutes. This is why it was decided to go with eight F-16s plus an escort of two F-15 Eagles. We thought that at least some of them would get through."

"They set out from Etzion Air Base in the Eastern Sinai, then turned and flew across the Red Sea into Saudi Arabia, flying at an altitude of 30 meters, so they wouldn't be detected by any radar systems."

Yaron shook his head. "It wasn't radar that spotted them. It was King Hussein of Jordan. He was vacationing on his royal yacht in Aqaba. He was a fighter pilot himself and immediately understood that the IAF's target was the Osirak nuclear reactor. He called headquarters in Amman and ordered that the Iraqis be informed that an attack was imminent. For some reason the information was never relayed."

"The empty fuel tanks were jettisoned over Saudi Arabia without any problems, and our pilots continued until they finally were approaching Baghdad. There was a war going on with Iran at the time, and Iran had tried, unsuccessfully, to take out Osirak less than a year before. When our pilots reached the Baghdad area, they expected the Iraqis to put up a strong defense. But there were no MIGs, no mirage jets, no defense at all!"

Tahlia was smiling. She had heard her father tell about this event before.

"Suddenly they saw the reactor ahead in their bombsights. They dived down, dropped the bombs, and soared up to an altitude of 12,000 meters and headed home…"

"Were you one of the pilots?" asked Nate.

"No, I was monitoring the mission from the ground," Yaron replied. "I debriefed the pilots when they returned. I can still remember every word. One of the pilots, Col. Ze'ev Raz, the leader of the attack, said: 'On the way back, no attempts were made to intercept us, no missiles, no radars, and no planes; but we saw something Israeli air-force pilots are not accustomed to. I had never seen such a thing! We flew into the sunset, and at our speed, we saw the sun as if it didn't move for the whole 45-minute journey. In Israel, an air-force pilot can't fly east to west for more than a few minutes, so we were faced with something we had never seen before: a vision of the sun suspended at sunset. It had us all thinking about what Yehoshua bin Nun experienced thousands of years ago: the shemesh b'Givon dom—may the sun stand still in Givon.'" **Joshua 10:12**

"Sweet!" exclaimed Nate. "That must have been something to see."

"It wasn't just that," said Yaron. "When they arrived back at Etzion, just before sunset on the eve of Shavuot, the pilots were brought in for debriefing. There really wasn't much to discuss, everything had gone so smoothly. The planes had all performed perfectly. None of the pilots reported even the most minor typical malfunction. Then one of the pilots put it into words: **'It was the finger of God.'**[15]

After a moment Yaron continued. "Whenever Israel is threatened, I read the report of the day the sun stood still."

"I'll tell you something," said David. "Most in Israel do not give the praise to HASHEM. I do not take away from those who fight, they are strong and courageous, each a hero. But it is HASHEM who gives protection and victory."

"If the leaders of Israel have faith, then perhaps it is enough for God to give mercy," said Yaakov.

Yaron agreed. "Menachem Begin believed the salvation of Israel came from HASHEM. He had faith in 1981."

"And now, the Prime Minister is having Bible study each week—isn't he?" asked Nate.

---

15   From an interview with Col. Ze'ev Raz.

"He is," David nodded.

"That would be interesting to go to," said Nate.

David smiled. "It is."

"Is this why you wish to join the IDF? So you will have a story to tell? "Tahlia asked.

Nate met Talia's gaze with a broad smile. "I want to fight for the winning team," he said, "in the final battle. The story has already been told."

"Enough of war talk," said Sara, glancing at Yosi and Gilana.

Changing the subject, Abigail asked Nate, "You have a family in America?"

"Yeah, my dad is in law enforcement, and Mom works at home taking care of the J's."

"Your mom takes care of birds?" asked Tahlia.

"No," Nate laughed. "The J's are my little brother and sister. Their names are James Justice and Jocelyn Joy—we call them 'the J's.'"

"How little are they? "Hannah inquired.

"They're four now." Nate saw the next question coming, so he explained, "I was an only child until I was fourteen. Then, along came the twins." Everyone smiled at that.

"And more family?" Hannah wanted to know.

"Lots of family. One set of great-grandparents, two sets of grandparents, uncles, aunts, cousins all over … the … place…" His voice trailed off as he realized that seated around this Shabbat table was a family who had lost nearly all of their relatives in the Holocaust.

"I tell a story," said Hannah, breaking the silence. "I do not speak of it until now, you see? It began when I was small—two years old, younger than Yosi. In the dark of night, my parents took me on a long bike ride. The Germans were coming, and my parents were bringing me to a family who would keep me safe. The man—my father was in the army with him during the First World War. We came to their house and I fell asleep. When I

61

woke up, my parents were gone. These people became my new parents. Such love they gave me! I didn't know then how much they risked having me in their home. They were Christian family. They took me to church, to Sunday School. They taught me about Jesus. 'Jesus loves you,' they would tell me. 'I love Jesus too,' I would say. I was Christian then, you see? The Nazis were in the Netherlands for five years. I was eight years old when the war was over. Everyone was happy! I didn't have to stay away from windows anymore or hide if a soldier came down the street.

One day I was looking out the window and I saw two people on bicycles. They stopped and came to the house. I ran and hid. I was still afraid. After they came in my parents found me and brought me to them. 'These are your momma and papa,' they said. I did not believe it. 'No!' I said and ran away, into the kitchen. The two bicycle people found me there. Then the woman said to me: 'May you be like Rachel and Leah...', the blessing my mother had said over me every day before the war. I remembered these words. Then I knew. These were my parents; I was Jewish. [16]

"They had survived, you see? The tabernacle of David is being raised up: Yosi, Gilana have family—mother, father, grandfather, grandmother, great-grandfather and great-grandmother. They have Aunt Tahlia..." Hannah smiled at Tahlia. "Someday an uncle and cousins."

Gilana, no longer sleeping, stared at Nate while Yosi struggled to stay awake. The Shabbat meal was drawing to a close. Yaron reached for his harp and played a few cords. He sang:

"When God restored the exiles to Zion it seemed like a dream,
Our mouths were filled with laughter, our tongues with joyful song.
Then they said among the nations: 'God has done great things
for them.'
Yes, God is doing great things for us, and we are joyful.
Restore our fortunes, O God, as streams revive the desert.
Then those who have sown in tears shall reap in joy.
Those who go forth weeping, carrying bags of seeds,
Shall come home with shouts of joy, bearing their sheaves."

---

16   From the account of a Holocaust survivor, name unknown.

David led the family in the blessing:

"Sovereign God of the universe, we praise You: Your goodness sustains the world. You are the God of grace, love and compassion, the Source of bread for all who live; for Your love is everlasting. In Your great goodness we need never lack for food; You provide food enough for all. We praise You, O God, Source of food for all who live.

"As it is written: When you have eaten and are satisfied, give praise to your God who has given you this good earth. We praise You, O God, for the earth and for its sustenance. Deuteronomy 8:10

"Let Jerusalem, the holy city, be renewed in our time. We praise You, Adonai; in compassion You rebuild Jerusalem.

"Merciful One, be our God forever. Merciful One, heaven and earth alike are blessed by Your presence. Merciful One, bless this house, this table at which we have eaten. Merciful One, send us tidings of Elijah, glimpses of good to come, redemption and consolation."

✿✞✿✞✿✞✿

Nate watched as the General's family gathered and said their goodbyes. Yaron and Abigail only had to walk across the courtyard to their home; Eyal and Yaakov's family were staying with them until Shabbat was over. Eyal grasped Nate's hand and handed him a folded paper. "What you bring here will find its way to me," he said. "Don't forget…"

"I'm on it," Nate said seriously. "I'll remember."

Seeing the General had his keys in hand, Nate turned to thank Hannah for having included him in her family Shabbat. "Sava," [17] Tahlia spoke up, "I'll drive Nathaniel. I'm on call, so I have to go in." Sweet, thought Nate, glancing at the General to see if it was okay with him. David slowly put the

17 Hebrew for *grandpa*.

keys back in his pocket, looking steadily at Nate. Then David nodded, a small smile on his face.

"So!" announced Hannah. "You will come again. I will write Grandmother and you will send it to her, you see? I will tell her you have a place here in Israel." Nate's wide smile was his only answer.

✿✿✿✿✿✿✿

"My family is from the Netherlands," Nate said as they drove down the nearly empty streets of Tel Aviv.

"A long time ago, in the 1800s, they came to America. I still have relatives there, I think."

"Savta[18] never talked about when she was little before, only when they were already in Israel," said Tahlia. "I'd like to talk to her some more, hear more stories."

"The General…"

"Told you all his stories," Tahlia interrupted with a smile.

"He took me to where he fought in '48 and '67; the road to Jerusalem, the Temple Mount…"

"There are more stories," Tahlia assured him. "Lipstick ammunition, cardboard ships, drainage-pipe cannons … I'll have to tell you those."

All of a sudden they were at the warehouse. "And you can tell me about your duffel bag, and how you got that medal," Tahlia said.

"Sure," Nate smiled, getting out of the car. "Talking about my duffel is my favorite subject! … Thanks for the ride."

"Wait," Tahlia said, grabbing a piece of paper and writing on it. "This is my number. Call me sometime."

Nate leaned over to take the paper. He saw wide brown eyes and an amazing smile. "I will. I'll call."

---

18 Hebrew for *grandma*.

Nate took a deep breath and watched as she pulled away. He definitely had to get a phone! It would be the first thing he'd do, after the Sabbath. And he'd look for a vehicle.

✡︎✝︎✡︎✝︎✡︎✝︎✡︎

Darryl pulled Nate into his office and threw his clipboard on the desk.

"You **can't** do that, man! You **can't** just **take** stuff and **bring** it wherever you **want**! We aren't **authorized** for that!"

Yeah, yeah, yeah, Nate thought as Darryl continued…

"You do **that** and we'll have the **whole board** of directors comin' down here!"

"You want **trouble** with the **Israelis**?! You want them breathing down our neck?!"

No, I just want them breathing.

Darryl looked at Nate's list. He rocked back on his heels. He looked at the ceiling. He looked at the floor. He looked at Nate. He crumpled the list and threw it in the trash.

"I'm havin' **nothin'** to do with this! **Nothin'!** You understand?! I don't want to see one **bandage** walkin' out of this warehouse!!"

Darryl stormed out of his office, slamming the door behind him.

Nate picked up the list and smoothed it out. He quickly read it. There were no bandages on the list.

✡︎✝︎✡︎✝︎✡︎✝︎✡︎

Nate carefully placed his tightly packed duffel bag under his bunk and kicked in front of it a pair of jeans lying on the floor. He fired up his laptop.

Re: Shabbat
Had a great time. Met the General's family.
His wife, Hannah, was saved from the Nazis by a Dutch family
His son, Yaron, Makes harps of David
Met Yaakov—he's stationed near Sderot
Yaakov's brother Eyal lives in a settlement in Samaria
Yaakov's sister Tahlia is an EMT with Magen David Adom
More later

Darryl watched as a woman driving a Magen David Adom ambulance pulled up in front of the warehouse. He watched as Nate opened the door and carefully put his duffel bag on the floor before getting in. He watched as they pulled away. "I see **nothing!** I know **nothing!**" he said, throwing the clipboard in the air.

-2-

Nate and Tahlia began spending all their free time together.

They delivered the medical supplies and traveled all over Israel. From Dan to Beersheba; from the Golan Heights to the Negev; from the Jordan River to the Mediterranean Sea; and everything in between.

They saw the battlefields, the archeological digs, the ancient cities.

They climbed the mountains, walked the deserts and swam in the Med, the Red, and the Dead Seas.

They followed in the footsteps of Abraham, David, and Y'shua.

Wherever they went, Nate read what the Scriptures told about the places they were seeing. And beginning with Moses and all the Prophets, Nate showed Tahlia all the things that had been written about Y'shua. He read her the accounts in Matthew, Mark, Luke and John, showing how Y'shua had fulfilled all that had been written.

Open her eyes, he prayed. Open her heart … just a little…

CHAPTER FOUR

Yad Vashem
-1-

And I will give in My house and within My walls
a monument and a name, better than sons and daughters;
I will give them an everlasting name that shall not be cut off.
Isaiah 56:5

"Lotta loads comin' in today! Be back at **decent time!** You can't be out **all day** with **that girl** and work **all night!** We got trucks goin' **north** tomorrow!" Darryl's voice followed Nate as he left the warehouse.

"Does he always yell?" Tahlia asked as Nate got into the car.

"Yeah," he replied distractedly.

Today they were going to Yad Vashem.

✡✝✡✝✡✝✡

Like a spear of light piercing the black heart of the mountain, Yad Vashem came into view as they approached Mount Herzl. As they got closer, Nate could see the spear of light was a triangular prism, shining in the morning sun with each end suspended, floating in the open air, on either side of the mountain. Nate couldn't take his eyes off the museum.

"That's pretty dramatic," he said. "Light piercing the darkness of the nations."

"It's a mountain, Nathaniel, the Mount of Remembrance."

"Yeah, well, in the Bible, mountains symbolize nations."

✡✝✡✝✡✝✡

They walked slowly through the exhibit, reading every document, examining every picture. The skylights that formed the prism brought in the light. They had entered the room that showed Jewish life before Hitler's rise to power. They saw photos of families: wedding pictures; bar mitzvahs; children.

"See how happy they are," Tahlia said as she wandered from one picture to another.

"Yeah," Nate replied. "They were enjoying life."

They followed the route, guided into the different galleries by impassable gaps in the prism floor.

The floor began to slope gently; as they continued their journey, the light began to dim.

The Nuremburg Laws...*Kristallnacht*...businesses destroyed... synagogues burning...

They looked at the pictures, watched the videos, listened to the accounts of the survivors.

Tahlia slipped her hand into Nate's as they watched films of the Jews being gathered and brought into the ghettos; she gripped tighter as they saw the brutality and starvation, the bodies piled up in the streets and the children with their pale faces and emaciated bodies.

Nate remembered what Goebbels had said: "We came like wolves descending upon a herd of sheep."

As they continued, they felt they were descending deep into the heart of the mountain.

Descending into hell, Nate thought.

They could feel the darkness enveloping them as they entered the galleries depicting the death camps. Auschwitz. Treblinka. Belzec. Majdanek. Dachau. Sobibor. Chelmno...

Nate stopped suddenly. A date had caught his eye. He read:

> **On 7 December 1941, as the first seven hundred Jews were being deported to the death camp at Chelmno, Japanese aircraft attacked the United States Fleet at Pearl Harbor. Unknown at the time either to the Allies or to the Jews of Europe, Roosevelt's day that would 'live in infamy' was also the first day of the 'final solution.'** [19]

19   From *The HOLOCAUST: A History of the Jews of Furope During the Second World War* by Marin Gilbert, pg 24.

They saw chimneys spewing columns of ash and death by day. At night the columns of smoke were filled with sparks of fire, each spark a life, a name. Each spark disappearing into the dark night.

They stood and watched as people were pulled off the trains, and felt their fear as they were confronted by snarling dogs and men with whips. Beings, dressed in black uniforms with death's-head insignias fixed to their hats, shouted orders. An officer carrying a hooked cane separated the terrified people. Families were torn apart. Those on the left were sent to immediate death. Those on the right, to a life that was slowly extinguished by starvation, disease and brutality.

They walked through barracks where people were stacked on shelves, living skeletons willing themselves to survive one more hour, one more day.

They saw row upon row of women, standing in the snow, freezing in their thin clothing, waiting to be counted.

Tahlia suddenly gasped. Nate followed her gaze to the picture. "What is it? What do you see?

Then he saw—there, in the second row—a face, a familiar face. Tahlia's face.

"Who is she?" Tahlia whispered. There were no names listed for the women in the photo, just a caption:

"WOMEN WAIT FOR ROLL CALL."

Nate put his arm around Tahlia, pulling her close. A little more than seventy years ago, that could have been Tahlia in the picture.

"These are my people; these are all my family," Tahlia said, trembling.

"I know ... I know," Nate replied gently.

Tahlia looked at Nate. "Why didn't they tell us?" she asked. Why didn't **they** warn us?"

"They had to deceive everyone," he answered. "They had to, or there would have an uprising—like in the Warsaw Ghetto. Then when those on the outside began to find out, it made it easier for them to deny it."

"Not the Nazis," Tahlia said, "the Prophets. Why didn't they warn us? You said God doesn't do anything without telling the prophets." [Amos 3:7]

Nate thought about that.

"Jeremiah wrote about it," Nate said. "He wrote about the Holocaust. He wrote that Israel would be saved out of it and that HASHEM would bring them back to the land He had given their fathers." [Jeremiah 30]

"There's a psalm," he said. "The words are like pictures." He led her toward one of the photos and quoted: "'For my days pass away like smoke, and my bones burn like a furnace. My heart is struck down like grass and has withered.'" Pointing to another picture, he said: "'I forget to eat my bread. Because of my loud groaning my bones cling to my flesh.'" Moving to still another, he continued: "'I lie awake …All the day my enemies taunt me; those who deride me use my name for a curse.'" And another: "'For I eat ashes like bread and mingle tears with my drink.'"

Tahlia was silent as she gazed at the pictures.

"This was so horrific, no one would have understood until it ended," Nate said. "The Psalm says: 'This will be written for a later generation.' This was written for our generation, so we would understand." Tahlia looked at Nate. He said, "It ends with a promise: 'Your servants' children will dwell securely and their offspring will be established before You.' It says: '… for the LORD will rebuild Zion…' [Psalm 102]

"This one," Nate said, pointing to another picture, "the prophet Ezekiel wrote about. The LORD asked Ezekiel, 'Can these bones live?' Then God said, 'Thus says the Lord GOD to these bones: Behold, I will cause breath to enter you and you shall live.' Then He says to Ezekiel, 'These are the whole house of Israel.'" [Ezekiel 37:3–5,11]

Tahlia nodded. "Even the Prime Minister said Ezekiel wrote about the resurrection of Israel."

The floor began to ascend as they entered the gallery of the Liberators. They saw the pictures and read the news reports that were now informing the world of the atrocities that had been found in the camps. They watched the graphic footage that had been released by the Signal Corps to the major newsreel companies, which had then been shown in Europe and the U.S.

They read the letter General Eisenhower had written to Chief of Staff George C. Marshall after seeing Ohrdruf, a sub-camp of Buchenwald. The letter was dated April 15, 1945.

"The things I saw beggar description... The visual evidence and the verbal testimony of starvation, cruelty and bestiality were ... overpowering ... I made the visit deliberately in order to be in a position to give firsthand evidence of these things if ever, in the future, there develops a tendency to charge these allegations merely to 'propaganda.'"

They read the dates the camps had been liberated in 1945:

January 27 - Soviet troops liberate Auschwitz, Poland
February 13 - Soviet Army liberates Gross-Rosen, Germany
April 4 - US 4th Armored and 89th Infantry liberate Ohrdruf, sub-camp of Buchenwald, Germany
April 11 - US 4th Armored and 104th Infantry liberate Buchenwald, Germany
April 11 - US liberates Dora-Mittelbau, Germany
April 12 - Canadian forces liberate Westerbork, Netherlands
April 15 - British army liberates Bergen-Belsen, Germany
April 23 - 90th US Infantry Division liberates Flossenbürg, Germany
April 29 - 42nd and 45th Infantry and 20th Armored Division of the US Army liberate Dachau, Germany

Nate felt a shiver go down his spine. He stared at the date Dachau had been liberated: April 29.

"What is it?" Tahlia asked, watching his face.

Nate shook his head. "It's nothing," he said. "Just a coincidence."

"So explain," said Tahlia.

"Dachau was liberated on my birthday," he replied. "Just a coincidence."

"Sava says there are no coincidences. He says everything means something."

"Yeah, and a soldier with my name liberated Dachau on my birthday. Does that mean something?"

✿✟✿✟✿✟✿

The floor continued to ascend, and the prism opened up again. Suddenly it seemed to burst out of the mountain. Jerusalem stretched out in the distance, the city bathed in light, its ancient stones gleaming like gold. As Nate and Tahlia drank in the beauty of the city, Nate began to sing softly:

"Jerusalem! Jerusalem! Lift up your gates and sing,
Hosanna in the highest, hosanna to your king!"

"Is that a real song, or are you making it up?" asked Tahlia.

"It's a real song," Nate smiled. "My family always sang it."

"Sing it all then. You sing. I'll listen."

Nate tried to remember all the words.

"Last night I lay a-sleeping, there came a dream so fair.
I stood in old Jerusalem beside the temple there.
The sun grew dark with mystery, the morn was cold and chill.
As the shadow of a cross arose upon a lonely hill,
As the shadow of a cross arose upon a lonely hill."

Tahlia had turned to look at Nate as she heard these words.

"And at once the scene was changed,
New earth there seemed to be,
I saw the Holy city beside the tideless sea;
The light of God was on its streets, the gates were open wide...
And all who would might enter, and no one was denied.
No need of moon or stars by night, or sun to shine by day...
It was the new Jerusalem, that would not pass away.
It was the new Jerusalem, that would not pass away!"

Taking a deep breath, Nate let the words ring out over the Holy City:

"Jerusalem! Jerusalem!

Sing, for the night is o'er!

Hosanna in the highest, Hosanna forevermore!

Hosanna in the highest, hosanna forevermore!"[20]

-2-

Nate and Tahlia walked slowly down the Avenue of the Righteous, reading the names on the plaques.

"Is the family that saved Hannah here?" Nate asked.

"I don't know. *Savta* never said their name." After a few minutes, Tahlia said: "Many of these Righteous Gentiles didn't believe in God. Hardly any were Christian; Christians have always hated us.

"Not all Christians," Nate said. "Hannah was hidden by Christians, I'm a Christian, and there are a lot of us who care about the Jewish people."

"I mean through history. It was always the Christians that made us suffer. Why?"

"I always wondered about that too. I've studied it a lot."

"Did you find out?"

"Yeah, I found some answers." Nate stopped and faced Tahlia. "I want to say—to you, to all the Jewish people—that I'm sorry, really, really sorry, about how the Church, Christianity has persecuted your people."

Tahlia looked into Nate's eyes and saw the sadness. "It's not you," she said, "not you and your friends. It's the other Christians that are, even today, after all this, siding with our enemies."

Nate nodded. It was true. The Christians who supported the Jewish State, fought against anti-Semitism, helped the Jewish

---

20 1892 song "The Holy City." Words by Frederick E. Weatherly, music by Stephen Adams.

people—they were only a small percentage of Christianity. The rest didn't think Israel or her people meant anything to God anymore. Most of the Church was silent. Others were taking up the cause of Israel's enemies.

"Look! Here's a name from the Netherlands. Maybe they're the ones who hid *Savta*."

Nate read the name and then took a picture of the plaque.

"What did you learn?" asked Tahlia.

Nate ran his hand through his hair, organizing his thoughts. "I learned that as the Church became more Gentile, it began to turn against the Jews—starting with the Jews who believed in Y'shua. This had begun by the end of the first century. By the second century, the Church leaders were saying that all the Jews, forever, were responsible for killing Y'shua. Then came Constantine. He made it illegal to observe the Sabbath or the Feast Days. It took a few centuries, but in the end, you couldn't be both Jewish and Christian. Even Y'shua wouldn't have been able to be part of the Church. It just escalated from there. At first it was discrimination; then persecution; then came the crusades, the inquisition and pogroms. The teachings of the Church against the Jews saturated the culture wherever the Church was. By the time Hitler came, it was just accepted as normal that the Jews would be persecuted."

"They always wanted the Jews to convert, to become Christians," Tahlia remarked. "They're killing us in the name of their Christ and then they want us to **convert**?" She shook her head.

"Yeah," Nate agreed, "It doesn't make sense. But—Tahlia, this is important—the way the Church acted toward the Jews is not how Jesus, Y'shua, wanted them to act."

"That's what confuses me," Tahlia replied seriously. "You read to me what the Bible says about Y'shua, and then I know what the Church has done to us."

"I don't think the Christian Jesus is the same as the Jewish Y'shua," she said.

Finding more names from the Netherlands, Nate continued taking pictures.

"There were always some in every generation, throughout the centuries that tried to protect the Jews," he said. "Not enough to stop what was happening, but there were always some that were willing to go against the Church and help the Jews. Members of the clergy tried to protect the Jews too—sometimes."

They wandered through the Garden of the Righteous and looked for a place to sit. Finding a rock wall, Nate set down his duffel bag and flexed his shoulders. "What are you thinking?" asked Tahlia.

"What you said. About the Christian Jesus not being the same as Y'shua in the Bible. They are the same. The love of Jesus, of Y'shua, just wasn't shown to the Jewish people by the Church. Remember how surprised you were when you learned Jesus was Jewish?"

Tahlia nodded.

"Well, there are a lot of Christians who are surprised about that too."

"They didn't know?"

"The Church made Jesus into a Gentile—it was like He was born a Jew and then became a Christian, a Gentile."

"And I thought **I** was confused."

They sat in silence for a long while, enjoying the cool of the garden, the scent of the flowers. It was so peaceful. Nate stretched out on the rock wall, laid his head on Tahlia's lap and closed his eyes. *I am so tired,* he thought as he began to drift away…

"Why did God let the *Shoah* happen?" asked Tahlia. "You say God has a purpose for everything."

Why did God allow the Holocaust… Nate thought, refusing to open his eyes. "I studied that too. It's complicated. I don't know if I can explain…"

"So explain."

"There's something else. I need to show you something else…you have to understand what else God allowed, for His purpose."

Tahlia reached into the duffel bag, took out his Bible and dropped it on his chest. "So explain."

Nate forced his eyes open and picked up his Bible. "Remember when Y'shua died on the cross?" he asked, turning to the passage. "Listen to what Isaiah wrote…

"See, My Servant will prosper; He will be exalted and raised up. Just as many were appalled at Him—so marred was His appearance, so disfigured, He did not look like a man, and His form did not look like a human being.

Just so He will sprinkle many nations. Kings will be silenced because of Him, for they will see what has not been told them, they will see what they have never heard. Who can believe what we have heard? To whom has the arm of the LORD been revealed? For He has grown up before Him like a tender plant, like a root out of dry ground.
He had no form or beauty that we should look at Him, no appearance that we would desire Him.
He was despised and rejected by men, a man of suffering, well acquainted with grief. As one who hid His face from us, like one people turned away from.
He was despised and we esteemed Him not.
Yet it was our sickness that He was bearing, our suffering that He endured. But we thought of Him as stricken, struck down by God, and afflicted.
But He was pierced because of our sins, crushed because of our iniquities.
He bore the punishment that made us whole, and by His bruises we were healed.
We all went astray like sheep, each going his own way;
And the LORD has punished Him for the guilt of us all."
(Isaiah 52:13–53:6; cf. John 1:11; 1 Peter 2:24–25)

Tahlia leaned over and studied the text. "I never heard that before. Are you sure that's Isaiah?"

"It's Isaiah. You can check in the Bible I gave you or in the Tanakh, when you get home."

"Keep reading," said Tahlia.

He was oppressed and afflicted, but He did not open
His mouth. Like a lamb led to the slaughter, like a sheep,
silent before her shearers.
He was taken away by oppression and judgment, and
who considered His fate?
For He was cut off from the land of the living; through the
sin of my people, who deserved the punishment.
And His grave was set among the wicked and with the rich
in His death—though He had done no injustice and had
spoken no falsehood.
But the LORD chose to crush Him, to put Him to grief,
that, if He made Himself an offering for guilt, He might
see offspring and prolong His days.
And that through Him the LORD's purpose might prosper.
Out of His anguish He will see it and be satisfied.

My righteous servant makes the many righteous. It is
their punishment that He bears.
Assuredly, I will give Him the many as His portion, and He
will receive the mighty as spoil. For He submitted Himself
to death, and was numbered among the sinners. He bore
the guilt of the many and made intercession for sinners.
(Isaiah 53:7–21; cf.Matthew 27:12–14, 38, 57)

Nate turned his head to look at Tahlia. She was just sitting there,
gazing out at the garden. He laid back and closed his eyes. *Help
her understand,* he prayed, *help her believe what she's heard...
help her understand...help her believe...help her...*

Soon he was sound asleep.

"Nathaniel," Tahlia shook him, waking him up. "Isaiah was talking
about Y'shua? This is what you wanted me to understand? That
God chose to make Y'shua suffer and die? That was HASHEM'S
purpose? For Y'shua to take our guilt and make intercession?"

"Yeah," said Nate, sitting up. "That's it. But Y'shua went
through all that suffering and death willingly. He chose to
suffer and die, to make Himself a guilt offering."

"And the reason is atonement? Like the Day of Atonement? A sacrifice, like when there was a Temple?"

"Yeah," said Nate, "a sacrifice, atonement for sin. But there's more to it. Y'shua made the final sacrifice. Now, anyone, any individual, who believes in Him and repents of their sin, will have their sins forgiven—forever. Not one year at a time, but forever." ^{Hebrews 10}

"Why? Why would He do that?"

"Because He loves us. The same reason He chose Israel. Just because. Nothing we did to deserve it. He just loves us. I don't understand it either, but there it is." ^{Deuteronomy 4:37, 7:8, 23:5, 33:3; John 3:16}

"And this is His purpose?"

"To provide a way, so no one has to face God's justice unless they choose to. He made a way for us to be reconciled to God our Father." Nate looked earnestly into Tahlia's eyes. "Y'shua took our guilt, paid the price of our guilt, and now we don't have to pay what we owe God for our sin—if we repent of our sin and believe in Y'shua..."

"What does that mean? To believe."

"Believe that Y'shua is who He said He is. That He was sent from God. That He came to do God's will. That He is God's Son. That He is the Messiah. He was born a human being and lived as one—but without sin. He died and God raised Him up. Now He's sitting at God's right hand."

"That's a lot more than what Isaiah said."

Nate closed his eyes for a minute, then said, "I can't explain everything. Only God can. Pray to the God of your fathers—to the God of Abraham, Isaac, and Jacob. Ask Him and He will let you know. Read the Gospel of Matthew...or Mark—it's a lot shorter..."

Tahlia didn't say anything for a long time. Finally she spoke: "I will. I will read. I will ask."

Nate put his Bible back in his duffel. He stood up and tried to work the kinks out of his shoulders. "Hungry?" he asked.

Tahlia looked up at him, "I'm still thinking," she said.

"You can think while I eat, "said Nate, pulling her to her feet.

✿♱✿♱✿♱✿

Nate let the buttery croissant melt in his mouth. Stuffed with grilled lamb and chopped vegetables, it was his favorite food in all Israel.

"The one Isaiah talked about," Tahlia said, "you say it's Y'shua. He suffered the same way that the Jews have."

Nate nodded. "That's true. The Jews were 'despised and rejected,' they were 'oppressed and afflicted,' they were 'led like sheep to the slaughter,' and 'by oppression and judgment' they were taken away. They were 'cut off from the land of the living.' The same things happened to the Jews as happened to Y'shua."

"You said HASHEM had a reason, a purpose for the *Shoah*," said Tahlia. "You said HASHEM doesn't let His people suffer for nothing."

Nate thought for a moment as he took another bite of his croissant. "Remember Y'shua was the atonement sacrifice?"

Tahlia nodded.

"Remember that on the Day of Atonement there were two goats for the sin offering?"

Tahlia nodded.

"Remember the lot was thrown for which one was the lot for the LORD and which one was for the scapegoat?"

Tahlia nodded.

"The lot for the LORD was Y'shua," Nate said. The sins of the people were laid on Him."

"And the purpose of the Shoah?" Tahlia asked.

Mopping up his plate with the last of the croissant, Nate said: "This is the way I understand it. The scapegoat that was sent into the wilderness—that was the Jewish people. The Jews settled in the Gentile nations. Every time there was a crisis the Jews were blamed. They were made the scapegoat for all of the problems of the Gentile nations."

"The world still blames its problems on us," Tahlia said. "We're still the scapegoat."

"Yeah, that's true," agreed Nate. "In the past they were forced out of the countries where they had been living—after being persecuted. When they were persecuted the people literally put their hands on the Jews. We just saw pictures of the Jews being beaten, we saw their suffering, and how people turned their faces from them. The sins of the nations were being put on the Jews."

"And now they want to drive us out of our own country," she said.

"Yeah," said Nate, eyeing her plate. "Aren't you going to eat?"

She pushed her plate over to him. "No, you can have it."

Nate handed her his Bible. "It's easier to explain if you read a couple of things," he said.

"Go to the book of Hebrews. It's in the last half—keep going to your right ... a little more... okay, go to chapter 9. Start at verse 7 and read to the end."

Tahlia read the passage while Nate took a bite of her croissant. When she finished, he said, "Now go to Leviticus. It's near the front..."

"I know where Leviticus is," said Tahlia.

"Chapter 16."

Nate finished the croissant at the same time Tahlia finished reading.

"Do you see where the bull and the goats were for a sin offering?" Tahlia nodded. "And the ram was a whole burnt offering—a holocaust?"

"What do you mean, a holocaust?"

"That's the Greek word for 'whole burnt offering.' When the Jews translated the Hebrew Scriptures into Greek, about 200B.C., that's the word they used."

Tahlia took a deep breath. "Are you saying the Jews were a whole burnt offering?"

"I'm sorry," Nate said. "… it's complicated… it's hard to explain."

"So explain."

"Now go to Numbers 29:12–32."

After reading the passage Tahlia said. "I don't understand."

"Those sacrifices were for the nations. Seventy bulls were sacrificed for the seventy nations that descended from Noah. When the Temple was destroyed, these sacrifices ended."

Tahlia didn't say anything. She looked out at the street, watching the people walking by.

"Tahlia," Nate said, drawing her attention back. "This is the conclusion I've come to. That the Jewish people were a sacrifice for the sins of the nations. The nations laid their sins on the Jews, and the Jews made the atonement for them. Now it's up to the nations. Will they accept the sacrifice and receive protection from the justice of God? Or will they continue to reject the Jews and Israel."

"That was HASHEM'S purpose for the Holocaust? So the nations could be saved from HASHEM'S judgment?" asked Tahlia.

"Y'shua's sacrifice was for each and every individual. Each person has the choice whether to accept His sacrifice or reject it. The Jews sacrifice was for the nations. The nations can accept it or reject it. That's the way I understand it."

Nate waited for Tahlia to say something. She didn't say a word.

"I could be wrong. I studied this a lot, and this was what I understood," Nate said as he got up.

"We have to get going," he said. "If I'm late again Darryl's going to chew me up and spit me out."

"He doesn't like you being with me," said Tahlia.

"He likes you all right. He just doesn't like me coming in late every time we go somewhere."

Standing outside the warehouse Nate held Tahlia a moment before he said, "We talked about a lot of things today, and I'm not that good at explaining…"

"It's okay, Nathaniel. I will read. I will ask HASHEM. Maybe He will answer."

✿✝✿✝✿✝✿

"**Finally!** Come on…" Darryl pulled Nate into the warehouse. "Had a guy from the **board of directors** here today!" Darryl turned and glared at Nate. "He was here with his little **calculator**, his little **pen**, his little **notebook**, lookin' at **everything**." Darryl opened the door to the medical supply room. "He comes in here. What do you think he saw?!"

Nate looked around. *Pretty empty,* he thought.

"**Shelves half-empty! That's** what he saw!" Darryl was waving his clipboard. "He's **punching** his little calculator. He's **writing** in his little notebook with his little **pen**. He says, 'Were you aware how fast you're going through medical supplies?'" Darryl looked at the floor. "My heart was **poundin'**, man. Thought I'd have a **heart attack**."

Darryl looked at Nate. "Know what he says **then**?"

Nate shook his head. *I have no idea.*

"He says: 'I'm going to have to **double** the shipments of medical supplies to you.'"

Darryl stared at Nate. "More than **half** of what we get **just disappears** and he's going to **replace** it with **double**!! Can you explain **that**?!"

The finger of God! Nate thought. "The finger of God," he said.

Darryl stood for a minute. He looked out at the warehouse. "Well, the finger of God isn't gonna get these pallets unloaded. I coulda used you **two hours** ago! **No sleep** for you tonight. Or **tomorrow.** We're bringin' these supplies up north."

-3-

The warehouse was quiet. Darryl was at his desk, and the rest of the guys had turned in. Nate was moving the last pallets into place.

"Nathaniel."

Startled, Nate looked around and saw Tahlia. It was five in the morning. What was she doing here?

"I had to talk to you. I couldn't wait," Tahlia said. Nate tried to read her expression. It was all mixed up—excited, serious, happy, tears in her eyes…

"Are you okay?" he asked, going toward her.

"I have to tell you," she said, tears beginning to run down her face. "I believe Y'shua is the Messiah!"

"You do?! Tell me! Tell me when you knew!"

"I prayed to HASHEM, I read all the Scriptures you gave me, and then I just knew. Everything we talked about. Everything in the Tanakh, in the Bible. My eyes were opened. I saw. I understood. I could feel my heart open, and love and thankfulness for Y'shua flooded in!"

Nate put his arms around her. *Thank You Jesus. Thank You Y'shua. Thank You Jesus.*

"This is the finger of God," he whispered in her ear.

PART TWO

THE FAITHFUL WITNESS

And from Jesus Christ the faithful witness,
the firstborn of the dead, and the ruler of the kings of the earth.
Revelation 1:5

Leaning heavily on his cane, the old man carefully shuffled his way across the busy Tel Aviv street. Rushing past him, in both directions, were other—younger—people. They were texting or talking into cell phones, distractedly hurrying to get to the other side. The old man gripped his cane as someone brushed against him. He barely kept his balance. Then he saw it. A truck speeding toward them! Ramming into the crowd! He knew he would not survive. "Hear O Israel," he whispered, "ADONAI our God, ADONAI is one…"

In that instant he felt strong arms around him, enveloping him, gently carrying him to the ground…rolling him out of harm's way…

CHAPTER ONE

Terror
-1-
Deliver me from those who work evil,
And save me from bloodthirsty men.
Psalm 59:2

"Are you almost ready?" Justine called up the stairs to the J's. "We're going to be late for the pool."

"Almost!" yelled JJ as he threw his towel, sandals, snorkel and goggles over the rail, nearly hitting Mommy.

"A mess, JJ," said Josie as she carefully stepped around JJ's gear.

"That all has to be in your bag before we leave," Justine reminded JJ.

"Whatever!" JJ raced down the stairs, almost knocking Josie over.

"You can wait in the car while I get some water and turn the TV off," Justine said to Josie. "Maybe your brother will be ready by then."

Justine took a few bottles of cold water out of the refrigerator. She looked around for the remote while she put the water in her bag. There it was, on the couch. She picked it up and pressed the power-off button just as the reporter was saying, "…terror attack in Tel Aviv…"

Justine stopped and turned the TV on again.

> On one of the busiest streets in Tel Aviv, four people are dead and many more injured. A man driving a truck rammed into pedestrians as they were crossing the street. He then jumped out of the truck and began stabbing whoever he could. He was heard shouting "Allahu Akbar" during the attack. Our Mid-East correspondent, Eric Strayer is on the scene. Eric?

*Yes, Carl—as you can see, the people here are in
shock. This is the first terrorist attack in Tel Aviv in
almost three years. Witnesses say the truck came
roaring out of nowhere. They say it stopped and
then backed up over those who had been knocked
down in the initial attack. Then the driver jumped
out of the vehicle with a knife and began stabbing
everyone he could. A couple of the men brought him
down, but not until he had done a lot of damage. He's
now in the custody of the Israeli Security Services.
We know there are at least four dead and there are
many more injured—we don't know as yet how many
or how serious the injuries are.[The camera panned
the chaotic scene behind Eric.] As you can see,
Magen David Adom is here. They are bringing all the
fatalities and the injured to the Sourasky Medical
Center in Tel Aviv.*

Justine leaned toward the screen. *What street was it? Was
it near where Nate worked?* She had a sick feeling in her
stomach. *Realistically,* she told herself, *what were the chances
that out of the hundreds of thousands of people in Tel Aviv,
Nate would be here? None.* She was sure he was fine.

Justine grabbed her cell and called Wes.

"Did you hear about the attack in Tel Aviv?" she asked.

"Tel Aviv was attacked?!"

"No, there was a terrorist attack **in** Tel Aviv. Four people killed
and a lot of injured."

"I'm sure Nate wasn't there."

"I don't feel so good about this."

Wes didn't say anything.

"Are you still there?" Justine asked.

"Yeah… okay. I'll call the Embassy. Let you know."

Justine watched one Magen David Adom ambulance pull away as another drove up. The camera zoomed in on the responders getting out of the ambulance. *Wait! Was that Tahlia?*

✿✞✿✞✿✞✿

Tahlia and Zvi ran toward the triage that had been set up. There was a lot of blood on the street and Tahlia nearly slipped. She had stepped on something hard and almost lost her footing. She reached down to see what it was. It was…she wiped the blood off…it was a small blue menorah, a medallion. She felt dizzy. It was Nathaniel's—he had been here! She looked around. Where was he?

"You coming?" Zvi called out. "We need you over here!"

Tahlia put the medallion in her pocket. She surveyed the area one more time before going to help with the injured.

✿✞✿✞✿✞✿

"Can we go now?" JJ stepped in front of the TV. "I'm packed up and waiting in the car!"

"No, were not going yet," said Justine. "Get away from the TV."

JJ turned and looked. "It's just news," he said.

"We're supposed to wait in the car!" Josie said to JJ, rolling her eyes.

"Look, you two," Justine said, pointing to the TV. "There's been an accident in Tel Aviv. We're going to watch this a little while before we go to the pool."

"Are there helicopters? Is Nate there? Did he wear his helmet?" JJ wanted to know.

"It's not that kind of accident," said Justine. "It was a terrorist attack."

87

"With planes?"

"No. A truck."

Josie was studying the TV screen. "Look! That's Nate's duffel bag!"

"What?! Where?!"

Josie pointed to the corner of the screen.

There on the street, next to an old man, was a battered green duffel bag.

✡✝✡✝✡✝✡

"There's a man over here," Eric said as he walked over to where an old man was standing, leaning on his cane. We're going to see what he remembers. ... Are you OK? Is there anything we can do for you?"

"I am standing, yes?" said the old man, straightening up and striking the ground with his cane. "Like an angel of the Almighty! Out of the way I was carried!"

"Who carried you out of the way?" Eric asked.

"Again I should be dead, yes? The young man. They took him away. To the hospital." Each sentence was punctuated by the sound of the cane tapping the ground.

"Which hospital?" Eric asked, sensing a human-interest angle to the story.

"Ichilov! And you will take me there!"

Eric faced the camera. "It looks like we're going to Ichilov General Hospital. It's one of the three hospitals that make up the Sourasky Medical Center. That's where the victims of this terrible attack have been taken. We'll see if we can locate the young man. Back to you, Carl."

"Eric, that old man looks an awful lot like Aaron Weiss. For our viewers who don't know who I'm talking about, Aaron Weiss is a very well-known and much-loved person in Israel."

88

"We'll get back with Eric at the top of the hour," said Carl. "He'll let us know who the old man is."

✿✞✿✞✿✞✿

Tahlia looked pleadingly at Zvi. "Go ahead," he said. "I'll take care of the paperwork. You go find your guy."

Tahlia threaded her way through the emergency room. Everything was still in chaos. Doctors and other medical personnel were coming in from all over to help. Everyone seemed to be running everywhere. She looked into each unit, searching faces, looking for a young man with dusty blonde hair.

Tahlia stepped into one unit that was relatively quiet and dimly lit. She could hear a respirator and could see someone...head wrapped in bandages...a tube down his throat. She felt her heart pounding. This was Nathaniel. He did not move—at all.

She picked up his chart: Fractured T12, L vertebrae compressing on nerves...pneumothorax...

"What have they done to you, what have they done?" she moaned.

She continued reading the chart. Broken back, severed nerves in spinal cord, punctured lung, right arm crushed...head injury. Tears filled her throat. "Nathaniel," she whispered. "Nathaniel..."

"He will live! Yes? I have talked to the Almighty and he will live!"

Tahlia turned to see an old man, leaning on his cane, shuffling toward her.

"He's all broken up," Tahlia said, tears in her voice. "Everything is broken."

The old man struck the floor with his cane. "He will heal! Yes!"

Tahlia stared at the old man. "Who are you? You look like... Aaron Weiss? Are you...?"

"I am Aaron Weiss, yes," the old man replied. "And you are his wife? Yes?"

89

"No," said Tahlia. "I'm his friend."

"More than a friend!" said Aaron. "Someday you will be his wife!"

Tahlia felt tears flood her face. *Would there be a "someday" for Nathaniel?*

✿✞✿✞✿✞✿

"The Embassy doesn't have the identification of those involved yet," Wes said.

"Nate was there," Justine said. Wes could tell she had been crying.

"We don't know that—"

"Yes, we do! We could see his duffel bag on the news."

Wes took a deep breath.

"We should have made him come home!" Justine sobbed. "We knew it was dangerous!"

"I'll contact the Embassy again," Wes said. "I'll let them know that Nate, an American citizen, was there."

JJ and Josie looked at each other. What could they do? They had to do something!

They put their arms around Mommy. "We don't have to go to the pool," said Josie.

"It's okay," JJ said, patting her back. "Jesus is watching over Nate."

-2-

Zvi pulled the ambulance into the MDA [21] station as Tahlia put her phone away.

"Anything?" he asked.

---

21 Magen David Adom.

Tahlia shook her head. "Same. He's still in a coma."

Since the truck-ramming attack that had put Nathaniel in a coma, vehicular and stabbing attacks had become a daily occurrence. Along with the usual calls, they had responded to two terrorist stabbing-attacks today.

They cleaned the ambulance and prepped it for the next emergency before heading inside.

"You're handling this really well," Zvi said. "Knowing you as well as I do, I've been waiting for you to fall apart." He opened the refrigerator, hoping there was something to eat that they wouldn't have to cook. There wasn't.

"I'll make some sandwiches if you make a salad," he said.

"All right," said Tahlia, taking a cucumber, a few plum tomatoes and green onions out of the fridge. "I'm doing okay. I'm waiting to see what God is going to do."

Zvi poured a little oil in a pan, letting it heat while he chopped an onion. "That's what I'm talking about. Before, you would have been frantic. Actually, you would have been hysterical. But you've been pretty calm. Why is that?"

Tahlia began slicing the cucumber she had just peeled. "I'm not doing this on my own strength."

Zvi added the onion to the oil before slicing the cold chicken breast he had found.

Tahlia looked over at him. "You might want to slice that a little thinner."

"I ask a question, and I get a cooking lesson," Zvi said. "I'm serious. You're acting different, and I want to know why. What does that mean, 'not your own strength'?"

Tahlia finished slicing the cucumber and started on the tomatoes. As she diced the tomatoes, she thought about telling Zvi about Y'shua; how believing in Him, knowing He was with her, had kept her from falling apart. But she was afraid to tell Zvi, afraid of how he would react. She chopped some green onion and mixed everything together with some parsley and pepper as she tried to decide.

Zvi sprinkled the chicken strips with cumin and paprika.

"You might want to add some pepper to that," said Tahlia. Zvi added some cayenne pepper and began to sauté the chicken along with the onion.

"You going to tell me?" Zvi asked. "You have to work with me every day, and I'm going to keep asking. Every day I'll be asking."

Tahlia didn't answer.

"Every day," Zvi repeated.

Tahlia sliced the pita bread in half and put it on the table with the salad. "Okay, I'll tell you."

She took a deep breath. "You know I was born in Israel and I've spent my whole life here. You know my family is religious—Torah religious, not rabbi religious, as my grandpa would say. We keep the Feast Days and we're 'Torah kosher'—we don't eat pork or shellfish, but pretty much everything else is on the menu. We keep the Sabbath, but we drive to see family or sometimes one of us would have to work—I'm an EMP and others are in the IDF, so sometimes we're on duty on the Sabbath; you know how that goes. We go to Synagogue, read the Tanakh and we talk about what it says."

"I haven't set foot in a synagogue since my bar mitzvah," said Zvi, putting the chicken on the table. "I forgot everything I learned."

"I would think about God all the time," said Tahlia. I always knew the God of Israel watched over us. When I was a little girl, I would look at the sky and imagine God living far away above the clouds. He was watching and protecting Israel and me. But He was always far away; too far to really know. As I grew up, I wanted to know Him like Sarah and Rebecca had. I wanted to know Him like Abraham, Isaac and Jacob had known Him. But He was far away. I spent the next years of my life waiting for God to come near to me. He was up there, I was down here, and that was the way it was."

Zvi pushed the hot chicken strips into a pita and topped it off with the cold salad.

"You're going to eat it like that?" asked Tahlia.

"Keep talking," said Zvi.

Tahlia picked some tomatoes out of the salad, remembering the Shabbat that had changed her life.

"Then I met Nathaniel. It wasn't long before we were spending a lot of time together."

"No kidding. He was all you talked about. Right then I knew I didn't have a chance with you."

Zvi stuffed another pita. "Keep talking."

"Nathaniel and I traveled all over Israel. I told him the history of the places we went, and he read to me what the Bible had to say. This was how I learned about Y'shua. Whenever we went someplace where Y'shua had been, Nathaniel would read about it in his Bible. Then he would tell me that Y'shua was the Messiah and show me the prophecies about the Messiah that Y'shua fulfilled in His life and death. Then he would tell me Y'shua was coming again, this time as the conquering king that we Jewish people expected." She glanced at Zvi.

"Keep talking," he said.

"One thing I learned about Nathaniel was he never went anywhere without his duffel bag and his Bible. Nathaniel seemed so close to God. He really seemed to know Him. I wanted that kind of relationship with God, where He was near all the time. I told Nathaniel I always felt far from God; how could he be so close? He told me it was Y'shua. It was through Y'shua that he was close to God. He said it's our sins that keep us separated from God, but that Y'shua made a way for us to be restored to God. If we turn away from our sin, and believe Y'shua did this for us, we will be close to God."

Zvi had quit eating and was listening intently.

"Keep talking," he said.

"I struggled with knowing that the Christian Jesus was the same as Y'shua. I knew that Christians, in the name of their Jesus, had been slaughtering our people for more than a thousand years. There was no way Jesus was the Jewish Messiah. Y'shua? I liked Y'shua—but was He the Messiah? I thought in my head that He was, but my heart resisted. I felt that to accept Y'shua as Messiah would be to betray my people."

Zvi nodded as he made another pita.

"Keep talking," he said.

"The day we visited Yad Vashem, Nathaniel read what Isaiah the prophet wrote about someone called the Servant. I had never even heard of this chapter. It was never read in the synagogue. I didn't even know it existed. Nathaniel tried to explain, but I was too emotional to understand. He said to read it in the Bible he had given me. He said to pray to know the truth."

"Did you?" asked Zvi.

"Yes. I prayed to the God of Abraham, Isaac and Jacob that He would show me the truth."

"Did He?" asked Zvi.

Tahlia went and got a Bible out of her bag. "This is the Bible Nathaniel gave me a few days before the attack. This is what he wrote on the first page." She opened it and read:

Tahlia, these things are written so that you may believe that Y'shua is the Messiah, the Son of God, and that by believing, you, Tahlia, may have life in his name. (John 20:31)

For God so loved Tahlia that He gave His only Son, so that when Tahlia believes in Him she will not perish but have eternal life. For God did not send His Son into the world to condemn Tahlia, but in order that she might be saved through Him. (John 3:16-17)

"Your name is in the Bible?" Zvi asked.

"No," said Tahlia. "I looked the verses up and saw that Nathaniel had put my name in them. Later I found he had done that all through the Bible."

Zvi took the Bible and read the verses for himself. Then he read the note Nathaniel had written: *"Read Isaiah 6:9–10. I'm praying for you, Tahlia, that you will open your heart to Y'shua, just a little bit."*

"Did you read this?" he asked.

"Yes," she answered, "and after I read it, I prayed that I would have eyes to see and a heart to understand."

"Then I read Isaiah from chapter 52:13 through chapter 53. Nathaniel had put notes in the margins with other passages to look up: Matthew 26–28; Mark 14–16; Luke 22:35–24:53, John 18–20 and Psalm 22."

"The more I read, the more I felt the presence of God. I felt like He was right next to me, nodding His head and pointing to the Scripture, saying *look at this*... the God that had seemed so far away was now next to me. I knew then that Y'shua was the Messiah—not just in my head but in my heart."

Tahlia looked at Zvi. "Can you understand how I was feeling?" she asked.

Zvi shook his head. "No."

"I was overwhelmed with different feelings."

"That's the Tahlia I know," said Zvi. "Overwhelmed."

"I was happy—I had found what I had been looking for— the way to be near to God was through Y'shua! ... I was awestruck—I was near to the Holy God of Israel with all my bad choices, all my sins, exposed. ... I was relieved—I knew Y'shua had already taken the punishment for my sinful actions and attitudes. Even though I had 'gone astray,' 'gone my own way,' because of Y'shua I would be 'counted as righteous' before God.

I used to think I could never know God, but now I know Him. I would have never known God, never had a relationship with Him if I hadn't asked Him to show me the truth."

Zvi made himself another pita."Keep talking."

"And I was scared. Scared of hurting my family. Scared of being disowned by them. Scared of being deserted by my friends. I was scared to tell you."

"Me? You were afraid to tell me?"

"Yes, you. You know how you are."

"How am I?"

"Opinionated, argumentative, condescending—you know."

"You're wrong about that. I let you have an opinion, even if you're uninformed or wrong."

"You just made my point."

"Keep talking."

"Nathaniel said he would be with me when I told my family, but before I could tell anyone, he was injured in the terrorist attack," Tahlia said, reaching for a piece of pita."Nathaniel always said God doesn't allow His people to suffer for no reason. I'm hoping we'll find out why this happened to him."

"You ate all the chicken?" she said looking at the table. "All of it?"

"You were talking," said Zvi. "Put some salad in it. Tastes pretty good."

"This is why you never had a chance," said Tahlia.

"Your guy would never do that, right?"

"He would ask first," said Tahlia, looking at her phone. "I'm going to go up and get some rest before the next call comes in."

"Anything?" asked Zvi.

"No," said Tahlia as she disappeared up the stairs.

Zvi waited a few minutes before he picked up Tahlia's Bible. He opened it to a page with a bookmark in it and began to read.

-3-

The faint sound of voices drew Nate to consciousness. As they grew louder, he could recognize the General's rough voice. The other voice was younger, and he was doing most of the talking. Nate opened his eyes a little and saw the General talking to a man who looked like a doctor. *Where am I?* He looked around the room. *Had to be a hospital.* Behind the General he saw an old man, sitting, leaning on a cane. *Who was he?* then—a woman's voice. Tahlia. *Tahlia was here!* He turned his head slowly toward the sound of her voice. She was seated beside him, holding his hand. He closed his hand tightly over hers.

Tahlia turned and looked at Nate. She saw his eyes open. "He's awake!" she exclaimed. "He's awake!" She leaned over and kissed Nate softly on each cheek.

I could wake up like this every day! Nate thought.

David turned and looked at Nate. He walked quickly to his bedside. "You're back," David said, looking down at Nate.

"I'll tell you something," said David. "This is the best hospital. Best doctors."

Nate tried to move. He couldn't. He felt like he was encased in concrete. He felt pain coursing through part of his body. *Feel like I've been run over by a truck,* he thought.

"You were in an accident," Tahlia said. "You were run over by a truck."

"Terrorist attack," growled David. "On the streets of Tel Aviv. Four people murdered. Nine injured."

Then Nate remembered—the truck, the crowd, the old man.

Dr. Ben Ari sat down next to him. "You are extremely fortunate," he said. "You are severely injured, but we have done all the surgery while you were in a coma. Your back has been broken in many places. Some of the nerves have been severed. You are at the beginning of healing, of recovery."

The doctor hesitated. "Healing, recovery will take many months. Then many more of therapy."

Nate squeezed back the tears that had begun to fill his eyes.

"As many as a year for healing…"

A year…or more…

The old man, leaning heavily on his cane, stood and walked slowly to Nate's side. "I say to you: 'Be strong and courageous. Do not be frightened, and do not be dismayed, for HASHEM your God is with you wherever you go.'" [Joshua 1:9] He struck the floor with his cane. "You are strong, you have much courage! Yes? To give your life for this old man," he struck the floor again, "like the arms of God!"

I didn't give my life, Nate thought. *I'm still here.*

The old man placed his hand on Nate's head. Raising his eyes to heaven, he said, "May the blessings of Avraham, Yitzak, and Yaakov fall upon you. May your name be written in the Book of Remembrance."

I'm not Jewish…

The old man peered at him.

"It is the second time Nathaniel Grange saved my life." The old man leaned over and looked into Nate's eyes. "Second time! Yes? It is true. The eyes, they are the same."

Second time?!

"Yes, yes! 1947. We were young, fighting on the road to Jerusalem. I was hit. Nathaniel, he shielded me. He took the bullets, yes? He died and I did not."

Nate thought about that. He remembered the road to Jerusalem. He remembered Sgt. Grange. He remembered the man who became the father of thousands in Israel. *Was this old man the one Sgt. Grange had given his life for?*

✿✞✿✞✿✞✿

Nate let the cool water wash his throat. He was finally off the ventilator, and what he had wanted most was water.

He remembered his duffel bag. "Where's my duffel?"

"It is safe. It is in your room," said David.

"My parents? Do they know?"

"They know," said Tahlia sadly. "They want to take you home."

✿✞✿✞✿✞✿

Everyone gathered around Nate as Face Time with his family began. They leaned in to see Josie and JJ.

"They are worried, you see?" said Hannah. "They wish you to be home."

Josie's eyes were very big as she looked at Nate. She saw all his big white bandages. She saw the tubes stuck in all over him. "You're all in pieces," she said softly. "You got broke and now you're taped together."

"Hey, Jos," said Nate, "Don't be scared. I'm put together again."

"Is God fixing you?" she asked.

"Yeah," Nate replied.

"Today?" Josie asked.

"God's using doctors," said Nate, "so it's going to take a little longer."

99

JJ pushed Josie aside. His eyes got really big when he saw Nate. "You okay, Nate?"

"God's using doctors," Josie said, "so it's going to take a long time."

JJ stared at Nate. He tried to touch Nate through the screen. "Maybe God's finger will touch you and all at once you're better!" he said to Nate.

"Yeah," said Nate. "Praying for that."

"Okay, you two," Justine's voice interjected. "Your father and I have to talk to Nate now."

Justine appeared on the screen. "You look much better today," she said.

"The Prime Minister came to see me," said Nate. "Can you believe that?!"

"Really! I'm impressed," she replied. "What's he like?"

"Strong, confident. He knows what he's dealing with."

"Well, that Iron Dome they have won't help with terrorists running people over with a truck," she remarked.

"He says the real Iron Dome is the *kippa,*" said Nate.

"Kippa??"

"You know—the little round cap people wear when they pray. He said it's the prayers of the people that keep Israel safe."

Wes leaned into the screen. "You can wear a *kippa* and pray from the States," he said. "We're making arrangements with the Embassy to bring you home as soon as you're able to travel."

"I don't think you should do that," said Nate. "I've been thinking I should stay here."

"Oh no you don't!" Justine said. "You thought you should stay last time and look what happened! No!

You are coming home where you can get proper care; where your family can help you."

"Son, you have to be practical," Wes said. "Our insurance isn't going to cover all your treatment if you're in Israel. You come home and it's 100%."

Nate hadn't thought about that.

"And where would you stay? You can't live in a hospital for a year," said Wes. "You need to be here, in the States, in your own home."

"You're coming home," said Justine. "You have family and friends here."

Her eyes filled with tears. "I love you, Nate. I want you to be safe. I'm your mother. I want to take care of you."

"I know, Mom," Nate replied. "I know."

Nate stared at the ceiling above his bed. *How long have I been in this stupid hospital? How long am I going to be in this stupid cast? How long am I going to be in this stupid bed?*

He didn't even know how long it had been. What he did know was that he probably was never going to walk again; that he was going to have to go home; that he would probably never see Tahlia again. He fought back tears. This sure wasn't what he thought God had wanted him to do in Israel. He always believed God doesn't make His people suffer for no reason. *There's a reason for this?* he asked God. *I know I'm supposed to be content whatever state I find myself,* Philippians 4:11 *but really? This? Really, God?!*

Nate closed his eyes. *Now I'm in trouble. Questioning God. Not good.*

Forgive me, Father God. I'm so sad. I'm so mixed up. I'm so frustrated!

Nate wished he could throw something, or better yet, kick something. *Yeah, that's a **great** attitude for prayer. Forgive me, forgive me, forgive me...heal me, O God. Please heal me... "make haste O Lord to help me."* ^{Psalm 70:1}

✿✝✿✝✿✝✿

Nate woke up to see the General staring at him. "I'll tell you something," David said. "You will stay in Israel."

"What?!"

"Everything has been made ready, you see?"

Nate turned his head toward Hannah. "You will stay in our home, in Netanya."

"What?"

"Your whole medical team is here, in Israel, Nathaniel," said Dr. Ben Ari. "We all think it best for your recovery that you remain here. We have one of the best rehabilitation centers in the world. We are the best equipped to prepare you for your future."

Nate took a deep breath. "I...we...my family can't afford for me to stay here."

"It is paid for, yes? The cost to you—nothing!" Nate heard the sound of a cane tapping the floor. He turned his head toward Aaron.

"What?"

"The foundation! They will pay, yes? All costs, they will pay."

"What foundation?"

"The Weiss Foundation," said David. "They help victims of terrorist attacks."

102

Nate looked at David, at Hannah and at Aaron Weiss, trying to absorb all this information.

"*Sababa!* I don't know what to say! Thank you!!" He took a deep breath. "Now all I have do is tell my parents."

-4-

"You **gotta** be **kiddin'**, man!" Darryl said, staring at the flat-screen TV that covered one of the walls in Nate's room. "How **big** is that? Five feet? **Six?**"

"Yeah, something like that." Nate grinned. "Look at this, everything is hi-tech." He handed Darryl a control board. "Go ahead—push a button…"

Darryl pressed a button, and a computer began to lower from the ceiling. Another press, and it went back up. Another button, lights on, lights off. He pushed yet another button, and the blinds inside the oversized glass patio doors opened. Another button opened the doors.

"This is **great!**" Darryl said. "Look at this **courtyard!** You can go outside **anytime** you **want**, man!"

"Across the courtyard is where Tahlia lives," said Nate. "You can't beat that."

"Is she **helping** you? Do you **see** her?"

"Every day. She comes every day."

Darryl was looking around Nate's room. "This place is **huge!** How'd they **do** all this? This must've cost the General **a lot** of shekels!"

"The Foundation paid for it. That's why I have all these toys. Did you see this?" Nate pushed a button, and his wheelchair, which was parked across the room, began moving toward the bed. When it got there, Nate pushed another button and the side came down; another button and the bed lowered to the level of the chair. Nate slid himself onto the chair and raised the side.

103

Darryl shook his head. "That's **unbelievable**, just un-be-**liev**-able!"

"Come on outside," Nate said.

Darryl followed Nate out to the courtyard.

"Got to ask your help," said Nate. "Need you to bring some supplies here." Nate looked steadily at him. "It's important."

"I told you, man, I want **nothin'** to do with that! **Nothin'!**"

"They doubled the amount of medical they're sending, right? You must be running out of room by now."

"We get **caught** doin' that…" Darryl shook his head. "We can't **risk** it, man."

"We already got caught—remember? Finger of God—remember?"

Darryl took a deep breath. He looked up at the sky. "**This** is how it starts," he said to God. "Say yes to **one thing** and…then there's **somthin' else**….and it just goes **on** and **on** and **on**…"

Nate waited.

"**Okay,**" Darryl finally agreed. "I don't **want** to, but I **will**."

"Tomorrow?" Nate asked.

"I'll **try**," Darryl replied. "But how 'bout we're a little **short-handed**? With you almost getting yourself **killed**?"

"The Hawks are playing…" bribed Nate.

"The **Blackhawks?** You get that **here?** The **Chicago** Blackhawks?"

"Yeah. On a six-foot screen."

Tahlia dumped the contents of Nate's duffel bag on his bed. She shook out the clothes to make sure there was nothing hidden in them. "How long have these been in here?" she asked.

"Awhile," Nate said. "Okay, look inside—see anything?"

"No," Tahlia answered.

"There's a big pocket, see it?"

"Yes, your Bible is in it." Tahlia took the Bible out and handed it to Nate.

"Anything else?"

Tahlia felt around the bottom of the pocket. "Nothing." She studied Nate's face. "What are you looking for? Something to help you understand who Sgt. Grange was?"

"No," said Nate. "Something to help me understand who **I** am."

"So explain."

Nate powered up his computer and pulled up the PDF of his family tree.

"Look at this," he said. "What do you see?"

Tahlia studied the screen. "What am I looking for?"

"A pattern. Do you see it?"

Tahlia shook her head.

Nate pointed to the first name. "This is a list of all the firstborn sons, starting with the first name that has a middle name," he said. "The middle name is the name of the mother's father."

He glanced at Tahlia. "The middle name becomes the first name of the firstborn son. See?" Nate pointed to each name as he read them off.

"William Matthew, Matthew Thomas; Thomas John, John Wesley; Wesley James, James Justice."

Nate looked at Tahlia. "Do you see the problem?"

Tahlia shook her head. "No."

"Wesley James is my father. I should be named James Justice."

Tahlia frowned. "That's JJ's name."

"Yeah. I'm named Nathaniel, and there's no one named Nathaniel in this whole genealogy."

"The only Nathaniel Grange is Sgt. Grange, and he's not in my family tree. At all. Anywhere. And I have his duffel bag, his medallion, and his Bible."

"Someone has to know something. "Your mom or dad or grandma … somebody." Then she asked, "Why don't you have your DNA done?"

Nate frowned. "I don't want to be in the system," he said. "Everyone who has their DNA done is in a huge database. I don't want to be in it."

"You could get some answers," said Tahlia.

"It's complicated," Nate said.

"So explain."

Nate didn't say anything. He stared down at his Bible.

"Like I said, it's complicated."

Nate picked up the Bible. He opened it and looked at the name in the front. Nathaniel Grange. Sgt. Grange's name. His name.

Nate turned to the back of the Bible. Maybe there was something he hadn't seen before. There was nothing. … Then he saw, in the margins of the book of Revelation…so faint he could barely make it out…words… verse references. *How come I never saw this before? I've read this like a dozen times.*

"What did you find?" asked Tahlia.

"Not sure." Nate handed the Bible to Tahlia. "Can you read these notes?"

"What notes? I don't see any notes." Tahlia gave the Bible back to Nate. "So explain."

Nate squinted at the faded writing, trying to make out the words. "Sgt. Grange wrote something in the margins. It might be important." He thought about that.

"I'm going to study Revelation," he said. "While I'm waiting to recover, I'm going to study Revelation."

-5-

"Hey General! How ya **doin'**?" Nate could hear Darryl as he came through the house. In a moment Darryl swung into his room wearing a Blackhawks jersey and carrying a large bag. "**Brought** ya somthin'," he said. "Look at this!" Darryl took some video games out of the bag. "These are the **best** games! On that **big screen** of yours, it'll be like you are **right there!**"

Darryl looked around for the General. "Your stuff is in here too," he almost whispered.

"It's okay, he knows you're bringing the supplies," Nate almost whispered back.

Nate looked at the jersey. "Mikita? He's a Blackhawk?"

"You **kiddin'** me?! Greatest Blackhawk ever! Played back in the **'70s.**"

"I was, like, not even born yet," said Nate.

"You're gonna **love** these games," Darryl said, throwing them at Nate one by one. "Help you pass the **time,** until you're up and **movin'** again." He paused. "You see Ben Ari? Any progress?"

"No," Nate said. "I mean, my head and arm are healing. My lung is good…back is healing. But the nerves aren't regenerating. Nothing. I can't feel anything from the waist down."

"This'll give you somthin' to **do**—*WORLD AT WAR*," Darryl read one of the titles.

"I'm going to study the book of Revelation."

"You're not **serious**!" Darryl replied incredulously. **Nobody** can understand Revelation! **Everybody** has a different opinion! **Pre**terists, **pre**-millenialists, **post**-millenialists, **a**millenialists, **dis**pensationalists, **pre**-trib, **post**-trib, **mid**-trib, Satan's wrath, God's wrath, **pre**-wrath, **post**-wrath—you'll be **wastin'** your time!"

Nate thought about that.

"Well, most of the verses in Revelation are from the Hebrew Bible, the Tanakh," Nate said after a pause. "The themes, the imagery—the majority are in the Tanakh. I'm planning to do a verse association study and find out what the Scriptures have to say about Revelation," he explained. "I'll be studying the whole Bible. Maybe the Holy Spirit will show me something."

"Yeah, **everybody** says the Holy Spirit is leading 'em, but everybody has a **different opinion**," Darryl remarked. "How does that work?"

"I'm going to rely on the Faithful Witness," Nate answered. "The Word of God."

CHAPTER TWO

Revelation

-1-

The revelation of Jesus Christ,
which God gave Him
to show to His servants the things
that must soon come to pass.

Revelation 1:1

David leaned back in his chair, studying a report on the rammings, stabbings and shootings that had been happening all over the country. It had all started in Tel Aviv when Nathaniel had been injured. No one could know where the next one would happen. People were on edge. David was thankful that the majority of Israelis had military training. The casualties would be much higher otherwise. All the terrorist attackers had been taken down by civilians. Some had been killed, others taken alive, held until the police arrived. All the terrorists were Palestinian. *I'll tell you something,* David said to himself, *you can't have peace with a people that want to kill you.*

He could hear Nathaniel and Tahlia talking in Nathaniel's room across the hall. "See," Nathaniel was saying, "This is all about Y'shua the Messiah. Look at this list…"

David wanted to see the list, but instead he took a Christian Bible out of his desk drawer. Nathaniel had said he should read the end of the Book, so he had gotten this Bible. David read:

"'Blessed is the one who reads aloud the words of this prophecy, and blessed are those who hear, and who keep what is written in it, for the time is near.'

"'Y'shua the Messiah, the faithful witness, the firstborn of the dead, and the ruler of the kings of the earth…who loves us and has freed us from our sins by His blood… made us a kingdom, priests to His God and Father.'"

David recognized some of these phrases from the Tanakh. That's what Nathaniel said he was doing: connecting the verses from the Tanakh with the Revelation.

"Listen to this description," he heard Nathaniel say. "This is Y'shua, the Son of Man…

"'He was wearing a long robe with a gold sash across His chest. His head and His hair were white like wool, as white as snow. And His eyes were as a flame of fire. His feet were like bronze being refined in a furnace, and His voice like the sound of cascading waters. He held seven stars in His right hand, and a sharp double-edged sword came from His mouth. His face was shining as bright as the sun at midday.'

"He looks like the 'man dressed in linen' Daniel 10:5–6 that Daniel saw," said Nate. "Remember how I heard this voice in the middle of the night saying I should take another look at the sword?" he asked. "I thought it was the double-edged sword that is the sword of the Spirit, but it's not!" Hebrews 4:12; Ephesians 6:17 It's a different Greek word," said Nate. The sword of the Spirit is the *machaira,* the short sword used by the Roman soldiers. *This* sword…" Nate paused dramatically. "…is entirely different! It's huge! It's anywhere from six to eight feet long! In Greek it's called the *rhomphaia.* It's a large, powerful, brutal and terrifying weapon!"

"It's coming out of Y'shua's mouth?" asked Tahlia.

"Yeah. That means He commands the sword. It's under His authority. It's His sword of judgment."

"So explain," said Tahlia.

"It's only in Revelation six times and once in Luke. It's always associated with Y'shua and judgment." Revelation 1:16; 2:12,16; 6:8; 19:15, 21; Luke 2:34–35

"It's in the Tanakh too," said Nate. "In the Septuagint, you know? When they translated it from Hebrew into Greek?"

"I know," said Tahlia.

"It's the sword of the Commander of Adonai's army," said Nate. "It's the sword of Adonai. … Look this up. Joshua 5:13." So she read the verse:

"'When Joshua was near Jericho, he looked up and saw a man standing in front of him with a drawn sword in His hand. Joshua approached Him and asked, "Are you for us or for our enemies?" "Neither," He replied. "I have now come as commander of Adonai's army."'"

110

"The General told me what the Jordanians saw over Jerusalem during the Six-Day War," Nate said. "It was a figure, shining as bright as the sun, carrying a huge sword of fire. It was Y'shua! Defending Jerusalem!"

David entered the room. Nate and Tahlia looked up at him. "I ask you something," he said. "You have notes on the Revelation?"

"Yeah. Mostly Scripture verses. I'm typing them all out."

"About this sword?"

"Yes. David took this sword from Goliath! He said, 'There is none like it'!" 1 Samuel 17:51, 21:9–10

"Send this to me. We will learn something together."

This is great! thought Nate. *Sababa! Maybe the General will find Y'shua like Tahlia did…!*

-2-

"Hey General! How ya **doin'**?" Darryl said as he came past David's office and into Nate's room. "Big game, **big game** tonight!" Darryl dropped a bag filled with medical supplies in the corner. He came over and peered at Nate's computer screen. "Learnin' anything **interesting**? What about those **churches**? Anything?"

Nate scrolled through his notes on Revelation 2 and 3. "There's a lot," he said.

"Just give me a few—**game's** gonna start—don't want to miss the **faceoff**," Darryl said, pacing around the room.

Nate pulled up the church at Pergamum. "Here's something interesting. The throne of Satan was in Pergamum. It was in a temple to Zeus that was built by Eumenes II, the local king. He was Antiochus IV Epiphanes' sponsor while Antiochus was building his influence and power, until the Roman Senate made him Seleucid king of the Syrian area," Nate read from his notes.

"This is the guy that **persecuted** the Jews, right? And offered a **pig** on the **altar** in the **Temple** in Jerusalem?" Darryl asked.

"Yeah, the Abomination that caused Desolation. Then the Jews revolted against him and they won!"

"That's **Hanukah**, right?"

"Right. Sgt. Grange wrote 'Berlin' in the margin here—see?"

Darryl leaned over and looked in the Bible. "I don't **see** anything."

"Trust me," said Nate, "it's there."

"The altar in Pergamum was excavated by a German archaeological team starting in 1879," he continued. "It was moved out of the Ottoman Empire, along with the entire temple, to Berlin."

Darryl had turned on the TV. "Keep goin', I'm **listening**. Just want to make sure this **screen** is warmed up."

"Fast-forward a few decades. Hitler has a replica of the Pergamum Altar made at the Zeppelin Tribune and Field and puts his podium right in the center. This is where he made all those huge speeches."

"Keep goin'…"

"Turkey wants the altar back but Germany won't return it. So Turkey is building a replica in the exact same spot the original one was."

"So the Pergamum Altar is the throne of **Satan**, and wherever Satan has his **throne**, there's going to be **persecution**," Darryl said, watching as the Hawks took the ice.

"Yeah, but more than that. Revelation 13 says the dragon gives the beast his throne."

Darryl turned up the volume. "**Love** how this guy sings!!"

"O SAY, CAN YOU SEE, BY THE DAWN'S EARLY LIGHT…"

✿✝✿✝✿✝✿

It was the end of the first period. No score. "They didn't come out **ready** to **skate**," Darryl said, pacing. "**Big game** like this, they should be **meltin'** the ice! … Give me another one, another church; we got about 15 minutes."

"Okay, how about Smyrna? 'Do not fear what you are about to suffer. Behold, the devil is about to throw some of you into prison, that you may be tested, and for ten days you will have tribulation. Be faithful unto death, and I will give you the crown of life.'"

Nate pulled up his notes. "Let's see … ah … Polycarp. A disciple of the Apostle John, and martyred around AD 156. He refused to deny Christ. He was faithful unto death. Burned alive."

Nate scrolled down. "Here's another time of persecution. 1402. The Muslim warlord Aksak Timur conducted a crusade of ethnic cleansing against the Christians in Smyrna. He boasted of 'washing the sword of Islam in the blood of the infidels.'"

"**Nothin's** changed!" Darryl exclaimed. "Look what **ISIS** was doin'! Puttin' Christians in **cages** and **burning** them **alive**! **Beheading, drowning,** even crucifying them!!"

"Listen to this," Nate said. "'In 1922 hundreds of thousands of men, women and children were caught in a human bloodbath on a scale that the world until that time had never seen before. When it was over, the *NEW YORK TIMES* would carry the headline 'SMYRNA WIPED OUT.'"[22]

"That's the **Armenian** Genocide, right? It was **all over** the news."

"Yeah. Smyrna was wiped out in 1922, but the Armenian Christians had already been nearly exterminated in 1915." He read: "It was this slaughter that led a Polish Jewish lawyer named Raphael Lemkin to come up with the word *genocide*. It means 'acts of extermination directed against the ethnic, religious or social collectivities, whatever the motive.'"[23]

"Like I said, **nothin's** changed! They **still** want to slaughter **anyone** who doesn't agree with them. Not just Christians and Jews. Even other **Muslims**!"

Darryl turned up the volume as the Blackhawks skated onto the ice. "Hope they're **ready** to play now!"

Nate leaned back and closed his eyes. What was happening all around Israel was so hard to watch. The rise of ISIS and the civil war in Syria had brought so much suffering. *Give Your people*

---

22   From *Hitler's Cross* by Erwin Lutzer

23   Ibid.

courage and strength to be faithful to the end, he prayed. *Make haste O LORD to deliver and help them.*^{Psalm 70:1} *And help me not to get discouraged. I'm not going through anything compared to them.*

"**YES!!**" Darryl shouted. "**SHOT AND A GOAL! Finally**! Did you see that?!"

"No," Nate replied.

"You're **kidding**, right? Watch the replay. Slick gets the puck…**passes** it to Svenson…Svenson **blasts** a high wrist shot **past** the goalie's stick side…! **Nate**, you **watchin'** this?"

"No," said Nate. "I'm thinking about the people who are faithful unto death. Those who conquer and get the crown of life."

Darryl stared at Nate. He shook his head. "**Stop thinking** for once! Watch the **game**! The **Hawks** are going to **conquer**! They win this, they go to the **playoffs**!"

Nate thought about the people, the refugees, who were pouring out of the Middle East and into Europe. The pictures on the news looked like a river of people flowing down the roads—a river at flood stage with refugees crossing borders like a turbulent river overflowing its banks.

Nate tried to remember who the General was who had testified at a U.S. Congressional hearing. *What was his name?* … Flynn! That was it—General Mike Flynn. He had said, "The Middle East is trying to give birth." If that was true, this flood of refugees was like water breaking. *Are these the birth pangs You told us about?* Nate asked the LORD. With all that was going on in Syria, maybe he should study how Damascus would "cease to be a city." Looked like that could happen any day. ^{Isaiah 17; Jeremiah 49:23–27}

-3-

Justine looked at the clock. 5 a.m. That would make it 1p.m. in Israel. Nate should be back from his appointment by now. She slipped out of bed, went downstairs and woke up the computer. She clicked on *Mail…Compose…Subject…*

Re: Medical

How are you today? How did your appointment go? Did you get your test results?

Nate read his mom's email. He really didn't want to talk about it.

Re: Medical
Yeah got my test results and saw the whole medical team. They aren't
hopeful. Now they're doubtful my nerves will regenerate. They are trying a
new experimental procedure. Putting injections in my spine. Whatever.
They'll know in a couple weeks whether this will do anything.
Pretty discouraged right now.

Re: Medical
I'm so so sorry the results are not what you and we hoped!
We will keep praying! Jos. 1:9.
[Joshua 1:9, "Wait for the LORD; be strong, and let your heart take courage;
wait for the LORD!"]

Re: Medical
I'm not strong. I'm not courageous. I'm a grasshopper.

Re: Medical
Nate, I believe you will look upon the goodness of the lord in the land of the living!
It may not be what you are longing for. It will be better than that. Ps. 27:14.
[Psalm 27:14, "Wait for the LORD; be strong, and let your heart take
courage; wait for the LORD!"]
Re: Medical
Whatever.
I'm still a grasshopper

Re: Medical
It's not over until Jesus says it's over.

Re: Medical
Yeah. I know. It's not over until the lion roars.

Re: Medical
Suggestion – make a list of all the good things and praise God for them.
Have to get the J's up for school now. I'll give dad your news.
Wish I could give you a hug. Sigh.

Nate leaned back and closed his eyes. *Thank you that I can use*
my arms. Thank you for the General and Hannah and Tahlia, he
prayed. *And for my family who keep praying for me.* Then he said
the Psalms he had prayed every night since the attack: *"I cry to*
you, O LORD, I say, 'You are my refuge, my portion in the land of
the living. Attend to my cry, for I am brought very low. Save me,
O God! I am weary with my crying out; Make haste, O God, to
deliver me! O LORD, make haste to help me!" Psalm 142:5–6; 69:1,3; 70:1

115

Nate repeated his prayer until he fell asleep.

✿✞✿✞✿✞✿

Tahlia ran her fingers through Nate's hair until he woke up. "You need a haircut," she said. "Long day?"

"Yeah."

"What did Ben Ari have to say?"

"It's doubtful I'll ever walk again. That's pretty much what they said."

"Can you accept that?"

Nate forced himself to look into Tahlia's eyes.

"I think," he said, "it would be good for you to spend more time with your friends. Maybe date a little."

Tahlia didn't say anything.

"There's really not much of a future for us," he said.

Tahlia didn't say anything.

"I'll probably have to go back to the States."

Tahlia didn't say anything.

"Could you say **something**?" Nate asked.

Tahlia didn't say anything.

She leaned over and kissed Nathaniel.

"Someday you will ask me to marry you," she said. "When you do, I'll say yes."

She leaned over and kissed him again.

"He asked to marry you!" Hannah said excitedly as she entered the room. "I knew this day would come. It's the way he looks at you, you see."

"No, ah, that's not what…"

"David, David! Our Tahlia and Nathaniel are to be married! Just now he asked!"

116

David came into Nate's room.

"He didn't ask," said Tahlia. "I just said that when he asked, I would say yes."

"I tell you something," said David, "you don't ask; you are *meshugah*. Crazy."

Nate looked at Tahlia. "I … I have a lot to think about. I have some stuff I have to sort out."

"It's okay, Nathaniel," Tahlia replied. "We can sort it out together."

-4-

Nate stared at the writing in the margin next to Revelation 4. *Was that word "courtroom"? I need a magnifying glass.* He held the Bible up to the light. *courtroom, Daniel 7, 2 Samuel 15:2, Exodus 28...* none of these verses matched the references printed in the center column of the Bible.

Nate read the passages Sgt. Grange had put in the margin. He looked up more verses. He typed all of them into his study notes. He looked up the words in his Complete Word Study Dictionary. He typed the meanings into his notes. He read everything again.

The chapter heading of Revelation 4 was "The Throne Room of Heaven." *This isn't the throne room in the Temple,* Nate thought. *This was different, a **place** of judgment. The throne was **set** in place, and the **place** it was set was by the **gate** of heaven. Just like the kings in the Hebrew Bible. The king would have a seat, a throne, set in the gate of the city on a special platform. The elders of the city would be seated around the king. This was where the king judged the people. The Throne room would be in the Temple in heaven. And God wasn't in His Temple.*

Nate turned to Revelation 15:8. "…and the Temple was filled with smoke from the glory of God and from His power, and no one could enter the sanctuary until the seven plagues of the seven angels were finished."

Before that, in chapters 8 and 14, angels were in and out of the Temple, so God wasn't in the Temple then. When God was in His Temple, no one else was.

117

Nate closed his eyes, recalling the day he and Tahlia had gone to Tel Dan. There was a gate to an ancient city, with a raised platform where the king's throne had been placed, and a long stone bench where the elders of the city sat. Nate swallowed the lump in his throat. He and Tahlia wouldn't be able to go there again.

Nate forced himself to focus on the rest of Revelation 4, picturing the scene: The throne of God surrounded by an emerald rainbow with seven torches of fire in front of it. Around all that were the twenty-four elders, seated on their thrones. Then there were the four living creatures, full of eyes, on each side of the throne: one like a lion, one like an ox, one with the face of a man, and one like a flying eagle. *Eyes all around? What was that about?*

-5-

Nate watched as Hannah, Abigail and Tahlia set the Sabbath table in the courtyard.

"We will eat outside, you see? It will be a beautiful Erev Shabbat," Hannah had said.

All the activity of the day had gradually faded until there was only this, the preparing of the table and the lighting of the candles. *It's so peaceful,* he thought. *Thank You, Father God, for the gift of the Sabbath.*

Nate rolled up to his place at the table, across from Tahlia.

"The Sabbath is a delight, the holy day of the Adonai..."

Hannah lit the candles, covered her eyes, and said the blessing, welcoming the Sabbath. In the silence that followed, each person offered a private personal prayer to Adonai. *Bless this family,* Nate prayed. *Reveal Y'shua Your Messiah to them as You have to Tahlia.*

Abigail placed her hand on Tahlia's head:

"May God make you like Rachel and Leah, who together built the house of Israel."

Nate was startled to feel Yaron's hand on his head, blessing him:

"May God make you like Ephraim and Menashe. May you grow into a multitude in the midst of the earth."

118

Nate felt a strange sensation. He felt as if this blessing had been said over him before. He remembered Hannah's story of when her parents had come for her, how she had known they were her parents by the blessing. He knew his father had never said the blessing over him. His father didn't know such a blessing existed. *Something's not right,* he thought. *Something's not making sense…*

✿✟✿✟✿✟✿

"Tahlia made this, you see?" Hannah said, passing a dish whose aroma had filled the courtyard.

Nate grinned at Tahlia. "She's beautiful and she cooks?!"

"You are *meshugah!*" David said to him.

"I'll tell you what's *meshugah,*" said Yaron. "A car ramming into people waiting at a bus stop. An old woman pulling a knife and stabbing a policeman. *That's* crazy!"

"A man was shot right inside the Jaffa Gate," said Tahlia, "and there are still attacks every week in Tel Aviv and Jerusalem."

"Eyal says no one is safe on the road near his settlement. Every car is a target."

"I tell you something," said David. "Lebanon, a hundred thousand rockets. Gaza, twenty thousand. All pointed at Israel. ISIS all over the Sinai. Tunnels everywhere."

"The war in Syria is going to spill over on us," said Yaron.

"Naharia is always full of injured Syrians," Tahlia said. "They come to us. We help them and then they go back."

"What's Naharia?" asked Nate.

"It's a major hospital we built near the Lebanon border. Syrian refugees come over the border in the dark of night. Sometimes they are so badly wounded they can't go any further. The IDF looks for them and brings them to the hospital. We take care of them."

Tahlia looked at Nate. "We're the only ones doing anything for these people. Even the United States isn't doing much."

"I wouldn't say that," Nate said. "This administration is doing a lot more than the last one!"

119

"It's Shabbat. Let us rest from this talk today," Abigail said.

"I'll tell you something," David finally said. "In the Revelation, where God's throne is. It is like the camp of Israel."

"What do you mean?" said Nate. "I didn't see that."

"In the camp of Israel, the Tabernacle is in the center, and the throne of God is above the cherubim in the Holiest Place. Around the Tabernacle is the Tribe of Levi, the priests. In the heavens the Throne of God is surrounded by the twenty-four elders. They are like the Levites."

Nate nodded. "Okay, I can see that."

"In the Tabernacle, in the Holy Place, in front of the veil is the golden menorah," David continued. "In front of the Throne in heaven are the seven torches of fire, like the seven branches of the menorah."

"Yeah. John calls them the seven spirits of God," said Nate.

"I'll tell you something. At the four corners of the camp of Israel are the tribes of Judah, of Reuven, of Ephraim, and Dan. Each with their standard. The lion for Judah. A man for Reuven, an ox for Ephraim, a flying eagle for Dan."

"I can see that now!" said Nate. "On each side of the Throne are the living creatures: a lion, an ox, the face of a man and a flying eagle. The flags of the tribes! They match four living creatures."

"Now I'll show you something," said David. "The order is not the same. Around the Throne, Ephraim is on the south. In the camp it is Reuven."

Nate thought about that. "Didn't they get switched? Reuven became last and Ephraim first?"

"Reuven slept with one of Yaakov's wives," Yaron replied. "His birthright was given to Ephraim."

David nodded. "They are the same then. The heavens and the camp."

"What I still don't get is the 'eyes all around and within,'" Nate told the General. "Or the scroll in chapter five."

"Someone I will call. He will know about the scroll," said David.

The night was the most beautiful Nate could remember. Dark and clear, with the stars shining so brightly, he felt he could reach up and touch them.

"You are one of those stars," Nate told Tahlia. "You are a descendant of Abraham. You're a star in the sky."

Tahlia looked at the stars. "I'm thinking about the throne of HASHEM above the stars. Above the cherubim."

Nate studied the sky. "There are four fixed constellations," he said slowly. "Leo, Taurus, Aquarius and Scorpio."

Tahlia closed her eyes. "So explain."

"Think about this," Nate said. "Leo—lion—is Judah. Taurus—ox—is Ephraim. Aquarius—man, the water-bearer—is Reuven." He paused. "Then there's Scorpio."

"What about Scorpio?"

"Scorpio is a scorpion, but Dan is a flying eagle. The eagle destroys the scorpion. I think the flying eagle is Aquila, which is part of Scorpio." Nate stared at the stars, trying to find the constellations.

"Are the constellations like the cherubim?" Tahlia asked.

Suddenly Nate turned to Tahlia. "That's it! The eyes all around and within! The eyes are stars!"

Tahlia gazed at the stars. "I'm from one of the tribes of Israel. I'm one of the stars in one of the constellations. I'm camped around the Tabernacle of God. In the heavens."

-6-

Re: family tree
Mom – this is important – why am I named Nathaniel? The first-born son is always given his father's middle name and the name of his mother's father is his middle name. So my name should be James Justice.
Mom should be up by now. Nate clicked the *Send* button.

Justine heard Wes come in as she read Nate's email. "You have to see this," she said.

Wes bent over her shoulder to read it.

"He wants to know," said Justine. "We should tell him."

Wes straightened up. He took off his gun and put it in the safe. "He's my son; that's all he needs to know."He took off his Kevlar vest, put it in the closet and went upstairs. Justine heard the shower running. She clicked *Reply.*

Re: family tree
You were born during a really difficult time in our lives. We named you
Nathaniel because you were a gift from God. YOU STILL ARE.

Justine leaned back in the chair and closed her eyes as she remembered that "really difficult time." **"ROOKIE POLICE OFFICER NATHANIEL ELLIS KILLED DURING ROUTINE TRAFFIC STOP"** was the headline that day. Wes, Nathaniel's best friend and fellow police officer, had brought her the news. It was the day she and Nathaniel were to be married. Justine had found out the week before that she was pregnant. When Nathaniel had finished his shift, they were going to go over to the courthouse and get married.

Somehow she had gotten through the funeral. Wes had been there with all the other officers, but he had walked beside her as she filed past the coffin.

A few days later Wes had taken her out to dinner. It was a nice restaurant with white tablecloths and no prices on the menu. "I'm keeping the baby," she had said.

After they had ordered desert, Wes had taken her hand. "I would be a good father," he said. "I would be a good husband." His hand had tightened around hers. "Will you let me? Will you give me the chance?"

She had started crying then.

"I know this isn't a good time," Wes had said. "I know it's too soon. I'm so sorry, Justine."

She had run to the ladies' room, sobbing.

A long time later she had come out. Wes was there, waiting.

He had driven her home in silence. Then he said, "I didn't mean you had to be a wife to me. Unless you wanted to be." She had gone into the house, avoiding her parents.

Later she called Wes. "If the baby is a boy, I want to name him Nathaniel."

Two weeks later they were married in a small ceremony in Wes's church. His brother had sung The Lord's Prayer, and close family had filled the front rows. Wedding cake and punch were served in the fellowship hall after the service. Years later she realized how Wes had wanted her to have a good memory of their wedding; that it had been a real wedding, in a church, with people who loved them.

The months before the baby was born were filled with emotion. She remembered crying until she threw up; yelling at Wes; not being able to sleep. She had nightmares about Nathaniel being shot and it turning out to be Wes.

Wes had been calm and patient. "It won't always be like this," he said to her.

At last Nathaniel had been born. He was so tiny, with so much blond hair. "He needs a haircut," Wes had said. The name on the birth certificate was *Nathaniel Grange*. They called him Nate.

They bought a house in the suburbs, and Wes brought home a puppy. Within a few months they were truly husband and wife.

✿✝✿✝✿✝✿

"You okay?" Wes asked, fresh from his shower. He put his arms around her as he read her reply. He clicked *Send*. "We're okay," she said.

✿✝✿✝✿✝✿

"I'm sure there's more," Nate said to Tahlia, reading his mom's reply. "I don't remember my parents ever having a 'difficult time.'"

"You can't remember when you were born," said Tahlia. "You can't—can you?"

"No, but I've seen all their pictures, I've heard all the stories. I never heard about 'a difficult time.'"

123

CHAPTER THREE

Seven Seals

-1-

Then I saw in the right hand
of Him who was seated on the throne
a scroll written within and on the back,
sealed with seven seals.

Revelation 5:1

Nate laid back and closed his eyes. His caretaker had just left. He was cleaned up and dressed, supposedly ready for another day. He just wanted to sleep. *I'm depressed,* he told himself, *but if I give in to it, it's all over. Father God, You said, 'You will call upon Me and come and pray to Me, and I will hear you.'* ^{Jeremiah 29:12} *I've been praying. All the time. Do You hear me? I'm not angry. I'm not bitter. I'm glad I was able to move Aaron out of the way. I just don't know how to live my life. How to be alive.* His eyes filled with tears. *I'm really tired, really sad, Father God. Really tired of living like this...*

✿✟✿✟✿✟✿

"Shlomo, look at him, it's just the same, yes?"

"Aaron, Aaron! It's not like Nathaniel—look at him. Can you see? Are you blind to colors?"

"I know the hair is not brown! It is the eyes. They are the same."

Nate recognized Aaron's voice. He opened his eyes and saw two very old men, leaning on their canes, staring down at him. Aaron he knew. The other one, the one with the black hat, white hair, thick glasses and a long black coat, he had never seen before.

"Do you see? Blue, not brown. Can you see blue eyes? Nathaniel's eyes, they were brown."

"The shape, Shlomo, yes? Not the color. One eye does not open all the way. This is how Nathaniel's eyes were."

"I'm Nathaniel," said Nate.

Both men straightened up. "Of course!" Aaron said. "Now you are awake, yes?"

"Yeah, I'm awake," said Nate.

"So. He is not healed," said Shlomo, looking at Nate's wheelchair. "Aaron, you say the Almighty told you he would be healed. I, a rabbi, do not have the Almighty talk to me. So he is not healed. Maybe it was not the Almighty you heard!"

"He is not healed yet. **Yet!** You doubt the Almighty can heal Nathaniel?"

"No, no. Aaron, Aaron! Listen to me. You maybe didn't understand."

Aaron struck the floor with his cane. "You hear the voice of the Almighty; you know it is HASHEM, yes? To believe! That is the difficult thing, yes?"

Shlomo stared at Aaron for a long time. Then he said: "You remember David? David Yaniv?"

"No, how can I remember? So many Davids in Ya'thom, yes?"

"Aaron, Aaron! Not in Ya'thom. In the IDF. Lt. Col. David Yaniv. My friend, Avram, was with him, and also later, in the *moshav*. [24] You do not remember?"

"I said no. You can't hear me, but you expect to hear the Almighty?"

"So. I will tell you then. About Ezra who was healed."

Nate closed his eyes and waited. Then he told Shlomo, "I'm waiting to hear the story of David Yaniv."

"So," said Shlomo, glancing at Nate. "After David and his wife were at the moshav for three years, he slipped and fell in the cowshed. He was in pain, so much pain. He went to the hospital, but they couldn't find anything wrong. The pain got worse and worse. Fifty painkillers a day! Think of it, Aaron, fifty! After three years a neurosurgeon discovered some slipped and smashed discs in his spinal cord. He was told he needed a

---

24 An agricultural community similar to a kibbutz.

minor operation. When he was awake from the surgery, he had no feeling from the waist down."

Like me, Nate thought.

"The doctor explained that something had gone wrong; that David would be paralyzed for life. David was very angry at everyone. He was desperate, but he did not turn to HASHEM. He was an atheist."Shlomo stopped talking. He was staring at Nate, thinking.

"So. A review. After WWII, his father had found out that two of his sisters and one brother and their families had been killed in Germany by the Nazis. The father, he took everything, the Tanakh and anything else that was religious, and threw it out. He would ask, 'Where was God?' and 'How could God allow such a thing to happen?'" Shlomo said. "Such questions? Who could answer?"

I asked those questions too, thought Nate.

"So. He is an atheist. Seven and a half years in a wheelchair. Then he gets sick with the flu. He is watching a program on Lebanese television called *The 700 Club.* An atheist watching a Christian program. Why is he watching?"

"Because it has stories about people who have been healed," Nate replied.

"You know this program? You are watching it, yes?" Aaron asked.

"No," said Nate. "My grandma, she watches it."

"Aaron. Nathaniel! Do you want to hear? So, the person, the host or co-host, whoever, always would ask the people watching to pray. One day David prayed. Something called the Sinner's Prayer. You know this prayer?" Shlomo asked Nate.

Nate nodded.

"So, David, he gets a Bible. He reads it. He reads the prophecies about the Messiah. Then he reads about Y'shua. He can't believe the Jewish people don't know about Y'shua being the Messiah."

"It is a hard thing to believe, yes?" Aaron leaned forward, almost falling off his cane.

126

"Aaron, Aaron! You yourself said, 'To believe, that is a difficult thing.'"

Aaron and Shlomo stared at each other. For a long time.

"What happened to David?" asked Nate.

"So, five months later, he is watching this *700 Club* again. The person on the program said, 'There is someone who has been paralyzed halfway down his body for many years. He will feel a warm sensation running through his body and he will be healed,'" said Shlomo. "The next morning David had feeling in his legs. He walked out of his room. Do you hear this, Aaron? He walked! A week later he met with twenty-five doctors. Neurosurgeons and neurologists. They said it was not possible. They said it was a medical miracle. David told them, 'This is not a medical miracle. This is Y'shua.'"[25]

"You believe this, yes?" Aaron inquired.

"So. I believe! The man is walking. I believe he is healed. Aaron, Aaron! I saw him myself!"

"Shlomo! I know he is walking! It is a miracle from Y'shua—that is your meaning, yes?"

"Yes, it is a miracle from Y'shua, Nate answered. "David said it himself."

Aaron and Shlomo turned and stared at Nate.

"What else could it be?" he asked.

✡✝✡✝✡✝✡

"Hey General," Nate said as David entered the room. "Can you get Aaron and Shlomo some chairs? I think they're going to fall over."

"I'll ask you something," said David as he slid a chair under Shlomo. "Did you bring it, the scroll?"

---

25 Adapted from the story of David Yaniy, whose story is available online and also in *The Miracle of Israel*.

Shlomo stared at David through his thick glasses. He thought for a moment.

"In your pocket. You put it in your pocket, yes?" said Aaron.

Shlomo began searching his long black coat's many pockets. After a moment, he triumphantly removed a paper. "So! A legal document—from the first century!" He unrolled the scroll. "This is the exterior," he said. "See the writing, Nathaniel? It is the same as the interior."

"Where's the interior?" Nate asked.

"Here. It is here, on the inside." Shlomo pointed to the unrolled part of the scroll.

"I'm not getting this," Nate said, confused.

Shlomo unrolled the scroll until he reached the part that was tied and sealed. "So, the inside, the interior, is tied together with knots. Then there is a wax seal on each knot. Nathaniel, so do you see my meaning?"

"Hmmm…not really."

"David. David! Get for me a paper! Over there." Shlomo pointed to the printer.

"So," he said, folding the paper in half. "This is the interior." He pointed to the top half. "The whole legal document is written here, with a little on the back. Now you see my meaning?"

"Yeah, okay."

"This is the exterior." Shlomo pointed to the bottom half of the paper. "Everything that is written on the interior is written on the exterior."

Nate nodded. "Okay."

"So, the interior is rolled up"—Shlomo rolled up the top of the paper—"and then it is tied with these special knots. Then, the wax seals on each knot."

"Why is it tied up like that?" asked Nate.

"No one can open it! No one can change it! No one can add anything or take anything. Nathaniel! Do you see my meaning?"

Nate nodded. He remembered the final chapter of Revelation, especially the verses warning everyone not to alter the words of the prophecy. *They wouldn't need to be warned if the scroll was still tied and sealed, would they?*

Shlomo pointed to the wax seals. "So. Each seal belongs to a witness. Each witness signs his name next to his seal. Seven seals, seven witnesses."

"I'll ask you something," said David. "Who can open the scroll?"

Shlomo looked at him. "So, Aaron. The scroll is a legal document. You are a lawyer. Who can open it?"

"The one who has the document drawn up, yes?" answered Aaron. "Or the one he gives authority to. An executor."

God the Father gave Y'shua authority to execute judgment, Nate remembered. **John 5:26–27**

"So," said Shlomo. "The first witness puts his name next to the first seal. He is the one who has the authority to open the scroll."

That would be Y'shua, Nate thought. *His name would be by the first seal. That's interesting.*

Nate opened his Bible. "It's the same. The scroll, the seven seals, written on the inside and the back. Now I understand why Y'shua had the legal authority to open the scroll. Because He conquered…" He read:

"'Weep no more; behold, the Lion of the tribe of Judah, the Root of David, has conquered, so that He can open the scroll and its seven seals.'"

"Shlomo, this Y'shua, he is the Messiah, yes?" asked Aaron.

"Aaron! I am a rabbi! I know these things," said Shlomo. "Our father Jacob blessed Judah. He said, 'Judah is a lion's cub.' Aaron, you know the blessing." **Genesis 49:9**

Aaron nodded.

"Isaiah, he prophesied, 'a shoot shall grow out of the stump of Jesse.' ^Isaiah 11:1 So, this is about Messiah."

Shlomo leaned back in his chair. He and Aaron looked at each other.

"Nathaniel, he always talked about Y'shua being the Messiah, yes?" said Aaron.

"Yes! I would tell him: 'Nathaniel, Nathaniel! We are fighting a war here! Talk about Messiah after the war!'" Shlomo answered.

"Then he died so I could live. Now this Nathaniel gives his life so again I live, yes?"

"I'm still alive," Nate said.

"So, Nathaniel, the war is over," Shlomo said. "Now you talk again about Messiah."

"I'm not *that* Nathaniel," said Nate. *Even I'm getting confused,* he thought.

Waiting, Aaron and Shlomo looked expectantly at Nate.

He began to read again:

"'And between the throne and the four living creatures and among the elders I saw a Lamb standing, as though it had been slain, with seven horns and with seven eyes, which are the seven spirits of God sent out into all the earth.'"

"So. The Messiah, the Lion of Judah …is also a lamb," said Shlomo. "A slaughtered lamb."

Nate nodded.

"With seven horns and seven eyes? Yes?" Aaron pressed.

"It's symbolism," Nate explained. "The eyes are the seven spirits of God."

"So. Horns are the power that comes out of his hand," Shlomo said.

"Really? His hand?" Nate asked.

"The prophet, Habakkuk, he says it," said Shlomo. [Habakkuk 3:4] "Another meaning: shofar. It can mean he has seven shofars in his hand. Do you see my meaning?"

"Yeah!" said Nate. "… I think I do." *Maybe Y'shua is holding the seven trumpets in His hand…and He gives them to the seven angels…* [Revelation 8:2]

"I am a rabbi! I know these things!" Shlomo said.

"I'll tell you something I know," said David. "Your driver is waiting. Soon it is Shabbat."

Aaron and Shlomo got up from the chairs, steadying themselves on their canes.

"Aaron. Aaron! We will read this Book about Y'shua. We must help Nathaniel with his studying."

"After Shabbat, yes? Then we will read the Book."

"So. Twice he saves your life, and you wait until after Shabbat? No, we will read it on Shabbat!"

Nate watched as the two stepped out the door. "How long have they been friends?" he asked David.

"A very long time," he replied. "They escaped the Nazis together. Together they fought in the Haganah."

"Shlomo knew Sgt. Grange too," Nate commented.

"I'll tell you something," said David. "Shlomo was a tough fighter and a hunter."

"Hunter?"

"After the war. Aaron took care of the widows and orphans. Shlomo? He hunted Nazis."

-2-

Nate rolled down the street, around the curve and headed for the walkway by the park. Walking was supposed to be good for depression. He couldn't walk, but he could roll. He powered his chair up the incline and entered the park. He saw Naomi walking her dog. *Ugliest dog I've ever seen,* he thought. "Hey, Naomi!" he called out. "How's the pup?"

"Isn't he just the cutest?!" Naomi gushed. "He gets cuter every day!"

Really, Naomi? Have you looked at him?! Nate thought as he rolled by.

A jogger ran past, narrowly missing his chair. *Hello! You could say something, or at least see I'm here! Same guy, every day.*

Nate cruised up to Reuven's Café. They had his coffee ready. Nate barely slowed as he put down his shekels and picked up the coffee. *This was the best coffee. It must be the chocolate they put in it.*

Nate rolled past Asa's Auto Repair, went another quarter-mile, and he was at his favorite spot overlooking the Mediterranean Sea. It was peaceful this morning. Waves gently washing up the beach; a lone fisherman soaking a line; a bird circling overhead. Nate remembered swimming here with Tahlia—at night, the water still warm, Tahlia laughing, a bright moon overhead.

Tomorrow Tahlia would be back and maybe they could come here together. But it wouldn't be the same.

He kept thinking about Tahlia and how they had traveled all over Israel. They'd hiked in the wilderness, following the narrow valley trails, staying clear of the Bedouin camps, and climbing to the hilltops. From there, in the desert, they had seen acres of date palm trees. They had seen hundreds of greenhouses. In the desert! With their own eyes they had seen the words of Isaiah being fulfilled.

Nate took his Bible out of the duffel. He read:

"The wilderness and the dry land shall be glad; the desert shall rejoice and blossom like the crocus; it shall blossom abundantly and rejoice with joy and singing." Isaiah 35:1-2

Tahlia had told him that Israel reclaimed nearly 90 percent of its sewage water. Then they used it to irrigate the Jordan

Valley, transforming what was once a desolate wilderness into one of the breadbaskets of Israel.

I won't be hiking anywhere with Tahlia again, Nate thought, swallowing the lump in his throat. *If I can't walk, I can't hike.*

Nate turned to another passage:

"In days to come Jacob shall take root, Israel shall blossom and put forth shoots and fill the whole world with fruit." Isaiah 27:6

Tahlia had told him that Israel ships fruit and flowers all over the world. It used to be, before the Boycott, Divestment and Sanctions movement, one-fourth of Europe's fruit came from Israel. She had also said that Israel ships 500 million flowers a day to the flower markets of the world. Amazing!

Nate remembered picking up Tahlia and spinning around, praising God for what He was doing in Israel. He could still hear her laugh.

They had gone down to the Dead Sea and smeared the mineral mud all over each other. They were both laughing then. That mud wouldn't help him now.

When they were down near the Dead Sea, they'd seen sinkholes that had filled with fresh water. Some of them even had fish in them. Green grass and bulrushes grew around them. Just as Isaiah had said:

"For waters break forth in the wilderness, and streams in the desert; the burning sand shall become a pool and the thirsty ground springs of water; in the haunt of jackals, where they lie down, the grass shall become reeds and rushes." Isaiah 35:7

They had hiked in Ein Gedi, cooling off under a waterfall, soaking their clothes. Tahlia had filled his boots with water and poured it over his head. Recalling that day, Nate almost smiled. Then, He realizing he'd never see that waterfall again, he almost cried.

Nate looked out over the Mediterranean. *Think about what God has done,* he told himself. *Do not think about Tahlia!*

God brought His people home a few at a time, Nate said to himself as he paged through his Bible. And those few prepared the way for the hundreds of thousands who would soon come. They had been faced with malaria-filled swamps, barren mountains and ruined cities. They had purchased land from the Arab and Turkish owners, who considered it worthless. These pioneers had drained the swamps, rebuilt the cities, planted trees and vineyards, and wheat and barley fields.

And God had blessed them with rain.

Nate found the verses in Ezekiel he was looking for.

"But you, O mountains of Israel, shall shoot forth your branches and yield your fruit to My people Israel, for they will soon come home. For behold, I am for you, and I will turn to you, and you shall be tilled and sown. And I will multiply people on you, the whole house of Israel, all of it. The cities shall be inhabited and the waste places rebuilt. And I will multiply on you man and beast and they shall multiply and be fruitful. And I will cause you to be inhabited as in your former times, and will do more good to you than ever before. Then you will know that I am the LORD." Ezekiel 36:8–11

Nate remembered seeing the mountains of Israel with rebuilt terraces planted with olive trees and grape vines next to the ancient crumbling ones. He and Tahlia had walked all over those terraces. They had looked down on the cattle grazing in rocky fields and had tasted the wine produced at the kibbutz that owned the vineyards and the cattle. "Look at how God is fulfilling His prophecies!" Nate had said to Tahlia. Nate felt tears falling from his eyes. *That life was over for him and Tahlia.*

Nate felt a chill as the air around him turned grey. He looked and saw two large ships standing out to sea. *Where had they come from? They hadn't been there before.* He looked around, at the street, at the houses. Everything was grey. Everything looked deserted. Abandoned. Nate turned and rolled slowly for home.

134

Reuven's was empty, the door ajar. A chair lay on the floor. *What was going on?* The park, which had been filled with people and beautiful flowers only an hour ago, was empty. Lifeless.

Nate closed his eyes. There was an odor in the air and a burning in his throat. *Father God, help me understand what's happening. Are You trying to show me something?*

Nate remembered the other times he had had visions of people rushing to get away. *Was this how it looked when they were gone?*

Nate opened his eyes as he felt the sun warm the air around him. He looked around. The flowers were red again. There were families in the park, and Reuven was serving coffee at the tables outside his café.

Something's not right, Nate thought. *Something is really not making sense.*

Nate powered up his chair and headed for home. Tahlia had been up at Naharia hospital for the last two weeks. Today she would be home.

It's really good for her to be away from me and my situation, Nate told himself. It's good for her to be around different people, in a different place. He sighed. *No wonder I'm depressed.*

Be the man! he told himself. *Re-focus! It is what it is!*

"Nathaniel."

Nate took a deep breath. Tahlia was back.

Tahlia put her arms around Nate and kissed him gently on each cheek. She looked deep into his eyes.

"You need a haircut," she said softly.

"I missed you too," said Nate.

Tahlia leaned over and gave him a hug.

"I've been thinking," she said, "About us."

Nate could barely breathe. "What have you been thinking?"

"One thing is, I'm not going away again, not for two whole weeks," Tahlia said. "And I've been thinking about how we can still do all the things we used to do together."

"I've been thinking how we can't do the things we used to do," Nate replied.

"'I'll tell you something, every problem has a solution,'" Tahlia said, quoting the General. "We have an appointment at Asa's tomorrow."

"At Asa's? What can he do?"

"You'll see. The three of us will figure it out."

Tahlia looked at Nate's computer screen. "What are you looking at?"

"Pictures of my family." Nate scrolled to another page. "Aaron and Shlomo—you know Shlomo?"

Tahlia nodded.

"Well, Aaron and Shlomo say I look like Sgt. Grange because of my eye."

Tahlia leaned over and looked at Nate's eyes.

"This one. This eye doesn't open all the way. I thought if it's genetic, someone else in my family would have it," Nate said. "I haven't found anyone so far, and I'm almost out of pictures."

"Why don't you find Sgt. Grange's picture?" Tahlia asked.

Nate stopped. He looked at Tahlia.

"I can't believe I never thought of that! Never once. Unbelievable!"

Nate typed "42nd Infantry Rainbow Division WWII images" into the search engine.

And there they were. Nate scrolled through the group photos. He and Tahlia studied each face. Nothing.

Some individual headshots came up next—and right in the middle was a face that looked almost familiar.

"He has my eye," said Nate.

"And your smile," said Tahlia. "That's just how you smile, all sideways like that."

"He has dark, curly hair. Mine is blonde and straight."

"And too long," said Tahlia.

"There are no names. How do I know it's him?"

"It has to be him. Who else could it be?" said Tahlia.

Nate stared at the picture. "This has been a really, um …a… really weird day," he said.

Turning to Tahlia, he told her what had happened that morning. Then he told her about what had happened at the airport, at the beach in Tel Aviv and at the Western Wall plaza. "I never told anyone about this before," he said.

"I think you should tell Sava," said Tahlia.

"Oh, no. No. The General already thinks I'm crazy."

-3-

"You're **crazy**! You **know** that, don't you?! **Everybody**, and I do mean **everybody**, is **watchin'** this game! Your **family** too!" Darryl glared at Nate. "Let's just **watch** the game, **relax**, have some **fun**…"

Nate stared at his Bible. He was studying Ezekiel's visions in chapters one and ten. He was having a strange sensation. It was as if he was seeing the chariot of the Almighty—not just visualizing it, but *actually seeing it.*

"You awake?" he said to Darryl. "You're awfully quiet."

"Score's **three** to one," Darryl answered.

"Who's winning?"

"**Not** the **Hawks**! I don't know **what** they're **doin'** out there. Not playin' **hockey**, that's for sure!"

"Look at this a minute then," Nate said. "Do you see anything, like a picture or something?"

He watched Darryl's face as he read.

"What'm I **s'posed** to see—did you see **that**?! They just got **another** one! **Four** to one. **Up** by **three**!" Darryl turned to Nate. "I can **tell** you what I do **see**! The **Hawks**! They better **regroup** before the second **period**!"

"I'm seeing the chariot of God," said Nate. "In the air, above a huge army…"

Darryl wasn't listening. His head was back in the game.

"**Yes! Yes!! Slick scores!**" Darryl jumped up and turned to Nate. "You **watchin'** this?! **Now** we got a **chance**!"

"No," Nate replied.

Nate tried to read the notes Sgt. Grange had written in the margin. He rummaged around until he found a magnifying glass. *Much better!*

"*Numbers 22–24*." Those chapters described what Balaam had seen. The whole camp of Israel, a vision of the Almighty.

Darryl paced around the room. "**One** more period. They can **do** this!"

"I'm trying to think," said Nate.

"Lemme **help** you," said Darryl. "Where you at?"

"Ezekiel 1. The chariot of the Almighty."

"Okay. **Listen**, there's **no** camp, **no** chariot! Just **wheels** and **cherubim**. It's just a **vision**! **Ezekiel** didn't even **know** what it meant! That's **it**! **Watch** the game!"

"I'm in the middle of this," said Nate.

"Think about **this**," said Darryl. "**Stanley** Cup! **The** Stanley **Cup**! They're only a **few games** away if they **win** this one!"

Nate saw the whole camp revolving—the whole camp of Israel. All the tribes camped around the chariot of the Almighty. He saw campfires and flashing swords of fire. It was different from other visions. *Why am I seeing this? What does this mean?*

"I have no idea," he said aloud.

"You talkin' to **me**?" asked Darryl.

"No," said Nate.

"Did you see that?! **Svenson** scores!! Are you **watchin'** this?" Darryl turned to Nate. "**Watch** the **replay**! Svenson's **pushin'** the puck down the ice…the Blues are **all over** him! He keeps **drivin'** the puck and then he turns…**swings** the stick behind his **back** and **nails** the puck **right into** the net! **Un-be-liev**-able! A **swirly-rama**! You won't see **that** again!"

"Yeah, that's pretty incredible," Nate said.

"He's the **only one** who does that!" Darryl paced around the room.

"One point to **tie, two** to win! We can do this!!"

Nate saw another verse Sgt. Grange had written: "*1 Chronicles 12:22-39.*"

The whole chapter was about the warriors from all the tribes of Israel coming to fight with David and make him king. *How did that tie in?*

"**What**!! Penalty on **Svenson**?! Nate, are you **watching** this?"

"No," said Nate.

"A **two-minute** penalty and only **two** minutes, **thirty-five seconds** left! This game is over. **Over**!"

Darryl grabbed the remote and clicked off the TV. "I **can't** watch this! I'm gonna have a **heart attack**, I'm **tellin'** ya!"

He turned the TV back on.

"Nate! **Watch this**!! … He's **outta** the box; he **grabs** the puck! He **scores**! Five **seconds** left and he **scores** the tying goal! We're in **overtime** now! Watch this! Watch the **replay**!"

"Every time you interrupt me, I lose where I am," said Nate. "My train of thought."

"You're **kidding**, right? Ezekiel's been around for **three thousand** years! This game is **once** in a **lifetime**! You keep **thinkin'**, you're going to **explode** your head!"

Where was I? Nate stared at his Bible. Right before his eyes, writing appeared in the margin. He was sure nothing had been there before. He was sure of that!

"Darryl, look at this a minute."

Darryl came over, keeping one eye on the TV. The Hawks were just coming on the ice.

"What'm I **lookin'** at?"

"The writing in the margin."

Darryl leaned over and peered at the margin. "Nothin' there. No writing. Nada."

Nate looked. The writing was still there. *Darryl's right,* he thought. *I'm going to explode my head.*

He read: *"Day for a thousand years / 2 Peter 3:8"*

What had Darryl said? Ezekiel had been around for three thousand years? What if…

What if God had been gathering his army for 3000 years? Nate thought about that. *Three thousand years was about up by now…*

-4-

"Nathaniel! My friend!" Asa was all smiles as he opened the door to his garage. "Come in!"

The inside of the garage looked like a junkyard dropped by a tornado. There was no space to come in to.

140

"What happened?!" Nate asked.

"For every solution there is a problem," said Asa spreading his arms. "Here I have the problem."

"How did this happen?" asked Nate.

"My friend, the lovely Tahlia, she brought to me the solution," said Asa.

"The lovely Tahlia"? Of course he would notice.

"She says to me, 'We will go all over Israel, just like we used to.'"

"We?"

"Of course! My friend! You and Tahlia—this is the solution. The problem"—he looked over his garage—"is to make transportation."

"Out of this?!" Nate looked incredulously at Tahlia. *Was she believing this?*

Asa hauled a large sheet of metal from under a pile of other sheets of metal. "My friend! This will lift your wonderful chair into the vehicle, right to the place of the driver."

"I'm going to drive?"

"Of course! My friend! You will drive all over the mountains of Judea. You will be like a Bedouin but much faster."

Asa found a tire. "This will take you everywhere. From the top of Mt. Herman to the Negev. My friend! There is no place you cannot go."

"I hope you have a few more of those," Nate quipped.

"Of course. Everything I need is right here!" Asa looked proudly over his garage's littered floor.

"Wow, Asa, this'll be … great," said Nate, glancing at Tahlia.

"My friend! This is the solution," said Asa. "But soon it will be also the problem!"

Nate watched as Asa made his way through the piles of junk.

"Do you think he can do this?" he asked Tahlia.

"Asa can make anything out of everything," she replied.

✿✞✿✞✿✞✿

Re: Picture
Mom –this is important – I found a picture of Sgt. Grange online
I have his duffel his Bible his medal and now his picture
See attached

Nate stared at the picture. It was almost like looking in the mirror. Almost. What would his parents think when they saw it? Would they see a resemblance? Should he even send it?

"Aaron and Shlomo are in the courtyard," Hannah said, entering his room. "They have been waiting, you see?"

Nate clicked *Send. There it goes,* he thought as he followed Hannah outside.

✿✞✿✞✿✞✿

"Shlomo, I said he would come, yes? And he is here," said Aaron.

"Aaron, Aaron! I can see he is here! Do you have the Book?"

"The Book? You have it. It is in your pocket, yes?"

Shlomo searched his pockets. "It is the Book of Y'shua," he said to Nate.

Finding it in an inside pocket, he held up a Bible for Nate to see.

"Now, to understand the Lamb that is slaughtered," said Aaron. "We will explain, yes?"

"Aaron, Aaron!" Shlomo said. "I am a rabbi! I will explain."

"First, a review. Y'shua is the Root of David. He is the *netzer*[26] that grows out of the Root."

Shlomo looked at Nate. "Do you remember?"

Nate nodded.

---

26 *Netzer* means "branch" in Hebrew

"Also, the Lion of Judah. The prophecies. Do you remember?"

Nate nodded.

"Shlomo, of course he remembers. It's a few weeks only, yes?" Aaron tapped the ground with his cane.

Shlomo glared at him.

"So, a review. Y'shua, born in Bethlehem, but also from Nazareth. Nazareth is a netzer. Nathaniel, do you see my meaning?" Shlomo asked.

Nate shook his head. "Now you lost me."

Aaron and Shlomo stopped and stared at Nate.

"You are not lost! You are here! Aaron, you see Nathaniel is here?"

"Nathaniel, you have come here. You were gone and now you are here, yes?"

Nate nodded. *Okay…*

"So. A review," Shlomo said, pulling himself to his feet and leaning on his cane.

"At the time of the Maccabeus—the Maccabeus, do you remember?"

"It is Hanukah, yes?" answered Aaron.

"Aaron! I am asking Nathaniel."

"I remember the Maccabeus," said Nate. "They rebelled against the Greeks. They won."

"So. To protect their borders," Shlomo said, "families are taken from the towns in Judea and sent to make towns in the Galilee. Do you see my meaning?"

"I think I do," Nate replied.

"From the city of David…"

"Bethlehem," Nate said.

"…the people went and made a town. They called it Netzereth…"

"Nazareth," Nate said.

"So. Nazareth is a *netzer* of Bethlehem. Now you see my meaning?"

"I never knew that!" said Nate. "Families from Bethlehem settled Nazareth! Yeah… I see it now. When people called Y'shua the Nazarene, they were calling Him the Branch!"

"So, it is what the prophet said—a branch from the root of Jesse—this is Y'shua," said Shlomo.[Isaiah 11:1] "I am a rabbi. I know these things!"

"The slaughtered Lamb, yes? You will now explain?" asked Aaron.

Shlomo sat down. He slowly paged through the Book. "So, a review. On the Passover, Y'shua is killed. It is the time of the evening sacrifice, when the lamb is slaughtered."

Shlomo adjusted his glasses. "A question. Is Y'shua the slaughtered lamb?"

"Yes," answered Nate.

"So why is He slaughtered?" Shlomo watched Nate. "Do you know?"

"To take away the sins of the world," said Nate. "So that whoever believes in Him will have eternal life." [John 1:29, 3:16]

Shlomo pulled himself to his feet. "The Passover lamb is not a sin offering. I am a rabbi; I know these things."

"I guess I never thought about that," said Nate.

"Now," said Aaron. "Now explain the slaughtered lamb, yes?"

"Aaron! I am explaining! There is an order to be followed!"

"So. The lamb of the Passover. A review. The lamb is slaughtered. The blood is put on the side and top doorposts of the house. The destroyer is not allowed to enter the house that has the blood." [Exodus 12:7,23]

Shlomo bent over his cane. "Do you see my meaning?"

Nate thought about it. "Yeah... I guess," he replied.

"The destroyer is the wrath of HASHEM. Do you see?"

"Yeah. I see. I just never really thought about it before."

Shlomo sat down. He opened the Book about Y'shua and turned the pages.

Does he have the whole New Testament memorized? Nate wondered, watching him.

"'Behold, the Lamb of God, who takes away the sin of the world," Shlomo read. [John 1:29]

"So, the Lamb of God, this is the lamb of the sin offering," he said. "Do you see?"

"Shlomo, it is in the Torah, yes?" Aaron said.

Shlomo paused, stared at Aaron, then turned to the front of the book.

So, there are two goats. One is the lot for HASHEM. One is the lot for the scapegoat."

"'And Aaron shall present the goat on which the lot fell for Adonai and use it as a sin offering. ... Then he shall kill the goat of the sin offering that is for the people, and bring its blood inside the veil ... sprinkling it over the mercy seat and in front of the mercy seat. Thus he shall make atonement for the Holy Place, from the impurities of the people of Israel and from their transgressions, all their sins.'" (Leviticus 16:9, 15–16)

"The goat that is killed, this is the lot for HASHEM. This is the lamb of God."

Nate frowned. "A lamb is different than a goat."

"This is the sin offering for the people! I know these things!"

"Yeah, I know," said Nate, "you're a rabbi."

Shlomo looked at Nate. "So. Now Y'shua is standing between the throne, the four living creatures and the elders. He is

145

the Lamb that is slaughtered. Do you see? He is the lot for HASHEM." Revelation 5:6

"Messiah died. He is the sin offering, yes?" Aaron tapped the ground with his cane. "Yes!"

"Now He is alive. Adonai raised Him from death. Remember?" Nate said. "Our sins are laid on Him, and we are forgiven."

Shlomo and Aaron thought about that.

"So. In Germany I was born to a religious family," Shlomo said. "My father was a rabbi. To obey God, to obey His commands, that was the whole of life. Yom Kippur was the holiest day of the year. If there were any commands we had broken, on Yom Kippur they could be forgiven. I asked my father, 'Are our sins forgiven now?' He said he hoped so. He 'hoped so'?" Shlomo shrugged his shoulders and shook his head. "He was a rabbi, but he didn't know. There were no sacrifices, no shedding of blood. So he didn't know. 'Keep the commandments, and maybe God will be merciful when you stand before Him,' he said." Leviticus 17:11; Hebrews 9:22

For a long time Shlomo didn't say anything... then he began.

"So, the Independence War, it ended. Nathaniel, you were gone. Aaron, he went to Ya'thom. He is doing good, taking care of the living. The widows, the children...

"I went out as an avenger of blood. I went and hunted ... Nazis...There were many of us. I was not alone. We knew who they were. We knew where they lived. We knew what they had done. ... So, we brought many to justice. They were tried in the courts. They were hung or shot or put in prison. Justice, we brought them to justice...you see my meaning?

"So. There were others, just as cruel, just as evil. They were living their lives. They had homes and families. They lived in towns and cities. They lived in comfort. They thought no one knew. ...We knew. We brought justice to them. We avenged the blood of our children...

"Our children, our little Jewish children. Murdered without mercy. Not to waste a bullet, little heads were smashed and

146

then… and then they were put back in their mothers' arms. … Little children, thrown in the air to be caught on the bayonet. Their little bodies dropped in the street. … Our little Jewish children, thrown alive into the pits…covered with dead bodies…to suffocate…to die…

"So. I avenged their blood. One … by one … by one … I hunted the Nazi murderers. One … by one … by one … they died. I was not cruel, but I was without mercy."

Nate remembered the Children's Memorial at Yad Vashem. He and Tahlia had walked into the darkness, a darkness pierced with thousands of tiny lights. Each light was a reflection of a life. Each light had a name. The names were spoken into the darkness, one… by one… by one. The names of one and a half million children. Each child had been murdered, one… by one… by one…[27]

"They were guilty, yes? There were witnesses," Aaron said. "Tell Nathaniel."

"So. Yes, two or three witnesses. For each Nazi. The witnesses, they told us who they were, what they had done. They told us all they had seen. They spoke for the dead. We wrote on paper what they told us. Each time I avenged their blood, I pinned the words of the witnesses on the bodies—two papers. Three."

"I executed evil men. It was justice. They did not deny their guilt."

I saw this! Nate thought. *I saw bodies lying scattered all over the place. Bodies with two or three papers pinned to them. I was reading my Bible when I saw these pictures my mind. I never knew what they were!*

"I had no remorse. My heart was black with anger and hate. I did not know that the darkness was covering my soul… but I had found no peace."

"So. Another war. A Six-Day War, but who knew? I came back to Israel, to fight."

Shlomo turned to Aaron. "Aaron, you remember? It was then you saw in me the darkness."

---

27 Imagery of "one by one by one" is taken from the documentary *Engineering Evil.*

"The light, it is in the Torah, yes?" said Aaron. "I said, 'Shlomo, study Torah, find the light.'"

"Nathaniel, you were hurt in the attack by the terrorists. You do not walk—maybe forever—but you are at peace. Where do you get this peace?"

"From Y'shua," Nate answered. "He gives me peace. Most of the time."

"So, this is where I also find peace," said Shlomo.

"You? You found peace in Y'shua?" asked Nate.

"It was Aaron. He sent me to find the light."

"So. I studied Torah. I become a rabbi," Shlomo stated. "I searched for peace, but I could not find peace. I am a rabbi, but this I did not know, how to find this peace."

Shlomo closed his eyes and rested his head on his cane.

"Is he okay?" Nate asked Aaron.

"He is thinking, yes? Shlomo, what are you thinking?"

"So, Aaron, he says to read Isaiah chapter 53." He slowly opened the Bible to Isaiah. "I am a rabbi, but this I never read in the Tanakh," he said. "The prophet Isaiah writes about a person who is innocent of all wrongdoing; a person who took all our suffering on himself. All of our guilt was laid on him, and he took our punishment. He was killed for our sin; he was an offering for our guilt. He is a slaughtered lamb."

"Then I give him the Book of Y'shua, yes?" said Aaron.

"So, I read this Bible, this Book about Y'shua," said Shlomo. "Who else can it be? The prophet is writing about Y'shua!" He turned to Nate. "There I read I must forgive my enemies. I read that HASHEM forgives in the same way we forgive. It says judgment is without mercy to one who has shown no mercy. How can I ask God for mercy when I gave no mercy?" James 2:13; Matthew 6:14–15

He continued: "So, I say to Aaron: 'Aaron. I cannot forgive. How do I forgive my enemy? How do I love my enemy? I have no peace.'" Shlomo's eyes were wet with tears.

"I tell him that to forgive does not take away their guilt," Aaron said. "Only Y'shua can take away guilt, yes?"

"I hated the terrorists that put me in this chair," Nate replied. "I hated them for all the people they killed or tried to kill. I didn't know how to love my enemy." Nate frowned as he remembered how he had struggled not only to forgive but to love the man who had paralyzed him. "Y'shua said to pray for the ones that persecute you. So I did. I prayed. I learned it is not possible to hate someone you pray for. Y'shua is helping me to forgive them, and I am asking Y'shua to forgive me." **Matthew 5:44**

Shlomo was silent for a long time, and then he spoke. "So, Y'shua gave to me the power to forgive the Nazis. He took away the bitterness. He took my pain and sorrow. It took a long time. A very long process. Some days I still have this burden."

"Nathaniel, on the road to Jerusalem, you talked of Y'shua the Messiah, yes?" Aaron inquired. "You said Y'shua is the Messiah. This you remember?"

I wasn't on the road to Jerusalem. ... They have me confused with Sgt. Grange—again.

"It is after the war, at Ya'thom, that I remember all you said," Aaron stated. "The children, so many were hidden by believers in Y'shua. One child had a Bible that told all about Y'shua, yes? This Book I read. Then I know that all you told to us was true. Y'shua is the Messiah."

Nate leaned back and closed his eyes. Sgt. Grange had told both Aaron and Shlomo about Y'shua, and now both were believers. This was a miracle of Y'shua; Shlomo had been healed just as surely as David Yaniv had been.

✿✝✿✝✿✝✿

Nate stared at the clock. 2 a.m. He was so tired, but he couldn't sleep. He didn't **want** to sleep. Every time he closed his eyes, he saw **him**—the rider on the pale horse. He wore a black

149

uniform with a death's-head insignia just above the brim of his hat. Behind him were piles of bodies, skeletons. Fire and smoke swirled around him. There were pits filled with more bodies. This was death. This was the grave.

Nate turned on the light. He knew the rider, whose name was Death. He was from the Death's-Head Unit of the *Waffen-SS*. He was one of the *Einsatzgruppen* who executed men, women and children—shooting them into huge graves, pits dug into the ground. He was a guard at the death camps, cruelly murdering hundreds of thousands, shooting or gassing them. He watched as others died of disease and starvation; he ordered the bodies piled in heaps because the ovens couldn't burn them fast enough. He was a wild beast.

Nate opened his Bible. *I'll finish reading Revelation,* he thought. *Then the Epistles of John. Then the Gospel of John...*

Hours later he read: "In the beginning was the Word, and the Word was with God, and the word was God. He was in the beginning with God. All things were made through Him, and without Him was not anything made that was made. In Him was life, and the life was the light of men.

"The light shines in the darkness, and the darkness has not overcome it."

Finally, Nate fell asleep.

Justine stared at the picture.

"Wes, take a look at this," she said. "Nate sent this picture of Sgt. Grange."

Wes peered over her shoulder. "What the… What?! It looks just like him! Like Ellis!"

Justine looked up at him. "What's going on? None of this makes any sense."

"It's Nate! In a army suit with a hat!" said JJ.

150

Justine quickly closed the picture.

"I want you and your sister to go up and get ready for bed," she said sternly. "Now!"

JJ raced for the stairs. "I'm faster!" he called to Josie.

"I don't care!" she yelled back.

"Can I see the picture?" she asked Justine sweetly.

"No," said Justine.

Josie started up the stairs. "It's not fair," she said softly.

"I heard that," Justine said.

"I don't care," Josie whispered.

"I heard that too," Justine remarked.

"We'll figure this out," said Wes. "I'll find out if Sgt. Grange is related to my family somehow. I'll find out how he's connected to Ellis."

"Nate said there's no Nathaniel in our family tree. Nate said Sgt. Grange was Jewish."

"We don't have any Jewish people in my family," said Wes.

"Ellis wasn't Jewish either," said Justine. "If he was Jewish, he would have said so. Wouldn't he?"

Wes thought about that.

"We'll find out," he said, hugging her. "Don't worry, we'll find out."

CHAPTER FOUR

Damascus
-1-
Behold, Damascus will cease to be a city
And will become a heap of ruins.
Isaiah 17:1

> There are many reports, coming from the refugee
> camps, of Jesus appearing to Muslims in visions and
> dreams. Because of these dreams, many Muslims are
> coming to believe in Jesus. This puts their lives in
> extreme danger! Anyone who converts from Islam to
> another religion has a death penalty over their head...

Nate was only half listening to *The 700 Club* as he checked his email. He had heard nothing from home about the picture he'd sent of Sgt. Grange. *Did they get it? Should he ask? Should he send it again?*

"Turn the channel," said the General, entering the room. "I'll show you something." Nate turned on INT News.

> Israeli fighter jets targeted a military convoy traveling
> north of Damascus near the Syrian-Lebanese border.
> The airstrike on the weapons convoy reportedly
> resulted in the death of a senior commander of
> Hezbollah. Israel has stated it will not allow advanced
> weapon systems to be delivered to Hezbollah. The
> IDF did not comment on the airstrike. A weapons
> depot outside Damascus was also targeted.

"They're storing weapons near Damascus?" Nate asked. "What kind of weapons?"

"I'll tell you something, they are the worst kind," said David. "Chemical, biological, also enriched uranium from Iran."

"Right by Damascus? By all those people?!"

"It is in a neighborhood, where families live. It is the largest storage bunker for Syrian biological and chemical weapons," said David. "With the war, no people are safe. I'll tell you something, Assad is still using the chemicals on his own people."

"Did the IAF destroy the bunker?" Nate inquired.

"No. This day, a smaller depot was destroyed. The roof of that bunker is 45 feet thick. All reinforced concrete. Filled with these terrible chemicals, it is dangerous to destroy."

"What kind of chemicals?"

"Mustard, cyanide, sarin; also VX nerve agents. These can be put on rockets. We cannot let these get into the hands of the terrorists. … Come. I'll show you something."

Nate rolled into the General's office—the war room, Tahlia called it. David pulled down a large map of Syria, Israel and Lebanon. He pointed to an area just north of Damascus. "Here is the large weapons bunker. It is between Al-Tal and Aysh Wurur."

He pointed to another spot just east of Al-Dumayr, on the north side of the highway. "This is a chemical weapons factory. I'll tell you something, it is under a berm over 40 feet high. The Iranians operate it."

Nate studied the map. He couldn't believe how close everything was. Close to Damascus. Close to Israel. "What would happen if these places were blown up?"

David also studied the map. "A disaster. I tell you something. These weapons would bring bacteria and viruses to people through food, through water, and even through the earth. With chemical weapons, even the air will become poison."

Both Nate and David were silent as they considered the implications of chemical and biological agents exploding into the atmosphere.

"I'll ask you something," said David. "Does your Revelation say anything about this?"

"I'm not sure," said Nate.

"The prophets, they say 'Damascus will no longer be a city,'" Isaiah 17:1 said David.

153

"Aaron. Aaron!" Shlomo called out. He looked at the empty courtyard. "Nathaniel is not here."

"He is not here; he is there, inside, yes?" Aaron said.

Aaron and Shlomo looked through the open patio doors into Nate's room.

"A woman is there. Aaron, do you see?"

"A woman. Nathaniel's wife, yes? You did not know?"

"I'm not his wife," Tahlia replied. "I'm his friend. Remember?"

"Someday a wife," Aaron said.

Shlomo looked at her. "So. A beautiful woman. A friend only? Nathaniel! You are meshugah! Ask her to be a wife! What can she say?"

"I can say yes," Tahlia remarked.

"We're sorting things out," said Nate.

"I'm wondering about Damascus," Nate said, changing the subject. "Has it ever been destroyed?"

"So," Shlomo answered. "Damascus always has been a city."

"Some people say it was completely destroyed in 732 B.C. Others say it was never totally destroyed." Nate read from his Bible:

"Behold, Damascus will cease to be a city and will become a heap of ruins." Isaiah17:1

Shlomo leaned on his cane. "So. A review. Damascus was a city even before Abraham. Josephus—you know Josephus?"

Nate nodded.

"Josephus writes Damascus was begun by Uz, a son of Aram. Then, it is ruled by Egypt, and after by Israel and Aram. Then, 732 B.C.—Tiglath-Pileser II, he conquers it and it becomes part of the Assyrian Empire. But it is not completely destroyed. This you can read in the Tanakh. As soon as Assyria conquered Damascus, King Ahaz went to Damascus to meet with Tiglath-Pileser, the king of Assyria. Do you know Ahaz?"

"He was king of Judah," Nate said. "He was the father of Hezekiah."

"So. When Ahaz comes to Damascus, he sees the altar that was in Damascus," Shlomo continued. [2 Kings 16:9–10] Do you see my meaning?"

"No," Nate admitted.

"The city, it was not destroyed! The altar, it still stood. The King of Assyria, he is having guests in the city. The city, it is still inhabited! I am a professor. I know these things."

"I thought you were a rabbi," Nate said.

"Nathaniel, he is both, yes?" Aaron clarified. "A professor and a rabbi."

"Really? Who knew!" Nate replied, impressed.

Aaron and Shlomo looked at each other.

"Everyone knew! Yes?"

"I knew," Tahlia agreed.

"Nathaniel, you only did not know," Shlomo said.

"So. A review," Shlomo continued. "572 B.C., all of Assyria is conquered by the Babylonians. Then it becomes a provincial capital of the Persian Empire. 332 B.C., it passes to the armies of Alexander the Great Murderer. Then it is controlled by the Seleucids, then Tigranes of Armenia. 64 B.C., Damascus becomes part of the Roman Empire under Pompey. Nathaniel, do you see my meaning? Always an important city. Always inhabited."

"Yeah, I can see that," said Nate.

"So, 335—after the Roman Empire splits in two, Damascus becomes a provincial capital of the Byzantine Empire. 635, now the Arabs occupy the city. 661, Damascus is the seat of the caliphate under the Umayyads. This is until 670. Then it is conquered many times—the Egyptians, the Karmathians, the Seljuk Turks, the Saracens, the Mongols and the Mamluks. It becomes a provincial capital of the Mamluk Empire. Never a capital city, only a provincial capital. Do you see my meaning?"

"Shlomo, of course he sees! He is listening, yes?"

Shlomo glared at Aaron. "Aaron! A point is being made!"

"So. A review. Damascus is a Provincial capital of the Mamluk Empire until1516. Now it is passed to the Ottoman Turks. For 400 years it is ruled by the Turks. Then, 1917—it is captured by General Allenby and Emir Faisal. Nathaniel, do you know Allenby?"

"Yeah, he took Jerusalem from the Turks on the eve of Hanukah!"

"So, after the Great War, Damascus becomes the capital of one of the French Levant States. Then, in 1941, Damascus becomes the capital of independent Syria. Do you see my meaning? For the first time since it is conquered by the Assyrians in732 B.C., Damascus is again the capital of the nation of Syria."

Shlomo sat down. He had made his point. Damascus had been continuously inhabited from the earliest times. It had never been completely destroyed. It had never ceased to be a city.

✿✞✿✞✿✞✿

"Shlomo, you have the paper, yes?" Aaron asked.

Shlomo searched his pockets. "So, an important paper—Aaron, it is in the Book. You have the Book!"

Aaron looked at the Book about Y'shua that was in his hand. He gave it to Shlomo, who opened it and found the paper.

Aaron and Shlomo stared at Tahlia. They waited. Tahlia looked at Nate. "Ah… I'm going to get something for us to drink," she said, getting up and heading for the door.

"So," said Shlomo, as soon as Tahlia had gone, "this is the place." He handed the paper to Nate. On it was the name of an Orthodox synagogue in Jerusalem.

"The place for what?" Nate asked.

"Nathaniel! The immersion, the baptism, yes?" Aaron answered.

"Believe, then the immersion," Shlomo stated. "All this time we believe, but now we will be baptized."

"And you will come, yes?" Aaron asked.

"You're going to be baptized at an Orthodox synagogue?!" Nate said, surprised.

"Nathaniel! Do you think in the Jordan? In the cold water?" Aaron replied.

"So, in a warm mikvah, we will be immersed!" Shlomo added.

"But…at an Orthodox synagogue?"

"Aaron. Aaron!" Shlomo said. He does not know in the orthodox there are believers in Y'shua."

"Everything is the same, but all believe Y'shua is the Messiah, yes?" Aaron said.

"Nathaniel, it's a Messianic synagogue," Tahlia explained, carrying a pitcher and glasses into the room.

"I want to be baptized too. I was going to, and then you were attacked. Remember we talked about it?"

"I remember," Nate told her. "It seems so long ago."

Aaron and Shlomo were startled. "Tahlia! You are a believer in Y'shua?!"

"Nathaniel, you did not tell of this."

"Tahlia! You are Jewish! You cannot be Christian! You cannot be baptized!"

Aaron, Shlomo, Nate and Tahlia all turned to see Hannah standing in the doorway, holding a plate of rugelach cookies.

"*Savta*, I can be a believer in Y'shua and still be Jewish," said Tahlia.

Shlomo pulled himself to his feet and leaned on his cane. He looked at Hannah. "So," he said, "I am a rabbi; I know these things. I know Y'shua is the Messiah. Also, Y'shua, He is a Jew. First, a review. He is born a Jew. He lives as a Jew. The Feast Days, He observes them all. He dies as a Jew. He is buried as a Jew." Shlomo looked at Hannah. "Do you see my meaning? Y'shua is the Messiah of the Jews. You see the list in the book of Matthew? All Jews!"

Hannah said nothing.

"So. Y'shua, He is the Messiah. He heals the sick; the blind ones see; the deaf ones hear; the lame, they walk; the dead are raised up. All this is the work of Messiah. He is then the slaughtered lamb, the Lamb of God who takes away the sin of the world. Do you see my meaning?"

Hannah said nothing.

"So, HASHEM raised Him from the dead and He is now at the right hand of HASHEM. Y'shua will come again to this earth as a Jew. The Lion of Judah. With the sword of fire. Do you see?"

"When I was a small girl, I loved Jesus," Hannah said. "When the Nazi soldiers walked down the street, I was afraid. My heart would beat very fast. I thought it was Jesus in my heart telling me not to be afraid."

"After the war, when my parents came, they told me, 'You are Jewish; you cannot be Christian.' I learned then, I could not be Christian, you see? But I did not know what it meant to be Jewish. I learned that Jewish people went to synagogue instead of church; that the Jewish Sabbath was Saturday instead of Sunday; that Jewish people said the *Shema*[28] instead of the Apostles' Creed. We celebrated the Holy Days of Passover, Shavuot, Rosh Hashanah, Yom Kippur and Sukkot, instead of the Christian Holy Days of Christmas and Easter. I learned about the Torah but not Jesus. His name was never spoken. I still loved Jesus in my heart, but never told anyone. Who could I tell? I was afraid I'd be shut out of the community. I was afraid my family would not understand, you see? I did not know Jesus was a Jew. I did not know Jesus was Y'shua."

"I ask you something," David said. Nate turned and saw the General standing in the doorway. "Do you believe this? Do you believe that Jesus is Y'shua and Y'shua is the Messiah?"

Hannah took a deep breath. She nodded her head.

---

28 "Hear O Israel Adonai our God, Adonai is one. You shall love Adonai your God with all your heart and with all your soul and all your might." Deuteronomy 6:4-5, Mark 12:30

David looked at Tahlia. "Yes, Sava, I also believe that Y'shua is the Messiah," she replied.

David spun around and walked away.

Sitting in his office, he thought about all he and Nate had talked about. He thought about all he had read in the Christian Bible. He thought about all he had heard Shlomo say. *Could it be true? Could it be that Y'shua was the Messiah? Had the Jewish people missed His coming?* David's face hardened. *No! When Messiah comes, He will be victorious over Israel's enemies. He will reign in Jerusalem as Israel's king. He will put an end to war. He will bring peace to the whole earth. None of that happened when Y'shua walked the earth.*

-2-

"Hey, **General**! How ya **doin'**? You **see** what's goin' **on** over there?" Darryl called to David as he came into Nate's room. "This is **all over** the news! You **watchin'** this?" he asked Nate.

"Yeah. They have a special report on now." Nate turned up the volume.

> ...major chemical weapons facility in the downtown area of Damascus, Syria's capital. The facility is only a short distance via underground tunnel from Al-Mazzeh military airfield in southwest Damascus. The tunnel is large enough to accommodate tractor-trailer-sized trucks and has exits to several buildings on the base. The path of tunnel leads to underground storage areas north and east of the airfield. The roof of the bunker is 45-foot-thick reinforced concrete designed to withstand a strike from U.S. Tomahawk missiles. The facility contains a variety of chemical weapons, from hand grenades filled with mustard-gas agents to various-sized rockets armed with chemical weapons...

"If that bunker gets busted and all those chemicals are blown into the atmosphere, it's going to be a disaster worse than anything we've seen yet," said Nate.

"**You** ain't seen **nothin!**" said Darryl. "If those chemicals are **weaponized**, we gotta **pray** it's like'91!"

> The Syrian military airport, located southwest of Damascus, was hit by several waves of airstrikes around 4:15 a.m. Because of darkness, the aircraft could not be identified, and the number of planes in each wave is unknown. Depots containing ammunition, bombs and missiles have been hit, the explosions shattering the normally quiet pre-dawn hours.

Nate and Darryl watched as footage of flames and pillars of smoke rose from the decimated airport.

> There has been no comment from Israel regarding the destruction of the weapons depots. Israel has stated that it has no interest in interfering with the Syrian Civil War, but will act to keep weapons out of the hands of terrorists like Hezbollah.

"What happened in '91?" Nate asked.

"The Gulf War. You don't **remember** that? You **gotta** be **kiddin'** me!"

"I know about it," said Nate, "but, I was, like, not even born yet."

"Well, I was **there** in Iraq, **chasin'** Saddam."

"You got him, right?"

Darryl shook his head. "That was the **next** Iraq War. Don't they teach you **nothin'** in school?"

"Yeah, so what happened?"

"It was a **miracle** for **Israel**, but there was a miracle **for me** and my **buddies** too!"

"I'm listening…"

"Okay. Iraq was threatening to use **chemical** weapons on **Israel**. Israel wasn't even **involved** in this war except being on the **receiving** end of **Scud-missile** attacks."

"Israel didn't respond? They always respond!"

160

"The **U.S.** didn't want them in this fight, so they **hunkered** down in their **sealed rooms** and waited it out. **Saddam** had threatened them with a **chemical-weapon** attack, so they were preparing for that. If **that'd** happened, **nothin'** would've kept the **Israelis** out of the fight. The attack **never** happened. The **wind** patterns shifted, and the wind began to blow **east** from Israel directly **toward** Iraq. Our military said the odd **weather** change probably was the **major** cause for the Iraqis' decision **not to use** chemical weapons. **Any** attack on **Israel** would have blown back on **Iraq**."[29]

"What about you? What happened with you?"

"Remember those **weapons** of mass destruction? We found **65,000** artillery shells filled with **mustard, sarin** and **VX** gas. Saddam was **plannin'** to fire these shells in front of **our** troops, one of which was **me**! You gotta **understand** the wind **always** blows from the **north** of Iraq and down through Saudi Arabia and Kuwait. On the night the **ground assault** on Iraq was supposed to **start**, the wind direction **changed**. For the **first time** in recorded **history**, the **wind** started to blow from the **south**. The Iraqis **couldn't** fire these weapons because the **gas** would have blown back on **them**. Saddam thought his generals were **lying** when they told him the wind had changed and they **couldn't** fire the **artillery shells** at us. He **shot** a couple of them before he found out they were telling the **truth**."[30]

"That was the Finger of God!" Nate exclaimed.

"We found out **later** those winds blew from the **south** for 100 hours, **exactly** enough time for the invasion!"

"Finger of God for sure!"

"I think **all** those WMDs are in **Syria** now," Darryl said.

"The General says there's a bunker near Damascus that's full of chemical weapons," Nate remarked.

---

29 https://UnitedWithIsrael.org/remember-miracles-in-israel-during-the-gulf-war

30 https://TheFederalist.com/2017/12/01/prayers-saved-life-many-american-soldiers-first-iraq-war

"Remember all those **trucks** headed for **Syria** before we invaded in 2003?"

"I was a little kid," said Nate. "I don't remember anything about that."

"I'm wondering if it's chemical weapons that force Israel to leave their land," Nate commented.

"**What**?! Are you **nuts**?! The **Israelis** aren't going to **leave** this **land**! Where'd you **get** that idea?"

"From the Bible," said Nate. "Revelation 12 says the woman, meaning Israel, flees into the wilderness."

Darryl grabbed Nate's Bible. "Hey! Be careful with that! It's starting to fall apart," Nate warned.

Darryl read Revelation 12:6, "'And the woman fled into the wilderness, where she has a place prepared by God, in which she is to be nourished for 1,260 days.'"

"Go down a few verses," Nate directed.

Darryl went down to verse 14: "'But the woman was given the two wings of the great eagle so she might fly from the serpent into the wilderness, to the place where she is to be nourished for a time, and times, and half a time.' …

"Maybe this already happened," Darryl said.

"Maybe, but I can't find it in history," Nate replied. "Look at Revelation 11. The Gentile nations are ruling Jerusalem for 42 months. When did that happen?" Revelation 11:1–2

"You're **kiddin'**, right? **Gentile** nations have ruled Jerusalem for what, **2500 years**? The Israelis didn't get the **whole city** 'till '67."

"What I'm wondering is, when did they rule for only 42 months? When were the two witnesses prophesying for 1260 days? That for sure hasn't happened yet," Nate stated. "And what about Armageddon? Do you think the Israelis are going to let the armies of the whole world assemble on the plain of Megiddo, in middle of their country, if they are in the land?"

Darryl thought about that.

"Maybe you're not **interpreting** it right," he said. "**You're** not **always** right, you know!"

"And then there's Isaiah 17," Nate added, ignoring what Darryl had just said. "Damascus is destroyed."

"We're **watchin'** the **start** of that right **now!**"

"Yeah, but it doesn't look good for Israel either. Look it up."

Darryl carefully turned to Isaiah 17. "'Behold, Damascus will cease to be a city and will become a heap of ruins. The cities of Aroer are deserted; they will be for flocks, which will lie down, and none will make them afraid. The fortress will disappear from Ephraim, and the kingdom from Damascus; and the remnant of Syria will be like the glory of the children of Israel, declares the LORD of hosts.'"

"What does **that** mean, 'the **fortress** will disappear from **Ephraim**'?" Darryl wanted to know.

"Well, fortress means defenses or defenders. So those will disappear from Ephraim," Nate answered. "I think Ephraim means northern Israel. If I'm right, it would mean an area all the way from the Golan to Jerusalem and Tel Aviv."

"That's **huge!** That's **half** the country," Darryl said. "There's no way **half the country** is undefended!"

"Yeah. Seems impossible, but something has to happen for Israel to 'flee into the wilderness.'"

"**Can't** happen! I'm **tellin'** ya, Israel is **never** going to leave Tel Aviv or Jerusalem **undefended!**"Darryl insisted. "How 'bout **Aroer**? Where's **that**? In **Israel**?"

"I'm not sure," Nate replied. "I'm going to ask Shlomo about all of this."

"**Shlomo**? The old **rabbi**?"

"Yeah, he used to be a Professor at Hebrew U."

Darryl shook his head. "**He's** full of surprises."

"You have no idea," Nate remarked.

Darryl continued reading: "'And in that day the glory of Jacob will be brought low and the fat of his flesh will grow lean. And it shall be as when the reaper gathers standing grain and his arm harvests the ears, and as when one gleans the ears of grain in the Valley of Rephaim. Gleanings will be left in it, as when an olive tree is beaten, two or three berries in the top of the highest bough, four or five on the branches of a fruit tree, declares the LORD God of Israel.' … You **sure** this didn't happen during the, **what'd** ya call it, **Assyrian** invasion? I mean this is **over** with, right?"

"Shlomo says no, but even if it did, what about Revelation?"

"What about that **verse** the PM always quotes in his **speeches**?" Darryl asked. **Amos** something."

"Yeah, Amos 9:15," Nate specified.

Darryl looked it up and read: "'I will plant them on their land, and they shall never again be uprooted out of the land that I have given them,' says the LORD your God."

Darryl and Nate thought about that.

"I could be wrong," Nate reflected. "I could be totally wrong. I hope I'm totally wrong."

✿✞✿✞✿✞✿

"Hey Darryl, what did you do after the war?" Nate asked. "Is that when you came to Israel?"

Darryl looked down at the floor. "When I got out of the army, I got a job as a warehouse foreman. I had a **family**, a **wife** and a **little girl**. Then…" He looked out into the courtyard. "It was winter. **February**. It wasn't even **snowing** when they went out. She had a doctor's appointment, regular checkup, some **women's** thing. By the time they got out of the doctor's, it had started **snowing**. Not just snowing, but a regular **blizzard**. Couldn't see **two feet**. Traffic was **crawling** along at maybe

20 miles an hour, tops. They hit a patch of **black ice** on a **downhill** slope, and that threw them into a **tree. Head-on.** By the time the paramedics got there, they were both... dead."

Nate was shocked. He couldn't think of anything to say.

"I can't even **remember** the visitation. I **cried** my way through the **funeral.** It was **freezing** cold that day when they put my girls in the **ground.** I walked away and I **never** came back, not once."

Darryl got up and walked around the room.

"I went to **that tree.** Almost **every day** I'd go and just **stand** there. I didn't pray. **At all.** I had **nothin'** to say to **God.** In the spring I made a little **cross** and put it by the **tree.** I planted **flowers,** pink ones. Real pretty, for my **girls.**"

Nate thought about the beautiful pink flowers that were all around the ELISHA warehouse. Darryl must have planted those.

"One day, I'm just **sittin'** there, by the **tree,** and I hear this **voice**—not out loud but in my heart. 'I **know** how much you love them. I know how much you're hurting.' So I get **up** and I'm **lookin'** at my little **cross** next to this big **tree.** That's when I realize God let **His** Son **die** on a tree. He **knows exactly** how I'm feelin'."

Darryl had stopped walking. He looked out at the courtyard again. "I **prayed** then. 'I don't know **what** to **do,**' I said to God. 'I don't know **how** to **live.**'"

I said that same thing to God, Nate thought.

"So I go **home** and there's an ELISHA FUND **newsletter** in the mailbox. I'm **readin'** it and on the **last page** it says they're lookin' for an experienced **manager** for their distribution center in **Tel Aviv.** Six weeks later I land at **Ben Gurion.** Been here ever since."

-3-

Wes leaned back in his chair and stared at the computer screen. Another dead-end. Nate was right: There was no Nathaniel Grange anywhere in the Grange family tree. He had searched the military databases for Sgt. Nathaniel Grange. He had found records that documented Sgt. Grange's entire military history, except for his enlistment and discharge papers.

"It's like he showed up in the army in 1942 out of nowhere and then disappeared after the war. He shows up again in Israel in 1947. He's killed just before their War of Independence," Wes summarized. "He's buried in Israel, and that's all the information there is."

"Isn't there a birth certificate?" Justine queried.

"No. No birth certificate, no marriage license, no driver's license—nothing."Wes shook his head. "He's just hanging out there with no connection to anyone."

"He has a connection to Nate," Justine remarked. "Somehow Nate has his duffel bag, Bible and that medal Israel gave him."

"All three Nathaniels have to be connected somehow," Wes remarked. "We know how Nate and Ellis are connected, but where does the sergeant fit in?"

"Any ideas?" Justine asked.

"I'm going to go over the Ellis genealogy again, see if I missed something," Wes replied.

✡✞✡✞✡✞✡

Nate woke up. His heart was pounding, and he was drenched with sweat. Not just sweat. His eyes were burning, and his nose was dripping. His throat felt like he had swallowed crushed glass. *It's a dream,* he told himself as he remembered the scene: *a crowd of people, running, pushing, trying to get away. Above them the sky seemed to be crumbling into pieces...and all around them, a grey fog.*

✡✞✡✞✡✞✡

"Come, I'll show you something," the General said. *He's got an odd look on his face,* Nate thought as he followed David outside.

166

Nate couldn't believe his eyes. There on the street was Asa with the strangest vehicle Nate had ever seen. It looked like half a Humvee, with a lot of tires. The front was scrunched in, and half the back was missing.

"Nathaniel! My friend! This is the problem to your solution! I will show you everything!"

Nate rolled around the vehicle. "This is insane!" he said in disbelief.

"Insane, yes, for you my friend," Asa replied. "The key is this." He held out what looked like a small remote. "The button, green, is power. Then, blue is the ramp." Asa pushed both buttons, and a ramp, which was the back panel of the vehicle, lowered to the pavement.

"My friend! Roll your wonderful chair up to the seat of the driver!"

Nate rolled up the ramp and found himself in front of a control panel, looking out the windshield. *This is insane! Am I really going to drive this?*

"Here! My friend! Everything you will need to go everywhere." Asa began showing him all the controls and how to use them. "This is showing the battery. Here you switch over to the second battery. First battery is recharging as you roll. One hundred miles, total recharge!"

Nate noticed the General was paying very close attention.

"I'll ask you something," David said. "There is no fuel? Only the battery?"

"Yes, yes! My friend! Only the battery; it is recharging by the turning wheels."

"No plug-in to electric?"

"For emergency only. My friend! It is contained in itself. It can go everywhere always!"

"Even up mountains and across deserts?" Nate asked.

"With the lovely Tahlia—from Mount Herman to the Negev. Across rivers, even the Jordan!"

"Power?" asked David.

"Power! Yes! My friend! Very much power, very fast speed!"

"This is insane!" Nate said again. Asa climbed in next to him. "Now we will drive. Reuven is waiting with the coffee. My friend! We will celebrate together!

✡✝✡✝✡✝✡

"That was one sweet ride," Nate gushed as he rolled into the General's office.

"Aaron. Aaron! He is here! I said he would be here!" Shlomo exclaimed.

"Shlomo! Right here I am sitting. I can see him, yes?"

"They say you have a question," David said.

"Yeah. Ah, okay… Darryl and I were talking about Isaiah 17," Nate began. Remember Shlomo? 'Damascus will no longer be a city'? You said it hasn't happened yet."

"So. Damascus. First, a review," Shlomo said, pulling himself to his feet.

"No, Shlomo, no review," Aaron stated. "He remembers, yes?"

"Nathaniel," David said. "Ask the question."

"It says the cities of Aroer are deserted, and the fortress will disappear from Ephraim. Where are the cities of Aroer?"

Leaning on his cane, Shlomo walked to the map behind David's desk. "So. Cities of Aroer are cities of ruin."He pointed to an area around the Arnon River in Jordan, near where it flows into the Dead Sea. "Not these cities. These are far from Damascus, do you see my meaning?"

"Yeah," Nate answered.

"So. Isaiah. It should not read 'the cities of Aroer are deserted,' but 'the cities thereof shall be deserted, a ruin.'"[31]

---

31 *The Jewish Encyclopedia.*

"And the 'thereof' is Damascus?"

"Of course Damascus. All around Damascus, to Lebanon; even the Bekaa Valley."

"That's Hezbollah territory," said Nate.

David was looking at the map. "They attacked us here two hours ago." He pointed to a spot near the Lebanon-Israeli ceasefire line. "The lead vehicle, hit by a rocket. The next, a rocket explodes over it."

"Hezbollah attacked?" Nate asked. "How many injuries?"

"And here, another attack. Three rockets." David pointed to a place near the Syrian-Israeli line. "The ones who attacked are destroyed. We have no injuries. I'll tell you something. Hezbollah uses chemical weapons, the Bekaa Valley will be destroyed! Syria uses these weapons against us, Damascus will be destroyed! All of it."

"General, I have a question for you," Nate interjected. "Is there anything that could possibly happen that would push Israel out of her land?"

David turned and looked at Nate. "You ask this question. Why?"

"They have all those chemical and biological weapons. If they used them against Israel? Would that make Israel fall back from the northern part?"

"We are watching so these weapons will not come into the hands of our enemies. I tell you something. An attack from these weapons would cause much suffering. We will destroy anyone who uses them."

"It says 'the fortress will disappear from Ephraim,'" Nate noted. "What could happen that would leave Israel undefended?"

David thought for a moment. "We have the Almighty to protect us. He is keeping watch. Today: no injuries. A direct hit and no injuries. It is the Finger of God!"

"Yeah! That's what I told Darryl when we were talking about the Gulf War. He told me about how the wind changed and Saddam couldn't fire his chemical weapons. Finger of God for sure!"

David picked up his Tanakh and opened it where a faded paper was stuck in the pages. He read: "'Come my people, enter your chambers, and shut your doors behind you; hide yourself for a little while until the wrath is past.'" Isaiah 26:20

He held up the old paper. "These are instructions from the Israel government to the people when the Gulf War began." He read: "'Do not use the bomb shelters; instead, prepare a room in your home by sealing the windows and storing food and water there. When there is a missile attack, gather everyone into the sealed room, shut the door tightly by sealing it with masking tape, and make sure that all keep their gas masks on until the all-clear signal is sounded.'"

"It's the same," Nate remarked. "The government is saying the same thing as Isaiah."

"Not everyone listened to the government," David said.

"Not everyone listened to Isaiah either," Nate returned.

"Aaron. Aaron! Remember the family running to the bomb shelter?" Shlomo asked.

"What family? Everyone was running, yes?"

"So. They ran and it was locked. No key could be found!"

"I remember!" Aaron answered. "They had to go to the sealed room."

"The shelter was hit by a missile! It was destroyed!"

"The family was safe, yes?"

"Yes, safe! The protection of the Almighty!" Shlomo declared.

"The Finger of God," Nate agreed.

"Nathaniel, I will tell you more!" Shlomo said. "The missile that went down the airshaft of the building. Aaron, you remember?"

"Yes, yes. Nine stories high with more than twenty apartments!"

"So, the missile did not explode. Everyone is safe."

"Shlomo, remember the missile that landed between the two buildings. It exploded, yes?"

"So. It exploded. It destroyed two buildings completely!"

"But did not kill any people," said Aaron.

"Finger of God!" said Nate.

"I'll tell you something, thirty-nine Scud missiles were shot at Israel during this war. Six weeks it lasted, and only two people killed by the missiles." David nodded his head. "The Israeli people. Many thought the missiles that missed targets, the missiles that didn't explode, and the people who escaped with only small injuries, were because the Scuds were badly designed, and the Iraqis were incompetent. At the end of the war they learned what the IDF knew. A Scud missile, only one, hit a U.S. Marine bunker in Saudi Arabia and killed more than forty men. Then they knew that Israel was protected by the Finger of God."

-4-

"Awugh… awugh… awugh…" Nate's screams began to wake him up. His heart was pounding. He couldn't breathe. He pushed his way through the crowd of people, people who had water pouring out of their eyes, blood pouring out of their noses, and long streamers of vomit hanging from their mouths. His arms swung around in the darkness, sending everything in reach crashing to the floor.

The light came on. "Nathaniel, we are here, you see?" Hannah's voice gradually reached Nate. He opened his eyes, looking anxiously around the room.

"There is blood all over," Hannah told David. "You must call Tahlia. She will know what to do."

Tahlia gently wiped the blood off of Nate's face, neck and arms. "You must tell Sava what is happening," she said.

"What is happening?" David asked. "Say something!"

"Okay." Nate sighed. "Remember the first day I walked into your office? I was supposed to go home but felt I was being turned around? That I was supposed to stay? Stay in Israel?"

David nodded. He remembered.

"At the airport, I saw, like, a vision or something, people frantically trying to get to the planes. They were trying to get away. I didn't know why. Then later, on the beach in Tel Aviv, I saw people trying to get to boats that were waiting for them. They were in a panic. I didn't know why. Then, that day we went to Jerusalem, I saw soldiers guarding the Western Wall plaza. They weren't IDF. I didn't know who they were, or why they were there."

David remembered that day. "You said nothing. Why?"

"I don't know. You would've thought I was crazy."

"Tell him about Reuven's," said Tahlia.

"A couple of weeks ago, I'm rolling through town, and all of a sudden, everything is grey. Everything is deserted, abandoned; Reuven's, the park, everything."

"And now this dream," said David.

Nate took a deep breath. "I've not only had visions, but I've been having dreams too."

"And this isn't the first one," said Tahlia.

"Say something," David ordered.

"Chunks of the sky are falling. Everything is grey. People are running. Sometimes they have sores all over them. Sometimes they can't breathe. Sometimes they are throwing up."

"And this dream? How did the people look?" asked Tahlia.

"They had water pouring out of their eyes. Blood streaming out of their noses. Vomit…"

Nate suddenly threw up all over his bloody sheets.

"No more talk," said Hannah. "Nathaniel is sick, you see?" She wrapped up the sheets and pulled them away. She took the blanket and tucked it around Nate.

Tahlia and David exchanged a long look.

"Nathaniel," said Tahlia, "these are all symptoms of contact with chemical weapons—sarin, mustard, VX…"

"I'll ask something," said David. "The dreams, they are why you ask what would make Israel leave their land?"

"That's part of it," said Nate. "The other part is what Isaiah says and what Revelation says."

Tahlia picked up Nate's Bible and handed it to him. "So explain."

Nate turned to Revelation 12. He read verses 6 and 14. "Israel flees into the wilderness to a place prepared by God, where she is to be cared for," he said. "That's why I'm asking what would make Israel flee to the wilderness."

"Maybe HASHEM is showing you what He is going to do," said Tahlia.

"Maybe He wants a place to be prepared," said David, "a place in the wilderness."

David, Tahlia and Nate thought about that.

"At the Bible study," said David, "I will say something."

"Who goes to that?" asked Nate.

"Many people: from government, from military, from archeology, from geology; rabbis, even a Christian minister," replied David.

"What are you studying?" asked Nate.

"The prophets," said David. "I'll tell you something, the prophets; they know the future of Israel."

173

"Look at this picture," said Justine. "This is Nate's vehicle. I can't figure out what it looks like!"

"Looks like the Flintstone-mobile, with extra wheels," Wes said.

"That must be why he named it Fred," said Justine. "He says it has lots of power and can go anywhere. ... And he wants to know if we got the picture of Sgt. Grange."

"I'm sure that picture is of this guy," said Wes, pulling up another screen and pointing to a name.

"It says Nathaniel Hanson," Justine observed.

"Let's start with Nathaniel Ellis and work our way back," said Wes. "His parents are Grace Hanson and Richard Ellis. Grace's mother is Claire Larke, married to Nathaniel Hanson. Claire died when Grace was born. Then Nathaniel Hanson disappears."

"What do you mean, 'disappears'?" asked Justine.

"No death certificate. No military service record—and this is during World War II. He disappears just when Sgt. Grange shows up. I think they're the same guy."

"That's not much evidence," said Justine.

"It's the only thing that would make any sense at all," said Wes.

"So why is his name Hanson? Why would he change it to Grange?" asked Justine.

"That's what I'm trying to find out," said Wes. "Like Sgt. Grange, there's no birth certificate. His brothers and sisters all have one, but there's none for Nathaniel.

He looked back at the screen. "Another thing—the first record that I can find of his mother is when she married Fredrik Hanson."

"No birth certificate for her either?"

"Nope. I checked immigration records for that time period too. Couldn't find anyone with her name."

"What is her name?" asked Justine.

"Eloise. Eloise LeMarais."

"Wes leaned back in his chair. "All of Nathaniel's siblings died young," he said. None of them lived long enough to have children. Ellis didn't have any brothers or sisters, did he?"

"No," said Justine. "He was an only child."

"If Sgt. Grange is Nathaniel Hanson, Nate is his only descendant." Wes looked at Justine. "Nate is the only one left."

✤✝✤✝✤✝✤

"I'll tell you something," said David. "What you have said is being taken seriously by everyone."

"They don't think I'm crazy?"

"It is extreme, but Israel must be prepared for everything, even the most impossible," said David.

"How can you prepare?" Nate replied. "The Bible doesn't say how or when it will happen."

"I have spoken to the Prime Minister. I have spoken to the military planners," said David. "I'll tell you something. Israel spends so much on defense, there is not much left to prepare a place in the wilderness for maybe a million people."

"Maybe ELISHA FUND can help," said Nate. "I'll see what Darryl says."

✤✝✤✝✤✝✤

"This is the **craziest thing** you've come up with **yet**! A **million** people? In the **wilderness**?!" Darryl paced rapidly around Nate's room.

"Might be two million," Nate said.

175

"Do you have **any idea** what you're talkin' about?! The **logistics**?! Lemme tell ya: 750 **tons** of food; 5.5 million **gallons** of water. For one **million people**! A **day**! **Every day!**"

"The Israeli government and the military would be partners. If ELISHA FUND can supply food, water, shelter, medical…the Israelis will do whatever…" said Nate.

"I'm **not talkin'** about this! I'm gonna **watch** the **game**!" Darryl quit pacing as the Hawks took the ice.

"Okay," said Nate.

"We're **barely** keepin' up our **inventory** now. Donations are **down**; we're **operatin'** on a **shoestring**!"

"Okay," said Nate.

"You sure **haven't thought** this through! … You **think** too much, you **know that**? Why can't you just **read** a couple a **chapters**, read a **devotional** and **get on** with your **day**? That's what **normal people** do!"

"Watch the game, okay?" said Nate.

"I'm **done thinkin'** about this! It's gonna give me a **heart attack!**"

"Watch the game," said Nate.

"You spend your **whole day** studying this!" Darryl picked up Nate's Bible and started waving it around.

"Be careful with that!" said Nate.

"You should be **doin'** somethin' **useful**! Take a **class**! Learn **somethin'**!"

Nate was insistent. **"Watch. The. Game."**

"And you could **get a job!** You gonna **live here** your **whole life?!** Or are you gonna **do somthin'** with your **life!**"

Nate felt a sharp pain as Darryl's words cut through him.

"You think I want to live like this?!" he yelled. *"There's nothing else I can do right now!! You think I don't want to have a job?! You think I don't want to marry Tahlia?! Have a normal life?! … And put my Bible down before you wreck it!!"*

176

Nate's Bible flew out of Darryl's hand, hit the wall and landed on the floor.

The General stormed into the room. "ENOUGH!" he commanded them. He then glared angrily at Darryl.

"You **always** wanna **say somethin'**," Darryl told David. "Say **somethin'** to **him**! Tell 'im this is **nuts**!"

"I'll tell you something," said David. "This is being discussed at the highest levels. It is taken very seriously."

"You're **kiddin'** me, right?" asked Darryl.

"We will do something," said David. "We will put out a fleece. Like Gideon. If it is from the Almighty, He will open the storehouses of heaven. He will fill your warehouse. It will flow out into the street. You will not have room even to sit, there will be so much."

"**Fine!**" said Darryl, grabbing his Blackhawks hat and smashing it on his head. "When I **see** that, I'll **believe** it!"

"I'll tell you something," David said to Nate as he followed Darryl out of the room, "we will soon know what to do."

Nate watched as the Hawks scored the final goal.

He watched as Slick lifted the Stanley Cup over his head.

He watched as Svenson took a victory lap, carrying the Cup.

Darryl waited all season to see this, Nate thought. *Now he missed it. Nate looked at where his Bible lay face-down and open on the floor. Serves him right.*

✿✞✿✞✿✞✿

Tahlia picked up Nate's Bible. She took the pages that had come loose and tucked them inside. "You can have it rebound," she said as she handed it to Nate.

"What if it's never the same?" asked Nate. "What if I can't see the notes? What if I can't see the pictures? You know what I'm talking about."

"It's just the binding, and the cover. Having it rebound won't change anything," said Tahlia.

Nate carefully put his Bible down. "I guess I don't have a choice. I'm afraid to even open it now. Don't want to make it worse." He looked at Tahlia. "Where should I bring it?"

"Ask Shlomo," said Tahlia. "He would know."

"Yeah, he's a rabbi. He knows these things."

CHAPTER FIVE

Storehouse of Heaven
-1-
The LORD will open for you His abundant storehouse,
The heavens, to give your land rain in its season,
and to bless all your undertakings.
Deuteronomy 28:12

Corp. Nahshon looked at the long line of trucks at a dead stop in front of them. "Sir?" he spoke to David. "We can sit here all day, all right? Or I go around."

"Go around," said David.

Nahshon pulled onto the shoulder and got up to speed, passing trucks of every description. "Are they all going to the ELISHA distribution center?" he asked.

"Soon we will know," said David.

Nahshon slowed nearly to a stop again. He threaded the vehicle through stacks of pallets, full of goods that were being offloaded onto the side of the street.

"This is all for the distribution center? Sir? This has to stop, all right? I'm going to park here and talk to the drivers."

David nodded. "I'll tell you something. The storehouse of heaven is open." He stepped out of the vehicle and looked around for Darryl.

"Not there, you **knucklehead**!" Darryl yelled at a forklift driver. "Read the **sign**! **Food** goes over **there**!" He waved his clipboard. "Not **there**! Ya gotta **leave room** to get **through**!" he barked at another driver.

"Hey, **General**! Did ya ever **see somethin'** like this? That fleece you put out? Can't even see it, there's so much **stuff** comin' in!"

David looked around. The parking lot was full; loading dock: full; warehouse: full.

"I need some **help**! I only got **three guys**, and they don't know **what** they're doin'!" Darryl said. "Not **there**! Are you

illiterate? **Read the signs!**" he hollered. "I'm gonna have a **heart attack,** I'm tellin' ya!"

David pointed at Nahshon. "He is here to help," he said as Nahshon walked toward them. "I tell you something. He was quartermaster in the U.S. Army. He made Aliyah. Now he's with the IDF."

"Am I **glad** to see **you!**" Darryl said. "You got any **ideas**? Can you get a **handle** on this?"

Nahshon pulled out his notebook. "All the trucks are going to the Negev, okay? Have one of your men give these coordinates to all the drivers." He handed a paper to Darryl while he thumbed a number on his cell. "Project Joseph is a go," he said into the phone. "First trucks should arrive in less than three hours."

"**Wait** a minute," Darryl interrupted, handing the paper to one of his guys. "You **can't** send all this **stuff** to the **Negev!** There's **nothin'** there!"

"We have a plan for this," Nahshon replied. "Now we start to execute it, all right?"

"I need to **inventory** all this **stuff,**" Darryl said. "I got a **board of directors** to answer to! I can't let it all **disappear!**"

"Watch your mail, all right?" Nahshon told him. "Every bill is coming straight to you."

"Sir? I'm taking a ride on one of these trucks, "Nahshon said to David. "You can explain to him"—he nodded toward Darryl—"how this is going to roll."

"Come in your office," David said to Darryl. "I'll tell you something about Project Joseph."

"You're **kiddin'** me, right? I haven't sat **anywhere** in a week! There's **no place** to sit. No **room** anywhere!"

"Project Joseph is a solid plan," David remarked, leaning against a stack of pallets. "It comes from the Strategic Planning Group. I'll tell you something. The best minds have put it together. Everything is planned. The storehouses, the encampment, the infrastructure. Everything is being prepared. At the right time, everything can be operational very quickly."

"Tell me **how** this is going to **work**," said Darryl. "How'd they **come up** with this plan?"

"We asked something," David replied. "We asked what would be needed to prepare a place in the wilderness for between one and two million people to live for about three years."

"And this **Project Joseph** is what they came up with?"

"Yes. ELISHA FUND will provide food, water, shelters and other relief supplies. Israel will provide infrastructure, personal and whatever else is needed."

"Like the **wilderness** and the **people**," Darryl commented.

-2-

Nate pulled 'Fred' into a parking space in front of the *Korach Seferim.* [32] "Here we go," he said to Tahlia as he unlocked his chair, lowered the ramp and backed onto the street. "Now we'll see if anything's changed."

"Darryl is really sorry," said Tahlia, opening the door to the shop. "Really he is."

"He's going to be even sorrier when he pays for this," said Nate.

"This is very unique," said the man who had rebound Nate's Bible. He set it on the counter. "Feel these pages. This is a patented paper that is no longer used. It was very costly to produce."

Tahlia handed Nate the Bible. Nate opened it—not to feel the pages, but to see if Sgt. Grange's notes were still visible.

They were.

"We bound it with the finest calfskin, as close to the original leather as possible," the man continued. "It should last another fifty years." He looked seriously at Nate. "As long as it is treated with respect."

Thanks a lot, Darryl, Nate thought. *Now this guy thinks I don't respect God's Word.*

The man handed Tahlia the bill. She handed it to Nate.

---

32 Hebrew for "a binder of books"

"Darryl's going to be really, **really** sorry when he sees this," Nate said.

"There is one more thing," the man said. "These pages were found, hidden in the spine." He handed Tahlia an envelope.

Nate rolled up and into 'Fred' and locked down his chair.

"See what it is," he said to Tahlia as he pulled into traffic.

"*Nathaniel, my dear son,*" she began to read. "It's a letter from your mom."

"Can't be," Nate replied. "Mom never wrote me a letter. She's never even called me Nathaniel."

Tahlia resumed reading.

"Nathaniel, my dear son,

Tomorrow you will be enlisting in the army of the United States of America. Today you must be told who you are. You are my son, this is true; however, as difficult as it will be for me, you must know who you are before entering this terrible war.

Many years ago, before I was born, there were many pogroms against the Jewish people in Russia and Ukraine. My parents fled to find refuge in a small Jewish community near Paris, France. My son, this is the first thing you must know: You are Jewish.

I was born at the turn of the century. My parents gave me the name Ester. Ester Galitz was my name. My father was a doctor. When the Great War began, I accompanied my father as he made his calls. He trained me to be a nurse. As the war progressed, and the wounded poured into Paris, I left my father's house. I went to Paris to help care for the wounded.

Among the wounded were American soldiers. There was one I spent much time with. After he recovered, we continued to spend time together. Then the war ended. He was sent back to America. He promised to send for me as soon as he was discharged. I never heard from him again. His name was Matthew Grange. This is the second thing you must know: Your true name is Nathaniel Grange.

182

"Whoa! Wait a minute!" Nate exclaimed. "Matthew Grange?! He's my great—no, make that great-great-grandfather!"

"Then you're related to Sgt. Grange," Tahlia said.

Nate thought about that. "Not exactly. "I'm related to Sgt. Grange's father, not to him."

"I wonder what your parents will say," Tahlia said.

"Probably nothing," Nate replied. "They don't seem very interested. They never even let me know if they got the picture I sent."

Tahlia looked back at the letter. She read more:

"Your birth is registered at the Guimard Synagogue in Paris, where our family went on Shabbat. The family thought it best that we should go to America, to a friend of my father who lived in New York. You and I went to live with him.

In France, before the war, there was some ill-feeling toward the Jews, but it was not until traveling to America that I experienced the hatred some people had for the Jewish people. It was then that I decided to conceal my identity. I would arrive in America as a young French war widow with a small child. My name became Eloise LeMarais. The only ones who knew my true identity were my father's friend, and later, my husband.

In America I soon found employment as a nurse at a nearby hospital. It was here that I met Dr. Fredrik Hanson, the man who became my husband and a father to you. Before we married, we determined it would be best to continue to conceal my Jewish identity. I would live as a Christian. You would be raised in the church. It was many years before I believed the Christian Jesus was the Messiah our people had been longing for. You, my son, believed before I did.

This is the third thing you must know: The Jewish people are your people. As you go to war, you are fighting not only for your country, but also for your people.

We have talked many times of how the Jewish people in Europe are suffering. You did not know that among them are your grandparents, uncles, aunts and cousins. We have heard such terrible rumors. I fear for their safety. I fear for their lives.

If you are able to find out the fate of our family, it would be a great comfort to me.

Their names are:

Yaakov and Rivka Galitz – my parents, your grandparents.

My brothers and their families:

Eliab and Naomi Galitz – their children: Yitzhak, Michael, Yoseph, Celia, Margot

Lucien and Tamar Galitz – their children: Chiam, Zivia, Judith

My sisters and their families:

Saul and Leah Taubis – their children: Simcha, Anna, Ethan

Shimon and Miriam Reiter – their children: Moshe, Yoel, Ariel, Michal

Micah and Rachal Mesika – their children: Sabina, Sharon, Shmuel, Sara

Do not be afraid, my son. The LORD your God who goes before you, will Himself fight for you. Deuteronomy 1:30a

I will wait for you with Grace.

"Did she sign it?" Nate asked.

Tahlia shook her head. "No."

Nate looked down at Sgt. Grange's medallion. *I can do something,* he thought.

"I'm going to see if any of them survived," said Nate. "I owe Sgt. Grange that much."

Re: Sgt Grange
Dad – this is important – this letter was found hidden in the binding of my Bible. Sgt. Grange's father is Matthew Grange. I think he's your great-grandfather. At the end of the letter is a list of his relatives who were in France during the Holocaust. Any way you could find out if any of them survived the war?

Nate scanned a copy of the letter and attached it to the email. Maybe they would answer him this time.

Nate's answer arrived the next day.

Re: Sgt Grange
I'll see what I can find out. Matthew Grange is his father? I'll see if there are any family stories about Grandpa Matt.

✡︎✝︎✡︎✝︎✡︎✝︎✡︎

"Hey **Nate**, how ya **doin'**?" Darryl said as he came into Nate's room. "Don't wanna **bother** ya."

"It's all good," Nate replied. "See this? I just got accepted at Tel Aviv U. I'm going to take some computer classes. I only have to go in for class twice a month."

"That's good, right?" Darryl asked.

"Yeah, a friend told me to take some classes," Nate said.

"I'm not sayin' **nothin'**," Darryl remarked, looking at the floor.

"Remember that when you see this," Nate said, handing him the bookbinder's bill.

"You **are** kiddin' me, **right**?" Darryl said. "I coulda **bought** you **twenty** Bibles for this!"

"Yeah, but this one is special. Look what they found hidden in it!" Nate handed Darryl the letter.

"You **related** to him?"

"My great-great-grandfather was his father."

"That's why **you** have his **Bible** and his other **stuff**?"

"Still haven't figured out how that happened. I don't think Matthew Grange even knew he had a son. I don't think he knew Nathaniel existed."

"Sirens are sounding in Tel Aviv! We are being attacked!" David said urgently as he strode into the room.

Nate grabbed the remote and turned to Israel National News.

185

> Early this morning, rockets were launched by ISIS toward locations in southern Israel. It appears they were attempting to destroy the storehouses recently built in the Negev. Three were intercepted by Iron Dome; the fourth was allowed to fall in an uninhabited area. The Hamas terrorists have also begun firing rockets from Gaza north toward Ashkelon and Ashdod. All the rockets have failed to reach their targets. All but one fell in uninhabited areas. The remaining rocket was intercepted by the Iron Dome Missile-Defense System.

Nate looked at the map on the TV. "Why did they build the storehouses so close to the Egyptian border? Isn't ISIS all over the Sinai?"

"Egypt is fighting ISIS in the Sinai," David said. "I'll tell you something. With the treaties Israel has with Egypt and Jordan, it is the safest place."

> For several hours, no rockets were fired from Gaza, but now it appears the attack has begun again. This time Hamas is using longer-range missiles. They are being fired in the direction of Tel Aviv.

"This is **not** good," Darryl said. "My **warehouse** is in **Tel Aviv!**"

"Yeah," Nate agreed, "all the business is in Tel Aviv. It's like attacking New York!"

> This is an INN news alert! We have a report that a missile has veered off-course and is headed toward Jerusalem. Its trajectory should have it landing just south of the city.
> We're watching…you can see it…there it goes!
> We have just received word that the rocket exploded in an empty field.

"Can you **imagine** if one of their rockets **exploded** on the **Temple Mount?!**" Darryl exclaimed. Think about it! It would start **World War Three!**"

"That place is explosive enough," Nate remarked."Doesn't need a rocket to set off a war."

Sirens are continuing to go off in Tel Aviv, warning of incoming missiles from Gaza.
Our sources say the Iron Dome battery has taken down three missiles.
This is a rapidly developing situation. Whatever information we get, we are immediately putting on air. Now this: The IAF is pinpointing the location of the rocket launchers and is expected to take them out momentarily.

David, Nate and Darryl watched the video feed intently.

We are watching in real time the rocket launchers in Gaza being blown up. That should put an end to the threat to Tel Aviv. WAIT... there is one last missile headed toward Tel Aviv! Iron Dome has failed—I repeat, failed—to intercept it—twice! There are just four seconds before this missile lands in a heavily populated area! Emergency services have been notified, and Tel Aviv is bracing for a mass-casualty incident.
What just happened?! It didn't land?! Somebody tell me something! It was blown out to sea? Is that possible?

"Something's not right," said Nate. "Something is not making sense."

We have with us on the phone General Izhar. General Izhar is very familiar with the Iron Dome Missile-Defense System. General, can you explain what just happened?
Yes and no. The Iron Dome precisely calculates the trajectory of missiles. We know, within a 200-meter radius, where a missile will land. This missile was on a trajectory to hit the central railway station, Azrieli Towers, or the Kirya. [33] It would have been a mass-casualty event, with possibly hundreds of fatalities. Both our first and second interceptors missed their target. I would like to emphasize that this is a very rare occurrence. Very rare! In addition to calculating the trajectory of missiles, Iron Dome also calculates wind speed and direction. Suddenly, only seconds before impact, Iron Dome indicated an extremely strong wind coming from the east. A wind so strong that it sent the missile out to sea! I was stunned! We all were. I witnessed this with my own eyes. The only explanation is that it was the Finger of God! [34]

---

33 Israel's equivalent of the Pentagon.

34 This is based on an actual event that occurred in 2014. See:
www.wnd.com/2014/08/israeli-soldier-testifies-to-miracle-in-gaza

"Unbelievable!" Darryl shouted. "If that rocket had come down just a **few blocks** farther **north**, it would have **leveled** my warehouse!"

"Do you think they are trying to hit the storehouses?" Nate asked. "Why would they do that?"

"I'll tell you something," David said. "The storehouses are life. Hamas is death."

-3-

"It is the Almighty that protects Israel, yes?" Aaron struck the floor with his cane. "Yes!"

"Aaron. Aaron! Show Nathaniel the paper!" Shlomo said.

"In your pocket, Shlomo, it is in your pocket," Aaron replied.

"So. Hamas knows the Holy One of Israel is keeping watch!" said Shlomo, finding the paper.

Nate read the headline:

"Their God changes the path of our rockets in mid-air," said a terrorist. [35]

"I was watching it!" Nate said. "No one could figure out what happened! It was so incredible!"

"The finger of God, yes?" said Aaron, striking the floor with his cane. "Yes!"

"Aaron, Aaron!" said Shlomo. "David Yaniv, you remember?"

"He's the guy that was paralyzed and God healed him?" asked Nate.

"Yes! Aaron, he saw the wind of God, you remember?"

"Shlomo, I remember. Tell Nathaniel; he does not know."

"Know what?" asked Nate.

Shlomo leaned forward on his cane. "First a review. It was the War of Yom Kippur, October 1973. The Golan Heights, on the Syria Israel border. Nathaniel! You have been there?"

"Yeah, I was there with Tahlia," said Nate.

---

35 Patrial quote as reported in the *Jewish Telegraph* on 7/18/2014. See: www.wnd.com/2014/08/hand-of-god-sent-missile-into-sea

"So, Lt. Col. David Yaniv is there with his men. It is night; the only light is from the full moon of Yom Kippur. Suddenly! They see they are in a minefield! 100,000 mines, buried! Where do they step? Where do they put their feet?" Shlomo stared at Nate.

"I have no idea," Nate answered.

"They do not walk; they crawl. They feel the ground ahead to find the mines. When they find one, it is disarmed using the bayonet. It is very slow, very dangerous. Aaron, you remember?"

"I remember! Your friend, he was there, yes?" said Aaron.

"Yes, Avram. He says they think they will not get through alive. Suddenly! A very strong gust of wind!

So strong they can feel pieces of the earth blowing into the air. Then—the moon comes out of the clouds and they see all the mines! Mines that were buried 25, 30 centimeters are exposed! Then the wind stopped! They walked out of the minefield alive."

Shlomo looked at Nate. "This is how God sends the wind."

"It is the finger of God," said Nate. [36]

✡︎✝︎✡︎✝︎✡︎✝︎✡︎

"The *Korach Seferim* makes it like new, yes?" Aaron asked, pointing to Nate's Bible with his cane.

"Yeah," Nate replied, "but look what they found hidden inside!" Nate took out the letter and handed it to Aaron. "It's a letter Sgt. Grange's mother wrote him before the war."

Aaron read the letter carefully and then handed it to Shlomo.

"I'm trying to find out if there is anyone of his family still alive," Nate said.

Shlomo read the letter. He sat silently with it in his hand.

"Shlomo, tell Nathaniel," Aaron said. "It is his family, yes?"

Shlomo said nothing. He stared at the letter.

"Tell Nathaniel," Aaron repeated. "How the Galitz, it was also your family."

36　From the account of David Yaniv, in the documentary *Against All Odds*

"Really?" Nate asked. "Are you related to Sgt. Grange?"

"Nathaniel, you did not talk about a family in France," said Shlomo. "I do not know about this until now."

After a long silence Shlomo spoke. "So. I came to Paris from Germany. I escaped over the border with the help of the Jewish Underground. In Paris I met Eliab Galitz. He was one who was helping the Jews who were pouring in from Germany. Aaron also escaped the Germans. It is when we met. Aaron, you remember?"

"I remember. Shlomo, it was difficult, yes?"

"We were poor, we were religious, we spoke no French. So. We were different from the French Jews. They had become part of the French people and did not like that we looked and acted so Jewish. But the Galitz family, who had come from Ukraine many decades before, they did not forget the hardships of being a poor Jew in a strange country. They had prospered in France. They were educated. Eliab was a doctor like his father. He had formed a committee with other wealthy Jews to aid the immigrants. He was also a member of the Jewish Resistance. All of the Galitz families were involved, either with the aid committee, the Resistance or the Underground. Not men only. Women also."

Shlomo was silent for a long time, then he said. "So. I met Ariel. Nathaniel, she is your cousin. Her mother, Miriam, is sister to your mother Ester."

He has us mixed up again, Nate thought. *He thinks I'm Sgt. Grange.*

"War had come to France and evil men rode through Paris. Soldiers were everywhere. The Gestapo filled their headquarters. I was in the Resistance and Ariel also. We knew we loved each other. We did not know how long the war would last. So. We were married."

"The war against the Jews, it does not end," Aaron observed. "When the world is at peace, still the Jews are hated."

Shlomo nodded his head. "The Fogel family. [37] Aaron! You remember? Murdered in their beds."

"I remember that too," Nate said. "It happened right here in Israel, only a few years ago."

---

37 The Itamar massacre, March 11, 2011. Ehud and Ruth Fogel were murdered, along with 3 of their children, one an infant.

"So. We were married," Shlomo continued. "But, when she became pregnant, it was decided: She would not work with the underground or Resistance."

"The roundups, Shlomo, tell Nathaniel how the Jews were swept away," Aaron said.

"So. The rounding up of the Jews," said Shlomo. "First, a review. The Germans, they decreed all Jews must register in a census. This is October 1940. Many of the foreign Jews refuse to register. We know these lists of names and addresses will be used against us. Some have no choice. The Galitz family. They are well-known. They must register. Do you see my meaning?"

"Everyone in Paris knows they are Jews, yes?" Aaron added.

"We do not register, Aaron and I," Shlomo said. "When the law to wear the star comes, we do not wear it. Ariel, her family, they must wear the star."

Shlomo was silent. Then he said: "So. When Ariel and I marry, it is without papers. A blessing from the rabbi, Aaron as witness, and we are married. We have false identity cards, false birth certificates and a false marriage certificate. We have a small room far from where the Jews live. Maybe we will be safe."

"What about Ariel's family?" Nate asked. "Didn't they go into hiding?"

"They were French Jews. They did not think they would be treated like the foreign Jews. They were supporting poor Jewish families, giving them food, medical care, finding them places to live, to hide; helping them to survive. They did not think of themselves, their own safety. It was a shock when wearing the star separated them from the French. … Soon the roundups began. "The first in May, then in August of 1941. Only foreign Jews, men were taken. Then, December 12—before dawn the raid began. This time it was French Jews they rounded up; men over fifty. Eliab and Shimon were taken with over 700 others. They were brought to the *Royallieu-Compiègne*, a camp operated by the Germans. Then they were handed over to the French and taken to Drancy. Do you know Drancy?"

"No," Nate shook his head.

"It is a suburb of Paris. A camp run by the French *gendarmes*, yes?" Aaron replied.

"The French guards, they were very brutal and cruel," Shlomo continued. The camp, filthy, full of lice and fleas. From there Eliab and Shimon were put on a train. It was March 27. This is the first train to leave France for Auschwitz. One thousand, one hundred and twelve men were on that train. In the first five months, 1008 died from starvation, exhaustion and abuse. The mass gassing, it had not yet begun. Still, Eliab and Shimon did not survive."

"Tell Nathaniel of *Jeudi noir*," said Aaron. "The Black Thursday."

"Aaron. Aaron! I am telling him! So.The great July roundup of 1942. It is when most of the Galitz family is swept away. There were rumors that there would be a raid. Many men slept away from their homes. Until now, only men had been taken. No one thought women and children would be rounded up. The raid began early morning of July 16. It lasted until 5 p.m., July 17. There were more women, more children taken than men. [38] Of the Galitz family, only Chiam, Ethan and Moshe remained free."

"How many were taken in the roundup?" Nate asked.

"Almost 13,000. ... They were divided up. Men and women without children under sixteen—they went to Drancy. The ones with children went to the *Vélodromed'Hiver*."

"What is the Vélodrome?" Nate asked.

"A sports stadium with a glass roof," Shlomo answered. "So. It was hot, with almost no ventilation. Do you see my meaning? More than 8000 people, half of them children, were packed into it. There was no food; water had been turned off; there was almost nothing to drink. Only a few toilets were open. There was no privacy. The stench was nauseating, overwhelming everything. For three days, for a week, they were kept at the *Vel'd'Hiv*. Then they were brought to *Pithiviers* and *Beaune-la-Rolande*, two other camps that had already sent their prisoners to Auschwitz. It is here that mothers were torn away from their little children. Only those

---

38   In total, 12,884 were taken: 3031 men, 5802 women, 4051 children.

older than fourteen could go with the mothers. The little ones were to follow in a few weeks. More than 4000 were transported to Auschwitz. About half were admitted; the rest were gassed. Only 35 survived. None from the Galitz family."

Nate was looking at the letter. "Who were they? Who had young children?"

Shlomo said, "Your cousins, they had the little children: Celia, Margot, Judith, Anna, and Michal. … The rest of the people from the *Vélodrome d'Hiver,* they were taken to the Drancy camp. They stayed only a few days before the deportations to Auschwitz. Only 47 survived. None from the Galitz family. … The little children, forced to stay alone at *Pithiviers* and *Beaune-la-Rolande*, were sent to Drancy and then to Auschwitz. Packed into cattle cars with no food, no water for the three-day trip. Little Jewish children, terrified, sick and starving. Do you see my meaning? None survived."

Nate looked at the letter again. Now only Chiam, Ethan, Moshe and Ariel were left alive. "What about the others?" he asked. "Did they survive?"

"They joined the FTP-MOI Second Detachment in Paris. [39] They had lost their families. They were looking for revenge. They put a bomb in a German hotel near the Iénastation of the Paris Métro. They threw grenades into a German army unit in the Place de la Nation. They attacked a truck full of German soldiers and threw a grenade into a German restaurant on Avenue Hoche. A bomb was thrown into the car of General von Schaumburg, the German commander of Greater Paris. There was retaliation. Chiam, Ethan, Moshe and many others were arrested. They were executed."

"Shlomo, what about Ariel?" Nate asked. "She survived, right?"

"No. My Ariel, my wife, did not survive. I was bringing identity papers to some Jews in hiding when it happened. I did not know until after they took her."

"The Gestapo, they took her," Aaron said to Nate.

---

39 The *Francs-tireurs et partisans - main-d'œuvreimmigrée,* an organization that was part of the France resistance.

"Eight months pregnant, she was not now involved in the Underground," Shlomo said. She did not look Jewish, with her light hair. She did not wear the star. She was picked up far from where the Jews lived."

"An informer, yes?" Aaron said."Shlomo, what else could it be?"

"So we try to find where she is taken, how she can be rescued," Shlomo said. He shut his eyes. After a long pause, he said, "They threw her body onto the *Rue des Rosiers,* a street where the Jews lived. She was beaten, tortured. Because of this, she had given birth to our son. Both of their bodies lay in the street…"

"We knew they were watching, to see who would come for them," Aaron explained. "Shlomo, you remember, yes? We could do nothing until dark. Nothing."

Nate closed his eyes. *This is so horrible.* He tried to get the picture out of his mind. He couldn't.

"Then there appeared a very old woman on the street. She carried a bucket, towels, and some sheets. She went to Ariel and knelt down next to her. She took towels and soaked up the pools of blood off the pavement. She took the baby, my son, and cut the cord. Tenderly, she washed the blood off his little body and wrapped him in a towel. Then she cleaned the blood and dirt off of Ariel. She took our son and laid him on Ariel's chest, so gently. She took the towels, soaked with the blood of their lives, and wrapped them in a cloth, and put it next to Ariel. She tucked a sheet around them and spread a cloth over them. Then, the old woman took her bucket, walked up the street and disappeared… [40]

"Night finally came. Fog rose up from the street, and we were able to gather them up without being seen. We brought them inside to a small room. Both of their faces were peaceful. It

_____

40 Jewish burial practices were often impssible to follow during WWII. Normally it was customary for the body to be washed completely with warm water, dressed in a simple white burial shroud and buried in a plain pine box. A person's blood was considered as holy as their life. If they had been injured and there was blood on the clothing, the washing was not done. Any blood on the ground was soaked up and buried with the body. Men were often buried with their prayer shawls. Some of the fringes would be cut off, rendering it ineffective.

was then I saw the cloth the old woman had spread over them. It was a *tallit*, a prayer shawl...

"Underground, beneath the buildings on the *Rue des Rosiers*, were tunnels. We carried my Ariel and my son down into the tunnels. We buried them there. ... So. Nathaniel. Only you are left."

✿✞✿✞✿✞✿

Wes and Justine read Nate's email about Shlomo and Ariel. Justine wiped away a tear and tried to swallow the lump in her throat. Finally, Wes said: "I understand why Shlomo went Nazi hunting. After what they did to his wife."

"And baby," Justine added.

The email alert went off. "Another one from Nate," Wes said.

Re: Shlomo and Ariel
Dad –this is important – I can't stop thinking about Shlomo and Ariel. He's like a hundred years old. When he dies he'll be buried all alone. He never remarried, he has no children. His whole family died in the Holocaust. He has his friend Aaron. That's it. So I've been thinking. What if we could find Ariel's body? And bring it to Israel? Then Shlomo and Ariel and the baby would be together. What do you think?

"Another impossible idea," Wes remarked. "His heart's in the right place, but I can guarantee the French aren't going to let us go digging under Paris looking for a body.

Re: Shlomo and Ariel
Nate– can't imagine how that could happen. The French would never allow it. I'm still looking for any relatives of Sgt. Grange who might have survived. Maybe Shlomo didn't actually check all the records. He was busy doing other things.

"I have an idea," Justine said. "You know that TV program *Underground Mysteries?*"

Wes shook his head.

"They go underneath cities and see what's there. You never watched it?"

"Never heard of it."

"Last week they were underneath San Francisco, showing the tunnels where shanghaied sailors would be taken."

"You think they might be interested in Shlomo and Ariel?

"They might. It's more interesting than kidnapping drunken sailors."

✿♱✿♱✿♱✿

On a ridge, high above a vast plain in the heart of the Negev, stood two men. They watched the activity below. Steady streams of trucks were arriving at the camp. They were being unloaded at one of the 42 storehouses that had been constructed along the base of the ridges that surrounded the plain. Teams of men were laying a grid across the dusty ground, preparing it for the housing that would be put in place. Solar towers were being erected. More groups were raising field hospitals at intervals around the site, as well as other large buildings.

"Will there be enough time?" the younger of the two men asked.

"The last time Israel camped here there were more than two million people," the older man replied. "The Holy One of Israel cared for them then. It will be ready at the appointed time."

"Will He again send bread from heaven? Our fathers ate manna in the wilderness, and they all died."

"This time He will give them the true bread from heaven," the older man answered. "The bread that gives life to the world."
John 6:31–33

As the sun sank behind the ridge, the two men pulled their cloaks around them, their long *tzitzits* spinning dust into the cool night air. They disappeared down the ridge and into the desert.

PART THREE

THE GREAT EAGLE

*But the woman was given the two wings of the great eagle
so that she might fly from the serpent into the wilderness,
to the place where she is to be nourished
for a time, times, and half a time.*

Revelation 12:14

NATHANIEL ... NATHANIEL.

The voice penetrated Nate's sleep. He opened his eyes and peered into the darkness of his room.

I thought I heard someone call me. He listened, but heard nothing. "Is someone calling me?" he asked. All he heard was silence. Nate closed his eyes and drifted back to sleep.

NATHANIEL ... I HAVE HEARD YOUR PRAYERS.

Nate opened his eyes.

DO YOU WANT TO BE HEALED?

"Yes," Nate whispered.

GET UP AND WALK.

Nate took a deep breath. Slowly he pushed himself up. He sat a moment before pulling himself to the side of the bed. He flopped one leg over the edge, and then the other. He felt the tears in his throat. His heart was pounding. He slid off the bed.

An electrical current shocked his body. It raced up his legs. It pulsed through his back. It wrapped around and around his hips, his thighs, his legs. Heat, like hot water, poured down his spine and flowed down his legs and onto his feet. And then—it stopped.

Nate stood, looking around. *I'm really scared right now.* He took one step, then another one. "Thank You, Jesus," he whispered. Another step; and another. "Thank You, Y'shua." Tears streamed down his face.

197

Nate walked back and forth in his room. Then he opened the courtyard doors and walked outside. He lifted his hands toward heaven. "Thank You, Y'shua. Thank You, Father God. Thank You, Y'shua, thank You, Jesus. I will praise You as long as I live!"

In the moonlight, Nate looked at his legs. Instead of thin and withered, they were strong and muscular. He began to jog around the courtyard. Soon he was running. He sang:

> "Great are you LORD and worthy of glory;
>
> Great are you LORD and worthy of praise."

NATHANIEL ... THE DAY YOU HAVE PREPARED FOR IS NEAR.

Nate slowed to a stop. He was breathing hard and sweating. "How near? Do I have time for a shower?"

IN TEN DAYS I WILL BEGIN TO DO GREAT AND TERRIBLE THINGS BEFORE YOUR EYES.

CHAPTER ONE

Wings Like Eagles
-1-

They who wait for the LORD shall renew their strength;
They shall mount up with wings like eagles;
They shall run and not be weary;
They shall walk and not faint.

Isaiah 40:31

Nisan 1 [41]

This is GREAT!! Sababa! Nate thought. I'm taking a shower ALL BY MYSELF!! Thank You Y'shua! Thank You Father God!! Thank You Jesus!!

Nate lathered up while he sang:

---

41 Nisan is the first month on the Jewish religious calendar. In this story, the first day of Nisan corresponds to the 10-day countdown to the beginning of 'GREAT AND TERRIBLE things.'

"My God is faithful,

My God is healer…"

Really need a haircut, he thought as he rinsed the shampoo out
of his hair.

"My God is an awesome God,

He reigns from heaven above,

With wisdom power and love

My God is an awesome God!"

Nate stepped out of the shower and grabbed his towel.

"Nathaniel, you are standing!" Hannah exclaimed, eyes wide.
"David! Look at Nathaniel! He is walking!"

Nate quickly wrapped the towel around his waist. "Yeah, it's
me. Standing! Walking! Y'shua healed me!"

"David, look, Y'shua has healed Nathaniel! All the prayers are
answered, you see?"

David was speechless. He stared at Nate. He looked for a long
time into Nate's eyes. Finally he nodded. "It is the finger of
God," he said. "Get dressed, then you will say something. You
will tell how it is you are walking."

✿✝✿✝✿✝✿

"I heard a voice, calling my name," Nate explained. "It woke me
up. The voice said He heard my prayers. He asked if I wanted to
be healed. I said yes. Then He said, 'GET UP AND WALK.'"

Tahlia burst into the kitchen. "Y'shua healed you!! He really
did!" Her eyes were full of tears as she threw her arms around
him. "I can hardly believe what I'm seeing!"

"Me either," Nate said. "I thought it was a dream! When my
feet touched the floor, I felt the power of God wrapping around
me and flowing through my body! Even then I thought I was
dreaming. Then I was walking. Then I was running!"

199

David and Hannah couldn't take their eyes off him. "It is not a dream, "Hannah said. "This is a miracle before our eyes, you see?"

"It was the finger of God!" David said. "I'll ask something. The voice, did it say more?"

"Yes. He said, 'THE DAY YOU HAVE PREPARED FOR IS NEAR.' I asked if I had time for a shower, and—"

"You asked Y'shua if you could take a shower?!" Tahlia asked.

"Yeah, well… I was all sweated up from running," Nate replied.

"Say something," ordered David.

"He said 'IN TEN DAYS I WILL BEGIN TO DO GREAT AND TERRIBLE THINGS BEFORE YOUR EYES.'"

"Ten days." David thought about that. "In a little more than ten days it is Passover. *Erev Pesac.*"He turned and left the room.

"I have to tell my parents," Nate said. He handed his phone to Tahlia. "Take some pictures. They're going to be shocked."

✿✝✿✝✿✝✿

"James Justice! Jocelyn Joy! Do **not** make me come up there!" Justine warned. "You should have been asleep hours ago!"

"They're driving me crazy," she said to Wes as the message alert went off on her phone.

"It's from Nate…he says…he says he's healed!" She looked at Wes. "What does he mean, 'healed'?" Justine looked at the pictures. "He's standing!" She looked at the video. "He's walking!!"

Wes took the phone and looked at the pictures. He watched the video. They were stunned. They looked at each other. They looked at the pictures. Again. Justine started crying.

Wes took out his cell, pulled up Nate's number and pressed *Call.*

"Nate? We just got your text!" Wes exclaimed. "This is incredible! What—how were you healed? … Wait, your

200

mother wants to talk to you." Wes put the phone on speaker before handing it to Justine.

"Nate, you're not kidding us, are you?" Justine asked. "This is for real, right?"

"Yeah, Mom, it's for real. I can hardly believe it either. We prayed for so long and then God answers and it's hard to believe! I've just been thanking Him. Over and over. And I will for the rest of my life!"

"Son, tell us what happened," Wes said. "We want to hear every detail of how God healed you."

"Why is Mommy crying?" JJ whispered to Josie. "Is Nate in another accident?"

"No," Josie replied. "She keeps saying 'thank You Jesus thank You Jesus thank You Jesus."

JJ and Josie tip-toed down the stairs.

"This is a miracle. You're walking! This is a miracle, thank you Jesus!" Mommy said again.

"JJ! Josie! Come down here!" Wes called as the J's came into the room. "We have something to show you!"

They looked at the pictures. "God got tired of waiting for doctors," Josie said.

"God touched Nate with his finger," JJ said. "Now he's walking out of his chair."

"Now you can come home," said Wes. "We all want to see you! Everyone who's been praying for you will want to hear what God has done."

"I don't think this is a good time," Nate replied. "I really need to stay a while longer."

"I don't understand," Justine said. "Don't you ever want to see us again?"

"It's not that," Nate said. "I really miss you! I really want to see you! It's complicated. There's a lot happening right now. That's all I can say."

201

"The PM wants to see you," David said. "I'll tell you something, he has to see you with his own eyes."

✧✞✧✞✧✞✧

"Nathaniel!" the Prime Minister said, grasping his hand and drawing him into the room. "We are all very eager to see you!"

Nate looked at the people who had gathered before dawn to see him. The only one he recognized was Dr. Ben Ari, who had gotten up to greet him. "To see you like this…" he said, "…completely healed—tell me, tell all of us, how this has happened."

Nate paced back and forth as he told how he had been healed. He saw the incredulous looks on their faces. "It was Y'shua's voice I heard. It was Y'shua who healed me," he said.

Ben Ari came and stood next to Nate. "There is no medical explanation for the healing of Nathaniel. The nerve ends in his spine were completely atrophied. There was no possibility of regeneration." He added,

"I am happy you are wearing shorts. All of us can see how muscular your legs are. … After more than a year in a wheelchair, Nathaniel had no muscle tone at all. If this was a medical miracle, he would have had to have months of therapy to regain muscle strength; he would have had to learn how to walk again."

"Nathaniel, I am Rabbi Eliezer Kahan. The visions and dreams you have had, we have wondered: Are they from God?" He turned to the others. "Nathaniel's healing is a sign from the Almighty! What we have been told to prepare for is truth."

"Gentlemen," the PM said, "when this idea was first brought up, we challenged the most brilliant minds in Israel to come up with a design for a self-contained, self-sufficient encampment in the middle of the Negev, with housing for tens of thousands of people. Within a few months these designs were completed, and work began. Publicly we announced that a camp, a *Machom Mishpan,* a place for the Tabernacle was being built—a place of worship and pilgrimage for the people of Israel."

He paused before saying, "This has made our enemies uneasy. … What has not been made public is that this camp is also to be a *Machom Mihlawt*, a place of refuge for those who may need to be evacuated from natural disasters or from the effects of war—events that may be soon be upon us. Gentlemen, we have a little more than ten days to finish our preparations. Today I will declare a major-emergency-readiness drill. It will be similar to Turning Point Three, which we conducted several years ago. However, this drill, when it happens, will be unannounced. Everyone must be prepared for immediate action. I will inform the people that if the sirens are sounded, it is a drill. If they hear the blowing of the shofars, it is a real emergency and emergency procedures must be followed." He turned to Major Harim. "Has the military been fully briefed?"

Major Harim nodded. "I have only to give the date. We are prepared for everything from an attack by one or all our enemies, any kind of natural disaster, or facilitating a mass evacuation."

"Adin?" the PM nodded to the head of Emergency Services.

"We're ready. MDA has trained local response teams to provide initial treatment, psychotherapy and social support until the EMS teams can arrive. We've completed a series of exercises coordinating our response between the various services. We worked out a few difficulties and we're ready. I'll give out the date later today."

"Corp. Nahshon?"

"Yes, Sir. The necessary infrastructure is in place. The solar towers are generating more power than we anticipate will be needed. We have sanitation trucks ready to roll and disposal sites prepared. Fuel tanks have been buried and filled. Cisterns have been dug. Water is flowing into them. We tapped into a deep aquifer, so water won't be a problem. The large community areas have been built, and we're rolling on the housing." Nahshon looked over to Rabbi Kahan. "Everything is prepared for the Tabernacle, okay? Bring it down. We even have the houses for the priests put together, all right?"

"Everything is ready for transport," said Rabbi Kahan. "The Tabernacle will be erected on this day, the first day of Nisan. The priests will be consecrated and all will be ready for Erev Pesac." He paused, nodding his head. "I also will address the people today. I will call them to go into the wilderness, to the Tabernacle of Adonai, to worship the God of Israel. I will tell them, for the first time since the destruction of the Temple, the lamb of Passover will be sacrificed, as Adonai commanded Moshe."

The Rabbi looked around the room. "Those who desire to worship Adonai at the Tabernacle will be under the wings of the Great Eagle, protected from the great and terrible things that will soon come."

"They still have the Tabernacle?" Nate asked as they turned onto Route 1, heading for Tel Aviv.

"It's a replica," Tahlia replied.

"It is made exactly to the pattern given to Moshe," said David. "I'll tell you something, it is a real Tabernacle. The Tabernacle and the furnishings have been made to the pattern in the Torah."

Nate took his Bible out of his duffel bag. He read: "'The table for the bread of the Presence, the golden menorah, the bronze altar, the altar of incense, the bronze basin, and all the utensils.' Exodus 26, 27 Who made all of these?"

"The SHILOH HERITAGE FOUNDATION. They have made everything. I'll tell you something, for the high priest, even the breast-piece of judgment they have made."

"There's a high priest?" Nate asked.

"The Sanhedrin appointed one of the most respected rabbis, a direct descendant of Aaron, to be high priest," Tahlia said.

"The Aaron from the Bible?" asked Nate. "How do they know?"

"With DNA and genealogies," said Tahlia. "They know.

"What about the Ark of the Covenant? Did they make one of those?"

"They did not make a new Ark." David looked over at Nate. "They may have the original."

"Okay, I'm listening," said Nate, a skeptical look on his face.

"I'll tell you something," said David. "It was when we rescued the Ethiopian Jews during the final days of their civil war. It was at this time that there was an account of the Ark of the Covenant being released to agents of the Mossad by the Ethiopian generals. There was a cost. Forty-two million in U.S. dollars. Then, Israeli special forces, all descendants of the tribe of Levi, secretly removed the Ark from the tunnels beneath the Church of Zion of Mary in Aksum. The Ark was taken to Israel and is protected in a secure location near Jerusalem. There were several credible witnesses, but all the information is classified. It was thought best to let it be forgotten. [42]

"What would that be like?" Nate wondered aloud. "To have the Ark of the Covenant in the Holy of Holies, in the Tabernacle, in the wilderness?"

"I think we'll find out," said Tahlia. "We'll find out together."

As they turned off Rt.1 onto the Tel Aviv exit, David said: "You say it is Y'shua's voice you heard. How do you know this?"

"He said the same things to me that He said to the paralyzed man in the Bible," said Nate. "I knew it was His voice." [John 5:6-8]

"And," Nate added as they pulled in front of the ELISHA distribution center, "the voice of HASHEM would have been too terrifying to hear. Remember Mount Sinai? The thunder, lightning and fire? Everyone was terrified to hear His voice."

✿✝✿✝✿✝✿

"Hey **General!**" Darryl started to say. "How ya do—" Darryl stopped... and stared... at Nate.

---

42 From an account relayed by Grant Jeffrey in his book *Unveiling Mysteries of the Bible*

"That **you**? **Nate**? You **walkin'**?!"

"Yeah, it's me. I can hardly believe it either!"

"What **happened**? How'd it **happen**? **When**? **Talk** to me!!"

Nate explained how early that morning he had heard a voice, Y'shua's voice, telling him to get up and walk.

"That's **it**? You just got **up** and **walked**?"

"Yeah, and then I ran, and then I took a shower!"

"We are here from the Prime Minister," David interrupted. "Nathaniel was told there will be about ten days before it begins."

"Before **what** begins?" Darryl asked.

"Everything we have been preparing for," Nate said. "Y'shua said 'great and terrible things.'"

"'Great and terrible **things**'? **What** things?" Darryl looked around the warehouse. "I got **ten days** to clear **this** out? You're **kiddin'** me, right?"

"You will leave a good amount of food and water," David instructed. "I'll tell you something, not everyone will evacuate. Some will be trapped, and some will choose to stay."

"Save out some medical supplies," Tahlia said. "Magen David Adom may need them."

Darryl looked at Nate. "You **sure** you're all **healed**?"

"Yeah! I'm good!"

"Okay, then, now that you're **on** your **feet**, you could help out! All these **trucks** need to be **loaded**!"

"Tahlia and I have plans," Nate answered. "Maybe tomorrow I can take a truck down to the Negev."

Waving his clipboard, Darryl turned away from Nate. "Where you **puttin'** that?!"he yelled at one of the workers. "Were you **born yesterday**? On the **truck**! The **truck**!"

-2-

Nate and Tahlia jogged down the street, around the curve and onto the walkway by the park.

"Hey Naomi, how's the pup?" Nate called. Naomi's eyes opened wide and her mouth opened, but no sound came out.

"Even her ugly dog looks good today," Nate remarked to Tahlia. They brushed by another jogger. Nate turned around and ran backward. "Hello! Do you see me now?" With a puzzled look on his face, the jogger slowed to a stop, watching Nate. "He doesn't even realize I'm the same guy he's been ignoring every morning," Nate told Tahlia. He looked over at her. "Isn't this **great**?! After everyone gets over the shock of me walking, I'm going to tell them about Y'shua and how He healed me!"

"You can start with Reuven," Tahlia said.

Reuven stopped in his tracks when he saw Nate and Tahlia. He closed his eyes, took a deep breath, opened his eyes … and Nate was still there, standing right in front of him. No wheelchair. Reuven looked at Tahlia. "What's going on here? I don't understand."

"Sit down," Tahlia said, taking the cups of coffee out of his hands. "Nathaniel will explain. So explain."

Nate told Reuven how God had answered his prayers and how Y'shua had told him to GET UP AND WALK. "It was about three o'clock this morning when I heard His voice," Nate said.

Nate explained that Y'shua was the Messiah, sent from God.

"I see you walking, standing, running. I say to myself, *Who is that with Tahlia?*" Then I see it is you. *How can this be?* I ask myself. Now you say it is Y'shua who has healed you. That Y'shua is the Messiah. What does this mean?"

"It means the Messiah has come," Nate answered. "He came two thousand years ago. God pointed Him out as the Messiah by doing signs and wonders through him among the people of Israel. He was crucified and killed by unbelievers, according to God's plan, to bring salvation to Israel and the world. Adonai raised Him up from the dead, and now He is the living Savior of all who believe." Acts 2:22–24, 1 Timothy 4:10

"Is God pointing Y'shua out as the Messiah by healing you?" asked Reuven.

"Yes," said Nate. "God wants all Israel to be saved." [Romans 11:26]

"What should I do?"

"Believe that Y'shua is the Messiah sent from God, and confess your sin. Y'shua has paid the atonement for our sins. God is faithful to forgive the sins of all who believe." [1 John 1:8, 2:1] Do you believe this?"

"Yes, this I will believe," answered Reuven.

✡✝✡✝✡✝✡

"Where's Asa?" Nate asked, seeing the *CLOSED* sign on the door of the auto-repair shop.

"I haven't seen him in a while," Tahlia said. "Hope everything is all right. He never goes anywhere."

"I was going to ask him to revamp Fred," Nate said. "I was hoping he could put a put a regular seat in so I don't have to use my wheelchair when I drive."

Nate and Tahlia ran down the trail that led to the Mediterranean and slowed to a walk when they reached the beach. A cloudless blue sky touched the sapphire waters of the Med. A light breeze cooled the air. *This is an almost perfect day,* Nate thought. *Just one more thing. It's now or never.* He turned toward Talia. He realized his heart was pounding.

"Tahlia, will you marry me?" he asked.

Tahlia stopped and stared at him.

She shook her head. "No," she said.

"No?! You said you would say yes when I asked!" Nate ran his hand through his hair and took a step back. "This is me, asking."

"I have some things to sort out," Tahlia replied.

Nate turned away and began walking up the beach. He shoved his hands in his pockets and kicked some stones out of his way. *I'm just going to do this,* he thought. *I'm not giving up.* He walked back toward Tahlia. He took her hand and put in it the ring he had carried in his pocket. "I would have asked weeks ago, but this wasn't ready yet. I didn't want to ask without having this to give you."

Tahlia examined the ring.

"I talked to your father. He said if you said yes, he would give his blessing."

"This is like the throne of God," Tahlia said breathlessly. "A diamond with emeralds around it, like a rainbow. And these seven smaller diamonds are like the seven torches that burn before the throne." She looked at Nate. "This is beautiful."

"The rubies all around represent the twenty-four elders," Nate explained. "And these four stones represent the four living creatures."

Tahlia slipped the ring on her finger. "Yes," she said.

"You can keep the ring even if you say no," said Nate.

"I needed to sort out if you waited until you were healed to ask," Tahlia said. "Now that's all sorted out."

Nate drew her into his arms. "I will sacrifice my life for you," he said softly. "I will protect you; I will provide for you. I will love you as long as I live."

"I know," said Tahlia. "I know."

-3-

Nisan 1 - Wednesday

This is Carl Roisen, INT News. There's a lot going on in Israel's Negev Desert. Over the past year, storehouses have been built and stocked; solar towers have been constructed; deep water sources have been located and tapped into. Housing for thousands of people has been constructed. Now, today, we're seeing a lot of activity at this site. Eric Strayer, our Mid-East correspondent, is on the scene. Eric?

Yes, Carl. We are in the middle of what was previously an uninhabited, desolate area. But today the entire site is swarming with activity. More housing is being erected and connected to the infrastructure, which is already in place. I'm told the goal is to have nearly 150,000 of these homes in place in less than two weeks.

What is the reason for all of this? Why are they building a settlement in the desert?

From what I've learned, this site is being prepared as a place for the Tabernacle. Earlier today, two trucks from the SHILOH HERITAGE FOUNDATION arrived. They brought a full-size replica of the Tabernacle and all the furnishings that go with it. It is being erected by members of the Levitical priesthood and will be completed before sundown.

But why there, in the Negev, Eric?

Passover is two weeks away. According to Chief Rabbi Kahan, a Passover lamb will be sacrificed. This will be the first sacrifice since the Temple was destroyed in 70 A.D. They are expecting over 100,000 people.

Are sacrifices going to be ongoing, or just for Passover?

I don't have an answer for that.

How about the Ark of the Covenant? Do you think they have it?

"I'm sure Nate is involved with this," Justine said to Wes. "It's probably why he doesn't want to come home."

Nisan 2 - Thursday

Nate pulled up in front of Corp. Nahshon's headquarters, jumped out of the truck and went inside. He still couldn't quite believe he was able to jump out of anything. Nahshon looked up as Nate walked in. "Hey Nash, I have a load from ELISHA for you. Where should I bring it?"

Nahshon looked at the site map on his desk. "Storehouse #24."

Nate looked at the map. "You know, that looks just like the wilderness camp of Israel."

"It is. That's the model, okay? We have the Tabernacle in the center, the Levites around that and the four main tribes at the corners. We have flags marking the different sections. You're with Gen. Yash'el's family—here." Nahshon tapped the map, showing four units in the section flying the Lion of Judah flag. "Gen. Yash'el has units J-4 through J-8. Front row, okay? Your housing should be connected to the grid in a day or two, all right?"

"*Sababa!*" Nate said. "I can't believe everything that's going on here!"

"We're just getting started, okay?" said Nahshon. "Take a look around. Today they're finishing assembling the bronze altar, and putting the furniture into the Tabernacle."

"Are they really going to have sacrifices? Other than the Passover lamb?" Nate wanted to know.

"Starting tomorrow," Nahshon replied. "The priests have to be ordained and the Tabernacle consecrated."

"It just seems so…so primitive," said Nate. "No wonder they're doing it here in the desert. I can't imagine offering sacrifices in Jerusalem."

"Don't forget this is all because of you, okay? You're the one with the dreams and visions," Nahshon remarked. "Without you none of this is happening, all right?"

✿♱✿♱✿♱✿

Nate backed his truck up to #24 and handed off the paperwork. While the truck was being unloaded, he climbed on top of the cab, took the binoculars out of his duffel and looked out over the camp. The Court of the Tabernacle was in the center of the camp. The sun reflected off the silver hooks of the curtains and made the pillars' bronze feet glow. The hanging curtain that formed the gate shimmered with blue, purple and scarlet threads. At the west end of the courtyard was the Tabernacle. Nate knew it was overlaid with gold, but it was covered with layers of cloth and skins, hidden from his eyes. He watched as the bronze altar was put in place. He hadn't realized it was so big. From where he stood on top of the cab, Nate could see that some sort of drainage system had been prepared for the altar. They're really going to do it, he thought. *They're really going to start the sacrifices again.*

✲✞✲✞✲✞✲

<u>Nisan 3 - Friday</u>

This is Carl Roisen, INT breaking news. Thousands of people have gathered in the Negev to observe the ordination of the priests and the consecration of the Tabernacle. Our Mid-East correspondent Eric Strayer brings this report. Eric?

Yes, Carl, earlier today the ordination of the High Priest, the priests, and the consecration of the Tabernacle began. The ordination and consecration will take seven days to complete. All the priests are Kohathites, direct descendants of the Biblical Aaron. They are to be washed with water and dressed in the priestly garments. The garments for the High Priest include an ephod made of gold, blue, purple and scarlet yarns; a breast-piece set with gemstones representing the twelve tribes of Israel; and a turban on which is fastened a plate of pure gold engraved with the words "HOLY TO THE LORD." The rest of the priests will be clothed with coats, sashes and caps. The High Priest will be anointed with oil, as will the Tabernacle and all that is in it. There will also be several animal sacrifices. A bull has been butchered and prepared for sacrifice. Its blood has been collected in a bowl and some of it has been put on the horns of the altar. The rest of the blood has been poured out at the base of the altar. The fat of the entrails, the liver and the kidneys are on the altar. The first sacrifice in almost two thousand years will soon be burned on this altar. The rest of the bull, the flesh and skin, have been taken outside the camp to be burned.
What is this offering for, Eric?

It's a sin offering for the priests. The next offering will be of one of the rams. This will be a whole burnt offering. The other ram will also be offered. This is the ram of ordination. It's a long process. The smoke from these offerings will be seen rising above the Tabernacle all week.

Are these the only sacrifices that will be offered?

No. The ordination of the priests and the consecration of the Tabernacle will take seven days. There will be morning and evening sacrifices every day.

That's a lot of animals. There might be a worldwide protest by animal-rights activists.

I spoke to the SHILOH HERITAGE FOUNDATION about that, Carl. They pointed out that thousands of animals are slaughtered every day for food. The animals here are humanely killed. Only certain parts of the animal are burned as an offering. The rest of the animal is eaten either by the priests or the people.

It just seems bizarre, Eric. Nobody does animal sacrifices anymore. Exodus 29, Leviticus 8

Nate took Tahlia into his arms and slowly danced around the courtyard. "One last dance before we go into the wilderness."

He sang softly:

"I'll always remember the song they were playing,

the first time we danced and I knew…

as we swayed to the music and held to each other,

I fell in love with you…"

"And I fell in love with you," Tahlia replied.

"Mom wants to know if we've set a date yet," Nate said as he took another slow turn around the courtyard. "She wants to start looking for airline tickets."

"Did you tell her anything?" Talia inquired.

"Yeah, I said I hoped there wouldn't be a problem with them coming. We really can't make plans until we see what's going to happen in the next few weeks."

"I was thinking of a fall wedding," said Tahlia.

"I was thinking of tomorrow," said Nate.

> "When we're together it feels so right...
> Can I have this dance for the rest of my life?"[43]

"Yes," Tahlia answered.

"Shlomo, he is healed, yes?" said Aaron as they came into the courtyard.

"Aaron. Aaron! I can see he is healed! You see how tall he is standing on his feet?"

"Just as the Almighty said, yes?"

Nate and Tahlia danced over to Aaron and Shlomo.

"Y'shua called out to me in the middle of the night," said Nate. "He said 'GET UP AND WALK.'"

"And now you walk; now you dance. Now you get married!" Shlomo said.

"Not yet," Nate replied.

"So. Still meshugah," Shlomo said.

"We'll be married soon," Tahlia said. "We're waiting to see what will happen."

"Happen! What can happen? Get married! Aaron, tell them!"

"Nathaniel will explain," Tahlia said, looking at Nate. "So explain."

"Y'shua said more than 'GET UP AND WALK,'" Nate began. "He also said: 'IN TEN DAYS I WILL BEGIN TO DO GREAT AND TERRIBLE THINGS BEFORE YOUR EYES.'"

What great and terrible things?" Aaron asked.

"I have no idea," Nate said. "That's what we're waiting to see."

---

43 From the 1980 song "Could I Have This Dance," written by Wayland Holyfield and Bob House.

"So. It is the plagues of Egypt," Shlomo said. "The great and terrible things done before the eyes of Israel. ^{Deuteronomy 10:21} Do you see my meaning?"

"You sure?" asked Nate.

"I am a rabbi. I know these things."

✿✞✿✞✿✞✿

Justine ripped the sheets off of Nate's bed and threw them down the stairs. She took the drawers out of his dresser and dumped them over the railing on top of the sheets.

JJ raised his eyebrows and looked at Josie.

"Hey, what's going on here?" Wes asked as he stepped over the pile of sheets and clothes and ran up the stairs.

"I'm cleaning out Nate's room," Justine replied. "He's probably never coming home again, and I'll probably never see my son again!"

"Calm down," Wes said. "Just calm down a little."

"I'm calm. See how calm I am?!" said Justine as she pitched a box of CDs down the stairs. "Did you see his email? All I asked was if they had set a date yet. All I said was I wanted to see about airline tickets. Know what he said?"

JJ and Josie cautiously began to pick up the CDs.

"No, but I'm sure you're going to tell me," Wes remarked.

"He said there might be a **problem** with us coming! A **problem**?! Really?! Thousands of people fly to Israel every day, but there's a problem with us?!" Justine dragged the mattress off the bed.

Wes leaned the mattress and the box spring against the wall. "I'm sure you're overreacting. "There's a lot goi—"

"**I'm** overreacting?! I'm **overreacting**?! REALLY?!"

215

JJ and Josie dove for cover as a box of sports equipment went flying down the stairs.

Wes re-read Nate's email.

Re: Wedding
No date yet waiting to see what happens in the next couple of weeks
There might be a problem with you coming

Then he read the email he had sent and Nate's reply:

Re: Wedding
We are all looking forward to seeing you and meeting Tahlia! As soon as you set a date we'll make arrangements to come. It will take an act of God to keep us away!

Re: Wedding
That's what I'm talking about.

Wes leaned back in his chair. What was Nate talking about?

-4-

Nisan 10 - Friday

The week of ordination and consecration had passed. The Tabernacle and the High Priest had been anointed with oil. Throughout the week the smoke of the offerings had risen to heaven. Now the time had come for the High Priest to bless the people of Israel.

Nate and Tahlia were among the thousands upon thousands of people who stood outside the Tabernacle courtyard waiting for the blessing.

"Look," Nate said, "see how the top layer of skins over the Tabernacle is the same blue as the sky?"

Tahlia looked. The skins that formed the roof of the Tabernacle faded into the sky, almost disappearing. "How many layers are there?" she asked.

216

"Four," Nate replied. "The top layer that we can see is made of some kind of sea mammal. Under that is a layer of ram skins dyed blood-red. Next is a layer of coarse black goatskins. Finally, an embroidered cloth separates the skins from the Holy places."

Nate knew the red ram-skins represented the blood of the Atonement sacrifice, which covered the black goat-skins, which symbolized the sins of the people. What the other two layers meant, he had no idea.

The people leaned forward in anticipation as the High Priest stepped out of the Tabernacle courtyard and onto the plaza in front of the gate. The golden plate on his turban was glowing in the sunlight, and the gemstones on his breast-piece were like coals of fire. He raised his hands and blessed the people as Adonai had commanded Moses:

> "Adonai bless you and keep you;
> Adonai make his face to shine upon you
> And be gracious to you;
> Adonai lift up his countenance upon you
> And give you peace.'" Numbers 6:23–26

And so he put the name of Adonai on the people.

As the blessing ended, far in the distance they could hear the low, ominous rolling of thunder. It grew louder and louder as the crystal-blue sky began to darken, turning an eerie green as a strong wind began to blow. Nate watched the darkening skies with a growing sense of uneasiness. Back home, in the States, this looked like tornado weather.

A great cloud, surrounded by brilliant light, filled with intense flashes of lightning, was moving toward the camp. All the people were watching it and looking around with fear in their eyes. Nate's heart was pounding. He put his arm around Tahlia and pulled her toward him.

Thunder exploded all around them, shaking the earth again and again. The flashing lightning became a great wall of fire, surrounding the camp. Tahlia was trembling. She pressed herself against Nate, and he tightened his arms around her as he watched the lightning strike all along the perimeter of the camp. The people were beginning to panic. The great booming thunder, the constant flashing lightning, was terrifying.

Suddenly... there was silence.

Then—from the middle of the great cloud, a bolt of lightning came down into the courtyard of the Tabernacle, striking the altar of burnt offering, consuming the sacrifice.

✡✟✡✟✡✟✡

Nisan 12- Sunday

"Hear O Israel! Adonai has only begun to show His greatness and His mighty hand. What God is there in heaven or on earth who can do such great and terrible works as what has been done before your eyes? You are a people brought out of the nations where Adonai your God had scattered you. With a mighty hand and an outstretched arm and with wrath poured out you have been gathered. You have been brought into the land of Israel, the land Adonai swore to your fathers to give you. He has brought you into the land that your fathers possessed, and you have again possessed it, and He has made you more prosperous and numerous than your fathers. Repent O Israel! Turn your faces away from all your abominations! Do not let your sins be your ruin! Put rebellion behind you and get a new heart and new spirit. Why should you die O Israel!"
Deuteronomy 3:24; Ezekiel 20:34,36:11 Ezekiel 14:6;18:30–31

"You **listenin'** to this?" Darryl asked Nate. "They've been **at it** all **morning**! One **stops** and the other one **starts**! You **hearin'** this?"

"Yeah," Nate replied. "Hard not to." He studied the two men who were preaching at the Tabernacle gate. They both looked pretty shabby, with worn sandals, dusty jeans, faded t-shirts, long, unkempt beards and hair, and what looked like some kind of *abayah*[44] with tassels on the corners draped around their necks."Where'd they come from?"

---

44 A bedouin blanket, usually white with black stripes along the sides.

"You're askin' me? This is the first time **I'm seein'** 'em."

Nate's eyes narrowed as he listened. "Do you notice anything?"

"**What**? What'm I supposed to **notice**? They **both** look like they belong in a **homeless shelter!**"

"Everything they're saying sounds like it's from the Bible."

"Is **that** supposed to **mean** somethin'?"

"Maybe…"

"It is not like when Adonai brought your fathers into the land, a land that was filled with great and good cities that they did not build, and houses full of all good things that they did not fill, and cisterns that they did not dig, vineyards and olive trees that they did not plant. You were brought into a land whose cities had been laid waste; a land where the heavens above were like bronze and the earth beneath like iron; a land with swamps and disease, a land where the rain was like dust from heaven, a land devastated by Adonai because of the sins of your fathers." **Deuteronomy 1:30; Ezekiel 36:8–12**

Nate and Darryl turned and began pushing their way through the crowd that had gathered. As they headed toward Corp. Nahshon's headquarters, the words of the Preachers followed them.

"Adonai your God brought you to prepare the way for the people who would soon be coming home. He brought you to drain the swamps, to rebuild the cities and houses and to fill them with all the good things Adonai your God is giving you. He brought you here to replant the vineyards and the olive trees, and to dig the cisterns. Adonai your God has blessed the work of your hands and has caused the early rain and the latter rain to fall upon the land. He has gathered you again from all the peoples where He had scattered you. Adonai your God has had compassion on you and has restored your fortunes. He has caused your enemies, who have risen against you to be defeated before you, for it is Adonai your God who fights for you. This you have seen with your own eyes." Deuteronomy 28

Nate remembered all the stories the General and others had told him. He remembered how God had fought for Israel. He remembered the finger of God.

"It is not because of your righteousness or the uprightness of your heart that Adonai your God has given you this good land to possess. It is because Adonai loves you and is keeping the oath that He swore to your fathers, that He has brought you out of all the nations where He scattered you in His wrath. Know now that Adonai your God is the faithful God who keeps covenant and steadfast love with those who love Him and keep his commandments, and repays to their face those who hate Him, by destroying them." **Deuteronomy 7:8–10, Ezekiel 36:21, et. al.**

There was a crowd of people around the headquarters, standing and listening to the preacher.

"And now O Israel, be careful to obey the commands that Adonai your God has given you. Do not add or take from them. Keep them and do them, so that Adonai your God will be near to you whenever you call upon Him. Take care, be diligent! Do not forget what your eyes have seen! Make them known to your children and your children's children! Now turn everyone from his evil ways and you will live in peace in the land I have given you!" Deuteronomy 12:32, 4:9, 6:7; Jeremiah 35:15

Nate and Darryl spotted the General and made their way to him.

"Do you know where they came from?" Nate asked David.

"I'll tell you something," said David. "Last night they were camped on the ridge. They came in from the desert. Nahshon sent someone to see. They said they were bringing a message for Israel."

Together they listened to the voice of the Preacher as it echoed off the ridges that surrounded the camp.

"Hear O Israel! Do not grieve Adonai your God as your fathers did! Repent and return to Adonai your God! Take the idols out of your hearts and remove iniquity from

220

before your face! Turn away from all your evil ways! You will be judged O Israel, every one according to his ways. Repent and turn from all your sins or your iniquity will be your ruin! The day of Adonai is near! A day of desolation and distress. A day of clouds and thick darkness. A day of fire and smoke! A day of wrath!" Ezekiel 14:6, 18:30, 24:14; Joel 2

Nate leaned against the outside wall of Corp. Nahshon's headquarters, watching as the leaders of the people began to file inside. The words of the Preacher echoed in his head.

"Come," said David. "Yaakov is here. He will tell you something."

✿✞✿✞✿✞✿

"Nathaniel!" Yaakov exclaimed. "It is the finger of God—you are walking!" He grasped Nate's hand.

"Yeah, I never want to sit again. Glory to God and to Y'shua who healed me!" Nate said.

"We have a plan for you," Yaakov told him. "You will train with the IDF."

"Really? I can join up?!"

"No, no. You are not Jewish or Israeli. But you will get the training. And then *Gibbor Chayil*."

"*Gibbor* who?"

"Mighty Men of Valor. Former commandos. They got together for the protection of the settlements. We need some *Gibbor Chayil* here in the Negev, especially with this huge camp. Eyal will be here tomorrow. He'll tell you more then."

✿✞✿✞✿✞✿

Major Harim waited until all the leaders of the camp were in the room before he spoke.

"Okay, people, listen up. We have seen, heard and felt the power of the most spectacular electrical storm ever recorded

221

in the Negev. This storm happened before our eyes. It did not happen to our ancestors, but to us. We were not told about it; we experienced it. We saw for ourselves a wall of fire encircling this camp. We saw for ourselves the fire from heaven consume the burnt offering."

The Major paused, his eyes meeting Nate's. "What you did not see were the rockets, fired from the Sinai by the Soldiers of Islam, seconds before the storm began. All three rockets were exploded in mid-air, far from the camp, not by Iron Dome but by bolts of lightning."

Nate saw the people looking at each other and nodding their heads as they absorbed this information.

"It may be that the God of Israel will protect this camp, but we also have to do our part. There are tens of thousands of people in camp as of this morning. We expect that number to double by the time the Passover Lamb is sacrificed.

"We have troops patrolling the perimeter and checkpoints on all the roads entering the Negev. We are urging everyone…"

The email alert went off on Nate's phone. He read the message:

Re: Ariel
Nate – I think I may have a way to get Ariel's body out of France. Details to follow.

Nate showed Darryl the email.

"**No! Nada! Not** gonna **happen!** I helped you **smuggle drugs,** I'm helpin' with this **whole thing,** but I am **NOT** gonna help you **smuggle a body** out of **France!**"

David turned and looked at Darryl. Then he turned to Nate and raised his eyebrows. "Tell me something."

"Nobody is smuggling anything," Nate said. *Yet.*

Re: Ariel
Dad – Thanks! let me know what the plan is.
I have great news! I'm going to be training with the IDF! And then I'll be protecting the camp with the commandos. Is that great or what?!

This camp is huge! It's set up just like the wilderness camp of Israel in numbers 2. It's divided into twelve sections, each one named for one of the tribes, and each section is flying the standard of that tribe. In the middle is the Tabernacle, and all around it is a huge plaza With the Israeli flags flying. Around that are where the priests and the Levites are housed. It's incredible to see!

I'm in the Judah section with The General's family. Tahlia and I will have our own unit when we get married. That'll happen After I'm trained up with the IDF. Remember the prayer I put in the Western Wall? God is answering my prayer! This is important – I need to get my own equipment. Can you help with that?

✿✝✿✝✿✝✿

Nisan 14 - Tuesday Evening

Nate watched the campfire up on the ridge. He could see the two men sitting by it with their cloaks draped over their heads. Who were they? Nate ran his hand through his hair. *Maybe I should go up and talk to them. I don't have anything else to do.*

As Nate began to jog toward the ridge, he saw the two men stand up. They looked ten feet tall in the firelight, silhouetted by the full moon. He slowed to a walk as they raised their hands heavenward.

"HEAR O ISRAEL! ADONAI OUR GOD, ADONAI IS ONE."
Their words rang out over the camp.

The ground suddenly shifted under Nate's feet. He staggered a few steps before he came to a stop. He looked up at the ridge. The two men and the fire were gone.

CHAPTER TWO

Shadow of His Wings
-1-

Be merciful to me, O God, be merciful to me,
For in you my soul takes refuge;
In the shadow of your wings I will take refuge
Till the storms of destruction pass by.
Psalm 57:1

Nisan 14 - Wednesday

Nate stood on the top of the ridge where the Preachers had
camped. There was nothing here except the remains of their
fire. *I wonder what they saw from up here,* Nate thought. He
took the binoculars out of his duffel and looked out over the
camp. *Sababa! This is sweet!*

Nate saw the twelve sections or the camp, each representing
one of the twelve tribes of Israel. He saw the forty communities
in each section, flying its tribal flag. The wide main roads of
the camp outlined a giant cross, and in the center of the cross,
more roadways formed a Star of David. In the center of the star
was the Tabernacle, the heart of the camp. The Tabernacle was
encircled by a spacious walkway with a large plaza on the east
side in front of the courtyard gate. *This is what Balaam must
have seen,* he thought, *the sign of the cross in the wilderness,
with the throne of God in the center.* [Numbers 24]

Nate scanned the camp, watching the preparations for the feast.
Each community had its own dining hall and courtyard. The
kosher butchers, all of them priests, were going from courtyard
to courtyard, ritually slaughtering the family Passover lambs
and collecting the blood in bowls. The lamb for the nation
would be slaughtered at exactly 3 p.m., and then roasted on the
Altar of Burnt Offering. In the courtyards, all the lambs would
be roasted at the same time as the Passover for the nation.

Suddenly Nate felt the ground sway beneath his feet and he
nearly lost his balance. Another tremor. He looked at the time.

The tremors had been coming regularly since last night. Not strong, just enough to feel something had happened.

Nate put the binoculars back to his eyes and watched as more housing units were being hooked up to the grid. *Was that Asa? Yes!* Nate put the binoculars back in his duffel and headed down off the ridge. Maybe Asa would have time to put a real seat in Fred.

As Nate approached Storehouse #32, he could hear Darryl's voice. "Are **you** telling' **me** you don't feel **anything**? The **ground** is movin', I'm **tellin'** ya!"

Now Nate could see Darryl, waving his clipboard in Corp. Nahshon's face. "This **keeps up**, all my **storehouses** are gonna **collapse**!"

"This happens in the Negev, okay?" Nash reassured. "We're near a fault line, so the ground shakes a little. The camp was built to be pretty much earthquake proof, all right?"

"Nobody's worried about this?" Nate asked. "These are coming at pretty regular intervals. Is that normal?"

✿✢✿✢✿✢✿

Nate climbed onto the roof of Unit J-5 and scanned the walkway for Tahlia. There she was, talking to Zvi. They would be leaving the camp as soon as the Passover meal was over, heading to the MDA station in Haifa. Everyone had to be on duty this week in case something 'GREAT AND TERRIBLE' happened. If there was nothing, then there would be an emergency-preparedness drill, the largest in the nation's history. Either way, Tahlia would be gone for at least ten days.

It was almost an hour before the sacrifice would begin. Nate thumbed through his emails, looking for the one his Dad had sent.

Re: Ariel
Nate – since you are determined to be involved in whatever is going on in the Negev, your mother and I are glad you are going to get some training. We'll do what we can to help out with the equipment. BTW your college fund is nearly empty.

225

About Ariel – I'm going to be meeting with the producer of a TV show called "Underground Mysteries." I told him just enough about Shlomo and Ariel to get him interested. He's coming to Chicago to film a program about Al Capone. I'll meet with him then.

Also – I've been researching the Galitz family. All of the adults were killed, just like Shlomo said. Ask him if he remembers any of the Galitz children. How many were in each family, boys or girls, names. Anything. It may be different than what was in the letter.

The camp sounds pretty amazing! The J's are all about the wilderness camp and the Tabernacle. I bought them a book about it, and they're even reading Exodus. Can you send some pictures?

Nate thought a moment before replying.

Re: Ariel
Thanks Dad! Let me know what happens. I'll ask Shlomo what he remembers. Could you maybe look at the Hansen family? Maybe Sgt. Grange has some family left in the States?
I went up on the ridge and saw the camp from above! It's incredible! Tell the J's I'm on it. Lots of pictures coming their way.

✿ ✤ ✿ ✤ ✿ ✤ ✿

"They're about ready to start," said Tahlia as she climbed on the roof.

"Yeah," Nate replied. "Look at Shlomo and Aaron. They've been sitting on that bench in front of the gate all afternoon."

"What do you think about this Passover sacrifice?" Tahlia asked. "You said Y'shua was the final, once-for-all sacrifice. So what about this?"

"I've been thinking about that," Nate said as he took a photo of Shlomo and Aaron.

"So explain," Tahlia said.

"Maybe it's so the people will have a visual aid for how the sacrifice of the lamb represents Y'shua. Maybe they'll understand that Y'shua was the Lamb for the nation."

Tahlia looked at Nate. "Somebody will have to tell them."

226

"Maybe the Preachers will," Nate said.

"They're saying to repent," Tahlia said.

"Yeah," Nate said. "So maybe we'll have to tell them how to be saved from the wrath of God."

Nate focused on the gate to the Tabernacle courtyard. Ten priests carrying shofars came out...*click.*

...and stood at intervals along the courtyard curtain. *Click.*

Two priests carrying silver trumpets came and stood on either side of the gate... *click.*

...and sounded a long blast. *Click.*

All the people gathered together, in their doorways, on their rooftops, on the plaza and all along the wide walkway that surrounded the Tabernacle courtyard. Shlomo and Aaron hadn't moved from their spot near the front of the gate.

The ten priests began to blow the shofars. The rest of the priests, hundreds of them, filed through the gate. They stood in rows on the walkway. They were all dressed in white linen and carried harps. *Click.*

"Are those the harps your father makes?" Nate asked Tahlia.

"They were going to save them for when the Temple is built, but they wanted to be part of this Passover," she replied.

Nate zoomed in on one of the harps, hoping he could capture some of the details. *Click.*

The shofars fell silent. The playing of the harps began. Then the priestly choir began to sing. Nate closed his eyes and listened. It was like being transported to heaven. He felt a shiver run over him. These were the most beautiful sounds he had ever heard.

"Do you feel it?" whispered Tahlia.

Nate nodded. "I'll never forget this," he said softly. "Never."

The courtyard gate opened, and the High Priest emerged leading the Passover lamb. *Click.*

227

The lamb was the purest white Nate had ever seen. Even from the rooftop they could see a sweet, curious expression on its face. Leading the lamb, the High Priest turned to the south and walked slowly around the courtyard to the sounds of the choir. *Click.*

As the lamb turned onto the north side of the Tabernacle, Nate could see him stop and look at the crowd of people that lined the walkway. Then he continued to follow the High Priest. *Click.*

"He has no idea he's being led to the slaughter," Nate remarked to Tahlia.

The lamb was led back into the courtyard. From the rooftop Nate and Tahlia could see over the seven-and-a-half-foot-high curtain fence. They watched as the lamb was held...*click.*

...and his throat was slit. *Click.*

The blood was sprinkled on the corners of the altar...*click.*

...and the lamb was skinned and butchered.

Nate put his camera down. The J's didn't have to see this. He didn't even want to watch.

Each family had been given a container holding a small amount of the blood of the lamb that had been slaughtered in the community courtyards. Nate watched as first Eyal, and then Yaakov, Yaron and the General put the blood on the doorposts and lintels of their units. *This hasn't been done in thousands of years,* Nate thought as he put the blood on Unit J-5. *What had Shlomo said? The 'great and terrible things' were the plagues of Egypt?*

"I guess it's time to go," Tahlia said as Zvi pulled up in an MICU[45] ambulance.

---

45 A Magen David Adom Mobile Intensive Care Unit ambulance

"Not yet," said Nate. He took the lid off of the container with the blood of the lamb in it and took a sprig of oregano out of his pocket. Stepping over to the ambulance, he put the blood around the doors. Zvi watched, raised his eyebrows, but didn't say anything.

"One more thing," Nate said. He kissed Tahlia, and then, dipping his finger into the blood, he traced the sign of the cross on her forehead. He leaned over and pressed his forehead against hers. "Blood of the Lamb," he whispered. Giving her a final hug, he helped her into the ambulance and watched it disappear.

✿✞✿✞✿✞✿

Nisan 15 Erev - Thursday

Nate stretched out on the roof, using his duffel as a pillow. The light of the full moon lit up the whole camp. This was a day he would never forget. He could still hear the trumpets and shofars. The harps and the singing of the priestly choir played over and over in his head. Brushing the blood on the doorposts, eating the Passover meal with hundreds of people, waiting for Elijah to join them—he had half-expected the Preachers to show up and drink the cup.

The sky was clear, and far from the brightness of the moon the stars pierced the darkness. The tremors that had shaken the earth most of the day had stopped. It would have been a perfect night if Tahlia was next to him.

Father God, he prayed, *watch over her, keep her safe. Guard her, bring her back to me. In the name Y'shua, and the blood of the Lamb...*

✿✞✿✞✿✞✿

A rumbling, a deep muted sound shook the earth. Nate was thrown nearly to the edge of the roof. He cautiously got to his feet and looked over the camp. Everything was swaying like

229

ships at sea, but none of the units were crumbling or falling. People were coming out, looking around anxiously. Nate took his binoculars and focused on the Tabernacle. It stood, solid as a rock in a rolling sea, luminous in the moonlight. He swung around to check the storehouses. They were swaying but standing. Then he looked far to the north. He saw a black hole in the sky, blocking out the stars.

The earth reeled again as Nate pulled himself over the side of the roof and dropped to the ground.

-2-

Zvi gripped the steering wheel, trying to keep control as the road beneath them writhed like a snake. Tahlia clung to the door handle as she prayed *Y'shua, keep us safe, Y'shua...*

Finally the ground settled and Zvi maneuvered over the crevasses where the road had split apart. He looked over at Tahlia. "What was that?! An earthquake?"

Tahlia turned up the radio. "Earthquake. We better head for Tiberius. A lot of damage there."

They drove in silence, listening for updates and then...the sky lit up over Golan Heights. Explosion after explosion ripped the night air. The sound of shofars blasted from loudspeakers as they approached Tiberius. This was not a drill!

The city was in ruins. Buildings had crumbled. Roads were nearly impassable. Power was out. Tahlia watched the skies over the Golan as she jumped out of the ambulance. "Are we being attacked?"

Zvi looked at Tahlia. "What do you think? What did your guy talk about?"

"Damascus," said Tahlia. "Damascus destroyed. A river of blood."

"Okay, people! Listen up! Sit down!" Major Harim addressed the section leaders who had gathered in his headquarters. "We are getting early reports of the cause of the explosions. We are not being attacked. We are not attacking anybody. The explosions are coming from the Al-Safa volcanic field. It seems the whole field is erupting."

The room started to buzz. "...thought that was dormant..." "...how can we hear it this far?" "... there has to be more to it..."

"Okay, people! Listen! A large earthquake has struck Al-Safa all the way down to Tiberius. This is what may have caused the eruption of the volcanic field. A lot of toxic gases are released with a volcanic eruption along with a lot of ash being pumped into the atmosphere," Harim said. "But more serious than that are the weapon storage depots in and around Damascus. If those blow, we have some serious issues."

"What kind of serious?" someone called out.

"There are enough conventional weapons stored in and around Damascus to level the city if they are set off," Harim replied. "And that's the least of our problems."

He waited again for the room to quiet. "Chemical and biological weapons are also stored in proximity to Al-Safa. If they get blown into the atmosphere, there's no telling where the wind will take them. The prevailing winds blow from the north. That would bring everything into northern Israel, maybe as far south as Haifa or even Tel Aviv."

"What kind of chemicals?" someone asked. The room began to buzz again. "Sarin?""Ammonia?" "Held in the ash, won't dissipate..." "VX?" ... "Mustard..." "...get in the ground... toxic for decades..."

Darryl and Nate made their way to where the General was standing.

"What about Tiberius?" Nate asked.

"I'll tell you something," David said. "A volcano we didn't plan on."

"What about the earthquake? How bad is it in Tiberius?"

"Okay, people! Listen!" Major Harim called out above the noise. "There are going to be thousands of people arriving in the next twenty-four hours, getting as far as they can as fast as they can from the toxic fumes and the other fallout of the eruption. We have a lot to do, people!"

Major Harim waited until the room was mostly quiet. "We didn't plan for this volcano to erupt, but the same evacuation plan will apply. The first point of contact with the refugees from the north will be the checkpoints. Not all will be brought here. Some will be directed to one of the other settlements."

He held up a piece of paper. "This is a directive from the Tabernacle Camp Council. Only the God of Israel will be worshiped in the Tabernacle Camp. There will be no worship of Allah or any other god in this camp. Is that clear?"

It wasn't.

"General," someone called out. "We can't have this camp run by a bunch of Orthodox rabbis!"

"No, we can't," Harim agreed. "That's why **I'm** running this camp. No worship of any other gods. Any questions?"

Nate stood up.

"Sit down, Nathaniel. Good question." Major Harim nodded at him.

Nate sat down. "I didn't ask anything. I didn't even say anything," he said to David.

"He knows something," David replied.

"Anyone who was here for the dedication of the Tabernacle knows that the God of Israel is in this camp." Harim looked at the section leaders. "I don't know about you, but I'm not going to insult the God of Israel by having a call to prayer to another god sounded in this camp." He responded to all the questions and statements about this directive in the same way. "No worship of other gods. Period."

"What about believers in Y'shua?" Nate asked. "We worship the God of Israel and His Messiah."

"Not all Christians believe Israel is legit; you know that," Harim said. "We can't have anyone in this camp who is going to oppose Israel, not at a time like this."

"Yeah, I get that," Nate said. "But a lot of Jewish believers in Y'shua are going to be coming. What about them?"

"That's why you're going to be at the first checkpoint. You can get them sorted out."

"But I'm working the storehouse."

"Not anymore." Harim studied Nate for a moment. "Nathaniel, we're here because of you. Now I want you to start figuring out what's next. Your Revelation tell you anything? About this volcano and all the earthquakes going off?"

Nate slowly shook his head, thinking. "There are more earthquakes?" he asked. "How many?"

✡✝✡✝✡✝✡

Nate looked at his phone. Tahlia hadn't answered his text. *Please,* he pleaded with God, *watch over her...*

✡✝✡✝✡✝✡

"Mom! Mom!" JJ yelled up the stairs. "You better come down here! There's trouble!"

"Honestly! I can't leave you two alone for five minutes..." Justine said, dropping a basket of laundry at the top of the stairs.

"It's not us," said Josie.

"It's the **world**!" yelled JJ. "It's exploding in pieces!"

As she came down the stairs Justine could hear the TV:

> This is an INT News Alert. We have just received a
> report of another earthquake! This one seems to
> have triggered an eruption of the Al-Safa volcanic
> field near Damascus. It is sending tons of ash and
> toxic gases into the atmosphere. It is located only
> 60 km SE of Damascus. Thought to be dormant, it
> has exploded with a vengeance! The fear is that the
> earthquakes and eruptions will set off the weapons
> depots in and around Damascus...

Someone handed the news anchor a paper. He looked stunned
as he read it. At last he looked into the camera and said:

> There has been an 8.3 earthquake along the Cascadia
> Subduction Zone. A tsunami is hitting the West Coast—
> Washington, Oregon, northern California...

"I told you—the world is exploding!" JJ said.

"This must be what Nate was talking about," Justine said,
"'great and terrible things.'"

Nisan 16 Erev - Friday

It was growing dark as Nate approached the Tabernacle Plaza.
There were people praying all along the curtain that fenced in
the courtyard, as if they were at the Kotel.[46] Nate carefully
folded the prayer he had written and put it in one of the brass
urns that had been set at intervals along the curtain. As Nate
closed his eyes, he pictured his prayers brought before the throne
of God. *Please, Father God, watch over Tahlia,* he whispered.

"So. Nathaniel," said a voice. "You are here! Aaron, Aaron!
Did I tell you tonight he would come?"

"I see he is here," said Aaron. "Now you will give it to him, yes?"

Nate opened his eyes and saw Shlomo peering into his face.

---

46 The Western Wall Plaza in Jerusalem.

234

Shlomo searched the many pockets in his long coat. He looked at Aaron. "Aaron! Aaron! It is lost!"

"No, nothing is lost. HASHEM, he knows where everything is, yes?"

Shlomo lifted his eyes to heaven. He searched the through his pockets again. Out of an inside pocket he took a small paper wrapped in tape. He held it up to Nate.

"So, this was my Ariel's." Shlomo held out the wrapped paper. He shut his eyes and slowly shook head, remembering. "Also, it was your grandmother's."

"You mean Ariel's grandmother's."

Shlomo leaned on his cane and stepped close to Nate. "Yes! Ariel's and yours also, Nathaniel. So I give it to you for your Tahlia."

"Shlomo, I'm not Sgt. Grange," said Nate. "Ariel's grandmother is not my grandmother."

Shlomo turned to Aaron. "You see? Still he does not know!"

"Know what?" asked Nate.

Shlomo put the paper in Nate's hand. "For Tahlia, to her you will give it." Nate carefully pulled the tape off the package and unfolded the paper. A small oval locket fell into his hand.

✿✝✿✝✿✝✿

Nate sat on the roof of J-5 and stared at the picture in the locket. It could have been a picture of him, the likeness was so exact. Not like the picture of Sgt. Grange, which had only a strong resemblance. *If it weren't for the clothes, anyone would think it was me,* he thought. *Who am I? Who am I?* After a long while he put the locket on the chain with the pendant from Sgt. Grange, and put both of them under his shirt. *What do Shlomo and Aaron know that I don't?*

Looking up, he saw that the moon was red. The camp looked bathed in blood. *It's nothing,* he told himself. *The ash and dust from the volcano makes the moon red. Nothing. It's nothing.*

A gritty dark cloud draped the sun like sackcloth. Nate had an uneasy feeling as he looked north. There was no volcanic ash fallout this far south, but Al-Safa was still erupting, even if he couldn't see it, with fire and smoke filling the sky. At over 200 miles away, the explosions couldn't be seen, but the continuing tremors from the earthquake could be felt. The ground under his feet hadn't stopped moving. It was as if a current was running through the earth.

The main road into the Negev was crowded with vehicles, ambulances and people walking. Nate thought about the visions he'd had about people fleeing Israel. Is this what the visions had meant? Were people trying to get on planes at Ben Gurion and on boats in the Mediterranean?

Nate had been at the checkpoint since dawn. He walked alongside the endless line of vehicles, handing out pamphlets, directing each vehicle to the appropriate turnoff, all the while watching for any sign of Tahlia. He glanced down at his phone. Still nothing from her. Or Zvi. *Where were they?*

He had looked at thousands of ID cards. He had seen hundreds of people who had been injured or were suffering from the effects of breathing in the toxic fumes and ash. He saw the stunned faces of people who had survived the earthquake in Tiberius. Nate couldn't imagine how bad it would be if Israel hadn't been prepared for an evacuation.

Down the line of vehicles, on the shoulder of the road, he spotted a MICU coming toward him. That had to be them! That was the type of ambulance they had taken.

Zvi had a strange look on his face as he slowed the ambulance and met Nate's eyes.

"Where's Tahlia?" Nate asked.

Zvi didn't answer.

Nate's heart began to pound. "What is it? Where is she?"

"Tiberius," Zvi yelled as he pulled through the checkpoint.

Nate stared as Zvi disappeared in a cloud of dust. Tiberius? He thought about the look on Zvi's face. *Something wasn't right. Something was* **not** *right.*

Nate ran to the checkpoint. He shoved the pamphlets inside. "I'm done here," he announced as he climbed into Fred and headed for the Camp.

✿ ✝ ✿ ✝ ✿ ✝ ✿

Nate followed Zvi into the emergency entrance of Tabernacle Hospital. "Where **exactly** is Tahlia?" he asked. "And Tiberius? What does that mean? Why isn't she here with you?"

"I'll tell you everything as soon as I get these people checked in," Zvi answered.

"Why did you leave Tahlia?" Nate asked, blocking the way.

✿ ✝ ✿ ✝ ✿ ✝ ✿

Fred roared over the rocky terrain spitting a cloud of dust. "Talk to me," Nate said to Zvi. "Tell me why you left Tahlia buried, **buried**! In Tiberius!" Nate glared at Zvi. Zvi looked terrified.

"We were heading for Haifa when we got the alert about the earthquake," Zvi said. "The ground was shaking under us, and by then the sky was exploding. Al-Safa was throwing fire into the air. We could see huge burning rocks falling like meteors. There was thunder, so loud it seemed like it was cracking the earth. Lightning was flashing all around." Zvi fell silent.

"Keep talking," Nate ordered.

"We could hear the shofar sounding. It was like hearing the voice of God." Zvi took a deep breath. "When we got to Tiberius, everything seemed to be rubble. Buildings down. The roads buckled. People trying to find those who were buried when the buildings collapsed."

"That's what happened?!" Nate said fiercely. "A building fell on Tahlia? And you left her buried? **Buried?**"

"It didn't happen right away. It seemed safe. We found a man first and then a kid. We got them out, then another earthquake. I thought Tahlia was right by me, but she wasn't…I looked around and couldn't see her." Zvi swallowed hard, holding back tears. "We looked. We looked everywhere."

"And then you left," said Nate. "You left her there. **Buried.**"

"Search and Rescue came with the dogs. They kept looking."

"I'm listening…" Nate said.

"And I had to bring the injured to the hospital." Zvi looked at Nate. "I'm sure they found her."

Nate listened as Search and Rescue told them they hadn't found Tahlia. He watched as they indicated all the areas they had searched. His hand rested on the soft head of one of the rescue dogs as his eyes searched for anything—anything—that might show where Tahlia had gone.

Abruptly he turned and walked away. *Where could she be? What had Aaron said? Nothing is lost… HASHEM knows where everything is. Father God, nothing is lost. You know where she is. Show me where Tahlia is,* he prayed. *Let my eyes fall on something that will lead me to her.* Running his hand through his hair, he stopped and began to walk in the opposite direction. He stared at the ground as he walked, examining every stone, brick and board.

Nothing.

He continued walking and praying. *Direct my path,* he prayed, *let my eyes see…*

The dog trotted past him, nose to the ground. It went from one side to the other, focused and intent. Nate followed a short distance behind. They both ignored the handler who was calling the dog back. The dog went in a tight circle and laid down. Nate's heart was pounding. *This is the place, right?* He knelt down and began pulling rocks and rubble away. Soon Zvi and the Search and Rescue guys were helping. *There!!* He could see clothing. *It was—yes! A Magen David uniform!*

Carefully, quickly, gently, he uncovered her face. Tahlia's eyes opened a little. "I knew you would come for me," she barely whispered. "I waited for you." Her eyes closed as they lifted her up. While they watched for the stretcher, Zvi said, "That dog just broke away. How did he know to come here, to this place?"

"Nothing is lost," said Nate. "HASHEM knows where everything is. He knew where Tahlia was. He sent this dog to this place to find her."

✿✤✿✤✿✤✿

"Where you **been**?! **Lookin'** all **over** for ya!" Nate turned to see Darryl running toward him.

"Do you have **any idea** what's been **goin'** on?!"

"I know what's going on," said Nate. "I was in Tiberius."

"Not **there**! At **home**! In the **States**!"

Now what? Nate thought. "What?"

"The Cascadian slipped!" said Darryl.

"The what?"

"The big **fault** line! You know! The **subduction**! By **California**! A tsunami **wiped out** the West Coast! Everything from the coast to the I-5 is underwater!!"

Nate spun around. "You're kidding, right?"

"No, I **ain't** kidding! I got an **alert** on my **phone**! Y'know, like what we get with **rockets** comin' in."An alert went off on Darryl's phone. "Like **this**, y'see?" He held his phone up.

"So what is it?" asked Nate.

Darryl looked at his phone, then stared at Nate. "This is **not** good!"

"What?!"

"They're going to have to **cancel** the whole **hockey** season!"

"What?"

"The New **Madrid** just went!"

Nate knew what that was. That was the fault line near where his family lived. The biggest earthquake in U.S. history had been along that fault line.

Justine paged through the channels. The Weather Channel was showing the NASA space shuttle image of the Al-Safa volcanic field. It was huge. It was so close to Damascus and the Golan.

Fox News was reporting on the tsunami that had devastated the West Coast.

> ... There are more than 100,000 fatalities, and more than 1,000,000 people have been displaced. Rescue efforts are continuing...

INT was interviewing Taylor Jones from the U.S. Geological Survey.

> The Laki volcanic system in Iceland is erupting— the whole system! A high volume of ash and other volcanic material is being expelled into the atmosphere, but more dangerous is the extremely large quantities of toxic gas. What kind of impact will these volcanic eruptions have? This has the potential to be a cataclysmic event...

"What's a cataclysmic?" asked JJ as the floor seemed to shift. The TV swayed...

"Get under the table!!" Justine yelled. "Now!"

She physically threw Josie under the table and shielded both of the J's with her body. The TV crashed and splintered everywhere.

"Do. Not. Move," Justine commanded.

"I want to see," said Josie. "Me too," said JJ.

"Close your eyes. Now!" Justine said as the bookcase fell, hurtling books all over the place.

-4-

Nate crammed the last of his equipment into his duffel. If Sgt. Grange could fit everything he needed for the whole of WWII into this duffel bag, he could fit what he needed for a few months of IDF training. He picked up his Bible and put it on top of everything else in the duffel. He took a look around Unit J5. Once he left, there would be nothing to show he'd ever been here.

Stepping outside, he was confronted by the General. "I will tell you something," David said.

Nate stopped, a feeling of uneasiness coming over him. It couldn't be Tahlia. He had just left her, had just said goodbye.

"What?" he asked.

"The black flags are flying over the Old City; from the Church of the Sepulcher, from the Hurva, from the Dome," said David. "From the Tower of David and Christ Church." Nate could swear he saw tears in the General's eyes. It had to be the Soldiers of Islam. They were the ones who carried the black flags.

CHAPTER THREE

Erev Sukkot
-1-

You have captured my heart, my treasure, my bride.
You have captured my heart with one glance of your eyes.
Song of Solomon 4:9

It was full dark as Nate approached Unit J-5 in the Judah district. The day had started with a sunrise run, in full gear, up to the top of Masada. The IDF's chief rabbi had blessed them, and they were formally inducted into the Israeli Defense Forces. All but Nate.

"It is good, Nathaniel," Yaakov had said. "You have the training and now also the freedom!"

"Yeah, but..."

"You are a soldier of HASHEM! This is good!"

"Yeah, but..." Nate remembered the sword of fire that had been over Jerusalem. *Y'shua is the commander of HASHEM's army. He has a drawn sword in his hand. Joshua 5:13–15*

Yaakov had put his arm around Nate's shoulder. "Go to the *Machom Mishpan*. See Tahlia. Get married. Eyal will be coming for you soon enough."

Nate stepped in the door, dropped his duffel and turned on the light. He looked around. He stepped back outside and checked the number. **J-5.** Yeah, this was it, but it was different.

There were curtains. Furniture. A couch, a table with three chairs. *Three?* A bed with a comforter in desert colors. Pillows. Pictures on the walls. The whole place was filled with Tahlia. She'd been making this cold unit into a home for them, but she wasn't here. The Gaza border had been exploding with violence. There had been injuries. Talia had gone to the field hospital near Gaza.

Nate looked longingly at the bed. He was so tired. *No, not until we're married.* He'd sleep on the roof tonight and every night for the next two weeks. They would be married then—on the day before *Sukkot.* [47]

---

47   Feast of Tabernacles.

✿♰✿♰✿♰✿

Nate stretched out on the roof and looked at the stars of heaven. There was barely a sliver of the new moon visible, making the stars seem even brighter. It was Erev Rosh Hashanah, the eve of the Feast of Trumpets. Tomorrow would be a Sabbath. He could sleep until he woke up—if he could just fall asleep!

He thought of all that had happened in the last six months: First Y'shua had healed him. Then the Camp of the Tabernacle was completed, and the Passover lamb was sacrificed for the first time in nearly 2000 years. Then the volcano in Syria erupted, spewing ash and fire into the atmosphere, along with a store of biological and chemical poisons. An earthquake leveled Tiberius, burying Tahlia alive. In the U.S., the Cascadia Subduction Zone fault line slipped, causing a tsunami that devastated the West Coast, taking over 100,000 lives and displacing over a million people. Then the New Madrid fault caused a huge earthquake that nearly destroyed Nate's parents' house. Earthquakes, tsunamis and volcanoes had been happening all over the earth. Huge ash clouds had blocked satellites, grounded planes and blacked out communications.

In the midst of all this chaos, the Soldiers of Islam were being called on to rise up all over the world. In the previous decades they had migrated from the Mideast and North Africa to Europe, changing the demographics of every country they had settled in. They had refused to assimilate to the Western cultures, and now they were answering the call to rise up. Terrorist attacks were a daily event in almost every major city in the U.S., Canada, Europe, Australia and seemingly everywhere else. The black flag was flying over major cities in nearly every country.

Worst of all, the Soldiers of Islam had overcome the Old City, and the self-proclaimed caliph had spread his tent on the Temple Mount under the black flags. They had not only taken control of Old Jerusalem, they were holding it hostage. Jews and Christians were living under the threat of instant death if the IDF or anyone else did anything to try to regain the city. All the holy places were wired with explosives, ready to be blown up if there was an attack.

And now…he and Tahlia were getting married…in two weeks…

Please, Father God, don't let anything happen before then.

✡✞✡✞✡✞✡

The message alert went off on his cell. *Where was his phone?* When he finally found it, Nate saw the message from Tahlia: **"Hamas rocket hit school in Beersheva! We're on our way there. Won't be back tomorrow as planned ☹ "**

Filled with longing for Tahlia, Nate closed his eyes. *Please, please, please bring her back safely …please, God…let us get married before the whole world ends.*

✡✞✡✞✡✞✡

Nate woke to the shofars sounding, his heart pounding.

Then he remembered—it was Rosh Hashanah. It was okay.

He looked toward the Tabernacle and saw the priests with the shofars. And there were Aaron and Shlomo, seated on their usual bench.

He had to talk to Shlomo about the wedding ceremony.

And he had to find Asa. He was the only one who could get what he needed to build the *sukkah.* [48]

✡✞✡✞✡✞✡

"My friend!" Asa said. "We have anything to make everything!"

Nate followed Asa through Storehouse #27.

"This! This is bamboo for the poles! All natural!"

Nate carefully stepped over the bundles of bamboo poles that Asa was tossing into the aisle.

---

48 Leviticus 23:42."'You shall dwell in booths for seven days…'" Sukkahs are booths constructed to simulate the original huts used by ancient Israel in the desert. The top of the sukkah is covered with branches so there is more shade than sunlight inside and the stars are visible at night. They are used for the seven days of Sukkot, the Feast of Tabernacles.

244

"This! This for the sides! The best cotton! All natural!"

A bundle of heavy cotton cloth nearly hit Nate in the head.

Rope, tent stakes, zip ties, and some things Nate didn't recognize littered the floor.

"My friend! The best *sukkah* in all the Negev!" said Asa, a grin covering his face.

"**What** the—**what**?! No! **No**! You **can't** do this! **This** is **not** authorized. **Nobody** signed off on **this**!"

Darryl rushed toward them, waving his clipboard. "**These** are for—" Darryl looked at his list. "—ah, **special** people. You can't just **take** 'em!"

"My friend, my friend," Asa said, coming alongside Darryl. "Be calm. No worries. … Who is more special than Nathaniel and Tahlia? It is for their honeymoon *sukkah*. It is our gift to them."

"Look," Darryl said. "There are **100,000** people who want to build a *sukkah*. He waved the clipboard at them. "Only **these** are supposed to **get the materials** from **here**. I tell ya, Nate, you're **givin'** me a **heart attack**!"

"My friend," Asa said. "We are borrowing only. After the honeymoon week, we bring everything back."

"Yeah, well, **Sukkot** will be **over** by then!" Darryl replied.

"Darryl," Nate interrupted, with a glance at Asa, "I want you to be my best man. Will you?"

Darryl stared at Nate. He didn't say anything. Then finally: "Yes! **Okay**! I'll be your **best man**! But I don't know **nothin'** about this stuff for the *sukkah*! **Nothin'**!"

"Okay," Nate agreed.

"Asa, **look** for those big **lounge pillows** in aisle 7! **Top shelf!**" Darryl yelled as he strode away.

Nate and Asa carried the materials for the *sukkah* up to the ridge overlooking the Camp. "You're sure the Preachers aren't coming back?" Nate asked.

"My friend, they will not be back. They have not yet gone through all the towns of Israel. They are being thrown out of the cities! Driven out of Tel Aviv—they are fortunate they are not killed!"

"You're kidding, right?"

"To preach repentance to people who love their pleasures?" Asa shrugged. "People were angry!"

"Where did they go?" Nate asked, securing the tarp over the pile of poles, cloth, stakes and hardware.

"The desert. Thousands of people are coming to hear them. They are asking, 'Who are these men?' They are calling them prophets!"

"Maybe we should go," Nate said.

"My friend! We will go and you will see the thousands of Israel coming to hear to the Preachers!"

-2-

The voice of the younger Preacher echoed across the desert floor, the words as clear as if he were standing right in front of them. Nate looked around. There were a least 5000 people. Most were sitting in small groups. Others were standing or walking, weaving their way through the crowd. Security personnel were around the perimeter, watching. Nate spotted the General walking toward him.

"Repent! Return to Adonai your God! He spreads out His hands to you day and night! You rebellious people; you who follow your own pleasures and not the commands of the Adonai your God!" Isaiah 65:2

This must be what he was preaching in *Tel Aviv,* Nate thought.

"Remember your God, O Israel! For you have not been forgotten by Adonai your God. He has swept away your transgressions like a cloud, and all your sins like a mist! Return to Him! He has redeemed you!" Isaiah 44:21-22

246

"I'll show you something," David said, coming up to Nate and Asa. "Look—the man with the green jacket. Watch him."

Nate and Asa scanned the crowd. There were a lot of men. No one was wearing a jacket in the desert heat. "Where?" Nate looked at the General.

"There—he's moving now," David replied. Nate spotted a man in a green jacket stand up, move through the crowd, then sit down again. A few minutes later he got up and moved a few yards before sitting again.

"Bring him to me," David said. "He plans to kill the Preachers."

Nate's eyes locked on the green-jacket man. "How about security?"

"I'll tell you something," David said. "He's watching for them."

"And if he doesn't want to come?" Asa asked.

"Show him something," David told Nate. "You have your Eagle?[49] Show him that."

"I'm on it," Nate confirmed.

"Seek Adonai while He may be found! Call to Him while He is near! Let the wicked abandon his way and the sinful one his thoughts! Return to Adonai your God so that He may have compassion on you! Return to your God, for He will freely forgive!" Isaiah 55:7

Nate and Asa sliced through the crowd until they had the man in the green jacket between them.

"My friend," Asa said, "you will come with us."

The man glared at them and started to dart into the crowd. Asa blocked him, and Nate pressed the Eagle into his spine as Asa removed the micro version of the Galil rifle concealed under the green jacket.

"Repent and return to Adonai your God!" the Preacher thundered.

"Where are you taking me?" the man asked.

"We're going to help you *repent*," Nate replied sarcastically.

---

49 The Israeli "Desert Eagle" handgun

"For Adonai your God loves you! He delivered you from slavery in Egypt and now He has redeemed you from the slavery of your sins! ^{Matthew 20:28} For Adonai your God loved you so much that He gave the Messiah, His beloved Son, as a ransom for you! Everyone who puts his trust in God's Son will not perish but will have everlasting life!" ^{John 3:16}

Nate and Asa, with the green-jacket man, headed toward David…

"Who is the Messiah? God's anointed Son! What is His name? Y'shua! Adonai your God did not send His Son into the world to condemn the world but that the world might be saved through Him! Anyone who trusts in Him is not condemned, but he who does not put his trust in Him is condemned already for not believing in His name. ^{John 3:17-18}

There was silence as they moved through the crowd. The people were leaning forward, listening…

"But now Adonai your God commands you to repent! He has set a day when He will judge the world by Y'shua, who, after He was nailed to a cross and killed, Adonai raised from the dead. ^{Acts 2:23, 17:31} He will come in judgment and with fire! He will separate the righteous from the wicked: the righteous to everlasting life and the wicked to the fire of destruction!" ^{Matthew 3:11}

Security grabbed the man in the green jacket as the Preacher's words seemed to shake the desert floor: "Repent and return to Adonai your God! Choose life!" ^{Deuteronomy 30:11-18}

✡✝✡✝✡✝✡

The older Preacher stood and looked over the multitude of people before him. His face was filled with compassion.

"Today is the day of salvation.
Adonai has gathered His people. The desolate land has been renewed.
The cities have been rebuilt.
The houses are filled with people.

248

Today, you hear our message.
Today, if you will see, if you will open your heart,
then you will understand.
Then you will repent and return to Adonai your God,
and you will be healed. Isaiah 6:10
Y'shua was wounded for our rebellion against Adonai.
He was crushed for our sins. He was beaten so that
we could be made whole. He was whipped so that we
could be healed.
Adonai laid on Y'shua the sins of us all. Isaiah 53:5-6

"My friend," said Asa, "look at David. He's thinking something…"

Nate looked over at the General. David's face was incredibly sad. *Open his heart, just a little,* he prayed.

"My friend! We must pray today is the day of salvation for David!" Asa said.

"Are you a believer in Y'shua?" Nate asked.

"My friend, before Y'shua, in this life I was lost. My only happiness was making everything out of anything. Then I would not think of how alone I was, how empty my life was. I knew I was different than the other people. My mind did not think the way they thought. People stayed away from me. But not Shlomo. With Aaron he would come and sit. Just watching me make or fix things. Shlomo would talk to Aaron. He would say: 'So, Asa makes anything out of everything. It is what Y'shua does.' One day I said, 'My friend, who is Y'shua? What is it He is making?' Then Shlomo tells me about Y'shua. He says Y'shua is making sad people happy; He is fixing the broken heart; to the ones without friends, He is being a friend; He is being a father to those whose fathers have left them; He doesn't go away; He is always there. He doesn't leave us when life is hard; instead He gives us strength."

Asa looked over at Nate. "So I ask, 'Can Y'shua make anything out of me?' Shlomo looks around my shop. Then he says, "So. Y'shua has anything He needs to make you everything that He wants." I ask, 'What does He want?' Shlomo says: 'To believe He is the Messiah sent from God, to trust Him.' Then he told me all about Y'shua. He's a rabbi. He knows these things. I pray to the God of my fathers and my eyes are opened. Then I believe. My friend, I gave to Y'shua everything. All my loneliness, all my sadness, all my emptiness. Now He is with me all the time. Now my life is full and I am never alone."

Nate nodded, thinking about that.

"I've been praying for the General for years," Nate said. "He's just so—so—stubborn!"

"Is anything too hard for HASHEM?" Asa replied. "He can bend a stiff neck."

"Father God," prayed Nate, "Don't let the General stiffen his neck against You. Open his heart so that he will not be able to resist Your Spirit."

"Amen!" said Asa. "May it be so!"

Justine looked at the empty space that used to be her home. There had been so much damage, they had to demolish what was left. The whole neighborhood looked the same: piles of rubble with trailers or tents where houses used to be. She was thankful they had power—*finally!*—and water. They even had internet again. They were going to try to get a small house framed out before winter; maybe by next summer they'd be able to live in it. The whole neighborhood was working together: carpenters, plumbers, electricians; everyone who knew how to do anything was teaching others, and they were all working together. The government was overwhelmed with the extent of the destruction, so they decided to help each other rebuild rather than wait for FEMA.

Going to Nate and Tahlia's wedding was out of the question. They would go to Israel when all this was straightened out. When the house was built. When the planes were safe again. Wes said they would get Ariel's remains from France. Then they would go. Justine sighed. *Just do the next thing,* she told herself. *And then the next and the next...*

Up on the ridge, Nate and Asa began securing the sides of the *sukkah* to the bamboo frame. Yom Kippur was over. It was only three days until the wedding, and Tahlia was coming back today. Nate watched the road from Beersheva, looking for anything that looked like an MDA vehicle.

"My friend, do not worry," Asa said. "She will be here soon. It's only an hour, not even an hour, from Beersheva. The *sukkah* will be up, and you will be together."

"She should be here by now," said Nate. "She sent a text saying they were on their way hours ago."

They both looked over the camp, toward the road.

Nothing.

✿ ✡ ✿ ✡ ✿ ✡ ✿

Asa and Nate sat down on the ridge. The sukkah was finished. Leafy branches formed the roof, letting the last of the sunlight in.

It was nearly sundown and Tahlia still was not back.

Nate looked at the text Tahlia had sent a few hours ago: **"Rocket exploded in middle of Bedouin camp. Everyone thought it had gone off in empty desert. Will bring survivors to Tabernacle Hospital."**

-3-

Nate sat on the roof of J-5, watching the activity on the Tabernacle plaza. Darryl was running around, clipboard in hand, as the *chuppah*[50] was being secured to four upright poles. "Make **double** sure that doesn't **fall** down!" he yelled. "I don't want anything happenin' to mess up this wedding!"

The canopy was like a large prayer shawl, with a menorah in the middle and embroidered with the Aaronic blessing. Under Darryl's watchful eye, *Tzitzit*[51] were fastened to the four corners. Curtains were hung and tied around the poles, leaving

---

50 The wedding canopy

51 Tassels put on the corners of a garment; see Deuteronomy 22:12

251

it open to the desert breeze. A small table, covered with a white cloth, was placed inside with two chairs. A bottle of wine with two glasses and a bowl of fruit were set on the table. Nate looked longingly at the fruit. Today had been a day of fasting. He had prayed the Yom Kippur prayers of confession and read from the book of Psalms. He had asked for forgiveness for every wrong thing he had ever done. He wanted to start his life with Tahlia free and forgiven. Now he just wanted to get married and to eat!

Nate watched as Shlomo and Aaron walked slowly to the *chuppah*. They stood there, leaning on their canes, as Shlomo placed a large paper on the table. *That has to be the ketubah,*[52] Nate thought. He scanned the entire area, hoping to catch a glimpse of Tahlia. She had finally gotten back, but whether she was still at the hospital or had come home, he had no idea.

More tables were set up around the *chuppah* on the Tabernacle Plaza. Tablecloths, vases of desert flowers and oil lamps were placed on each table.

"**Eight** chairs! Not **ten**! Can't you count?!" Darryl waved his clipboard. "Each table has **eight** chairs!" Darryl checked his watch. He looked up at Nate. "What're ya **doin'**? You have to get **ready**! Sundown's in **one hour!**"

As Asa set up the video cameras, Nate came down off the roof. Asa gave a thumbs-up: The video feed was working! Nate took a deep breath. In one hour he would see Tahlia. *One more long hour…*

✿✟✿✟✿✟✿

Wes brought the TV screen out of the trailer and secured it to the outside under the awning. He hooked up the cables from the computer. He turned everything on… *Yes!!* Everything seemed to be working. In less than an hour they would be watching the wedding on a live feed from the Negev.

Justine spread a tablecloth over the table. She put a small vase of flowers in the middle and added candles on each side. Wes came over and put his arm around her. "It'll be okay, hon; it'll

---

52 The wedding contract

almost be like we're there." He kissed her cheek and wiped the tear that had escaped her eye.

JJ and Josie watched them and rolled their eyes.

"Why get ready now?" JJ asked. "The wedding isn't till tomorrow night!"

Josie stared at him for a long moment. "No, it's today."

"Nope," JJ replied, shaking his head. "It's on Tuesday night, and today is Monday."

Josie thought about that. "We're behind Israel, so their day is first."

JJ frowned.

"And their night is before the day."

JJ frowned harder.

"So Tuesday night is Monday night."

Josie looked at JJ. "Okay?"

"No," said JJ. "Everything is all mixed up!"

"Time to get ready," Justine called. "We don't want to be late!"

"How can we be late?" JJ asked. "We're not going anywhere!"

JJ and Josie got up. "I get to wear my pretty dress," Josie announced.

"I have to wear a shirt. With **buttons**," JJ said, kicking up a cloud of dirt.

Justine glared at him. "James Justice! Don't you dare get dirt on this table!!"

"What**ever**!" said JJ as he climbed into the trailer.

✿✞✿✞✿✞✿

Nate laid his wedding clothes out on the bed: tan dress pants, white linen shirt, vest and *kippa*. *No tie, no tux—thank You, God*—he picked up the vest and tried to read the words Tahlia had embroidered. She had said it was the Song of Solomon— the entire book, every word. The gold thread made the whole vest look golden.

Nate looked at the pants and shirt. The pants were okay, but the shirt was wrinkled. He hung it near the shower and turned the hot water on. Steam began pouring out of the bathroom. Soon the shirt would be wrinkle-free… it had worked before. He couldn't go to his own wedding with a wrinkled shirt, could he?

He ran his hand through his hair. *Really need a haircut. Every time something important happens, I need a haircut…*

Nate remembered the first time he had seen Tahlia. Her smile… Her eyes softly reflecting the candlelight. He took a deep breath. Tonight was the night he'd been waiting for. Soon… soon he would see her and they would be together … forever. If nothing happened in the next hour… no earthquakes or rockets or anything else … *please God, don't let anything happen…*

CHAPTER FOUR

My Beloved
-1-
I am my beloved's and my beloved is mine.
Song of Solomon 6:3

Justine watched as the sun sank like a glowing ember behind the ridge overlooking the wilderness camp. She watched as the full moon rose, bathing the Tabernacle Plaza in soft white light. She watched as the oil lamps on the tables around the wedding canopy were lit. Her eyes followed the camera as it panned the camp. She saw crowds of people standing on the rooftops, lighting the small oil lamps they carried.

"Look," she said to Wes as she lit the candles on their table. "It looks like all the stars of heaven have come down to witness Nate and Tahlia's wedding."

She saw Darryl watching as the guests were seated at the tables. Tahlia's friend Rivka gently plucked the strings of a large harp that was opposite the *chuppah*.

Rabbi Shlomo Levi sat quietly on a chair, leaning on his cane.

Then Justine saw Nate take his place under the canopy.

"He needs a haircut," said Wes.

"No tux or tie, I get that," Justine remarked, "but he could've at least buttoned the vest."

✿✝✿✝✿✝✿

Nate rocked slowly side to side, watching as the white runner was rolled out. Then his eyes focused on the end of the aisle, where Tahlia would soon appear.

A shofar began to sound, softly at first, then gaining strength, and finally fading away.

Tahlia stepped onto the white runner, her linen dress shimmering with reflected moonlight, the oil lamp in her hand flickering slightly in the breeze, a breeze that had lifted the edge of her dress so that she seemed to be floating in the air…

Nate's heart was pounding as he stepped out from under the *chuppah* and walked toward her, as if in a dream.

Reaching her side, he saw the soft light of the oil lamp glowing in her eyes as he lowered the veil over her face. [53]

"Are you ready?" he whispered.

"Yes," she breathed.

A single violin began to play *Agnus Dei* as Tahlia put her hand in his and they walked together toward the wedding canopy.

The guests all stood. They said:

Blessed is the one who comes in the name of Adonai. We bless you from the house of Adonai.

Under the chuppah, Tahlia circled around Nathaniel as she softly sang:

I will betroth you to Me forever; I will betroth you to Me in righteousness and justice; love and compassion; I will betroth you to Me in faithfulness; and you shall know Adonai. Hosea 2:19-20

Rabbi Shlomo Levi stood. "So," he began, "this is what Adonai has said…"

"It is not good for man to be alone; I will make a companion for him to be a helpmate to him." So Adonai caused Adam to fall into a deep sleep. He took a part of Adam's side and closed up the place from which He had taken it. Then Adonai made a woman from the side and brought her to Adam. And he said: "She is a part of my own flesh and bone. She will be called 'woman' because she was taken out of a man." … For this reason a man leaves his father and mother and is joined to his wife, and the two are united into one. Genesis 2:18,20-24

---

53 A ceremony called *bedeken* ("covering"), signifying that his love for he is for her inner beauty.

Shlomo put his hand on the *Ketuba*, moving it slightly toward Nate and Tahlia.

Tahlia set her lamp on the table. Nathaniel and Tahlia each signed the marriage contract.

The witnesses, Darryl and Rivka, signed beneath them.

Then Shlomo said:

He who is majestic over all, He who is blessed over all,
He who is great over all, May He bless Nathaniel and Tahlia.
And he put his signature on the *Ketuba*.

Rabbi Shlomo took a cup of wine, and lifting it up said:

Blessed are You, Adonai our God, King of the Universe,
who has made us holy through His commandments,
and has commanded us concerning forbidden unions,
forbidding us those who are betrothed, permitting us
those who are wedded to us.
Blessed are You, Adonai, who sanctifies His people Israel
through the rite of the chuppah and sacred covenant of
marriage.

Nate and Tahlia took the first glass of wine from Shlomo's hand, and they each took a sip.

Nate took the ring, a plain gold band. Holding it ready to be placed on Tahlia's forefinger, he said:

Behold, you are consecrated to me by this ring in
accordance with the law of Moses and of Israel.

Darryl picked up the marriage contract. Putting it on his clipboard, he read:

On the third day of the week, on Erev Tishrei the
fourteenth, in the year 5780 in the State of Israel, in the
Negev, in the camp of the Tabernacle, before the gates of
the Tabernacle, Nathaniel Grange and Tahlia Yash'el have
come together under the chuppah. On this day they
enter into the holy covenant of marriage with Adonai and
all the stars of heaven as their witnesses.

257

Darryl looked up and said, "These are the terms and conditions of the marriage contract, in the words of Nathaniel and Tahlia." He read:

I, Nathaniel, vow to protect Tahlia, even shedding my blood for her and giving my life for her.
I vow to provide for her, sacrificing my own desires for her welfare.

Nate said: "This I vow."

Darryl continued:

I, Nathaniel, and I, Tahlia, vow: We will love each other as Y'shua has loved us, and as Y'shua has pledged never to leave or forsake us, so we pledge never to leave or forsake each other. As Adonai has shown mercy to us through the Messiah Y'shua, so we will show mercy to one another, forgiving one another as Adonai has forgiven us. Together we will love Adonai our God with all our heart, mind, soul and strength. We will love each other as we love ourselves, and together we will love our neighbor. We will build a house of love, faith, and commitment to Adonai and to each other.

Nate and Tahlia both said: "This we vow."

Darryl held up the Ketuba, showing it had been signed. He said:

Before Adonai and these witnesses, we seal this document.

Rabbi Shlomo then took the second cup of wine. He pronounced over it the seven blessings:

Blessed are You, Adonai our God, King of the Universe, who creates the fruit of the vine and who has given us the true vine, Y'shua the Messiah.

Blessed are You, Adonai our God, King of the Universe, who has created all for His glory.

Blessed are You, Adonai our God, King of the Universe, Creator of mankind.

Blessed are You, Adonai our God, King of the Universe, who made humanity in His image, the image of His likeness, and out of His very self formed a building for eternity.

Blessed are You, Adonai, Creator of mankind.
Blessed are You, Adonai, who gladdens Zion through her children, as her children return to her in joy.
Blessed are you, Adonai, who gives joy to the bridegroom and the bride.
Bring great joy to these loving friends, as You gave joy to Your creations in the Garden of Eden.
Blessed are You, Adonai our God, King of the Universe, who created joy and gladness, bridegroom and bride, happiness and jubilation, cheer and delight, love, fellowship, peace and friendship. Soon, Adonai our God, may there be heard in the cities of Judah, and in the streets of Jerusalem, the sounds of joy and gladness, the sounds of the bridegroom and bride, the joyous sounds of bridegrooms from their wedding canopy and of young people at their feasts of song.

Blessed are You, Adonai, who makes the bridegroom rejoice with the bride.

Shlomo gave the cup of wine to Nathaniel, and then he raised his right hand, his left hand gripping his cane.

He blessed them, putting the name of Adonai on them:

Adonai will bless you and protect you;
Adonai will smile on you and be gracious to you;
Adonai will look with favor on you and give you His peace. Numbers 6:24–27

Nathaniel and Tahlia drank the second cup of wine.

Shlomo declared:

Nathaniel and Tahlia have bound themselves together in the holy covenant of marriage before Adonai and these witnesses. They are now husband and wife. They are no longer two but one.
Let no man separate them, for Adonai has joined them together.

Nate and Tahlia looked at each other and waited… and waited … and waited.

Nate whispered, "Shlomo, Shlomo! What's next? Can I kiss my bride?"

"So," Shlomo said, straightening up, "kiss her already! What is it you are waiting for?"

As Nate bent down to kiss Tahlia, both of them were trying not to laugh.

Placing the cup in a small bag, Nate said,

We pray for the peace of Jerusalem. Let there be peace within your walls... For the sake of our family and friends, we will say 'Peace be with you. For the sake of the house of Adonai our God, we will seek what is best for you, O Jerusalem." (Psalm 122:6–9)

His foot came down on the cup, smashing it into pieces.

"Mazel Tov! Mazel Tov!" All the guests cheered, wishing them a future full of love and hope and prosperity.

"Mazel Tov!" called all Israel as they stood on their rooftops and in the streets.

Shlomo walked slowly from under the wedding canopy as Nate gathered Tahlia in his arms and kissed her again. Darryl let down the curtains, drawing them closed on the four sides of the chuppah. The violin began to fill the air with the sounds of Hallelujah.[54]

Rivka began to sing:

Hallelujah, Hallelujah, Hallelujah, Hallelujah
Nathaniel planned to fly away
But his heart was asking him to stay
He turned around and then he found Tahlia
With love they walked all through the land
From mountain heights to desert sand
They raised their hands and sang *Hallelujah*

---

54   Song by Leonard Cohen; new lyrics written by the author for Nathaniel and Tahlia's wedding

Hallelujah, Hallelujah, Hallelujah, Hallelujah
And then the day of terror came
A truck hit Nate and left him lame
And he cried out for mercy to Yah
They found comfort in your word
And learned about your fiery sword
They raised their hands and sang *Hallelujah*

Hallelujah, Hallelujah, Hallelujah, Hallelujah
A voice called out into the night
Calling for Nate to stand upright
He stood and walked, trusting in Y'shua
And now they've reached this special time
Of love and faith and hope combined
To raise their hands in praise and glory to Yah
Hallelujah, Hallelujah, Hallelujah, Hallelujah

-2-

"Why are they in the little tent?" Josie asked.

"Because they just got married," Justine replied. "They want to be alone."

"What do they do in there?" asked JJ.

"They're kissing," Josie told him.

"They're having something to eat," Justine said. "They haven't eaten all day."

"Well, I'm hungry too!" JJ said, as he watched platters of food being placed on the buffet tables set up around the Tabernacle plaza.

"Okay, young man," Wes said, "you can help bring out the food."

"I never saw a wedding like that, at night, under the stars," Justine said.

"It was different," Wes agreed.

They watched as the remains of the wedding supper were cleared away and the wedding cake was brought out.

"Look," Justine said to the J's, "the little bride and groom are under a little *chuppah*!"

They watched as Nate and Tahlia walked hand-in-hand to the middle of the plaza as a familiar song began to play.

"This is our song," Wes remarked. "Did you tell Nate this was our song at our wedding?"

Justine shook her head. "I've never said anything about our wedding to Nate."

Wes stood up. "May I have this dance?" he asked. "For the rest of my life?"

"I'm still saying yes," Justine replied, as they began to dance.

Josie looked over at JJ. "I have my pretty dress on," she stated.

JJ folded his arms over his shirt with buttons and turned his head.

"Dance with your sister," Wes told him.

JJ turned and glared at Josie.

"Be the man," Wes ordered.

"What**ever**," JJ muttered as he took his sister's hand and dragged her onto the patio.

✿✝✿✝✿✝✿

Justine, Wes and the J's watched as the camera panned over the Tabernacle plaza. It was empty now. The wedding was over. They watched as the camera showed the night sky and then focused on a small *sukkah* high on the ridge, glowing with the light inside of it.

"Are Nate and Tahlia eating in that little tent too?" JJ asked.

"They're still kissing," Josie said.

Justine and Wes smiled. "I'm sure they are," Wes said.

✡✝✡✝✡✝✡

On the ridge, in the little *sukkah*, Nate and Tahlia lay in each other's arms, looking through the leafy branches at all the stars of heaven.

"Remember when you told me I was one of those stars?" Tahlia asked.

"Yeah," Nate answered. "And now here we are, camped around the Tabernacle of God."

PART FOUR

ALIYAH

Many nations will come and say,
"Come, let us make aliyah
to the mountain of the LORD…"
Micah 4:3

A small circle of light followed the traces of disturbed earth deep in a tunnel beneath the *Rue des Rosiers*. A shred of fabric, barely a thread, was found. Simcha carefully brushed away the dirt.

Wes watched as more of the cloth was revealed. "You getting this?" he asked the cameraman.

At last Simcha stepped back. "Prayer shawl," he said. "I think we've found our girl."

CHAPTER ONE

Ariel

-1-
When God comes to your aid,
you are to carry my bones up from here.
Genesis 50:25

Nate watched as Justine and the J's came off the plane. He hadn't realized until now how much he had missed them. "There's Nate!" JJ shouted. Both the J's broke away from Justine and ran to him, throwing their arms around him. Nate bent down and hugged them tightly.

Justine watched them. The J's had missed their big brother and had done nothing but talk about seeing him for months. And there he was. She could hardly believe her eyes. He was bigger, taller, than when he had left home a few years ago. Now he was married—and a father. Justine was overcome with emotion. To see her son again, to be in Israel, to meet Tahlia and her new little grandson, was more joy than she could have dreamed of.

Nate put his arms around his mom and pulled her close. "I missed you," he said.

"There were times I thought I'd never see you again," Justine said.

"Mom threw all your stuff down the stairs!" JJ announced.

"Even your CDs!" Josie chimed in.

"Really? All of them?"

"Yep!" the J's said in unison.

"Did you find any you liked?" Nate asked as he led them to where Fred was waiting.

"Is this safe to ride in?" asked Justine. "I don't see any seatbelts."

Nate threw the luggage in the back, leaving just enough room for the J's. "Stay low and hang on," he said.

"Nate, I'm serious."

"No one's fallen out yet," said Nate. "You ready?" he asked the J's.

"I'm so excited to see little Nathan," Justine said. "I just can't wait to hold him!"

"You'll have plenty of time for that," Nate said. A shadow of sadness passed over his face.

Justine frowned. Something isn't right. "Is everything okay?" she asked.

"Yeah," Nate said. "It's all good."

"You said you weren't going to name him Nathaniel," she said, watching Nate carefully.

"We didn't. His name is Nathan Eli. Totally different."

"Really?"

"Yeah, Nathaniel means 'gift of God.' Nathan Eli means 'gift of my God.' Totally different."

"Totally!" said JJ.

Justine watched the bleak landscape—empty, brown, rocky, filled with nothing.

"This is a real wilderness," she said. "There's nothing but earth and sky."

"Yeah, but over there…" Nate pointed, "…is Qumran. That's something." He turned to the J's. "You know what that is?"

"Yep!" JJ said.

"It's the dead scrolls," Josie said.

"We'll go see it while you're here," Nate told them.

"See over there? That's the Dead Sea." Nate pointed to his left.

Justine looked and saw green houses and what looked like palm trees. Lots of them. "I thought you were in a serious drought."

"We are. So is everyone else."

"You must be getting water from somewhere."

"We recycle 90% of our water. And we can get water out of the air, and out of the Mediterranean."

"Really?!"

"It's like I wrote you, Mom. The desert is blooming."

"Blooming!" the J's repeated.

"Look! High up on that mountain, what do you see?"

Josie stood up to get a better look.

"Sit down! Now!" Justine ordered.

"See those buildings on top?"

"Yep!" JJ confirmed.

"No," Josie answered, glaring at Justine.

"That's Masada. Do you know what that is?" Nate asked.

"It's where everyone killed everyone," JJ replied.

"So they wouldn't be slaves," Josie added.

"We watched a movie about it," Justine explained.

"Do you know about the prophecies?" asked Nate.

The J's looked at each other. They shook their heads.

"During an archeological dig at Masada, they found a small room next to the synagogue. It was a room that was used to store worn out scrolls before they could be properly buried in a Jewish cemetery. They found two scrolls. One was the last two chapters of Deuteronomy, and the other was from Ezekiel, mostly chapter 37."

"Know what that chapter is about?" Nate asked the J's. "Bones, dem bones, de, dry bones..." he sang.

"...and the foot bone's connected to the ankle bone..." the J's chimed in.

"What prophecies did they find?" Justine asked.

"Well, let's see. They found some in Deuteronomy 33,where Moses is blessing the twelve tribes. When Israeli Geologist Tovia Luskin read the blessing about Joseph, he realized it was a perfect description of an oil field. He founded an oil company that eventually found a site that had more than a billion barrels of oil."

"Really!"

"The next chapter is when God shows Moses the whole land of Israel, all the land that He had promised to give to the descendants of Abraham, Isaac and Jacob. They found these scrolls after the Six-Day War, after God miraculously gave Israel all of Jerusalem, Judea, Samaria and the Sinai."

Nate pulled off the paved road onto a barely visible dirt track in the desert. "Also, another prophecy, in the Ezekiel scroll, starts with God telling Edom, which is part of Jordan today, that He will make them desolate. The next passage is how God is going to restore Israel. Ezekiel 37 is about the valley of the dry bones. The bones represent the whole house of Israel, without life after the Holocaust. Ezekiel writes that God was going to restore Israel and that they would become a great army. That is exactly what has happened. The prophecy isn't totally fulfilled yet—all Israel hasn't been saved yet—but it will be!"

"Yep!" said the J's.

☆✞☆✞☆✞☆

Dust swirled around Fred and the J's hung on as they bounced over the desert. "I'm taking you to a special place," Nate said as Fred powered its way up the ridge. When he stopped at the top, Nate said, "This is where our honeymoon sukkah was."

"It was a wonderful wedding, "said Justine. "Tahlia was just beautiful."

"I had to dance with my sister," JJ remarked.

"I had on my pretty dress," Josie said sweetly.

"You were beautiful too," said Justine.

Nate took the binoculars out of his duffel and handed them to Justine.

"This is pretty impressive," she said, looking over the camp. "It's bigger than I thought."

"It's set up for about 140,000 people," Nate commented.

"Where do you live?" Justine asked.

"Do you see the Tabernacle?"

Justine nodded, watching a column of smoke rising.

"Around that is the housing for the Levites. Then on the east side is the flag of Judah. That's where we live. Under the Lion of Judah."

"I want to see!" Josie exclaimed.

Justine handed the binoculars to JJ.

"See that guy down there? The one walking around waving the clipboard?"

"Yep," said JJ. "Is he crazy?"

"No, that's just Darryl."

"I want to see!" Josie grabbed for the binoculars.

"Give those to your sister," said Justine.

JJ glared at Josie.

"I'm waiting," Justine said.

"Whatever!" said JJ, handing them to Josie.

"I'll take you there later, okay?" said Nate.

✡✞✡✞✡✞✡

Justine could hear Nathan crying before they even got inside of Unit J-5. She looked at Nate. "Everything's okay? It's all good? Really?"

"He cries all the time," said Nate. "The doctor says its colic, nothing to worry about."

"He says it won't last forever," Tahlia added, handing Nathan to Nate.

Tahlia looked exhausted. Justine put her arms around her, giving her a comforting hug. "You need some rest. While I'm here you need to get some sleep."

"Abigail and Hannah help out," Nate explained, "but the only time he's not crying is when he's nursing. Only Tahlia can do that."

Justine took Nathan from Nate. "Shhh, shhh, little one," she whispered. She spread his blanket on the table and laid him down. She gently began to massage his little body and carefully turned him one way and then another.

Gradually Nathan's cries became whimpers, and then he was quiet.

Justine wrapped him tightly in his blanket and picked him up. Holding him close, she began to rock back and forth.

"What just happened?" asked a surprised Nate. "What did you just do?"

269

"Explain…" Tahlia said, staring at her sleeping, not-crying baby.

"It's not complicated," said Justine. "There were a lot of years between you and the J's. For a long time it looked like you were going to be an only child."

"But then we came!" the J's interjected.

"Let Mom talk," Nate replied.

"When you started school I began to volunteer with a group called CRYING BABIES. We helped out moms who had babies with colic, or who had crack babies, or had babies with other problems."

"The babies were cracked?" asked Josie.

"Let Mom talk," Nate repeated.

"Before we could help with the babies, we had to take a course in baby massage and a more advanced course in Infant Chiropractic Technique." Justine patted little Nathan's back. "That's what I just did. It doesn't always help, but most of the time it does."

Nate and Tahlia watched Nathan quietly sleeping.

"I don't think babies want to cry all the time," said Justine. "It almost becomes a habit. They just don't know how to stop. This helps them learn they don't have to cry in order to breathe. I'll teach both of you."

-2-

With great care and even greater respect, Simcha and Wes wrapped the bones of Ariel and put them in a backpack. Tears in their eyes, they wrapped her baby's tiny bones and placed them with Ariel's. They gathered what remained of the cloths, dark with dried blood, and put them in another backpack, laying the tattered prayer shawl on top.

Jessie, the cameraman, turned off the camera. "We're finished here," he said into his cell phone.

Robert Maltz, producer of *Underground Mysteries*, followed the French guide out of the tunnels. It had been a successful shoot. They'd filmed the tunnels where the French Underground met during WWII. They had found the room where anti-Nazi flyers had been printed. In another tunnel they found where documents had been forged. They also found where the Partisans made the bombs they used when they attacked the German commander of Paris. Even without Ariel, this episode would be the highlight of the season. Now all they had to do was get Ariel out of France. As they stepped into the daylight he noticed his cameraman, Jessie, the Israeli archeologist and Wes blending in with his crew. They all got into the van without raising any suspicion.

"You got everything?" Maltz asked.

"We have her," Simcha said.

"I got some great footage," said Jessie. "It's pretty intense."

"Keep it with you," said Robert. "I don't want any problems getting back to the States. And when you get to Israel, I don't want any publicity. None. No newspapers, no TV, no radio, no Internet. Can you make sure of that?"

"We'll keep it private," Simcha promised. "Real quiet. The Israelis don't want the publicity either. Nobody wants an international incident."

"Are you all set to get out of France?" Maltz asked Wes.

"Our biggest challenge is getting from here to the Embassy. Once we get to there, the Israelis take over."

✿✞✿✞✿✞✿

Nate, Tahlia and Justine sat on the roof of J-5. The stars were shining and everything was peaceful. Justine looked at her little grandson, lying quietly in her arms. *Sleep in heavenly peace,* she thought.

"He's hardly cried at all today," Tahlia remarked.

Looking up, Justine noticed Tahlia's necklace.

"That's a beautiful locket," she said. "Unusual, antique-looking."

"Nate gave it to me for our wedding."Tahlia took it off and handed it to Justine.

Justine opened the locket and looked at the picture. "We did this once, dressed up in all old-fashioned clothes and had our picture taken. Remember?"

She looked at Nate and then back at the picture. "This isn't you, is it?" she said.

"No. Shlomo gave it to me to give to Tahlia. He said it belonged to Ariel's grandmother, and that she was Sgt. Grange's grandmother too. Then he said she was my grandmother. Shlomo and Aaron always get me confused with Sgt. Grange."

"Did you ever wonder why you look like Sgt. Grange? Why you look like his grandfather?" Justine asked, staring at the picture.

"Yeah—all the time," Nate replied." Sometimes I think I'm going to explode my head."

As she handed Nathan to Tahlia, Justine said, "I have something to tell you about you, about our family."

She took a deep breath before continuing. "Before Wes and I were married, I was engaged to someone else. We planned on getting married, but when I found out I was pregnant, we decided to get married right away. We never had a chance. He was killed during a routine traffic stop on the day were to be married. He was your father's partner, his best friend."

Justine paused, remembering those difficult times.

"Wes asked me to marry him. He said he would be a good father to you. We got married two weeks later. No one ever realized he wasn't your biological father. We never even thought about it. You were our son. Wes was your father. This is what you need to know. Your biological father's name was Nathaniel Ellis."

"Is he related to Sgt. Grange?"

"It's complicated, but yes. Yes, he is."

"I'm listening."

"Nathaniel Ellis' mother was Grace Hansen. Remember the letter from Sgt. Grange's mother? Where she said she'd 'wait

272

with grace'? That was a name, Grace. Sgt Grange's daughter. She married Richard Ellis."

"When did you figure all this out?" Nate asked. "When I sent you the letter?"

"That was when we learned that Sgt. Nathaniel Grange and Nathaniel Hansen were the same person."

Nate got up and started walking around, running his fingers through his hair. "You knew this?! You couldn't tell me?!"

"Like I said, it's complicated."

Nate looked at Tahlia. "So explain," he said to his mom.

"Your father, Wes—he said you were his son and he was your father and that was all you needed to know. He was afraid of losing you."

"Yeah, well, that'll never happen. He'll always be my father. … What about my duffel bag? Sgt. Grange's Bible? And his medal? How did I get those?"

Justine shook her head. "I don't know. I just don't know."

"Somebody has to know," Nate mused.

JJ and Josie put their heads over the top of the stairs. They had listened to all the complicated talking.

"Ask him," JJ instructed.

"We'll be in trouble," Josie whispered, looking at her pajamas.

"Whatever!" JJ said. He climbed on the roof and asked Nate, "Are you still our brother?"

"Yeah," said Nate. "I'll always be your brother."

-3-

General David Yash'el watched as the El Al flight landed on the most desolate landing strip in the Negev.

He had made sure there was no one here to see the plane come down. He paced impatiently. He wouldn't relax until this precious cargo was on the ground.

273

He watched as Simcha Lackpor, the archeologist, Wes Grange, and the cameraman from *Underground Mysteries* disembarked from the plane. He watched as Simcha carefully rolled a heavy, hard-sided suitcase off the tarmac. He watched as Wes slung a backpack over his shoulder and raised the handle on another, smaller suitcase. He watched as the cameraman unloaded a rolling footlocker. He watched as a man carrying a metal briefcase got off the plane. The man gave him a nod. Relief washed over David. It had arrived, with no one the wiser.

Wes, Simcha, and the cameraman walked over to David.

"We got our girl," said Simcha patting the hard-sided suitcase. "Ariel is finally making aliyah."

David smiled. "I'll tell you something, I was beginning to be worried."

"We had a little trouble getting to the Embassy," Wes said, shaking David's hand. "But your guy ran interference and we made it okay."

"He is one scary guy," Simcha remarked. "Doesn't talk much, though."

David watched as the scary guy put the briefcase into a partially hidden vehicle and then sped away. Wes watched the dust trail hanging in the air.

"I can film this, right?" Jessie asked. "Ariel's arrival in Israel?"

All it took was one glare from the General, and he put his camera down.

"How soon before Shlomo can be told?" David asked Simcha.

I'll have her ready tomorrow," Simcha answered. "Then you can tell him."

"Nathaniel will tell him," David said.

"Dad! Dad! We saw the Tabernacle!" JJ yelled.

"And deer climbing trees in the Gedi!" Josie yelled.

"And the dead scrolls!"

"Whoa, slow down," said Wes. "Let me see your brother a minute." He threw an arm around Nate's shoulders and grasped his hand. He shook his head. "Thought I'd never make it."

"Did you bring her?" Nate asked.

Wes nodded. "Simcha says you can tell Shlomo day after tomorrow."

Wes drew Nate off to the side. "Ariel wasn't the only one on that plane. There was a dangerous-looking man carrying a metal briefcase."

"I'm listening…" Nate said.

"As soon as we landed, he took the briefcase, got into a car that had been concealed, and drove away."

"The General say anything?"

"No, but he looked relieved. That level of secrecy wasn't just for Ariel."

"Yeah," said Nate. "Something's not right…"

✿✞✿✞✿✞✿

"This is quite the setup," Wes commented as he looked over the camp. He saw people standing and swaying, prayer books in hand, as they stood on the walkway, facing the curtain that fenced the Tabernacle courtyard. He saw two old men sitting on a bench on the Tabernacle Plaza, facing the gate. He watched as the smoke rose from the Altar of Burnt Offering.

"I thought you said they were only going to have a sacrifice on Passover," he said to Nate.

"Yeah," Nate said, "that's what I thought, but they're sacrificing every morning and evening."

Wes saw families walking leisurely, pushing strollers. He saw groups of men sitting at café tables, talking. He saw kids running and playing. "Everything looks so peaceful."

"Yeah, it is peaceful. We have almost no crime."

"People are people. There's always going to be crime."

"Seriously, Dad, there really is very little. Everyone in this camp worships, or at least acknowledges the God of Israel. There was a huge revival when the Preachers were here. Everyone at least tries to follow the Ten Commandments. When you wake up every day and see the smoke rising over the Tabernacle, it's an incentive."

"They're called mitzvot—good deeds," Tahlia explained. "Everyone tries to do good for each other."

"The Commandments are a hedge of protection around this camp," Nate said. "With everyone living within this hedge, life here is pretty safe."

"When the Bible was taken out of schools and the Ten Commandments taken off the walls, our crime rates started to climb," Wes observed.

"It's gotten to where people don't even know right from wrong anymore," Justine remarked. "I wonder what kind of world our little Nathan is going to grow up in."

"He'll be fine," Wes said, looking down at Nathan. "He's got a good mom and dad."

"If I'm a good father," Nate said, looking steadily into Wes' eyes, "it's because you've been such a good father to me."

Wes bent over to kiss Nathan's little head, hiding the tears that suddenly came.

"You know he needs a haircut, right?"

"We hardly have any sickness either," Tahlia added. "Other settlements have had epidemics; we've had nothing like that."

"The finger of God!" said David as he stepped onto the roof. "I tell you something. In Beersheva, hundreds died last year from this disease. And the terrorists! They are coming up from the ground, right into Israel. Into the settlements, even into bigger towns. This is since the black flags are flying over the Old City. Even Arabs who used to be peaceful are joining the Soldiers of Islam."

276

"Nothing like that in the Camp of the Tabernacle," Nate said. "We are protected by the God of Israel."

"We all like to think that," said Wes.

"Not even rockets can touch us," said Nate.

"So explain," said Tahlia. "Tell about the rocket."

"It was the day of the Priestly Blessing," Nate began. "Right after the Blessing, there was lightning flashing all around the camp, like a wall of fire! What we didn't know was that rockets were being fired at us from the Sinai. These were serious guided rockets, not like the ones from Gaza. They were all exploded in mid-air by the lightning."

"I'll tell you something, lightning is God's Iron Dome," David remarked.

"You remember that verse?" asked Nate. "'Adonai will appear above his people, his arrows will fly like the lightning.' Zechariah 9:14. That's what happened. God's arrows shot down the rockets!"

"Not those rockets," Tahlia said to Nate. "Tell about the one that could have blown you to pieces."

"Okay. Yeah…" Nate got up and began walking slowly. "So I'm out on patrol at the Sinai border. It's me, Eyal, Zvi and a couple other guys from Gibbor Chayil. We know there's something on the other side of this high berm, but we can't see. So we send up our drone."

JJ and Josie loved it when Nate told stories. He always acted them out. They felt they were on patrol too. They watched as he sent the drone up…

"Then we're all huddled around this little screen and we can see the terrorists with their faces wrapped in black. They're carrying rocket launchers. All of a sudden a rocket lands right in the middle of our huddle! It actually brushed Zvi! We froze. We hardly dared to breathe."

JJ and Josie held their breath…

"Then we started backing away, very, very slowly. When we got far enough, we just took off running. Then the whole thing blew. BOOM!!"

JJ and Josie jumped.

"It left a crater as big as this building! No kidding. If it had gone off right away we would have all been blown to bits."

"The guys said it didn't go off because God is with Nathaniel," said Tahlia. "They said if Nathaniel's with them, they'll have God's protections too."

"Yep!" said JJ. "So I'm going on patrol."

"No you're not," said Justine.

"God's protecting me too."

"You. Are. Not. Going," Justine firmly told him.

"Dad, you could go with us," Nate said.

"No," Justine said.

"We'll talk about it," Wes stated.

He's going to come, Nate thought.

-4-

The sky was dark with barely a sliver of moon to light the way. The vehicle moved carefully, without any lights showing. Nate and Wes followed Eyal and Yoav across the desert.

"What are we watching for?" asked Wes, scanning the landscape with night-vision goggles.

"Anything that looks out of place, any movement," Nate answered. The vehicle in front of them came to a halt. "They've spotted something."

Eyal signaled them to come up.

"The Preachers," said Yoav, "and they're not alone."

Nate could see four men standing around a small fire.

"The General is there," Nate said.

"And the man from the plane," said Wes, "the one I told you about."

"What plane?" asked Eyal, keeping his eyes on the men.

"The one I came in on."

"And this man, why did you notice him?"

"He looked dangerous," said Wes.

"If he was dangerous, he wouldn't have made it out of the airport."

Wes looked at Nate and barely shook his head.

Eyal turned and looked at Wes. "Unless he was with the General."

"What is the General doing out here?" Nate asked.

"Sava is involved in something," said Eyal. "Something with the Preachers."

"Talk to me," said Nate.

"He's been tense and secretive lately," Eyal remarked. "You notice?"

"Yeah," Nate agreed, "I noticed."

-5-

It was early morning when Nate approached the bench where Shlomo and Aaron were already sitting.

"Hey, Shlomo," he said sitting down next to him.

Shlomo looked at him. "Aaron, Aaron! It is Nathaniel. He has come to tell us about his family."

"They have come to Israel, yes?" asked Aaron.

"Yeah, they're here now," said Nate. "They brought someone very special with them."

"So? You will tell us who this someone is?"

"Shlomo, remember when you told me about Ariel? How you and Aaron buried her in the tunnels under the streets in the *Le Marais*?"

Shlomo bent over his cane. He nodded his head. "So. I am remembering."

"My dad, he went to Paris to find her."

Shlomo sat up straight. "He has found my Ariel?"

"Yeah, he found her," Nate answered. "And your son. He found them both."

"In the tunnels, yes?" asked Aaron.

"They took her out of the tunnels and brought her here to Israel."

"Aaron, Aaron!" Shlomo pulled himself to his feet. "My Ariel has made aliyah."

He looked at Nate. "Where have they brought her?"

"She is at your house," said Nate. "We will come and sit Shiva with you."

"So." said Shlomo. "Now we can bless her memory. Now we can mourn."

✿✙✿✙✿✙✿

Shlomo stood, his hand resting on the plain pine box that held the bones of Ariel and his son. Great tears rolled down his face as sobs shook his body.

"It is the first time he can mourn, yes?" Aaron said. "He has carried his grief, hidden deep inside. Now it comes out."

"It's not too much for him, is it?" asked Nate.

"No, no," said Aaron. "It is good to weep for those we lose, yes?"

At last Shlomo sat. He looked again at the plain pine box. Then he closed his eyes.

After a while Nate asked, "Is he sleeping?"

"He is remembering," Aaron answered.

Shlomo opened his eyes. "There is someone in this room I do not know."

"This is Jessie, a filmmaker," said Nate. "He is making a film about Ariel so she will never be forgotten."

Shlomo struggled to his feet. Leaning on his cane he looked at the camera. "So. First a review."

Shlomo began to tell the story of Ariel.

He told how she was working with the Resistance during WWII.

He told of how they had fallen in love, that they had gotten married and she had become pregnant.

He told of the roundups of the Jews in Paris and how Ariel's whole family had been murdered by the Nazis.

He told how she had been tortured and how because of this she had given birth to their son.

He told how she had been killed by the Gestapo and how her body and that of his son had been thrown onto the *Rue des Rosiers*.

He told how he and Aaron had taken her and buried her in the tunnels.

Then he sat back down.

Jessie turned off the camera. They sat in silence for a long time.

✿✞✿✞✿✞✿

When Nate arrived early the next morning, Aaron was waiting.

"He is with Ariel," Aaron said. "They are always together now, yes?"

Nate went inside and found Shlomo lying on the floor. His cane had fallen, and his hand was reaching toward the plain pine box.

✿✞✿✞✿✞✿

The funeral was small. Only Aaron, the General and his family, Nate and his family and Darryl attended. Ten were needed to say the Kaddish. There were barely enough to make up a minyan.

They prayed:

God, full of compassion, who dwells on high, God of
forgiveness, who is gracious and compassionate, slow to
anger and abounding in kindness, may He grant pardon
of transgression, nearness of salvation, and perfect
rest beneath the wings of the Divine Presence, in the
exalted places among the holy and pure, who shine as the
brightness of heaven, to who has gone to his eternal home.
We pray to You, Adonai of compassion: remember to him
with favor all the worthy and righteous deeds which he did
on earth. Open for him the gates of righteousness and light,
the gates of pity and grace. Shelter him for evermore under
the cover of Your wings; and let his soul be bound in the
bonds of life. Adonai is his heritage; may he rest in peace.
Let us say Amen.

Mourner:
Magnified and sanctified my His great name be, in the world
He created by His will. May He establish His kingdom in
your lifetime and in your days, and in the lifetime of all the
House of Israel, swiftly and soon—and say: Amen.

All:
May His great name be blessed forever and all time.

Mourner:
Blessed and praised, glorified and exalted, raised and
honored, up lifted and lauded be the name of the Holy
One, blessed be He, beyond any blessing, song, praise
and consolation uttered in the world—and say: Amen.
May He who makes peace in His high places, make peace
for us and all Israel—and say: Amen.

-6-

Nate walked across the Tabernacle Plaza and stood in front
of the bench Shlomo and Aaron had sat on every day for the
last year. There should be a plaque, he thought, in memory of
Shlomo and Aaron. He hesitated a moment before sitting down.
It was a little unsettling to sit on 'their' bench. He brought the
TABERNACLE TIMES – EXTRA EDITION to read here, in
this special place. On the cover was a picture of Aaron. Nate

remembered the first time he had seen him: an old man trying to cross a street in Tel Aviv. That meeting had changed his life.

Nate opened the *Times*. Inside was a headline: THE FATHER OF THOUSANDS IN ISRAEL. And more pictures, one of them captioned: "Thousands attend the funeral of Aaron Weiss." Another photo showed the long funeral procession that stretched from the Tabernacle Plaza all the way to the cemetery. The Weiss families were all buried on the Mount of Olives, but with the black flags flying over the Old City, Aaron would be buried here, next to Shlomo and Ariel.

Aaron Weiss, one of the most beloved figures in the State of Israel, was laid to rest in Tabernacle Cemetery early yesterday," the article began."In one of the most well-attended funerals in the history of the Jewish State, Aaron was eulogized by prominent members of the Knesset as well as the Prime Minister.

"Aaron was born in Germany in the year 1922," the article continued. "It was in this same year that the *Stosstrupp-Hitler* (Shock Troop) was established. This is the organization that became the *Schutzstaffel*—commonly known as the SS.

"Aaron's parents both died from the Spanish Flu pandemic that was ravaging Europe in the years following WWI. By age six, Aaron had become an orphan. He was taken in by an uncle until, at the age of thirteen, he left to make his own way in the world.

"After *Kristallnacht* Aaron escaped to France and joined the Jewish Underground. He helped many Jews escape from Germany and other German-occupied countries. When the Germans conquered France, he joined the Resistance, providing the leadership with necessary information, false identity papers, ration cards for refugees and hiding places. As a member of the Jewish Underground he smuggled Jews, primarily children, out of occupied France.

"When the war ended, Aaron began taking orphaned Jewish children out of Europe and into British Palestine. He was not always successful, and many children were detained by the British or returned to Europe.

"When the War for Independence began, Aaron joined the *Palmach* and fought for Israel. Having survived the War, Aaron again thought of the children. He focused his energy on finding a place for all the orphaned and misplaced children who had survived both the Holocaust and the War of Independence. He decided on Ya'thom Kibbutz. It was a fitting name: Ya'thom means to be fatherless, to be lonely. He brought into his Kibbutz thousands of fatherless children. He was a father to them all."

Nate remembered that David's parents had founded Ya'thom and that he had been born there. After the War of Independence, David had returned to Ya'thom. Nate remembered that Hannah had come there with her parents in 1948, and that they had become parents to many of the orphans living there. David and Hannah met at Ya'thom and were later married.

In 1952 Aaron married Miriam Goldstein. They had three children—Rachel, Oren and Zechariah—and twelve grandchildren. His grandchildren made their fortunes in the high-tech industry. They established the Weiss Foundation to continue their grandfather's work: caring for orphans and other victims of war and of terror.

Nate thought about the Weiss Foundation. It had provided for him financially and had made it possible for him to stay in Israel. If he had gone back to the States, he wouldn't have married Tahlia. He wouldn't have a son named Nathan. He would have never learned about Sgt. Grange. And he wouldn't be sitting here, in front of the Tabernacle of God, watching the smoke of the morning sacrifice rising to heaven.

-7-

"THE TUNNELS OF LEMARAIS," the premiere episode of the newest *Underground Mysteries* season, aired at 8 p.m. Eastern Time on September 14.

A year later, *ALIYAH – ARIEL'S LONG JOURNEY HOME* won an Emmy for Best Documentary.

Ariel, may her memory be blessed, will not be forgotten.

CHAPTER TWO

The Camp of the Almighty
-1-

For the LORD your God walks throughout your camp to protect you and deliver your enemies to you...

Nate looked around the room and sat down reluctantly. *What am I doing here?* He asked himself. Around the large conference table sat some of the most powerful men in Israel, the decision-makers. High-ranking military, leaders in technology, members of the Knesset and the Prime Minister, were already seated. *I'm the only regular person here.*

Nate and the General had left the Camp early that morning for Jerusalem. There was a meeting, David had said, with the Prime Minister. As they approached the modern city, slowed by layer after layer of security, they could see the black flags flying from every high point in the Old City. It seemed the entire IDF was doing nothing but keeping the Soldiers of Islam confined within the Old Cities walls. As they walked to a plain, ordinary building, Nate heard a familiar voice: The Preacher! The words echoed over the entire city. Nate looked around. Where was it coming from?

"I'll tell you something," said David. "Every day they are preaching from the Old City. Their voices are heard everywhere, even here."

"Adonai is giving you time to repent! Turn from this false god! You shall not worship any God but Adonai! Adonai is a jealous God and will not share your worship with another!" Deuteronomy 5:7-9

"Everyone knows that," Nate said as they entered the building. David just raised his eyebrows and kept walking.

The meeting was being held in what seemed to be an underground bunker. They took their seats just as the Prime Minister was standing up to speak.

"Today Israel faces the greatest challenge of survival in the history of the Jewish people. Greater than the Egyptians, the Assyrians, the Babylonians, the Persians, the Greeks, or the Romans. Greater than the Holocaust."

He paused, letting that sink in.

"The State of Israel is surrounded on all sides by the combined forces of nearly every military in the world," he continued. "Our only ally, our only friend, has been under siege in his own country. Radical elements from every spectrum are at war with each other and the President. As the President himself tweeted, 'The barbarians are at the gates while Congress does nothing!' Violence is on nearly every street, and the military has been deployed in all the major cities. I could go on, but you get the picture—despite the President's support, we will not be getting any help from the United States."

Nate's face was grim. His family was living in this nightmare. Once the insanity—which was what his dad called it—had reached a certain level, it had accelerated so rapidly, no one was able to stop it. Every attempt by law enforcement was rejected by the courts. "Our Constitution was designed to govern a moral people; take that basic morality away and the Constitution is a weapon in their hands," he had said.

The Prime Minister's voice broke through his thoughts. "Evangelical Christians have been our biggest supporters, but now they are being persecuted to a degree never thought possible in the West. Churches are being burned to the ground, Christian pastors imprisoned, and in some areas Christian believers are being slaughtered. This is not only happening in the Middle East or Africa, where Christianity has been all but eradicated, but in Europe! Australia! Canada! And even in parts of the United States!"

It was frightening. Nate realized how much danger his family was in. Two years ago, when they had come to Israel, they had been worried about his safety. Even with the danger Israel was in today, it was much safer here than anyplace else in the world.

286

He remembered studying the seven churches of Revelation. His family was definitely in line for the "crown of life." Revelation 2:10

"We are here to discuss our options," the Prime Minister said. "General Ghehrem, we'll start with you."

Gen. Ghehrem slowly rose to his feet. His face was troubled as he began to speak: "The armies we are facing on our borders are unlike anything we have faced or even conceived of facing before. Thousands of tanks are amassing on the Sinai border, and nearly 500,000 troops are on the Jordanian side, from the Dead Sea to Eilat. The navies of seventy nations are in the Mediterranean, and their armies are beginning to gather on the Plain of Jezreel. If you do the math, we're outnumbered 200-or-more to one."

The room was silent.

Gen. Ghehrem cleared his throat. "Gaza has been quiet. In our present circumstances, the people of Gaza realize that one rocket; one incident of any kind will result in all of Gaza being totally obliterated. The people there are keeping Hamas in check. The Golan and the northern Galilee have been neutralized by the volcanic eruption and the resulting chemical and biological contamination. Hezbollah has moved from Lebanon with their tens of thousands of missiles, and are setting up operations in Jordan. Iran may be supplying them with nuclear warheads."

"Solutions?" asked the Prime Minister.

"The Samson Option." The General sank into his seat, and looked at the table, shielding his eyes.

"Dr. Issachar," said the Prime Minister, breaking the silence that had enveloped the room, "will brief us on any possible technology or scientific solutions."

Dr. Issachar stood and gave David a quick look. *What was that about?* Nate wondered.

"We have been working very hard on developing a new weapons system that would, in theory, neutralize all the threats just described by Gen. Ghehrem." He rubbed his forehead,

"Unfortunately we have not finalized our work. Another year, maybe two…"

"We do not have another year. It may be we don't even have another month," Gen. Ghehrem stated.

Again Dr. Issachar glanced at David. *Something isn't making sense,* thought Nate. He looked at the General. David's face was set in stone, his arms crossed in front of his chest.

"We are working as quickly as we can; we are doing everything humanly possible!" Issachar said.

"With God all things are possible!" [Matthew 19:26] Rabbi Eliezer Kahan, the chief rabbi of Israel, pushed his chair back and struggled to his feet. His snow-white beard flowed down his chest, nearly touching the table, and despite his great age he stood upright. "It may seem impossible to you. You are discouraged and fearful. But do you think this is impossible for Adonai? This is what Adonai has said, 'I will rescue my people from the east and from the west. I will bring them home again to live safely in Jerusalem. They will be my people, and I will be faithful and just toward them, and I will be their God.'" [Zechariah 8:6–8]

Rabbi Kahan looked at each of the men seated at the table. "Today is the day of repentance! All of the people of Israel must come and stand before Adonai, with fasting and weeping, and mourning. We must turn to Adonai and give Him our hearts! He is gracious and merciful; He is filled with kindness and faithful love." [Joel 2:12–13]

The old rabbi swept the room with his stern gaze. "Every day we hear the words of the Preachers from the roofs of the Old City calling us to repent, to humble ourselves before Adonai and to turn from our wicked ways! Today is the day of repentance! O Israel! Put your hope in Adonai! He will hear your cries!"

Again the room was silent.

"Tomorrow we begin the Forty Days of Repentance. Let each person search their heart and come repenting before Adonai. In the synagogues, on the streets, in every place where people gather, let them weep and repent. Each day let shofars be blown throughout the land, at the times of the ancient sacrifices—at 9 in the morning, and at 3 in the afternoon. It will be as it is on the days of remembrance: All the people will stop what they are doing; they will stop and remember their sins, and they will confess them to Adonai. They will turn from their sin in true repentance, and Adonai will forgive their sin and save them from their enemies."

Rabbi Kahan again looked at each of the men seated at the table.

"Adonai is the one who searches your hearts. He knows your thoughts. He will know if your repentance is true."

The men moved uncomfortably in their chairs.

"Nathaniel." Startled, Nate looked up. *The rabbi knew his name?*

"Yeah," he said.

"At the Tabernacle, you will make sure the silver trumpets are sounded morning and evening."

"I can do that," said Nate.

"This is what Adonai says, 'When you are in your own land and go to war against your enemies, you must sound the alarm with these trumpets so Adonai your God will remember you and rescue you from your enemies.' [Numbers 10:9] Do not forget!"

"I'm on it," said Nate.

The meeting was over. They would gather again after Yom Kippur.

Nate and the General were pushing back their chairs when Nate heard his name again. This time it was the Prime Minister. "Do you have any thoughts? What does your Revelation say?"

Nate watched as Dr. Issachar took the General aside and began talking earnestly.

"What the rabbi just said," Nate said distractedly. "Y'shua says to repent. Revelation says to obey God and keep the faith of Y'shua. Y'shua will deliver those who are faithful." [Revelation 2–3]

A moment later they stepped outside. They could hear the Preacher:

"This is what Adonai says, 'No matter how deep the stain of your sins, I can remove it. I can make you as clean as freshly fallen snow! Even if you are stained as red as crimson, I can make you white as wool. If you are willing to obey me you will eat the good things in the land. But if you keep turning away and refusing to listen, you will be destroyed by your enemies!'" Isaiah 1:18-20, NLT

-2-

The rumbling of thousands of tanks, idling just beyond the border; the engines of thousands of trucks revving up in the morning heat; the movement of thousands of troops—it all made the ground vibrate under the wheels of the Sufa.

"Pull over," said Eyal. "We need to get our bird in the air."

Nate brought out the drone and sent it up. They watched the screen but saw nothing but exhaust and swirling dust beneath the drone.

"Bring it down a bit."

They could just make out row after row of tanks.

"Send it further out."

Nate sent the drone further over the border, deeper into the Sinai. All they could see was tanks, trucks and troops, like water piling up behind a dam.

"They're on the move now," said Eyal.

They waited until they could see the lead tanks nearing the border.

Bringing in the drone, they put their vehicle in gear and headed into the desert.

There was a strange sound, one they had never heard before—a loud sucking sound. *What was that?!*

Nate looked over at Eyal, who was totally calm while Nate's heart was pounding through his chest.

Eyal stopped the Sufa and looked back.

"Send it up," he said.

Nate sent up the drone again. He stared in disbelief at the small screen.

"Look at this," he said to Eyal. "What do you see?"

Eyal narrowed his eyes as he watched the screen. He turned the Sufa around and headed slowly back towards the border. Now they could hear crashes and shouting. On the screen he could see tanks—tanks!—tipping into a jagged opening in the ground.

Eyal had his binoculars glued to his eyes. "What is the time?"

The time, the time, Nate thought rapidly. What is the time? Finally he found it. "It's 9:16."

"We are watching the destruction of our enemies by Adonai," said Eyal.

Nate took the binoculars out of his duffel and watched as row after row of tanks, column after column of trucks full of troops, tipped over the edge of the earth and disappeared. He watched as the tanks and trucks exploded, sending flames into the air, a column of smoke and fire.

Didn't they see what was happening?! Why do they keep coming?! On and on they came, this great army, flowing like a flood. The vehicles behind seemed to be pushing the ones ahead of them, sweeping them into the chasm, into the flames.

And then they stopped. Men were jumping out of their vehicles and running toward the edge of the deep gash in the earth. Then they turned and ran, shouting to each other, fleeing into the desert.

"The earth just swallowed them up," Nate said, stunned. "Huge tanks, trucks—just gone!"

Then it felt as if the earth lunged forward. The great canyon that had opened, swallowing the enemies of Israel, closed. Violently. Eyal and Nate felt the earth tremble.

✡︎✞✡︎✞✡︎✞✡︎

Nate walked into J-5, scooped up Nathan, and called for Tahlia.

"You won't believe what happened today!" he said.

"I heard!" Tahlia replied. "Zvi said the wall of dust was thirty feet high!"

"The what?"

"He said it was like the pillar of cloud! He got some video on his phone." She pulled some chicken out of the refrigerator. "Hungry?"

"Yeah," said Nate.

"Zvi said it nearly buried the army, but didn't cross over into Israel at all! It sat right on the border like a barrier." Tahlia poured olive oil into the pan, then added onion and garlic. She started cutting the chicken into strips.

"It was the Finger of God," Tahlia said. "The army was just starting to move toward Israel and out of nowhere comes this storm! Zvi said it stretched along the border as far as he could see!"

"What border?" asked Nate.

"Southern Jordan." Tahlia looked puzzled. "I thought you were there."

"I was at the Sinai," Nate replied. At the Sinai border, the earth just opened up and swallowed tanks and trucks and soldiers…"

Tahlia added the chicken to the pan, stirring it around, before she said: "Was it a sinkhole?"

"No," Nate answered, "it was like the earth ripped apart all along the border."

"So explain," said Tahlia.

Nate told how the tanks tipped over the edge and disappeared; how they were crushed, catching on fire. He told how it looked with the smoke and fire ascending out of the chasm, like a great pillar of fire.

Tahlia put a plate of steaming garlic chicken in front of Nate.

"I can't eat," Nate said. "I don't think I'll ever swallow anything again, after today."

Finally he said, "It was about nine o'clock, the time when the trumpets were being blown at the Tabernacle. That was when God remembered us and rescued us from our enemies."

✿✝✿✝✿✝✿

The next day the headline of the *Tabernacle Times* read:

PILLAR OF CLOUD - PILLAR OF FIRE
The God of Israel protects our borders

-3-

"I'm tellin' ya, I'm hearin' things every night!" Darryl waved his clipboard in Nate's face. "You're supposed to be protectin' this camp! What're ya going to do about it?"

Nate looked at Eyal. "What kind of things?" he asked.

"Motors runnin', horses, people talkin'!"

"Horses?"

"I'm tellin' ya, horses!"

"Where would we find these horses?" asked Eyal.

"Over there! The other side of the ridge! Past the wadi!" Darryl took a deep breath. "I tell ya, I'm gonna have a heart attack!"

"Settle down," said Nate. "We'll take a look. Relax."

✿✞✿✞✿✞✿

Eyal maneuvered the Sufa over the desert behind the ridge and over the wadi. He stopped and said, "Take a look over that hill."

Nate grabbed his duffel before Eyal took off. He climbed up the small hill and looked out over a flat plain. The sun had gone down, but it wasn't dark yet. He didn't hear anything. There seemed to be a mist rising out of the ground. Then, in the mist, he saw a flash of light, and then another.

Nate walked slowly down the hill, taking the binoculars out of his duffel. At the bottom, he sat on a rock and looked over the plain. Peering through the mist he began to see what appeared to be vehicles and horses, all blurry around the edges. He saw what looked like campfires with men sitting around them, their weapons gleaming in the light. He stared at the men, not sure of what he was seeing: men dressed the way warriors from Bible times dressed; men dressed in WWI and WWII uniforms; men wearing desert camo and IDF uniforms.

This is a vision. It has to be a vision, like the others I've had.

Now Nate could hear the noise of the encampment. Engines running, horses neighing, men shouting…

Moving among the men were other men carrying what looked like torches of fire. He focused in on the vehicles: tanks, half tracks and trucks; wagons, horses and chariots. *This is an army,* he said to himself. He scanned the plain, not believing his eyes. This was a great army. An army of hundreds of thousands, stretching as far as he could see. cf. 1 Chronicles 12:22–23

Then he saw, high above the camp, a brilliant green rainbow. In the middle of the rainbow was a sapphire throne. The

294

rainbow and the throne seemed to be suspended in the air, over the entire camp. Resting on the ground, the great wheels that carried the throne, glowed like amber. On the throne was someone who had the form of a man. He gleamed like polished brass, and shone like the radiance of the sun.

Nate was frozen with fear. This was Y'shua! This was the camp of the Almighty! The Army of Adonai!

"Adonai, who will not fear and glorify Your name?" he whispered. Revelation 15:4

As he spoke, the vision of the throne, suspended above the camp, disappeared into the mist.

Taking a deep breath, Nate raised the binoculars to his eyes and continued to watch the activity in the camp. Weapons were being cleaned and polished, vehicles were being made ready, and baggage was being loaded into trucks and wagons. This army was preparing to move.

Then, out of the mist he saw a man coming toward him. A soldier.

Nate slowly got to his feet. The soldier had on a WWII uniform.

He began to back away as the soldier approached.

"It's okay," the man said. "Don't be afraid."

"You're him," said Nate, his heart pounding. "You're Sgt. Grange."

"And you are Nathaniel. My grandson."

"Great-grandson," Nate corrected.

Sgt. Grange nodded. He put his hand on Nate's shoulder.

Nate could feel the weight of it. *This is not a vision…not a vision…not a—*

"I have come to tell you the final battle is going to be soon. You must be ready."

Nate took a deep breath. "I'm ready," "I am ready, aren't I?"

"Yes, you are. But not everyone is ready, and the time is near."

Nate thought about David, who was still resisting Y'shua.

Sgt. Grange ripped something off the sleeve of his uniform, studied it a moment, and then put it in Nate's hand. It was a patch. A patch with a rainbow on it. Nate knew what it was: the patch of Sgt. Grange's WWII 42nd Infantry Division, also called the Rainbow Division.

He looked up and saw Sgt. Grange disappearing into the mist.

"Wait!" He called. "How did I get your Bible? And your duffel bag?"

✧✞✧✞✧✞✧

Eyal pulled up and slowed just enough for Nate to get in.

"Did you hear anything? See anything?" he asked.

"Yeah," said Nate. "I saw a great army. The army of Adonai."

✧✞✧✞✧✞✧

"I met him," said Nate.

"Met who?" asked Tahlia."…Nathan Eli! You're going to break that!" Tahlia picked up Nathan's toy tank off the floor. "He's been running it off the side of the table all day," she explained.

"Sgt. Grange," Nate continued.

Tahlia stood up and looked at him. "So explain," she said.

"Eyal dropped me off to take a look over this hill. When I did I saw an army gathering. It was the army of the Almighty!"

"A vision," said Tahlia, nodding her head.

"One of the soldiers started coming toward me. He had on a WWII uniform. When he got closer, I recognized him. It was Sgt. Grange."

"A vision, you were having one of your visions," said Tahlia.

"He gave me this." Nate took the rainbow patch out of his pocket and handed it to Tahlia.

"This was no vision," he said.

Tahlia looked carefully at the patch. "You sure this didn't come out of your duffel?"

"Remember when you searched the duffel bag?" asked Nate.

Tahlia looked up at Nate. "It was empty," she said, "except for your clothes."

She handed the patch back to Nate. "So explain," she said.

"He ripped this patch right off of his uniform. As soon as I saw it I knew what it was." Nate stared at the patch. "I knew it was the 42nd Infantry 'Rainbow Division' Patch."

"Did he say anything?" Tahlia asked.

"He said the final battle is going to be soon," said Nate. "He said we must be ready."

Tahlia picked up Nathan. "We're ready," she said. "We are ready, aren't we?"

"We need to talk to the General," Nate replied.

CHAPTER THREE

The Sign

*Then the sign of the Son of Man will appear in the sky,
and then all the peoples of the earth will mourn...*
Matthew 24:30

Negev, Israel, 3 a.m.

For no reason at all Nate woke up. He listened to Tahlia
breathing and then reached over her and rested his hand on
Nathan, who was curled up next to Tahlia. Everyone was
sleeping peacefully—except him. He slipped out of bed
and looked around. He picked up his Eagle and walked
quietly through Unit J-5. *Something is not right,* he thought.
Something is not right...

He remembered how the Fogel family had been slaughtered
in their beds by teenaged Palestinians so long ago. But that
had been in Judea, in a settlement. *The Machom Mishpan is
the most secure place on the planet,* he told himself. It was
guarded by Adonai Himself. He checked the door and then the
windows. They were all secure.

So why do I feel so uneasy...?

He climbed up onto the roof. The entire camp was at peace.
There were a few people praying at the Tabernacle, but that was
all. He looked at the heavens overhead. Even they were at peace.

Illinois, USA, 7 p.m.

Justine looked out the window at the J's. It was time for them
to come in. The sky had an eerie look, and it was getting
darker. There had been no rain in the forecast, but this looked
like bad weather coming.

The J's were looking around, frightened. Then she felt it: the
floor was shifting.

298

This couldn't be another earthquake!

"We better get outside," Wes said, pushing her toward the door. "We don't want the house falling down on top of us."

Negev, Israel

Suddenly Nate felt the earth shift, rising all around him. It was like the earthquake three years ago: the camp rolling like a raging sea, the houses like ships riding the wild waves. Only the Tabernacle was stable, unmoving, as it had been last time. It was solid as a rock, glowing in the night.

Nate carefully made his way back to Tahlia and Nathan. Nathan was crying, and Tahlia looked terrified.

"Outside," Nate said, grabbing his duffel and taking Nathan from Tahlia.

They raced for the Tabernacle Plaza as a sound, loud and terrifying, filled the air.

The gate to the Tabernacle courtyard was open, and they ran inside. Clinging to each other, they looked around. Nate's eyes were riveted on the Tabernacle. The curtain that had closed off the entrance of the Holy Place had been pulled aside.

Then, as Nate watched, the Holiest Place, the Holy of Holies, opened, and the Ark of God's Covenant appeared, radiating light.

Illinois, USA

Justine pulled the J's close to her as Wes' arms encircled all three of them. They looked around apprehensively, waiting for the next tremor.

Lightning filled the sky, and thunder crashed in the distance.

Then—a loud and terrifying sound began to fill the air.

"What is that?!" Even Wes had fear in his voice.

Justine had heard that sound before, but not like this, not this loud.

Negev, Israel

Nate and Tahlia stood, hardly able to breathe, their eyes riveted on the Ark of God.

Lightning flashed all around the camp and the deep rumbling of thunder rolled over the desert.

The sound of the shofar had been growing louder and louder, and seemed to make the very air shake in terror.

Nathan buried his face in Nate's chest, his little body trembling. Tahlia clung to Nate as he pulled her close to him. She was trembling too.

Pulling his gaze from the Ark, Nate watched as sparks of light flew into the air from all over the camp.

Illinois, USA

"It's a shofar," said Justine. "It's the trumpet of God." Her heart was pounding as she looked around. Sparks of light were rising from the earth, flying high into the air.

Then the sky was torn open, from east to west, as far as she could see.

She grasped the J's and felt Wes tighten his grip around them.

Negev, Israel

Nate looked up at the heavens as they opened. A brilliant light, brighter than the sun shining full strength, poured out of the opening.

He saw the Army of the Almighty, riding gleaming white horses, wearing pure white linen.

He saw the Commander of the Army of Adonai.

His eyes were blazing, and He had a drawn sword, a sword of fire.

Illinois, USA

"It's the coming of the LORD!" Justine shouted. "If you don't believe in Jesus Christ, you have only a few seconds to repent and believe!!" Suddenly they were drawn into the light…

Negev, Israel

In an instant Nate, Tahlia and Nathan had become one with the light. They joined with all the armies of heaven as they praised Adonai, saying: ^{Revelation 11:15}

THE KINGDOM OF THE WORLD HAS BECOME THE KINGDOM OF ADONAI AND OF HIS MESSIAH! HE WILL REIGN FOREVER AND EVER!

THE DREAM

The final chapter of *Wall of Fire* is based on a dream I had in
November 2015…

In the very early hours of November 1, 2015, around 3 a.m.
(my eyes have gotten so bad that when I woke, I couldn't tell
if it was 2 or 3), I had a dream or a vision, or maybe I was just
thinking while asleep…

We were having a family dinner, and my children and grandchildren
were all over. It had gotten very dark outside even though it was
afternoon. Some of us went outside to see what was going on. The
sky was full of dark rolling clouds, and thunder was beginning to
rumble all around. We turned on the TV and the screen was dark
except for the text scrolling at the bottom. It read: *"Extreme weather
warning … stand by … extreme weather warning."*

Lightning began flashing all around as the thunder was booming
louder and louder. Then a loud trumpeting sound—I knew
immediately it was the sound of a shofar—began. "What is
that?" someone asked. "A shofar, the trumpet of God!" I said.

My heart was pounding so hard I could hardly speak. Then
the earth started to shake. The bookcases in the living room
fell over, and outside the trees were bent to the earth. **"What
is going on?!"** everyone was asking, looking around, scared.
I replied, "I think it's the resurrection of the dead in Christ."
I felt I was barely breathing. "If you don't believe in Jesus
Christ, you have only a few seconds to repent and believe!"

Then … we looked up. The dark clouds had been rolled back.
There was a light so bright … brighter than the sun…

Then I was looking down on the earth from the light.

I woke up, wondering what had just happened. I looked at the
clock. It was 3 or maybe 2 in the morning.

I

ONE MORE THING...

I am often asked what prompted me to write this story. The answer is simple: my children and grandchildren. I wanted to share with them the glory of God that I had seen while studying His Word. I wanted them to know that the God of the Bible is a covenant-keeping God. I wanted them to understand that the prophecies that had been written in the Bible thousands of years ago were being fulfilled in our day, before our very eyes. I wanted them to be filled with the same wonder and awe that I have been.

I wanted to give praise, with them, to our God and Savior for all He has done and is going to do in the future.

I knew that they would not read my thousands of pages of study notes, but perhaps they would read a fictional story based on those notes, a story that would be interwoven with a selection of the miracles that God had performed in the land of Israel during her many wars.

Part I and the beginning of Part II of *Wall of Fire* were written during the years 2010–2013. Then I had to put this project aside for a time. When these first pages were written I had never known a Jewish person. I had never been to Israel. Then, in 2015, the LORD blessed me with many Jewish friends, who I met at a small messianic congregation near my home called New Jerusalem House of Prayer. New Jerusalem offered Hebrew lessons and I began learning the Hebrew language. In the fall of 2016 we went to Israel and celebrated the Feast of Tabernacles in the City of the Great King—Jerusalem! Hallelujah!

It was during this trip that Jill and Sam Wat read the first part of what would become this book. Their enthusiasm for the story and their encouragement gave me the confidence to continue. At this time we realized there might be a wider audience for a novel of this type. That wider audience would be both the Jewish people who believed in Y'shua and those who did not. It would also be a reminder to the Church that God has not replaced Israel but continues to provide for her and protect her.

It was at this point that I felt I had completely lost control over the storyline.

I was having dreams and nightmares.

I had a character show up in a dream saying he wanted to be in the story.

I would sit down at my computer and something entirely different from what I thought I was writing would appear on the screen.

It is my prayer that I have been faithful with what God has given me to write. It is my prayer that the miracles and testimonies woven throughout this narrative will be a witness of God's faithfulness to His covenant with Israel. It is my prayer that those who do not yet believe that Y'shua is the Messiah would come to know Him.

So why did I write this book? The answer is simple: to give praise to the LORD, and to bless His name. To tell of His mighty acts, and His wonderful miracles; to share the story of His goodness, mercy and loving kindness. Psalm 145:4–7.

✡✝✡✝✡✝✡

The phrase "Finger of God" is a Hebrew idiom for the power or Spirit of God (Exodus 8:19; Matthew 12:28; Luke 11:20). It is a phrase used to indicate the intervention of the God of Israel in the events that affect the people and the land of Israel. From the time of the Exodus from Egypt—when the phrase was first used—until the present day, the God of Israel has taken action on behalf of His people. These actions have been most visible during the wars of Israel.

Although the story itself is solely from my imagination, the accounts of the miracles, which have been woven throughout the fictional storyline, are true. Each true story has been adapted to fit the narrative while still being faithful to the true account.

The characters in this story have been suggested by people I know, both family and friends. They are not, however, a representation of the actual people. People, personalities, actions, words—all are a product of my imagination.

Several of the characters in this story come to believe that Y'shua is the Messiah. Their testimonies have been adapted from actual testimonies from real Jewish people who have found Y'shua the Messiah.

The testimonies of each character can be found in the appendix titled "I KNOW Y'SHUA IS THE MESSIAH."

This story is not intended to be a definitive interpretation of the events that are to occur before the return of Y'shua, the Lion of Judah. Its only intent is to bring glory to the God of Israel and to His Son, Y'shua the Messiah.

I KNOW Y'SHUA IS THE MESSIAH

Several of the characters in this story come to believe that Y'shua is the Messiah. Although the characters are fictional, the testimonies are authentic, adapted from the testimonies of real Jewish people who came to believe that Y'shua is the Jewish Messiah and who have put their trust in Him for their redemption and salvation. These testimonies can be found at:

OneForIsrael.org

ChosenPeople.com

JewsForJesus.org

The testimonies below are written in the voices of the story's characters.

AARON

I was an orphan, yes? Both my parents died from the influenza by the time I was six. I was taken into my uncle's house, who was very religious. We kept the Sabbath, the Feast days and the kosher food. We went to the Synagogue and the Hebrew school.

My uncle had many children and was very poor. He spent his days studying Talmud instead of working. He was not a father to me. I knew from the Torah that God was the Father of orphans. God, not my uncle, was my father. My uncle obeyed the command to take care of the orphan, but there was no love. I was another mouth to feed. If there was not enough food, I was the one who didn't eat.

After my bar mitzvah I left my uncle's house. I trusted that my Father in heaven would protect me and provide for me. I lived on the streets and found ways to survive. This was good experience, yes? For when the Nazis came. After the *Kristallnacht* I escaped to France, where I met Shlomo and other many other Jews who were fleeing from the Nazis. When the Nazis came to France

V

we helped many to escape or to hide. I knew the Almighty was watching over me, like a good father watches over his children.

It was when Israel fought the War for Independence that I met Sgt. Nathaniel Grange. He was an American soldier, a Jew and a Christian. Always he would talk about Jesus, Y'shua, being the Jewish Messiah. He would say "Jesus died so you can live." He would say "Aaron, God loved you so much that He gave His only Son, so that if you believe in Him, you will not die but have eternal life." He said Y'shua paid what I owed God for my sins. He would tell me to read Isaiah, the chapter 53 in the Tanakh.

One day during a battle on the road to Jerusalem, my gun jammed. Bullets were coming right at me when Sgt. Grange covered me with his body. Seconds later he was dead and I was not. He had given his life that I could live, yes?

After the War I found the Ya'thom kibbutz. It was the place I brought the orphans from the Holocaust and from the wars of Israel. The Almighty, the God of Israel, my Father in heaven— He provided all we needed to care for the children. We had food and houses and clothes and education. Most of all the children had love. I thought all my good works, taking care of the fatherless children would pay for my sins. I thought of Nathaniel who had given his life so I could live. I wondered about Y'shua, if he could have been the Messiah. There was no one I could talk to, no rabbi I could ask.

The children—many were hidden by believers in Y'shua. They were followers of Y'shua, and they were willing to risk their lives or even die to save Jewish children. One child had a Bible that told all about Y'shua. In this Book I read about Jesus. Y'shua is called Jesus, yes? I read there is no atonement for sin without the shedding of blood. I know that my good works will not pay for my sins.

I am drawn close to Y'shua. Like my Father in heaven, He has compassion, He is gentle and kind. He loves the children. I feel a stirring in my heart. I feel love for Him.

VI

I read about the way He is killed, and I understand that He died so my sins are paid for, yes? I remember that Nathaniel said Y'shua was killed for me, so I can live. I know that all Nathaniel told to us was true. Y'shua is the Messiah. It is then I feel the tears on my face.

When I pray I thank my Father in heaven for not letting me die until I know who His Messiah is. I thank Him for sending Nathaniel to tell me. I thank Him that Y'shua died so my sins are forgiven. I thank Him that Y'shua died so that I will live with my Father in heaven forever.

SHLOMO

So. In Germany I am born into a very religious family. My father, he was a rabbi. To obey God, to obey His commands, that was our whole life. Yom Kippur is the holiest day of the year. If there were any commands we had broken, on Yom Kippur they could be forgiven. So. I asked my father, "Are our sins forgiven now?" He said he hoped so. He hoped? He didn't know? There were no sacrifices, no shedding of blood. So he didn't know. He said, "Keep the commandments and when you stand before God maybe He will be merciful." Maybe?

Then … the Nazis come. They were people without God. They had their own laws, laws against the Jews. After Kristallnacht my family knew Germany, it was not safe. My Father was arrested. Our synagogue was burned. My mother, she sent me away. "You can escape," she said. "You can help others to escape." I asked, "Has God has turned His face from us?" All the years of the war I asked, "Where is God?"

I never saw my mother, myfather, or any of my family again. I helped save many lives, but my family, them I could not save. The Nazis, they killed my wife and son. God had turned His face from us. I was filled with hatred for my enemies. I wanted vengeance. I thought it would bring me peace.

VII

During the Independence War, I meet Sgt. Nathaniel Grange. He is a Jew, but he believed the Christian God, Jesus, was the Messiah. If he was the Messiah, why were the Christians always killing the Jews? He said they weren't real Christians. He said real Christians loved the Jews because Jesus is a Jew. He called Jesus by His Jewish name, Y'shua. He always talked about Y'shua. I did not have time to listen. "After the war," I told him, "then talk about Y'shua." But he died. He was killed saving my friend Aaron's life.

After the Independence War, I took vengeance. I hunted down the Nazis. I did not forgive what they had done. The darkness of bitterness and hatred covered my soul. I had no remorse. My heart was black with anger and hate. I did not know that the darkness was covering my soul … I had found no peace.

Then, another war. A Six-Day War, but who knew? I returned to fight. It was then that Aaron saw me in the darkness. Aaron said the light was in the Torah. He said to study the Torah. So, I studied to become a rabbi like my father before me. I tried to find the light in the Torah. The Torah says forgiveness only comes after repentance. The Nazis did not repent, and I did not repent for killing them. … So, still I had no peace. I searched for peace but could not find it. I was a rabbi, but this I did not know, where to find the peace.

So, Aaron, he says to read Isaiah, the chapter 53. I am a rabbi, but this I never read in the Tanakh. The prophet Isaiah, he writes about a person who is innocent of all wrongdoing; a person who took all our suffering on himself. All of our guilt was laid on him, and he took our punishment. He was killed for our sin; he was an offering for our guilt. He is a slaughtered lamb. I read that he is the one who brings us peace.

Then Aaron gives to me the Book of Y'shua. So, I read the Book. All that Isaiah has written is the same as what happened to Y'shua. I know this must be Y'shua. I did not want to believe this. I know Y'shua is the same as the Christian Jesus, but I do not think a Jew can get peace from a Y'shua who is Jesus.

VIII

I turned my face from the truth. Then I remembered how I thought God had turned His face from me. I didn't want to turn from God. I want to know He will be merciful to me. I want to have this peace.

So. I read this Bible, this Book about Y'shua. There I read I must forgive my enemies. I read thatHASHEM forgives in the same way we forgive. It says that judgment is without mercy to one who has shown no mercy. How can I ask God for mercy when I gave no mercy?" James 2:13; Matthew 6:14–15

I say to Aaron: "Aaron. I cannot forgive. How do I forgive my enemy? How do I love my enemy? I have no peace. The Book about Y'shua says I will be forgiven as I forgive others. It says that judgment is without mercy to one who has shown no mercy. I showed no mercy when I took my vengeance. How do I forgive? How do I receive mercy? I want to know that my sin is forgiven, and God will be merciful. I want peace."

Aaron, he says to pray and ask Y'shua to forgive me and to give me the power to forgive.

So. I pray. I say, "Y'shua, I know now that You are the Messiah. I know You are the one who forgives sin. Forgive my sins that I confess today. Give me the power to forgive, today. Give me the power to let go of my hate, today. I know You are the one who brings peace. Bring me peace, today."

Right away I can feel the darkness, it is lifted from me. The hate is gone. Now I can forgive. Now I am forgiven. Now God will have mercy on me. Now I have peace.

He took away the bitterness. He took my pain and sorrow. It took a long time. A very long process. Some days I still have this burden. But I found peace in Y'shua.

James 4:13 For judgment is without mercy to one who has shown no mercy. Mercy triumphs over judgment.

Psalm 18:25 With the merciful You show Yourself merciful...

Matthew 6:14–15 For if you forgive others their wrongdoing, your heavenly Father will also forgive you, but if you do not forgive others their wrongdoing, neither will your Father forgive your wrongdoing.

Matthew 5:44 But I say to you, Love your enemies and pray for those who persecute you.

TAHLIA

I was born in Israel and have spent my whole life here. My family was religious—Torah religious, not "rabbi religious," as my grandpa would say. We kept the Sabbath, but we would drive to see family or sometimes one of us would have to work. I'm an EMT and others are in the IDF, so sometimes we're on duty on the Sabbath. We went to Synagogue, read the Tanakh and would talk about what it said. We kept the Feast Days and were 'Torah kosher'—we didn't eat pork or shellfish, but pretty much everything else was on the menu.

I always knew the God of Israel watched over us. When I was a little girl, I would look at the sky and imagine God living far away above the clouds. He was watching and protecting Israel and me. But He was always far away, too far to really know. As I grew up I wanted to know Him like Sarah and Rebecca had. I wanted to know Him like Abraham, Isaac and Jacob had known Him. But He was far away. I spent the next years of my life waiting for God to come near to me. He was up there, I was down here, and that was the way it was.

And then I met Nathaniel.

One thing I learned about Nathaniel was he never went anywhere without his duffelbag and his Bible. Nathaniel seemed so close to God. He really seemed to know Him. I wanted that kind of relationship with God, where He was near all the time. I told Nathaniel I always felt far from God, how could he be so close? He told me that it was through Y'shua that he was close to God. He said our sins keep us separated from God, but Y'shua paid what we owe to God for disobeying Him. If we turn away from our sin, and believe Y'shua did this for us, we will be close to God.

Nathaniel and I traveled all over Israel. I told him the history of the places we went, and he read to me what the Bible had to say. This was how I learned about Y'shua. Whenever we went someplace where Y'shua had been, Nathaniel would read about it in his Bible. Then he would tell me Y'shua was the Messiah and show me the prophecies about the Messiah that Y'shua fulfilled in His life and death. He told me that Adonai had raised Y'shua from the dead and that He is at the right hand of Adonai in heaven. Then he would tell me Y'shua was coming again, this time as the conquering King, the Lion of Judah.

I struggled with knowing that the Christian Jesus was the same as Y'shua. I knew that Christians, in the name of their Jesus, had been slaughtering my people for more than a thousand years. There was no way Jesus was the Jewish Messiah. Y'shua? I liked Y'shua—but was He the Messiah? I thought in my head He probably was, but my heart resisted. I felt that to accept Y'shua as Messiah would be to betray my people.

The day we visited Yad Vashem, Nathaniel read what Isaiah the prophet wrote about someone called the Servant. I had never even heard of this chapter. It was never read in the Synagogue. I didn't even know it existed. Nathaniel tried to explain, but I was too emotional to understand. He said to read it in the Bible he had given me. He said to pray to know the truth.

So I did. I prayed to the God of Abraham, Isaac and Jacob that He would show me the truth.

When I got home, I took the Bible Nathaniel had given me a few days before and opened it. On the first page he had written:

Tahlia, these things are written so that you may believe that Y'shua is the Messiah, the Son of God, and that by believing, you Tahlia, may have life in His name. (John 20:31)

For God so loved Tahlia, that He gave His only Son, so that when Tahlia believes in Him she will not perish but have eternal life. For God did not send His Son into the world to condemn Tahlia, but in order that she might be saved through Him. (John 3:16–17)

My name was in the Bible? I looked the verses up and saw that Nathaniel had put my name in the verses. Later I found he had done that all through the Bible.

Nathaniel had also written a note:

Read Isaiah 6:9–10. I'm praying for you, Tahlia, that you will open your heart to Y'shua, just a little bit.

After I read the passage, I prayed that I would have eyes to see and a heart to understand.

I read Isaiah from 52:13 through 53. Nathaniel had put notes in the margins with other passages to look up: Matthew 26–28; Mark 14–16; Luke 22:35–24:53, John18:2 and Psalm 22.

The more I read, the more I felt the presence of God. I felt like He was right next to me, nodding His head and pointing to the Scripture, saying, Look at this…The God that had seemed so far away was now next to me. I knew then that Y'shua was the Messiah; not just in my head but in my heart.

I was overwhelmed with different feelings.

I was happy—I had found what I had been looking for—the way to be near to God was through Y'shua!

I was awestruck—I was near to the Holy God of Israel with all my shortcomings exposed.

I was relieved—I knew that Y'shua had already taken the punishment for my sinful actions and attitudes. Even though I had gone astray, gone my own way, because of Y'shua I would be 'counted as righteous' before God. I used to think I could never know God, but now I know Him.

I would have never known God, never had a relationship with Him, if I hadn't asked Him to show me the truth.

I went to tell Nathaniel I believed Y'shua was the Messiah and to ask him what to do next.

I was scared. Scared of hurting my family. Scared of being disowned by them. Scared of being deserted by my friends. Nathaniel said he would be with me when I told my family, but before I could tell anyone, he was injured in the terrorist attack.

While we waited to see if he had any chance of recovering from being paralyzed, Nathaniel and I began to study the Bible. We studied everything the Scriptures said about the Messiah. We studied everything Y'shua taught. My belief in Y'shua grew stronger, and Nathaniel said he needed to spend a lot of time with Y'shua and the Bible to keep him from getting discouraged. Nathaniel was mostly happy, mostly at peace, and mostly patient. I wanted to have that kind of trust and peace in God.

Nathaniel always said God doesn't allow His people to suffer for no reason. I always will remember how Y'shua suffered for me, so I could be close to God.

HANNAH

When I was a small child, only three years old, the Nazis came to the Netherlands where I lived. In the dark of night my parents took me on a long bike ride. The Germans were coming and they were bringing me to a family, a Dutch friend of my parents, who would hide me. We came to their house and I fell asleep.When I woke up my parents were gone. These people became my new parents. They loved me. They took me to church, to Sunday School. They were Christians. They taught me about Jesus. They told me Jesus loves me. I would say, "I love Jesus too." I was a Christian then, you see?

The Germans soldiers hated me, but Jesus loved me. When the soldiers walked down the street, I was afraid. My heart would beat very fast. I thought it was Jesus in my heart, telling me not to be afraid.

The Germans were in the Netherlands for five years. I was eight years old when the war was over. Everyone was happy! I didn't have to stay away from windows anymore, or hide if a soldier came down the street.

One day I was looking out the window and I saw two people on bicycles. They stopped and came to the house. I ran and hid. I was still afraid. My heart was beating very fast, so I knew Jesus was telling me not to be afraid.

After they came in, my parents found me and brought me to them. They told me that these people were my momma and papa. I did not believe it. I ran away, into the kitchen and hid in the cupboard. The two bicycle people found me there. Then the woman said to me: "May you be like Rachel and Leah…", the blessing my mother had said over me every day before the war. I remembered these words. Then I knew. These were my parents.

I told my real parents about Jesus, how He was in my heart, telling me not to be afraid. They were very angry. "You are Jewish! You cannot be Christian!" they said. Then I knew I could not be Christian, you see? But I did not know what it meant to be Jewish.

I learned that Jewish people went to synagogue instead of church; that the Jewish Sabbath was Saturday instead of Sunday; that Jewish people said the Shema instead of the Apostles' Creed. We celebrated the Holy Days of Passover, Shavout, Rosh Hashanah, Yom Kippur and Sukkot instead of the Christian holy days of Christmas and Easter. I learned about the Torah but not Jesus. His name was never spoken.

The Feast Days and the Shabbat, they were the heartbeat of our lives, you see? I loved preparing for Shabbat. The aroma of chicken roasting and challah baking filled the house. Just before sundown we would gather around the table and my mother would

XIV

light the Shabbat candles. Blessings would be said over the wine and the bread. My mother would bless me saying, "May you be like Rachel and Leah..." I soon loved being Jewish.

In all these years, I never told anyone about Jesus. Who could I tell? I was afraid I would be shut out of the community. I was afraid my family would not understand. I was afraid David would be angry. But I did not forget about Jesus, and I often thought about Him in my heart.

One day Aaron and Shlomo came to visit our Nathaniel. This is when I learn that Aaron, Shlomo and Tahlia, my granddaughter, are all believers in Y'shua. They all believe He is the Messiah.

Shlomo tells me that Jesus is Y'shua. He tells me Y'shua is a Jew. He tells me Y'shua is the Messiah. He tells me Y'shua is born a Jew, He lived as a Jew, died as a Jew, and was buried as a Jew. He says HASHEM raised Him from the dead and that Y'shua will come to Earth again as a Jew, as the Lion of Judah. Shlomo is a rabbi, you see? He knows these things.

Then Shlomo says Y'shua takes away our sin, that He is the Lamb of God, and that He is the sin offering. I remember this from long ago, from Sunday School. I remember being taught that Jesus died for our sins.

I did not say anything for a long time. I knew this all must be true, but I was afraid. My heart was beating very fast, and I remembered that as a child I thought it was Jesus in my heart telling me not to be afraid. When David asked if I believed this, that Jesus, Y'shua, was the Messiah, I said the truth. I said yes. David was angry with me. He was very cold to me for a long time.

When he saw that our life did not change, that we still went to synagogue, still kept Shabbat and the Holy Days that I still lived as a Jew, he began to accept that I believed in Y'shua. The warmth of our marriage returned over time, but David? He never would talk about Y'shua with me, you see?

ASA

My friend, before Y'shua, in this life I was lost. My only happiness was making everything out of anything. Then I would not think of how alone I was, how empty my life was.

I knew I was different than the other people. My mind did not think the way they thought. People stayed away from me.

But not Shlomo. With Aaron he would come and sit. Just watching me fix things or make things. Shlomo would talk to Aaron. He would say: "So. Asa makes anything out of everything. It is what Y'shua does."

One day I said, "My friend, who is Y'shua? What is it he is making out of anything?" Then Shlomo tells me about Y'shua. He says Y'shua is making the sad people happy; He is fixing the broken hearts; to the ones without friends, He is being a friend; He is being a father to those who have no father; He is not far away, He is always there. He doesn't leave us when life is hard; instead He gives us strength."

So I ask, "Can Y'shua make anything out of me?'"

Shlomo looks around my shop. Then he says, "So. Y'shua has anything He needs to make me everything that He wants."

I ask, "What does He want?" Shlomo says: "To believe He is the Messiah sent from God, to trust Him." Then he told me all about Y'shua. He's a rabbi. He knows these things. So I pray to the God of my fathers and my eyes are opened. Then I believe.

My friend, I gave to Y'shua everything. All my loneliness, all my sadness, all my emptiness. Now He is with me all the time. Now my life is full and I am never alone.

REUVEN

I met Nathaniel after he had been hurt in a terrorist attack. He was paralyzed; it didn't look like he would ever walk again. He

XVI

would come by in his wheelchair, roll up to the café, grab a cup of coffee, and go down to the Mediterranean. He would sit there and read his Bible; sometimes he would sing, praising Adonai. I didn't understand it, but he was mostly happy. Then one day I was bringing some coffee out of the café and standing right in front of me was Nate. *Standing.* I could hardly believe it.

Nate told me that God had answered his prayers and had told him to get up and walk. Then he said it was Y'shua who had healed him. I didn't know who Y'shua was, but Nate said He's the Messiah. I didn't even know what that meant.

Nate said that in the Tanakh, God promises a Messiah who will come to save His people, not only from their enemies but from themselves, from their own sins. He said the Messiah came two thousand years ago to bring salvation to Israel. That He was crucified and killed by unbelievers and then Adonai raised Him up from death and now He is the living Savior of all who believe. Nate said that God showed that Y'shua was the Messiah by doing signs and wonders through Y'shua.

Telling Nate to "get up and walk" looked like a sign and a wonder, but what did it mean for me. Nate said God wants me to be saved, to confess my sin. He wants me to trust in Y'shua and believe He is the Messiah sent from God. I said that I believed. How could I not? Nate was standing and walking right in front of me!

When I went to the Kotel, I confessed my sin to Adonai and told Him I believed in His Messiah.

ZVI

It was because of Tahlia that I came to believe in Y'shua. After Nate was injured in the attack, Tahlia was pretty calm. Normally she would have been frantic, hysterical. I asked her what was going on with her, why was she so calm.

She just said she was waiting to see what God would do. "See what God would do"?!

You have to understand, Tahlia never waited for anything. She was all about action.

She didn't want to talk about it, but I kept after her.

Finally she said she knew the God of Israel was watching over Nate. She said how she and Nate talked about God and about the Messiah. She told me that Y'shua was the Messiah. She said Nate showed her all the prophecies in the Tanakh about the Messiah, and then he showed her how they had happened in the life of Y'shua.

She said that she was close to God because of Y'shua. She explained that we are separated from God because of our sin but if we trust in Y'shua, then we could be restored to God and be close to Him. She said Y'shua had come to bring salvation to Israel, to remove our sin. [Psalm 103:12] I remembered something like that from the Tanakh, from when I was young. I hadn't been in a synagogue since my bar mitzvah, so I wasn't sure.

There was one more thing: Tahlia said that the Messiah was coming a second time, this time as a conquering King to bring us deliverance from our enemies. All I could think of was: "What's He waiting for?! We're surrounded by our enemies! On all sides! Even on the streets of our cities!"

Tahlia said trusting Y'shua changed her, but I didn't want to change. I was happy with my life. I had women in Haifa, Tel Aviv, Elat—all over the place. I drank, I partied—I had a great life. I didn't think of God at all, at least then I didn't. But I was curious. I read her Bible a little when she wasn't there.

Then things started to happen. Nate started walking. He says Y'shua healed him.

Then we're building this huge camp in the middle of the Negev. Nate says God said to build it.

Then there's a powerful earthquake. It levels Tiberius, and Tahlia is buried.

XVIII

We can't find her, but God shows Nate where she is.

I start to think about what Tahlia said about God and Y'shua. Tahlia said she prayed to the God of our fathers, the God of Abraham, Isaac and Jacob. She prayed that she would know the truth about Y'shua. What can it hurt, I ask myself? I pray the same prayer. After that God begins to open my eyes. Every day I'm meeting people who believe in Y'shua, who believe He is the Messiah. These people are everywhere in Israel, and I think I met all of them. It is now easier to believe than not to believe. I tell Adonai that I believe Y'shua is the Messiah, that I put my trust in Him. My whole life is changed.

DAVID

General David Yash'el resisted believing in Y'shua.

He believed in the God of Israel, but did not believe in His Son.

He believed the Messiah was coming but not that He had already come.

He believed the coming Messiah would save Israel from her enemies, but was not willing to believe that the Messiah had come, to suffer and die and to be raised up by Adonai, two thousand years ago to save her people from sin.

He listened when his family spoke about Y'shua.

He listened to the Preachers, and he discussed Y'shua with them.

He listened to Aaron and Shlomo as they told him how they came to believe in Y'shua.

He listened to Asa, Reuven and Zvi when they told him they knew Y'shua was the Messiah.

He knew they loved him.

He knew they prayed for him.

He knew their hearts were broken because he would not believe.

He knew they were filled with grief because he was unwilling to believe.

He knew they were overcome with bitter sorrow because he would not trust in Y'shua, the Messiah.

They said, "There is salvation only in Y'shua. There is no other name to call on to be saved." Acts 4:12

They said, "There is one way to be right with God through trusting Y'shua the Messiah."

They said, "Confess that Y'shua is the Messiah and believe in your heart that Adonai raised Him from the dead, and you will be made right with God and you will be saved. Romans 10:9–10

They said, "All who believe in God's Son have eternal life ... the wrath of God remains on those who do not believe." John 3:36

He said, "My life is in the hands of HASHEM; He has watched over me this far."

He said, "It is up to God if He will show mercy to me or not."

Hebrew Words

Abayah – Bedouin blanket with black stripes on the sides

Aliyah – to go up, to immigrate to Israel

Ariel – Jerusalem, a Jew in exile

Chuppa – wedding canopy

Eretz – land

Gibbor Chayil – mighty valor

HaShem – The NAME

Kaddish – mourners' prayer for the dead

Korach Seferim – a binder of books

Machal – foreign Jewish volunteers in Israel's wars. Fought with the IDF

Machom Mihlawt – Camp of Refuge

Machom Mishpan – Camp of the Taberanacle

Mashiach – Annointed One - Messiah

Merkiva – chariot, Israeli tank

Meshugah – crazy

Minyan – number, quorum of 10 required for certain religious obligations

Mishmar Ha'am – home guard

Mitzvot – commandments, good deeds

Sababa – great!

Sar-El – Service for Israel – volunteers supporting the IDF

Sava / Savta – grandfather / grandmother, respectively

Shauvot – Feast of Weeks

Shiva – the 7 days of mourning

Siddur – prayer book

Sufa – Israeli offroad vehicle, like a jeep

Sukkah – booth

Sukkot – Feast of Tabernacles

Tallit – prayer shawl

Tzitzoit – tassels on edges of garments

Ya-thom – Fatherless, lonely, bereaved

Hebrew Names

Asa – to make – son of a king (1 Kings 15:8)

Abigail – fathers joy, gives joy (1 Samuel 25:3)

Adin – gentle, tender (Ezra 2:15)

Ben Ari – son of the lion of God (Genesis 49:9)

Eyal – courage (Hebrew name dictionary)

Ghehrem – strong (Genesis 49:24)

Gilana – joy (Psalm 43:4)

Hannah – favor, grace (1 Samuel 1:2)

Harim – mountains (Genesis 7:20)

Kahan – to mediate as a priest (Genesis 14:18)

Lackpor (chaphar) – to dig (Deuteronomy 8:9)

Nahshon – enchanter – son of Amminadab, tribe of Judah (Numbers 7:12)

Nathaniel – gift of God (Numbers 1:8)

Nathan Eli – gift of my God (2 Samuel 7:2)

Reuven – see, a son (Genesis 29:32)

Sara – princess (Genesis 17:15)

Simcha – joy (1 Samuel 18:6)

Tahlia – dew of God (Exodus 16:13)

Yaron – he will sing (Hebrew name dictionary)

Y'shua – Jesus

Yoni – gracious (Genesis 43:29)

Zvi – deer, stag (Song of Solomon 2:9)

ABOUT THE AUTHOR

Jan is a storyteller with a purpose. Skillfully weaving together true accounts and fictional storylines, she writes to reveal the glory and salvation of God.

Over a decade ago Jan began to write a story that became *Wall of Fire*. Although the fictional storylines are compelling and entertaining, it is through the factual accounts that we get glimpses of God's glory.

Wall of Fire is Jan's way of sharing how God is fulfilling the prophecies written in the Bible. Prophecies of His restoration of the land of Israel, the rebuilding of the ruined cities, and the regathering of the Jewish people back to their land.

Wall of Fire also tells the true stories of God's miraculous protection of Israel during her wars and how the people are being restored to Him through Y'shua the Messiah. Within the framework of the story, Isaiah 53 is explained and Jewish opposition to Jesus, Y'shua, is discussed.

Jan has studied Jewish history and the prophecies in Scripture for many decades. Her desire to know and understand Jewish history began at an early age. When Jan was eight years old, she read, without understanding much of it, *The Rise and Fall of the Third Reich*. What she read made her heart break for the Jewish people and gave her a love for them that even she doesn't quite understand. When she realized that the Jewish people in that book were the same as God's people Israel in the Bible, she began a lifelong search for how something as horrific as the Holocaust could happen. Some of what she learned is included in *Wall of Fire*.

More than two decades ago Jan was told that "nobody read the Bible cover to cover." Jan took that as a challenge. She went out and bought a large-print Bible and began to read it as she would a novel: no studying, no meditating, no note-taking, no underlining, no highlighting. She read it straight through in less than three months. It was so captivating she read it again. And again. Three times in one year.

Jan was fascinated with how all of Scripture was tied together; how the themes were repeated over and over; how over a period of 1500 years and 42 different authors the Bible was consistent in everything that was written. This began years of Bible study, which Jan calls verse-association studies, letting the Bible be its own commentary. When Jan also began to see how accurately and detailed the prophecies in Scripture were, and how so many of those prophecies had come true in her lifetime, she was overwhelmed with the glory of God and His faithfulness to His Word. In order to share what she called 'glimpses of Gods glory,' Jan began to write *Wall of Fire*.

Jan Holtrop is the mother of two, grandmother of five, and great-grandmother of one. Many years ago she began writing stories for her grandchildren as a way of sharing her faith and trust in God. Among these stories are the JJ AND JOSIE STORIES: *The No-No Room, The Long Summer* and *Stars of Light*. These children's stories are available as free downloads on her website (see below).

Jan can be contacted by email at **brushbowbooks@outlook.com**. She will be happy to hear from you!

Jan and her husband Dale live in West Chicago, Illinois, and attend New Jerusalem House of Prayer, a Messianic congregation where both Jews and Gentiles worship God our Savior together. It is a place of prayer, worship, learning, and fellowship. Jan is part of the Chain-Breakers Prayer Group, and participates in the weekly Bible Study.

For more information about New Jerusalem House of Prayer, please visit **www.NewJerusalem.info** or email them at **info@NewJerusalem.info**.

www.WallofFire.info

Made in the USA
Monee, IL
02 November 2019